Faith Martin has been writing for thirty years and has published over fifty novels. She began writing romantic thrillers as Maxine Barry, but quickly turned to crime! It was when she turned to writing detective stories as Faith Martin that she became more widely known. Having lived in Oxfordshire all her life, both the city and the countryside often feature in her novels. The fauna and wildlife of a farming landscape has always played a big part in her life – and often sneaks its way onto the pages of her books.

Also by Faith Martin

MURDER
BY
CANDLELIGHT

FAITH MARTIN

ONE PLACE. MANY STORIES

HQ
An imprint of HarperCollins*Publishers* Ltd
1 London Bridge Street
London SE1 9GF

www.harpercollins.co.uk

HarperCollins*Publishers*
Macken House, 39/40 Mayor Street Upper,
Dublin 1, D01 C9W8, Ireland

This edition 2024

1

First published in Great Britain by
HQ, an imprint of HarperCollins*Publishers* Ltd 2024

Copyright © Faith Martin 2024

Faith Martin asserts the moral right to be
identified as the author of this work.
A catalogue record for this book is
available from the British Library.

ISBN: 978-0-00-858998-1

This book contains FSC™ certified paper and other controlled
sources to ensure responsible forest management.

For more information visit: www.harpercollins.co.uk/green

This book is set in 11.4/16 pt. Meridien by Type-it AS, Norway

Printed and Bound in the UK using 100% Renewable Electricity at
CPI Group (UK) Ltd, Croydon, CR0 4YY

For my literary agent, Kate Nash, for
putting up with me for so long

ENGLAND: SUMMER 1924

CHAPTER ONE

'Oh, hello, Mr Swift, might I just have a quick word with you about my ghost?'

Now this somewhat unconventional greeting would no doubt have disconcerted anyone other than Mr Arbuthnot Lancelot Swift. However, Mr Swift – known simply as 'that young fool Arbie' to his more discriminating friends and family – was made of sterner stuff. Or so he'd like to flatter himself. The more honest explanation for this display of savoir-faire, however, lay in the fact that, having just written a best-selling book about some of the nation's more prominent spooks, ghouls, spectres and the odd banshee or two, it could be argued that he was better placed than most to take this sort of thing in his stride.

'Oh, good morning, Miss Phelps,' he said, turning around to address the tall, grey-haired lady who was looking at him from a pair of thoughtful, watery blue eyes. 'Lovely day and all that,' he added cheerfully.

Naturally, that worthy lady batted away this piece of frippery with barely an acknowledgement.

Miss Phelps, he supposed, must now be in her late sixties, and was one of the wealthiest members of the Cotswold village of Maybury-in-the-Marsh. As a lifelong resident of the village himself, he was very much aware of the older lady's standing in the community – not to mention her notoriously gimlet eye – and could only hope that his Oxford bags and knitted jumper passed sartorial muster.

Her family had held sway at the Old Forge for generations, her antecedents starting out as mere humble smithies, but through luck, judgement, hard work and notorious parsimony had built up a business that was now the envy of many. But it had been her deceased brother who, like many industrialists, had made their biggest fortune from the Great War, and now the Phelps name could be seen written large on many a factory wall. Not to mention on the doors of a string of garages and scrap metal merchant yards in three counties.

Not surprisingly, Miss Phelps, as one of the very few remaining members of her family, bore evidence of her prosperity easily and without any apparent effort. Today, this took the form of an immaculately shabby tweed suit, specially tailored to fit her five feet eleven inches, a set of truly perfect pearls, the softest of kid-leather gloves and some sort of reptilian-skin handbag that even Arbie (not the most reliable judge of women's accessories) could tell was probably the envy of every woman for miles around.

But for once, Miss Phelps wasn't acting quite her self-important self. Normally she could be seen walking through the village like a member of minor royalty deigning to mix with the peasantry, but this morning she seemed to be lacking some of her usual vim and vigour, and her eyes darted nervously up and down Old Mill Lane.

'I was so hoping I might run into you, Mr Swift. I think you're just the person to advise me,' she said, though not sounding particularly convinced by her own statement. Which Arbie had to acknowledge was fair enough. It was rare indeed for anyone to ask his advice about anything. 'Since you know all about restless spirits and that sort of thing, I mean,' she added weakly.

Even as she made this request, the pale blue orbs of her eyes were running over him with obvious misgiving. No doubt she was recalling all the times when, as a boy, he'd regularly scrumped her pears, gooseberries and plums, and, on one occasion, had been directly responsible for the rapid entrance of a cricket ball through her (regrettably closed) dining room window.

'Oh, er, really?' he responded uncomfortably. Whilst it behoved one to help out one's neighbours when called upon, of course, it was not something a chap actively encouraged.

A lanky youth of six feet one with plentiful dark brown hair and fine grey eyes, he sought desperately to think of a way of disentangling himself from what looked like becoming a bit of a tricky situation. For the truth was, the last thing he wanted to do was discuss ghosts and their doings. He'd set out that lovely summer morning to stroll to the village shop for the papers and some tobacco and had intended to do nothing more strenuous afterwards than indulge in a spot of fishing in the river which ran along the bottom of his grounds.

Now, it was fair to say that everyone who knew Arbie well had been frankly astonished and bamboozled to see his first literary enterprise, *The Gentleman's Guide to Ghost-Hunting*, become such a roaring success with the British reading public. His best friend from Wadham, Walter Greenstreet, who had gone straight into his family's long-standing publishing business had, likewise, been utterly wrong-footed by it also.

The Gentleman's Guide to Ghost-Hunting had only come about at all when the two young men had met up in their club one day, and over a very boozy lunch indeed, had found the conversation turning to the nation's fascination with all things spook and spectre related. Everyone, it seemed, had a ghost story to tell, or an old family home that was haunted by a white lady, headless horseman or some other inconvenient poltergeist. Arbie had responded to this observation in an off-handed manner by saying that it was all too bad, and that someone should take the matter in hand in a logical and orderly way and publish a guide to it all, rather like the hill-walking or cycling tour guides that were currently so popular. Only instead of visiting historical monuments or natural wonders, the tourists could indulge their appetite for spirits (of the non-alcoholic kind) instead.

Why, it could become more popular than bird-watching or nature study, he'd declared airily, getting somewhat carried away. (In his defence, the club's fine port may have had something to do with his growing fervour.) Arbie had waxed so lyrically and enthusiastically at this bright new idea of how to titillate the bored well-to-do, that Wally had challenged him to go ahead and compile such a volume. After all, he'd pointed out with a wry smile, Arbie had nothing better to do with his time since he was determined not to work for a living, and writing such a guidebook might be a bit of a lark at that. But only if he was up to it, that is.

Naturally, Arbie hadn't been able to ignore the challenge or back down in the face of his friend's provocation, and had said grandiosely that he'd write it if Wally's firm would publish it, fully expecting that to spike his friend's guns. However, Walter, thus hoisted by his own petard, had instantly agreed to such an enterprise, and had had a contract ready for his friend to sign before the week was out.

This, obviously, left Arbie in something of a pickle. Apart from the fact that he now had only the vaguest of recollections of what they'd discussed at lunch, the same sense of honour that had resulted in the production of the contract had obliged him to take up the challenge and sign the dratted thing.

And so it was that one fine morning he'd found himself with an unwanted publishing deal under his belt and a book to write. And after some weeks of gloomily cursing fate and his treacherous friend – not to mention the club's fine port – Arbie had set off on a tour of the south of England, suitcase and portable typewriter in hand, in search of ghosts.

And had found, rather to his surprise, that it *was* all a bit of a lark. Oh, not the actual ghost-hunting itself. That had been tedious in the extreme and usually consisted of sitting in the dark and waiting for something to happen, which never did. But the actual travelling around in his black Alvis saloon had been a delight. Moseying along from seaside towns to attractive villages and staying at accommodating village inns or boarding houses as the whim – or hot tips about local ghosts – had taken him, had given him a wonderful sense of freedom. And since the majority of his commercial hosts and hostesses were willing to bend over backwards to make his stay comfortable in exchange for a good 'write-up' about their establishments in his new guidebook, the fact that Arbie had lived like a king might have had something to do with his enjoyment of the venture.

Once he'd returned home, he tidied up his 'working notes' and delivered the completed manuscript to Walter. His old pal had then, naturally and somewhat hastily, passed it over – unread – to a junior editor to deal with and had promptly forgotten all about it.

Until it was published three months later – and became something of a sensation. For some reason, a vast percentage of the reading public liked Arbie's easy, witty style. His habit of describing various holiday hotspots, mixed with his self-effacing 'tussles' with ghosts, vastly amused and entertained everybody from housewives to country solicitors, farmers to bus drivers, dowager duchesses to kitchen maids. And Walter Greenstreet, blast him to the moon and back, had all but taken to camping out on Arbie's doorstep and waving a contract under his nose, desperately promising a higher and higher rate of royalties every time his friend showed his face.

But Arbie's lazy nature had had ample time to reassert itself, and the thought of actually producing a second book was giving him a case of the jitters. For the last month he'd been so determinedly fending off Wally's pleadings to take up the ghost-hunt again, that finding himself unexpectedly accosted by a member of his own village asking him about ghosts was the last thing he needed. If Walter's big ears got to hear about it, he would insist that Arbie had no excuse whatsoever for not starting a new book now that he had a 'case' right on his doorstep.

So it was that Arbie cast what he hoped was a winsome smile on the wealthy spinster in front of him and said, 'Well, Miss Phelps, as a matter of fact I've sort of retired from all that sort . . .' but the lady, he could see, was going to have none of it. He could tell by the way her spine stiffened, with her upper lip following suit, that he was not going to be allowed to wiggle free. Manfully, he reminded himself that he was a mere boy no longer, and fought against the instilled urge to buckle under her gaze.

'And honestly, I'm not really such an expert on ghosts as all that, you know,' he began hopefully. 'Writing what was really a glorified holiday guidebook isn't . . .' but it was no use. He was doomed, for already Miss Phelps was opening her mouth to cut across his stumbling efforts to extricate himself. She simply wasn't going to accept anything other than his promise to come and investigate her wretched spook for her – which would probably turn out to be nothing more than the wind in the chimneys or a tree twig scratching against a windowpane somewhere.

With slumping shoulders, he resigned himself to the inevitable. Perhaps, he comforted himself, he could be in and out in one quick visit, before his publishers even became aware that he'd been asked to investigate at all?

'But you have to help me, Mr Swift,' the usually stalwart Miss Phelps said rather piteously. 'You see, this is no ordinary ghost. I think it's trying to kill me.'

'Eh?' squawked Arbie, thoroughly rattled.

It was not, perhaps, a particularly erudite response from one of the nation's favourite authors. But it conveyed his feelings pretty adequately, nonetheless.

It was at this moment, whilst Arbie was gaping at Miss Phelps like a stunned mullet, that he saw movement out of his peripheral vision, and turned his head slightly to see a familiar sight.

Maybury was a small village with one major road – Old Mill Lane – running through it. On this road most of the village's prominent residences and amenities had been built, including The Dun Cow Inn, the manor house, the Old Forge and the village shop. Off it, however, ran a few minor lanes and tracks, leading to various cul-de-sacs of cottages, and Church Lane, which led to the Norman church, its adjacent vicarage and finally, Arbie and his uncle's own residence, a converted chapel. And it was from this direction that a large black boneshaker of a bicycle had turned onto the main village street, bearing astride it a striking figure.

As usually happened whenever Arbie saw Valentina Olivia Charlotte Coulton-James, the vicar's daughter, whizzing along on her bicycle, he could hear in the back of his head the stirring music of Act 3 of *Die Walküre*, and Richard Wagner's rousing piece, 'Ride of the Valkyries'. This may have been due to the fact that Val, at five feet eleven, was a strapping girl, former hockey champion at her school and all-round athlete. Tennis, swimming, archery, whatever the sport, Val could beat anyone hands down. Or it may have been the fact that she had long, very straight and very fair hair that streamed out behind her in a rippling stream as her muscular legs pumped up and down, getting astonishing speeds out of her hand-me-down vehicle.

More likely, it was probably his memories of their shared schooldays at the village primary school, when Val had regularly duffed him up in the playground.

Now, if someone had told Arbie earlier that morning that he'd be pleased to see Val bearing down on him with her usual expression of mild scorn mixed with reluctant affection, he'd have told them to go boil their head. But as she applied the rather haphazard brakes on her contraption and brought herself

9

to a shuddering halt just in front of himself and Miss Phelps, he did indeed feel inordinately happy to see her.

If anyone could deal with beleaguered ladies with a persecution complex, it was Val. As one of the vicar's huge brood (how many children did the Reverend have now – eight, nine, ten?), she was used to dealing with anything.

'Ah, Val, you're just the ticket,' Arbie said gratefully.

Val put one sturdy foot on the ground to balance herself and looked at him suspiciously. 'Oh?' This was not the sort of greeting she'd been expecting. In her experience, Arbie Swift usually lived up to his name whenever he saw her, and swiftly made excuses to depart. So perhaps she could be forgiven if her gaze travelled suspiciously from his innocent smile to Amy Phelps's unhappy visage and then back to him again. As she sensed the atmosphere, her face darkened.

Arbie shuffled his feet, which was his usual response to being put on the spot.

'Have you been upsetting Miss Phelps?' Val demanded flatly.

'What? No! As if I would,' Arbie yelped, stung by her immediate assumption that, whatever was going on, he was to blame. Just for that, he had no more qualms – not that he'd ever had any in the first place – in setting about transferring his problem onto her sturdy shoulders.

'As a point of fact, Miss Phelps was just telling me about a little problem she has that really needs your father's sensitive touch,' he informed her loftily. Sensing that Miss Phelps wasn't happy with this opening gambit and was about to put her foot in it by saying that she'd asked for no such interference from the church, Arbie rushed on. 'And you're just the person to help arrange it. Miss Phelps you see—'

'Miss Phelps can speak for herself, thank you,' the lady interrupted firmly. 'Good morning, Miss Coulton-James,' she added, giving the vicar's daughter a gracious inclination of her head. As she did so, she cast her eyes disapprovingly over the mannish trousers and loose jersey that Val wore when out on her bicycle.

In her day, women rode side-saddle on horses with dresses down to the ankle.

Val, easily interpreting the other woman's glance, did her best to ignore her unspoken censure and continued to scowl at Arbie. 'Daddy's always very busy, you know, and right now he's got a visit from the Bishop in the offing, so the whole house is in uproar,' she said dampeningly. Although she might not know exactly what was going on between her two disparate neighbours, she was confident that whatever it was, Arbie was, as usual, trying to duck out of something.

'Ah, but I'm sure your father is never too busy to help a parishioner in distress,' Arbie shot back.

At this, Amy Phelps bridled. 'Mr Swift, I'll trust you not to break my confidences. I told you about my ghostly difficulties only on the tacit understanding that you would be both professional and discreet.'

Now it was Val's turn to shoot her a bemused look. 'I'm sorry, Miss Phelps, did you say *ghostly* difficulties?'

'Exactly so. Which, I'm sure we all agree really does fall under the purview of the Church,' Arbie slipped in triumphantly. 'If Miss Phelps needs some sort of exorcism perfor—'

'Exorcism?' hissed Miss Phelps, scandalised.

'Exorcism?' Val hissed, at the same time, even more scandalised.

Under the barrage of their combined displeasure, Arbie miserably shuffled his feet. 'Er, well, you know . . .'

'I'll have nothing to do with exorcisms,' Miss Phelps said, mortally offended.

'Daddy really doesn't do exorcisms,' Val added, equally as mortally offended.

Arbie shuffled his feet some more.

Both women looked at him in disgust for a moment longer, then mutually but tacitly acknowledging that he was a broken reed, turned instantly to one another to get things sorted out properly.

11

'What's the problem, Miss Phelps?' Val asked kindly. 'I'm sure between us we can see a way clear.'

'Well, Miss Coulton-James, it's like this . . .' Miss Phelps hesitated and glanced around cautiously. Although the small village was never exactly crammed with passers-by, there were always one or two people about, going to or from the shop, or working in their gardens. And the last thing she wanted was gossip about her family running rife all over the place. 'Perhaps you and Mr Swift could come to tea later on and we can discuss things more comfortably?'

'We'd love to, wouldn't we, Arbie?' Val said instantly, shooting him an acid smile.

Knowing when he was beaten, Arbie inwardly heaved a deep sigh but outwardly shot out a smile. 'Of course, Miss Phelps, we would be delighted,' he lied smoothly.

Miss Phelps, having achieved her aims (when had she ever not?), nodded in satisfaction, bid them good day until later and marched off. Arbie sadly watched her go. Then, turning to his satisfied companion, said reproachfully, 'I say, Val, what on earth did you let us in that for?'

Val regarded him with an aloof and disappointed air. 'Oh, Arbie, couldn't you see that underneath all that prim and proper-ness that poor lady was really worried about something? I mean, genuinely upset and not just, you know, playing the "grand dame" or something?'

'Well . . .' Arbie felt himself flushing. Because, in truth, he had found it discomfiting to see the usually imperious Amy Phelps so unlike her old self. Why was it that Val had always been able to make him feel like a worm with just a few snappy words and a pleading glance from her big blue eyes?

Sensing weakness, Val pressed home her advantage. 'You know Miss Phelps. When has she ever asked anybody for help?' she demanded.

'Well . . .'

'Exactly! Her generation would rather die than admit to any kind of weakness. But it was as plain as the nose on your face that she was worried sick. And there you were, dithering about, and trying to wriggle out of any unpleasantness, as usual. Well, this time, you can jolly well step in and do your bit. Now, what's all this about exorcisms and ghosts and things?'

'She says the Old Forge is haunted,' Arbie said, a shade sulkily.

'Well, everyone knows that,' Val said dismissively. 'Half the village is said to have ghosts flitting about. Isn't the Old Forge haunted by a past smithy who was said to have died after falling into his fire or something?'

'No, actually,' Arbie said, glad to be able to correct her. As a bit of an expert now, he knew about such things. 'He just died of pneumonia, brought on by TB.'

'Oh,' Val said, a little crestfallen. 'That doesn't sound like something a person would get particularly upset about and start haunting a place for, does it? Didn't a lot of people die of things like that? What's he got to complain of any more than anyone else?' Even the dead, it seemed, weren't safe from Val's firm view of how things ought to be.

'Ghosts aren't exactly known for their reasonableness,' Arbie pointed out dryly. 'And this one seems to have been very cross indeed about something or other.'

Something slightly gleeful in his tone made Val look at him closely. Sensing that Arbie wasn't as thoroughly subdued as he might appear, her chin came up pugnaciously. 'Oh?' she said cautiously. 'Why do you say that?'

'Because if Miss Phelps is to be believed, this family ghost is trying to kill her,' Arbie said nonchalantly.

'Oh,' Val said blankly.

'Still looking forward to taking tea at the forge, old thing?' he asked jovially.

CHAPTER TWO

'Did you hear, they say they're going to be bringing electricity to the village within the next seven years?'

The voice seemed to come out of the ether, and both Val and Arbie paused, their teacups in hand and hovering just in front of their faces.

They had dutifully wandered down to the Old Forge at a quarter to four, Val in her Sunday best frock and Arbie in a beautifully tailored summer suit, to take tea with Miss Phelps. Val, as ever vaguely annoyed by his effortless sartorial elegance, affected not to notice how handsome he looked, and the walk to the far end of the village had been done in a mutual, testy silence.

The Old Forge had, like many buildings, morphed over the centuries, this particular one from being a simple smithy into something of a rambling country-house residence, with various outbuildings attached: not exactly a squire's residence, but not the home of a mere artisan either. Neither fish nor fowl, it was built of the local creamy Cotswold stone, had a plethora of grey-slated roofs of various heights and designs, and was consequently prone to odd twists and turns both inside and out. Small, mullioned windows in some parts gave way to the wide sash-windows favoured by the Georgians in others. Higgledy-piggledy chimneys marched up and down in various heights and widths, giving the whole building a curious but definite charm. An ageing and beautiful wisteria that clambered and flowered all over a rather lackadaisical porch and south-facing wall helped significantly.

Neither Val nor Arbie, though they'd lived in the village all their lives, had ever set foot in the place before. Miss Phelps usually saved her entertaining for the relicts of Victorian society, such as herself. So when they finally walked up the gravelled driveway and pulled down on the intricate iron doorbell handle (probably made by a past smithy in this very spot in days of yore), they didn't know exactly what to expect.

The door had been answered by Mrs Brockhurst, Miss Phelps's housekeeper of the past thirty years or so. The 'Mrs' was purely a courtesy title, since the woman herself had never been married, but she was a well-liked and respected member of the village community. She had smiled on them a genuinely warm welcome and proceeded to usher them through a rather dark and shadowy hall into a sun-filled parlour that faced the expansive back garden.

Here, Miss Amy Phelps had risen from a Queen Anne chair and greeted them a shade formally. Within minutes, Arbie and Val found themselves seated at a large round table and began the usual meaningless, polite social chit-chat that was such a prerequisite of an English tea party, whilst Mrs Brockhurst brought in trays laden with delicious things. Apart from the actual tea itself, which was housed in a heavy silver teapot and poured out into exquisite Spode teacups, there were plates of dainty sandwiches – with the crusts removed, naturally – savoury and sweet scones, cake, jam, clotted cream and delicate brandy snaps.

Miss Phelps had just been mother and poured out the first of the tea when the excited voice had interrupted the tableau with news of electricity coming to the village.

A second later another lady moved silently into the room, her face slightly flushed. She was, Val gauged, somewhere in her mid-sixties. Petite, with a neat bun fixed firmly atop her head, and big brown eyes set in a complexion of roses and cream, she eyed the two youngsters with a slightly squinting glance that gave away the fact that she probably needed glasses. Either she was too vain to wear them or had been absent-minded enough to forget to put them on.

'Ah, this is my dearest and oldest friend, Mrs Cora Delaney. She's staying with me for a few weeks this summer for a little holiday,' Amy said, somewhat curtly. 'Cora, Miss Coulton-James, the dear vicar's daughter, and Mr Swift.'

'Oh, our celebrity guest,' Cora said, casting Arbie an inquisitive look. 'I enjoyed reading your book, Mr Swift. So amusing, and so informative, if you like holidays in resorts. And I have to say, I thought that the methods you employed to try and capture evidence of the supernatural sounded most, er, intriguing.' If her tone was rather on the dry side, Arbie decided not to notice.

'I'm glad you enjoyed it,' he said instead, trying his best to look modest. In truth, he still found himself genuinely buzzed that he'd produced a work that anyone bothered to read at all – even such a light, nonsensical piece as *The Gentleman's Guide*.

'What was it you were saying about electricity?' Amy, like Val, had little appetite for feeding Arbie's already healthy ego, and ruthlessly changed the subject. 'I won't have it here. I'm still not used to these awful gas lights,' she said, casting a withering glance at an inoffensive glass gas lamp on the wall beside her.

'Oh, but I was talking to the proprietor of the village shop this morning, and she was telling me how she got it from the clerk who works in the council offices that the electricity board is proposing a motion to run the pylons out your way in the next few years,' Cora related sedately, her tone now definitely dry. A lifelong resident of cities, she occasionally found village life to be entertaining. Sitting down and carefully arranging her skirts, she eyed the table and its contents with a bird-like eye, reminding Arbie of a hungry sparrow.

'Won't that be exciting for you, my dear Amy? Of course, we've had it for years in our place,' she added, addressing the remark to Arbie whilst eyeing the Dundee cake. 'It's so much cleaner, and you don't get the smell like you do with gas light.'

And selecting a plate, she swooped on the cake, waving a silver slicer with expert balance.

'Do help yourself to the teapot,' Amy said, her own tone so arid that it would have made the Sahara Desert sit up and take notice. 'And I tell you now, *I* won't have it in *this* house. It's positively dangerous, or so I hear. Killing people left and right, it seems. Nasty stuff! Now, where do you suppose . . . Oh, here is my other summer visitor.'

Both Val and Arbie noticed their hostess soften a little. 'Reggie, I'd thought you'd forgotten we had guests for tea.'

As she spoke, a slender, silver-haired man sauntered in and eyed the bulging tea-table with a happy smile. 'Ah, Mrs Brockhurst's scones. Amy, I swear half the reason I come here every year is because of Mrs Brockhurst's scones.'

Cora smiled minimally at this, but Amy's smile seemed genuine enough. 'I dare say that's true, you old rogue,' she even went so far as to tease him.

Arbie and Val watched this display, both fascinated and dumbstruck. Who'd have thought Miss Amy Phelps capable of such a feat!

Perhaps their hostess caught something of this, because she waved a hand vaguely in the air. 'Oh, you mustn't mind Reggie, and his odd ways,' Amy Phelps informed them airily. 'He's a bit of an artist, you know, like my dear late mama, and likes to amuse himself over the summer indulging his various hobbies and nestling down in Mama's old studio. Our families have known one another for so long, we've practically merged. Reggie and my late brother Francis went to school together, and he was always running about here in the school holidays.'

'My parents were in India at the time,' Reggie put in by way of explanation, sitting down and reaching for a plate and purloining a healthy selection of sandwiches.

Arbie, sensing that he had a rival in the food stakes, quickly followed suit. With a hard stare, Val watched him pile up his plate. Cora also looked on, much amused, from behind her teacup.

'Yes, Amy's right – during the school holidays Francis and I ran loose around here like a pair of wild animals.' Reggie sighed happily. 'And we just kept the tradition going after we'd grown up, somehow. I would often spend almost as much time here as in my own home, didn't I, Amy m'dear? Of course, we liked to knock about the Continent a bit together too, or take longer trips away and get off the beaten path. Francis was a great one for finding little out-of-the-way places up in the mountains someplace, where we'd live off goat's cheese and figs.'

At the mention of her late brother, Amy let out a small sigh. 'I do so miss all my siblings, but Francis most of all. I know I shouldn't say that, but I'm afraid it's true. He had such a way with him. He was Mama's favourite too,' she added matter-of-factly, and without any evidence of jealousy.

'But at least you have your nephew and niece as living reminders of the others,' Cora put in, sotto voce.

At this, Arbie and Val, who were looking at Amy, noticed the older woman's face shut down. It wasn't in any way subtle, and even the affable Reggie appeared a little uncomfortable to see it. Cora, however, didn't seem to notice her friend's sudden coolness. Perhaps her eyesight was more defective than she realised, for she carried on obliviously, 'Didn't I see Phyllis arrive just a little earlier?'

'Yes, she'll be down shortly,' Amy said primly. 'She went upstairs to wash her face and hands after the train journey. She only lives in the next county, but travel is such a dirty, grimy business, I'm glad I have little to do with it,' she added firmly.

Unaware that she was under discussion, upstairs the woman herself cautiously opened a door and peered around to check that she was alone. It was not, however, the door to one of the house's few bathrooms that she was exiting. Satisfied that the narrow corridor on either side of her appeared to be deserted, she tiptoed out, closed the door carefully behind her and hurried towards one of the Old Forge's many twisty staircases.

As she did so, Mrs Brockhurst, a short, tidy-looking woman who'd been coming up another set of stairs that let out behind her, paused for a moment. Her face was totally expressionless. For a moment, she watched Phyllis Thomas, the only child of Amy's sister Moira, as she hurried away, and only when the younger woman had turned a bend in the passageway and was safely out of sight did she herself move forward.

The housekeeper hesitated for a moment outside the bedroom door from which Phyllis had just emerged but did not open it to look inside. She had no need to. She knew very well that the room belonged to Amy Phelps, the mistress of the house. And whilst Miss Phelps tolerated the housekeeper's necessary intrusion into her domain strictly for cleaning purposes, she wouldn't have liked it at all if she knew that anyone else had been in her private quarters, for Amy had always been a secretive person who fulsomely guarded her privacy.

Quietly, Mrs Brockhurst carried on towards the airing cupboard, where she neatly deposited the set of towels she'd been carrying, before heading back down to the kitchen. Nothing about her would suggest that she was unduly concerned by what she had just seen, although in fact, she was thinking to herself that she wished Miss Phyllis would be more careful about how she went about things.

*

Downstairs, Phyllis was now smiling at Arbie and shaking his hand, then she turned a slightly less impressed smile on Val. 'How nice it is to meet you both,' she said, taking a seat and then accepting a cup of tea from Arbie, who had been quick to see to her needs. 'I was saying to Cora only a little while ago, I've never met a famous author before. Have you really seen ghosts?'

Val sighed gently and wondered just how many more fawning females the man was going to collect.

'No,' Arbie answered, honestly. 'That is . . . Not seen one, as such. But I think I may have heard one.' This, he knew, was the kind of thing people liked and expected from him, and he'd been dining out on his supposed area of expertise for long enough now that he knew how to sing for his supper. Nothing too frightening, but just enough to scintillate, that was the ticket.

As expected, Cora smiled coolly and said, 'Ah, that sounds interesting. Please do tell us all about it.'

'Yes, Arbie, do spill the beans,' Val said, turning to look at him fully. 'We all can't *wait* to hear about it.' And if there was something slightly mocking in her eyes, or suspiciously sardonic in her tone of voice, Arbie manfully ignored it.

'Yes, where was it? On one of the cases that you covered in your wonderful book?' Phyllis prompted, far more sincerely.

'As a matter of fact, no. It was in my own house, right here in the village. When I was twelve,' he added. Then he sipped from his cup, apparently in no hurry to continue. Leave 'em wanting more – that was the thing.

Reggie looked at him approvingly from benign eyes. 'This is more like it, young fellow – a bit of entertainment to give us all a little boost, eh? Well, go on, don't leave us all in suspense.'

Arbie shrugged. 'I'm not sure I can promise to be entertaining, Mr Bickersworth. Only honest.' At this, Val's eyebrow lifted sceptically, and he shot her a slightly hurt look. The story he was about to tell was true enough . . . well . . . in essence.

'You see, when my friend asked me to write *The Gentleman's Guide*, although I was a bit taken aback, in truth, I wasn't all that averse,' Arbie began. Of course, that was stretching things a bit but there was no point boring everyone with the true origins of his writing career, was there? 'Because of what happened in the chapel,' he added tantalisingly.

'The chapel?' Phyllis asked, puzzled. 'I thought you said it happened in your own house?'

'So it did,' Arbie rushed to explain. 'You see, I was orphaned when I was only three years old. My parents died in a boating accident, and so I came to live with Uncle, here in the village. And he'd just recently purchased the chapel. It was originally built in the early 1800s for the workers in the nearby clay pits who were nearly all Methodists and so wanted nothing to do with the local church. But when the pits were all worked out fifty or so years later, and the workers left, the chapel began to moulder a bit. Well, Uncle, being Uncle, bought it for a song and set about renovating the big awkward beast to his own . . . er . . . tastes.'

Here Amy Phelps drew in a sharp breath. 'Your uncle always has been, shall we say, someone who forged his own path in life,' she acknowledged tightly.

At this, both Cora and Reggie sat up a little straighter. Now it sounded as if some dirt was going to be dished.

But Arbie was having none of it. Whilst it was all right for him to suspect his relative of all manner of dodgy deeds and less-than-salubrious practices, he wouldn't stand for it from others. 'Yes, I suppose Uncle always has been a bit of a black sheep,' he admitted cautiously. 'But when disaster struck, he didn't hesitate, you have to give him that.' Here Arbie paused to take a decorous sip of tea, and let the point sink in. 'And even though he had no wife to help him, he took me in without a murmur, and saw to getting me a nanny and then overseeing my schooling and such.'

'Yes, that *was* admirable,' Amy acknowledged grudgingly. 'But I still maintain he was not the ideal guardian for a young boy.'

'Well really, you know, I had a jolly time as a young 'un, dashing around that cold old building,' Arbie chided gently. 'I think I must have learned enough to be an architect had my inclinations been that way, watching as Uncle put in staircases and dug out a cellar and extended into the attic and what have you.'

'Yes, you really must see it some time, Reggie,' Amy said dryly. 'The conversion of the Old Chapel into a private residence is really . . . er . . . remarkable. You'd appreciate its eccentricities, I think.'

Arbie openly grinned. 'What Miss Phelps is too polite to say, old boy, is that the place is an utter horror! Oh, it has no fireplace, for instance, but is wonderfully centrally heated – my uncle designed and built the system himself. He's something of a mad inventor, I'm afraid. It has bespoke furniture all over the place, but the pulpit is still in the living room, as well as the fully functioning organ! And as for the kitchen – it has all the mod cons, but the arched windows are still all stained glass. It's neither fish nor fowl. My bedroom is in the loft and has rafters and the original bell still dangling over my bed, right over my head. I only hope the rope holding it in place really is as stout as Uncle says it is, otherwise one day it'll come down and brain me!'

'Oh my!' Cora said dryly.

'How brave of you to sleep under it! I'd never get a wink!' Reggie said, eyes twinkling.

Phyllis, who was made of sterner stuff, smiled upon him a shade impatiently. 'It all sounds utterly charming, Mr Swift. But you were going to tell us of your ghost?'

'Ah, yes, so I was. Well, it was when I was around twelve. I was home for the school holidays, and it was a foul night.'

22

'Oh really. Not a thunderstorm, Arbie?' Val protested. The last thing she was in the mood for was listening to Arbie spouting utter tosh to his adoring fans. 'Wind howling around the rafters and thunder and lightning crashing and flashing all over the place? It really is too Frankenstein's monster for words.'

'Actually, there was no thunder and lightning,' Arbie told her with dignity. 'Just a lot of wind and rain. A typical British summer in fact.'

At this, everyone smiled wryly. They could all tell their own horror stories about British summers.

'Anyway, it was dark, and I'd been in bed some time when I heard it,' Arbie said, his voice lowering dramatically a little. And even though they were all perfectly aware that he was only doing it for effect, everyone was now hanging on to his every word.

'What? What did you hear?' It was, a little surprisingly, Amy Phelps who asked the question. Arbie would have said that, of them all, she'd be the least taken with his tale, but then he remembered that she had ghostly troubles of her own, so perhaps she was feeling less sceptical than she might have been otherwise.

'I heard the organ playing,' Arbie said. And as he spoke, he was once more back in his bed on that night, waking up and hearing the unmistakable sound of the pipes letting forth.

'Is that all, old chap?' Reggie said, sounding a little disappointed. 'It was probably your uncle having a bash. Bach was it? A bit of Mozart?'

'Uncle hasn't got a musical bone in his body,' Arbie scoffed. 'He's a painter. Inventor. Man of business. Or a combination of any of those things – according to Uncle that is,' he added with a gentle laugh. 'But I can testify to the fact that he has a tin ear when it comes to music.'

'So he couldn't have been playing then?' Cora nodded. 'So what did you do?' For the first time, the no-nonsense woman sounded genuinely interested.

'Well, like any curious boy, I got out of bed and sneaked to the top of the stairs to have a peek,' Arbie said truthfully. And once again, he was there that night, creeping along the short landing and peering over the banisters and looking down into the cavernous main living room below. 'Uncle, you have to understand, was doing odd bits and bobs to the building for years. Adding this here, taking that out there, as the whim took him. And I seem to remember, that holiday, that he had had the big main entrance door removed because it was going rotten at the bottom and was in the process of having another big oak thing installed instead. I was half inclined to wonder if he'd forgotten to secure the doorway properly, and some tramp or other had wandered in out of the weather and thought he'd play a tune to cheer himself up.'

'Was it a hymn?' Phyllis asked. 'It being a former chapel, I mean?'

Arbie smiled. 'No. Funnily enough – it was "Greensleeves". I could just about recognise it.'

'Oh. It wasn't being played well then?' Reggie asked, exaggerat-edly forlorn. 'Bit of a letdown that. You'd think a ghost would be able to do better than that, somehow.' He smiled gently. 'It would be nice to think you'd be given accomplishments in the afterlife that had evaded you whilst in the land of the living.'

Val gave him a warm look. He had a jolly, easy way about him that was soothing, and she could well see why he was a regular visitor at the Old Forge.

'I know. But there you are,' Arbie responded to his sally philo-sophically. 'There I was, twelve years old, listening to the organ playing by itself a rather hit-and-miss rendition of old Henry the Eighth's greatest hit!'

'You mean, there was nobody there actually playing it?' Phyllis asked sharply.

'Not a soul,' Arbie said, for once stating nothing but the truth.

'When I looked down, I could see the organ and the stool in front of it, and although the pipes were emitting sounds, nobody was pressing down on the keys. Well, nobody alive that is,' he added gruesomely.

Of course, when he'd told his uncle this tale the following morning, Uncle had explained it away with ease. What with the huge draught coming from the ill-fitting temporary doors, not to mention with the wind howling down the experimental chimney that he'd put in (and three years later discarded), it was simply a case of a major draught getting into the organ pipes and emitting a series of random notes. Notes which his half-awake schoolboy mind had interpreted as being 'Greensleeves', a tune that he and his fellow schoolmates had been forced to learn a few years earlier, courtesy of a particularly sadistic music master.

And whilst his now adult and rational self believed that his uncle's explanation was probably the true one, nevertheless, Arbie did still sometimes wonder. That organ *had* sounded as if it had played 'Greensleeves' that night. And what with that, and one or two other minor incidents which he hadn't seen fit to tell his uncle about over the last decade, it did give him pause to ponder. Like that time . . .

'I see. And this incident fed your interest in the supernatural?' Phyllis interrupted his musings. 'My friend Janice swears by a medium that her mother sees regularly.'

'Stuff and nonsense, my dear,' Reggie broke in kindly. 'Oh, I know it's all the rage nowadays, these seances, and table-rapping and what have you. But so much of it is fakery. The Victorians, bless them, came to the same conclusion decades ago.'

'Oh, I agree with you there, sir,' Arbie said, finding pleasure in taking a little of the wind out of the old duffer's sails. 'When I was researching *The Gentleman's Guide* the literature given over to exposing the amount of trickery by so-called mediums would make your hair turn white.'

Cora looked at him with her head cocked a little to one side. 'Are you saying you don't actually *believe* in ghosts then, Mr Swift?' she asked uncertainly.

'Of course he does, Cora, haven't you been paying attention? It's mediums he doesn't believe in, not the possibility that ghosts don't exist,' Amy cut in sharply. 'That's why Mr Swift is going to help me with my own manifestations. Aren't you, young man?' she said pointedly, shooting him a glance.

Arbie nearly choked on his tea. 'Oh, er, quite, Miss Phelps,' he finally managed to stutter.

In her chair, Val grinned widely. It wasn't often the usually eloquent Arbie was lost for words and she was thoroughly enjoying the spectacle. 'So, why don't you tell us all about your woes, Miss Phelps?' she said sweetly. 'I'm sure we can help. Isn't that right, Arbie?'

Arbie eyed her with a growing sense of doom. What was all this 'we' business? he thought warily. But what he said was, 'Oh yes, rather. So, who is it exactly that is causing all the fuss? Do you know?'

'My ancestor of course. The smithy,' Amy said flatly. 'You've probably heard the story about our family ghost – the whole village must have – but do you know the more interesting parts of the family legend? No? Well, it concerns my great-grandfather, Wilbur Phelps. He was only twenty-eight when he died of tuberculosis. Before that, however, he'd been a big strapping man who worked the forge and was very ambitious to get on in the world and improve the family's already growing fortune. It was his long-term business plan that helped shape the family's future successes.'

She said all this with a curious mixture of complacency, matter-of-factness and determined bravado – as if the humble origins of the Phelps family legacy were a matter of pride and yet, underneath it all, she was grudgingly aware that something about it was not quite nice. She would undoubtedly have preferred it if her family fortune and power had come about as the result of inherited wealth from a genteel family background, but since it wasn't, she was determined to make the best of it.

Val, the daughter of an impoverished vicar who happened to be the very minor younger son of a father who was himself a very minor younger son of a lord, understood this distinction at once, but would never have publicly admitted it.

'He married young and produced only one child, luckily a son, but he always lamented a lack of more heirs,' Amy swept on majestically. 'In those days, child mortality was so high you can understand his fear, I suppose. If he died without issue his line would be lost, and the power and growing fortune of the family would be scattered amongst a few distant relations. When he knew he was dying, he made his young son promise to strive hard and grow and protect the family, making sure that the Phelps name lived on forever. All very dramatic, I'm sure,' she added dryly.

Her listeners sighed a little in relief at this sign of levity. The tale had been in danger of becoming somewhat hoary.

'When he was buried, they went through the usual ritual of tying a piece of string on his big toe, and attaching it to a bell above ground,' Amy continued matter-of-factly.

But this bombshell statement made Val start. 'Oh my! What on earth for?' she asked, sounding genuinely alarmed. 'It sounds so macabre.'

Reggie reached over and patted her hand gently. 'There, there, my dear, don't fret. It was a common practice back then. Don't forget, in past times the doctors weren't quite so, er, proficient as our modern quacks! Sometimes they mistook unconsciousness for death, and a few poor unfortunates found themselves waking up six feet under.'

Val couldn't stop herself from giving a faint squeak at this, and even Arbie felt a cold shiver of horror scuttle up his own spine.

'For that reason,' Reggie hurried on, 'people did the sensible thing, and whenever someone was buried, they tied a bell on a piece of string and attached it to the dear departed's toe. That way, should there be any little mishaps, all the poor soul had to do was waggle his foot up and down and the bell would ring, and alert anyone out and about that they needed to be dug up again pronto.'

'I think if I were passing a churchyard and heard a little bell ringing, I might die myself,' Cora said crossly. 'Just imagine it!'

For a moment, everyone in the room *did* imagine it.

'Yes, quite.' It was, of course, the redoubtable Amy who broke the appalled silence. 'Be that as it may. Legend has it that, ever since, any Phelps family member who seemed to be in danger of putting the family legacy in danger could expect a visit from the ghost of Wilbur – heralded by the ringing of a tiny bell – forcing them back onto the straight and narrow. My grandmother always swore that her husband, who had taken to drinking far more than he should have, was shocked sober one night after one such visitation. Myself, I think it far more likely that Grand-papa just fell in the river one night when a little the worse for brandy, and it was the near-drowning experience that did the trick.'

Everyone laughed obligingly.

Amy sighed gently. 'Well, for some reason, my ancestor seems to have taken against me. I can't think why. I think I've been a steady guardian of our legacy after losing the last of my dear siblings. But it seems Wilbur doesn't think so. Recently, a few odd . . . things . . . have been happening that lead me to suspect that he's unhappy with me.'

'Oh, come now, Amy, surely you're exaggerating,' Reggie said gently. He looked at her with obvious concern, but before he could say anything more comforting, he was forestalled.

'Who's this who would dare to be unhappy with you, Aunt?' A hearty voice broke into the tense atmosphere, as a man in his early to mid-thirties swept in through the open parlour door. 'Just give me his name, and I'll soon sort the blighter out.'

Everyone turned to look at the interloper. Not particularly tall, he was just a little portly, with a head of thick brown hair and a pair of dark brown, penetrating eyes. A button nose rather spoilt an otherwise classically handsome face, and he was wearing an expensive business suit made by a tailor who knew his business.

Val looked at him with distinct interest.

Phyllis looked at him with quickly disguised dismay.

Cora and Reggie both acknowledged him with muted pleasure.

But it was the look on Amy Phelps's face that struck Arbie the most, as it was so hard to read.

'My nephew, Murray Phelps,' Amy introduced him dryly. 'I wasn't expecting you, Murray. How nice of you to call in.' If there was a slightly mocking edge to her voice, her nephew didn't seem to hear it.

'Not at all, Aunt, not at all. Always glad to see you, you know. Oh, hello, Phil old thing.' He tossed the greeting casually at his cousin, his eyes quickly going from Val to Arbie and back again. 'So what's all this then?' he said, a distinct challenge in his voice.

'Mr Arbuthnot Swift and Valentina Coulton-James, the vicar's daughter,' Amy said. 'You've probably seen them both around the village from time to time, since they're lifelong residents,' she added laconically.

Arbie did, in fact, vaguely recognise the man, having seen him fleetingly once or twice about the village, this relative obscurity being mute testimony to the older man's lack of interest in the residents of Maybury-in-the-Marsh. Something told Arbie that this man had not set foot in The Dun Cow Inn, nor yet spent any of his pennies in the village shop. No, this was the sort of man who would patronise only fine-dining places, and the haughtiest of emporiums.

'Swift? Why does that name ring a bell?' Murray asked,

bending down absently to deposit a rather hit-and-miss attempt at a kiss on his aunt's cheek.

'Oh, Murray dear, you must have read *The Gentleman's Guide to Ghost-Hunting* by now. Almost everyone else in the country has,' Cora teased him drolly. 'Such a witty, light-hearted guide to some of the country's best ghosts and places to stay and all that?'

Murray's face cleared. 'Oh yes, I have as it happens. Good wheeze that. Jolly useful holiday guide too, and those little stories of yours about ghosts and things – most amusing.'

Arbie waved a vague hand in the air, pretending that he hadn't detected the patent insincerity in the other man's tone. 'Oh, it passed the time for me nicely, writing it,' he said airily. 'Once a chap's come down from Oxford he has to find something to do after all.'

Murray shot him an ill-concealed look of vague disdain. 'Wouldn't know, old chap. I've been toiling in the family business since I was in short trousers.'

'Don't exaggerate, Murray,' Amy Phelps said sharply, a definite chill in her voice now. 'And you make it sound as if you've been forced to work in a coal mine, instead of holding an executive position in a thriving business.'

'Oh, only teasing, Aunt. You know Phelps Industries is my very life.' He put a hand mockingly on his heart, making Cora tut and Reggie guffaw obligingly at his antics.

'Well, sit down, Murray, since you're here, and have some scones,' his aunt said flatly. 'I was just about to show Mr Swift and Miss Coulton-James the gardens.'

This was news to Arbie and Val, but both abandoned the bread and butter and Mrs Brockhurst's triumphant strawberry scones to follow her outside. 'I'm sure your cousin and our summer visitors can keep you entertained, Murray,' Amy tossed imperiously over her shoulder as she passed through the open French windows.

30

CHAPTER THREE

It wasn't until they had travelled some way through the gardens, which were indeed splendidly full of lupins, roses, sweet williams, love-in-a-mists and climbing clematis, that Amy unbent enough to sigh and sink wearily onto a wooden garden bench.

'Please, sit down, my dears,' she said, sounding almost human now.

Val took one swift look at her, noted her rather greyish complexion and stooping shoulders and sat beside her, laying a hand gently over hers. The poor dear really did look, under all her starch and vinegar, as if she was at the end of her tether, and as usual, she felt a flood of determination to help if she could. She was not a vicar's daughter for nothing. 'Now, why don't you tell us what's really worrying you, Miss Phelps?' she said encouragingly. 'Arbie and I will do all we can to help, won't we, Arbie?'

Arbie nodded. Although Val might think he was a bit of a clod, he could see as well as she could that the old girl was in dire need of some bucking up. 'Rather,' he said. Then added, with an acuity that had Val almost gaping at him, 'It's not really your family ghost that's worrying you though, is it?'

Amy Phelps regarded him thoughtfully. 'You know, you're not such a fool as everyone thinks, are you, young man?' she said devastatingly.

Arbie, not sure whether he'd just been utterly insulted, or had been given the biggest compliment of his life, simply blinked.

'Lost for words?' Val said, giving him one of her rare affectionate smiles. 'Not a good thing for an author, eh Miss Phelps? But don't you worry – between the three of us we can sort it all out. But we do rather need to know what it is that *needs* sorting out,' she prompted gently.

At this, the older woman nodded wearily but began to look uneasy. 'Yes, I know, I know. But it's very difficult. Sometimes, the things you think in your head sound utterly ridiculous if you say them out loud. And it's not as if I was sure . . . It's not as if I have anything solid to get a *hold* of, that's the thing. Nothing I can point to and say, "There, you see? Someone *is* trying to do me harm." It's all so . . . nebulous. And it really *might* be Wilbur haunting me after all, you know. That's the worst of it. I can't be sure.'

She twisted her hands restlessly in her lap, as Val exchanged worried and puzzled looks with Arbie.

'Do you honestly believe in the supernatural then, Miss Phelps?' Arbie asked gently, trying to get some sort of a feeling for what was expected of him.

'Well – before this, I would have said no,' the woman said with a somewhat tremulous smile. 'I mean, it's all very nice having a family legend and ghost and what have you, but it's hardly something you give much thought to, is it? But just lately . . . I'm beginning to wonder. Except of course, common sense . . . ' She trailed off and sighed heavily.

This time, Val tried to find a starting place. 'Well, have you *seen* the ghost? Wilbur, I mean?'

'Oh no. Well, not seen him exactly. But sometimes, at night, I'm sure I'm being watched . . . No, this won't do.' Miss Phelps stiffened her shoulders, and her head came back. Something of her old iron sparked in the back of her eyes. 'I'm burbling along like a silly young gel! Young man, I want you to do one of your investigations at my house. One of your ghost-watches. You can do that, can't you?'

Arbie, thus straight-forwardly challenged, instinctively felt his own shoulders stiffen and said simply, 'Yes, of course, Miss Phelps, I can do that. If that's what you really want.'

'It is,' she said firmly. And then, in her return to her former and alarmingly uncharacteristic vagueness, added, 'Then at least I'll know one way or another where things stand.'

Val caught Arbie's worried eye and gave him one of her 'do something' looks. All his life he'd been the recipient of such looks from Val, and they usually ended in him getting into trouble.

'It'll probably all turn out to be nothing but a mare's-nest you know,' he said to Amy Phelps gently. 'Most family ghosts and curses and whatnot turn out to be nothing more than pie in the sky. Do you remember the chapter in my book about the Brighton Banshee? That turned out to be nothing more than—'

'Yes, yes, I know,' Amy interrupted him testily. 'I'm not in my dotage yet, young man. I know it's probably all stuff and nonsense. But you see, I need to be *sure* before I act, especially about something so important as . . . Well, never mind that. I just need to be sure I'm right about things, just in case I'm not, and it really *is* Wilbur at work. Oh, I know how silly that sounds.' The older woman broke off, looking from one to the other and silently daring them to agree with her. Naturally, Arbie and Val remained tactfully silent. 'But believe me – there is *something* going on in that house, Mr Swift,' she said, glancing over at the Old Forge. 'I can feel it. All this summer, I've felt . . . uneasy. And I don't like it. And I mean to see to it that it stops,' she added, going so far as to slam the palm of her hand down on the wooden armrest of the bench. 'One way or another – ghost or no ghost – I won't be bullied!'

'Bravo,' Val said. 'That's the spirit!' Then, realising that her choice of words might not have been the wisest, added hastily, 'I'll tell you what, Miss Phelps, we'll hold a ghost-watch this very night. Won't we, Arbie?'

Arbie shot her an appalled look. 'Look here, what's with this "we" business all of a sudden, Val?' he protested. 'You oughtn't be involved at all. And tonight might not be—'

'Oh, I'd be so grateful if you could,' Amy broke in, not wanting to hear any excuses Arbie might make. 'And of course, Miss Coulton-James, you're welcome to stay the night too. I'm sure the presence of myself and Cora in the house will act as an adequate chaperone, should your dear papa be in any way concerned.'

'That's settled then,' Val said, clearly pleased with her afternoon's work. She understood that whilst the reticent older woman wasn't willing to discuss what was truly bothering her with outsiders, it was as plain as a pikestaff that something needed to be done. And besides – she was intrigued. She sensed adventure in the air and shot Arbie an arch look. 'Isn't it, Arbie?'

Arbie looked at Val's sparkling eyes and Amy's unhappy ones and knew when it was time to resign himself to the inevitable. 'We'll see you later then, Miss Phelps,' he said helplessly, ruminating morosely that his uncle would probably laugh himself sick when he had to confess to the old reprobate just what he'd let himself in for now.

*

When they returned to the salon, it was to find Reggie benevolently fending off the teasing barbs of Murray Phelps whilst petting an enormous and astonishingly beautiful cat which sat on the man's lap. The fluffy cat, predominantly black with a few tiger-ish ginger stripes, raised enquiring turquoise eyes to watch them as they stepped in from the garden, and Arbie immediately went over to it.

34

'What a beauty,' he said admiringly, but without making any move yet to touch it. Although cats, dogs and horses (in fact, most animals) took to him on sight, he'd learned some of his lessons the hard way when it came to being overfamiliar with members of the animal kingdom. Ever since Mr Jupp's donkey had taken a chunk out of him when he was still in short trousers, he maintained a healthy respect for their privacy. 'Can I pet her? What's her name?'

Reggie beamed. 'Of course. Empress Maud adores adoration, don't you, darling?' he drawled at the cat, who proved her master true to his word by setting up a purr that almost vibrated the rafters as Arbie ran his hand along her luxuriant fur.

'She's taken to you! You don't want a kitten or two by any chance, do you?' Reggie asked eagerly.

Phyllis half-laughed and half-shook her head in warning. 'Be careful what you say, Mr Swift. Reggie re-homes unwanted animals with a panache that can leave you reeling,' she said, with obvious affection. 'Why, I've seen him rehome copious amounts of white mice with the most timid of old ladies.'

'Yes, just how many waifs, strays and lost causes does that little outfit of yours cater to now?' Murray asked him with a laconic grimace.

'Oh, hundreds I expect,' Reggie said with a shrug and a smile. 'I lose count. Of course, our volunteers in the village are simply marvellous – we wouldn't be able to do it without them. Mrs Possett alone has been known to take ten kittens into her own home at a sitting, and eventually pass them on to friends and family. Then there are the youngsters – teenage girls simply adore looking after broken-down ponies and all our other equine casualties. It's just as well they do – there's no way I could afford to pay them anything. It's as much as we can do to feed them all.'

'Ah, but it's such a good cause,' Amy Phelps said, taking a seat and looking with benign bemusement at the antics of Empress

Maud, who was now reaching out her chin so far in quest of Arbie's tickling fingers that she looked in danger of tumbling off Reggie's knees and onto the floor. 'I got my dear Hamish from Reggie, remember? Alas, he's no longer with us – but I did keep him until he was nearly eighteen.'

'Ah yes, and a dear little chap he was too, Amy,' Reggie said with a fond, reminiscent smile. 'Which reminds me – I have another West Highland terrier just come in that needs a good home. Do you think . . . ?'

Murray shook his head. 'You're shameless, Reggie old man.'

Reggie sighed theatrically. 'Yes, I suppose I am.'

Everyone smiled, but Murray seemed to be in a bullish mood. 'You know, instead of confining yourself to good works, with a bit of effort you could turn your little hobby into a viable business. Selling pedigrees and so on. Might help you out with keeping the tax man from your door. Who knows, you might even be able to stay on in the summer at your own place instead of leasing it out to those dreadful Norwegians, or Swedes, or whoever it is gullible enough to take on that crumbling hovel of yours. You're going to have to keep the wolf from the door somehow. It's not as if you have dear old Uncle Francis to help you out anymore,' he added smoothly.

At this, there was a tense silence, and their hostess drew in a swift breath. She had gone a little red-faced, whilst Reggie had gone pale.

'Leave him alone, Murray,' Amy reprimanded. 'You know all the best people nowadays have to tighten their belts and letting out their homes for the summer to discerning people is a respectable way of doing so,' she said, deliberately ignoring his last words.

'Speaking of unpleasant things,' Amy said sharply, 'I've had to ask Mrs Brockhurst to have a word with Doreen again.' This had the effect of making Cora and Phyllis shoot quick, knowing glances at each other, whilst this time it was Murray Phelps's turn to go slightly red-faced. 'It's simply not good enough. That's twice now I've seen that young madam loitering about the vicinity when she knows she has no business here now.'

Arbie and Val, sensing the uncomfortable turn in the atmosphere, tactfully chose that moment to start making their farewells, and gave their promise to return later that night. At this, everyone in the room looked surprised, but Amy seemed disinclined to satisfy their curiosity, being in no mood to explain the situation.

*

Once outside in the lane, Arbie let out a long breath. 'Phew. That was all a bit fraught, wasn't it?'

'It was a bit,' Val agreed, stepping with Arbie to one side and onto the grass verge to let a horse and farm cart pass by. The horse, a big white mare, plodded on placidly, whilst the group of farm labourers, on their way to the fields, touched their caps and looked at Val with open enjoyment.

Val took no notice.

'What was all that about this Doreen person, do you suppose?' Arbie asked, once the road was clear and they set off again towards their respective houses. 'I thought Murray Phelps looked like he'd swallowed a caterpillar at the very mention of her.'

'Oh, you know Doreen Capstan. Her family live in one of the terrace cottages opposite Cooper's yard,' Val said brusquely.

Arbie nodded. He had a vague image of several Capstan youngsters running about the place – predominately red heads if his memory served him well.

'Well, she used to work as a maid at the Old Forge, but left under something of a cloud, according to village gossip,' Val swept on. 'I thought everyone knew that.'

Arbie sighed. 'It seems to me someone or other is always being picked apart by village gossip. It'd be nice if all the old moggies in this place minded their own business once in a while.'

Val didn't disagree with him, but since the village thrived on drama, the likelihood of Arbie's dream coming true was about as likely as she herself growing a pair of wings. 'So what do you think has got Miss Phelps in such a tizz then? The old bean really is in a flap about something, though she's determined not to let on of course. Too stiff upper lip for words, isn't she?'

'Yes, she is, and I've no more idea than you have. But I doubt it's got anything to do with the family ghost,' Arbie said dampeningly. 'And I do wish you hadn't let us in for this ghost-watch tonight, Val. I had to do enough of that last summer.'

'But you need more material for the next book, don't you?' Val said bracingly, looking at him closely as he muttered something indistinct. 'You *are going* to write another book, aren't you?' she asked suspiciously. 'Everyone's expecting one. The whole village, all your many readers, not to mention your publisher.'

Arbie muttered again.

Val stopped and stared at him. 'Arbie Swift, you can't let that poor mope Walter Greenstreet down. Isn't he supposed to be a pal of yours?'

Arbie nodded gloomily. 'I suppose so,' he agreed reluctantly.

'And didn't he go out on a limb to help you get *The Gentleman's Guide* published?' Val continued. 'And isn't the family firm on at him to get you to sign another contract? You simply can't let him down, you cad!'

'What's he been saying?' Arbie cried, stung at the insult. 'Don't tell me the blighter has been crying on your shoulder, Val?'

'What else can he do? He knows how lazy you are as well as I do,' Val said with her usual lack of tact. 'He has to do *something* to kick your lazy bones into action, and I promised to help him.'

'Val!' Arbie protested feebly at this rank treachery.

'Well, he was really down in the dumps, poor old thing,' Val muttered, feeling a little abashed now and not liking it at all. Trust Arbie to give her one of his 'kicked puppy' looks and make her feel all guilty! 'Come on, Arbie, buck up do. You can't laze around doing nothing *all* your life. I know you come into your parents' money soon, and you've no need to do another day's work and all that, but it'll do you good to write another book.'

Arbie, who had been invited by an old school pal of his to do some fly-fishing in a very nice chalk stream on his estate next weekend, followed by a bit of boating on the Broads, courtesy of yet another acquaintance who was looking for someone to help him crew his large yacht, muttered something unintelligible. He'd been looking forward to lazing around on the water with no particular agenda, and bitterly resented being forced into a corner by his friends and neighbours.

Val simply glared at him. 'I'll see you tonight then,' she said firmly. 'What time do you start ghost-watches by the way?' They had now turned into Church Lane, which housed only the church, vicarage and at the very end of the no-through lane, the Old Chapel itself. Beyond that, an old five-barred gate led onto the water meadow, currently being grazed by cattle, that dipped down to the river, where Uncle had had a jetty built. Nobody knew why – Uncle didn't own so much as a canoe.

'When it gets dark of course,' Arbie answered her question sulkily.

'Right-oh,' Val said. 'You'll pick me up around ten then?' And with that, she turned off into the vicarage, a pleased smile lighting her face.

It wasn't until Arbie had almost reached the entrance to his own home that he realised the fact that she didn't know when ghost-watches started proved that she'd never read a single line of his book!

*

39

Uncle was in the shed when Arbie passed and called out to him cheerfully. 'Oi there, boy, just the one I want. Come here and stick your finger on this thingamabob, will you, while I crank it? Don't fret, it won't kill you.' He offered this addendum automatically now, ever since an incident nearly eight years ago, whereby he'd inadvertently given Arbie an electric shock which had made his fingers go numb for nearly two hours.

With these typical and alarming words, Arbie reluctantly entered his uncle's domain. The 'shed' was, in fact, a light stone outbuilding with tall windows, its own generator, cold running water and a reassuringly weather-proof tiled roof. In one area nearest the largest set of windows, a raised dais had been added and was set up as his uncle's painting studio. But it was to the far long wall, where his nearest relative kept his workshop, that he was led.

Although Uncle had a given Christian name it had somehow become lost over the mists of time, and in the way that sometimes happened in villages, his identity had become subsumed, until he was known by one and all – and not only his legitimate nephew – simply by the sobriquet of 'Uncle'.

In his early sixties, he was of average height, neither fat nor thin, with receding grey hair and grey eyes. He was usually to be found dressed in something reprehensible – either his painter's smock, so stiff with oil paint it could probably stand up on its own – or oil-besmirched overalls the smell of which had been known to frighten the horses. Or worse yet – in some old Victorian relic of a black-tie-and-tails if he was forced to attend a theatre or dine out.

Today he was in the overalls and working on something that looked like a cross between a stationary engine and a knife-grinding machine. Arbie didn't dare ask what this latest invention of his was, lest his guardian attempted to explain it. The properties of mechanics, in Arbie's case, tended to flow in one

40

ear and then pass straight out of the other without bothering to put his brain to any unwanted trouble. 'Put your finger on this and don't take it off until I say,' Uncle muttered now, placing Arbie's unwilling digit on a greasy lever.

Arbie sighed and stood there patiently, holding the lever firmly down, whilst his uncle tinkered for a bit, but Arbie's general air of gloom didn't go unnoticed for long.

'So, what's biting you then, boy?' Uncle finally asked with a grin. 'You've got a face like a wet weekend.'

'Women,' Arbie said truculently.

'Ah. Say no more,' Uncle said.

So Arbie didn't.

CHAPTER FOUR

'What time is it?' Val whispered.

'About six minutes later than the last time you asked,' Arbie responded wearily.

They were sitting in the hall of the Old Forge, and the grandfather clock ticking ponderously in the corner had just roused itself to churr and strike the half-hour after eleven. It was, Arbie knew, going to be a long night. Usually when he'd done this sort of thing for *The Gentleman's Guide* he'd been alone and able to sit in peace and read a book or even doze. But with Val by his side, wide-eyed and constantly on the lookout for ghostly goings-on (which in Arbie's experience never actually happened), he had already abandoned all hope of an easy night.

'Did you hear that?' Val suddenly hissed, clutching his arm with tight fingers.

Arbie nodded. 'It was the stairs creaking. They often do that a little while after the last person has gone to bed. The wood, which had been tramped down a bit, suddenly pings back into place. On really old staircases, it can sound just as if someone unseen is walking down them, one after another, which is one of the main causes for false reports of ghosts. If you'd read my book, you'd have known that.'

'Oh,' Val said, momentarily rebuked and subsiding back into

her chair. 'And I *have* read your book,' she said, almost truthfully. She'd begun to read it when it first came out, expecting Arbie to have made a bad fist of it, but on finding herself regularly chuckling over his silly little ghostly exploits, or becoming generally interested in the holiday resorts he was writing about, had decided to abandon it. She was used to the handsome and feckless Arbie Swift being someone she could easily dismiss as being an irrelevant addendum to her normal life and seeing him in any other light tended to confuse and worry her.

In the dark gloom of the Old Forge's main hallway, she sensed that Arbie was tossing her a speaking glance and flushed guiltily.

'Well, some of it,' she muttered.

For about a minute and a half there was silence once more. Then Val began to fidget, and then, another twenty seconds or so later she said, 'Isn't it midnight yet?'

'No,' Arbie said miserably.

'Is it true that's really the "witching" hour, when you get most activity?'

'No,' Arbie said again. 'If you'd read my book you'd know that I haven't encountered real "activity" at all. Only a few instances of people playing the fool – though yes, they did tend to concentrate their antics around midnight.'

Val sighed. 'They *will* do it, I suppose.'

'Hmmm,' Arbie said. Then added, without much hope, 'You know, Val, we're supposed to sit here in silence and observe. Ghosts like their peace and quiet.' And so, it had to be said, did Arbie.

Val's whispering subsided, for about eight minutes.

Outside a tawny owl hooted, and its partner answered. From above came the odd faint creak, as the various inhabitants of the old house turned in their beds. Despite a recent long run of warm summer weather, for some reason it had now decided to turn almost chilly, in that rather lackadaisical manner to which

43

English summers were prone, and Arbie was beginning to wish he'd brought a coat.

Then Val said sharply, 'Arbie, that shadow's moving.'

Arbie, who'd had his eyes closed and was trying to catch a surreptitious forty winks, opened one eye and glanced at the wall opposite. 'There's a full moon tonight. It's shining through the shrubbery outside and the breeze is moving the leaves. It gives you the impression of something more substantial moving about. Ignore it.'

'Oh.' Val supposed, crossly, that even Arbie Swift, when given a task to do, was bound to become something of an expert eventually.

The big wheezy clock finally roused itself to strike twelve. Val held her breath. Arbie let out a very soft snore. Val looked at his sleeping form and shook her head in disgust. She just knew it. Trust him to fall asleep. She'd bet her entire – and meagre – allowance that he'd slept through every ghost vigil he'd ever kept. No wonder *The Gentleman's Guide to Ghost-Hunting* had never recorded a single real instance of a ghost. And there she'd been, willing to give him the benefit of the doubt! Oh, he'd have everyone believe it was creaking stairs, or draughts that blew newspapers off tables, or human forgetfulness that accounted for vases of flowers swopping places on mantel shelves overnight. She should have known he'd just been asleep on the job and not paying proper att—

Suddenly Val's heart leapt into her throat. Something, somewhere above her in the darkness, was moving. Definitely moving and not mere shadows on the wall. Stealthy, careful, precise movement. She reached out and grabbed Arbie's arm.

Arbie awoke from a nice dream where he'd just been about to land a splendid brown trout, and found himself not in his own bed, but an uncomfortable chair. And with someone shaking him soundly! But with the resilience of youth he became aware almost instantly of where he was, and the circumstances surrounding his lack of a comfortable bed, and he turned to scowl at his unwanted companion.

Before he could make a noise, however, Val put a finger to her lips and pointed upwards. Because of the full moon shining through the windows, he was able to make out quite a lot of his immediate environment and could clearly see that Val's finger was shaking as she pointed towards the stairs.

And then he could see for himself what had given her the jitters. A tall human form was slowly descending the stairs. It was wearing something white and seemed to have a white head. It was not the outline of a big strapping smithy though, dressed in his leathers and bearing with him the ghostly smell of iron and smoke. Moreover, Arbie noted that the shape was taking care to keep very carefully to the outer edges of the stairs, thus avoiding the worst of the creaking boards.

And why, he mused, would a proper ghost need to do that? He sighed gently, got up and began to walk carefully towards the foot of the stairs. He noted, with extreme pleasure, the shocked 'O' forming on Val's pretty mouth, and grinned. No doubt she'd expected him to turn tail and run a mile instead of fearlessly heading into the unknown! Well, that would teach her to take his lack of manhood for granted.

When he'd reached the bottom of the stairs, however, it was to find Val supportively by his side and, in a moment, both of them could clearly see the identity of their visitor.

Amy Phelps was dressed in a white flannel nightdress and over it, a large housecoat in a shade of heavy cream. Her long grey locks were primly hidden under a lacy white nightcap. She nodded at them silently and beckoned them into the nearest room – which turned out to be a library-cum-study.

'Sorry to disturb you, Mr Swift, Miss Coulton-James. I couldn't sleep and was wondering if you were making any progress,' she murmured softly.

'It's a little early yet, I'm afraid,' Arbie chided gently. 'It's usually well into the early hours before one can expect anything . . . er . . . interesting.'

Amy nodded. 'I thought as much,' she said. 'I feared I was being precipitate, but when you're lying alone in bed and worrying . . . well, the need for action becomes overwhelming, doesn't it?'

Arbie nodded. Leading her to a chair, Val hot on his heels, he helped Amy to sit, then took the chair nearest her. He leaned forward fluidly, letting his hands rest lightly on his knees, his head bent towards her in a confiding manner. 'I was hoping I might get you alone for a bit, Miss Phelps,' he said. 'You know, when we first spoke this morning, you said something that's been rather gnawing away at me all day.'

'Oh?' Amy said stiffly.

'Yes,' Arbie said firmly. 'You said . . . or rather, I seem to recall, you intimated that you thought the ghost had, er, somewhat alarming intentions towards you.'

Amy sat up straight in her chair. 'Let's not shilly-shally about the bushes, young man,' she said repressively. 'I believe I said that it wanted to kill me.'

'Yes, er, quite,' Arbie said a little helplessly. 'I was rather hoping you'd expand a bit on that at tea, but I gather you had second thoughts?'

Amy let out a rather dry chuckle. 'Well, it's hardly the kind of thing you can discuss with your family and friends all around you, is it, Mr Swift?' She shook her head, making her lace cap dance. 'They'd either think I'd gone potty, or else that I had been hitting the gin!'

In the darkness, Arbie grinned. Say what you like about Miss Phelps, she was a game old bird!

'Yes, I can see that they might,' he conceded smoothly. 'But perhaps now – between just us – you can be a bit more forthcoming? I'm sure Val won't repeat anything you have to say, will you, Val?'

'Of course not,' Val said staunchly, and meant it. 'Daddy always says gossip is the devil's work,' she added primly.

Amy Phelps sighed but nodded. 'Yes. I can see I owe you some sort of an explanation, especially when you're doing all this for me,' she added, waving a vague hand in the direction of the darkened hall. 'It's just that I know it's all going to sound so tentative and feeble when I say it out loud. It's not going to convey the real horror of what I've been feeling for the past week or so.'

'Just state the facts, Miss Phelps, that's best,' Arbie advised.

'Right. Well, it began with finding one of Wilbur's hammers on my chair. His heavy one,' Amy said. 'Well, naturally that gave me a bit of a turn.'

'Sorry?' Arbie had to interrupt. 'His *hammer*?'

'Yes,' Amy said, a shade impatiently. 'Our family kept all of Wilbur's original smithy tools and such in the original forge, that's now where the car and gardening things are kept. Wilbur had, as you might expect, a whole range of implements, which he used to shoe horses and make ironwork and what have you.'

'Ah, I see.' Arbie nodded. 'And naturally you wouldn't want to part with the family heirlooms, so to speak. But, pardon me, why did finding one of them on your chair give you such a case of the old goose bumps?'

'Well, for a start, what was it doing there? It had no business being there. And who put it there?' she demanded. 'The only people in the house were my immediate household. And Murray, who'd come over to collect some strawberries from the greenhouse.'

Arbie, who was beginning to feel like that member of the audience who'd come in halfway through the play and thereafter had to struggle to pick up the plot, settled himself down with patience. 'Sorry again, Miss Phelps, but when did this happen?'

'Last Tuesday, I think it was.'

'No, sorry, I mean what time of the day was it? Evening or . . . '

'Oh, just on dusk, I would say. I hadn't asked Mrs Brockhurst to light the lamps yet anyway.'

'And your two guests for the summer were both here in the house, you say?' he asked.

'I think Reggie had gone back to his studio by then – he spends so much time there on his photography and painting and things, so it was only Cora. And Murray, as I said. He arrived just as we were sitting down to coffee and took himself off to the greenhouse. The greedy boy always did like more than his fair share of the strawberries. The thing is, my chair was empty when I left it to go in to dinner. And when Cora and myself came back after we'd eaten . . . there it was.'

'Ah,' Arbie said. 'And Mrs Brockhurst . . . ?'

'Naturally I asked her if she knew anything about it,' Amy said shortly. 'And she was as puzzled as the rest of us.'

'She denied putting it there, in fact?' Arbie nodded.

'She did, young man, and I believe her. To have left it in my chair, she'd first have had to go out and find it, and would have probably got filthy in doing so, as the place, as you can imagine, is full of old coal, motor oil and who knows what else! And she was her normal neat and tidy self. What's more, in the dark of the Old Forge shed, she'd have needed to take a candle with her to see, taking up the use of one of her hands. And since the hammer was a very heavy thing indeed, made of solid oak and a heavy piece of iron, I doubt she could have carried it far one-handed with just her free hand. And besides which, why should she?'

To this, Arbie had no ready answer. Because, for that matter, why should anyone bother relocating an old hammer? What was the point of it? 'And is that all . . . ?' he asked gently.

'Of course not,' Amy Phelps said witheringly. 'The next thing was the poker.'

'Poker?' This time it was Val who found herself repeating Amy's words.

'Yes. The big poker Wilbur used to keep his forge fires hot and burning. A big iron thing, with a curled handle, handmade by Wilbur himself, naturally,' Amy said, with pride.

'And you found this on your chair one day too?' Arbie asked, hoping he didn't sound as bewildered as he felt.

'I found it,' Amy Phelps corrected him coldly, 'thrust into a ball of my knitting wool one morning after I'd had breakfast.'

'Oh,' Arbie said.

'It was a pretty powder blue in colour, and I was knitting myself a bed jacket. It had been thrust through not only the ball of wool itself, but through the ribbing I'd done the day before, making a hole in it. I had to unpick it and start again,' Amy said, aggrieved.

Val had to stifle a giggle, but Arbie managed to keep a straight face. 'I see. And again, nobody admitted to putting it there? You know, it could have been some sort of practical joke . . . '

'Reggie and Cora don't play those sorts of games, Mr Swift, I assure you. Such malarkey is the province of the young and foolish. And although Murray happened to be staying overnight on that occasion, I would have thought his prank-playing days long over.'

Crushed, Arbie could see she had a point. 'But children from the village . . . they could have sneaked in . . . '

'I doubt they'd get past the eagle eyes of my gardening staff, let alone Mrs Brockhurst. Besides . . . that's not the only thing,' Amy said, looking around nervously. 'It's what happened on each occasion just before I found these things that really made my blood run cold. Something that puts it beyond question that the legend surrounding the ghost of my ancestor is somehow involved.'

Her voice had taken on a distinctly quavering quality all at once, and Arbie stiffened and shot Val a quick look. And in her shining blue eyes he saw an answering excitement in her expression that must have matched his own. Now they were coming to it!

'Yes, Miss Phelps? What happened, exactly?' he asked gently.

Amy Phelps swallowed hard and drew her housecoat further around her. She leaned a little forward, as did Arbie and Val, until their three bent heads formed a neat circle. Amy's voice lowered dramatically. 'Each time, just before I found Wilbur's warning messages to me, I heard something most peculiar. And sinister.'

'What was it?' Val all but squeaked.

Amy looked at her tiredly. 'My dear, can't you guess? I distinctly heard the tinkling of a bell.'

Val opened her mouth and closed it again. 'A bell?' she repeated faintly. 'You mean, like the one that had been tied to Wilbur's toe, in the churchyard . . . '

'Exactly. And before you ask, young man,' Amy said, giving Arbie a firm look, 'it was not a bell like the chiming of one of the old clocks, or the bell one would use to summon a servant, nor yet the bell that someone such as a postman would have on his bicycle and which might have drifted in through the window from the lane outside. I know all the sounds of the various implements used in the house and this was something I'd never heard before. It was the small, gentle tinkling of a tiny bell. And what's more – every time I heard it, I went immediately towards the sound, but could find no earthly agency for it. Nobody was there! I was quite alone.'

Amy sat back and nodded firmly. 'And I'm not the sort to imagine things. Indeed, on the very first occasion I heard it, before I even found the hammer in my chair, why on earth should I be thinking of bells or any such thing anyway?' she demanded reasonably.

Arbie could see she had a point.

'I can see why such an odd set of circumstances would unnerve you, Miss Phelps,' he acceded gently. For a moment he was silent, thinking things through. Her assertion that she went immediately to seek out the source of the sound he dismissed at once. On the first occasion she heard it, she wouldn't have been human if she hadn't paused to wonder if her ears were deceiving her before setting off in pursuit of the origin of the sound. And on later occasions, once she was aware that someone was conducting a campaign of intimidation against her, she could be forgiven even more for hesitating for a moment or two in trepidation before seeking out the culprit. As formidable as Miss Phelps was, she *was* human! And any small delay meant that the practical joker could ring his or her wretched bell and then hastily exit the area with ease. So the fact she hadn't been able to find a human agency for the bell-ringing was not surprising. What he found very hard to understand, however, was who would want to frighten someone like Miss Phelps. And why?

He would have to be careful how he questioned her though, since it was becoming apparent that only one of those close to her could be responsible. And she was far too proud to admit such a thing readily.

He shifted a little in his chair. 'You must have thought about these events a lot over the past few days, Miss Phelps,' he began, with a massive understatement. 'Have you come to any conclusions about what they might mean?'

Amy shrugged helplessly. 'It makes no sense,' she said, somewhat crossly.

Arbie coughed delicately. 'And have you, er, done anything that might, er, incur the displeasure of your dead ancestor?' he asked, deciding he might as well try a different approach. If he could get her to abandon her hopes that an actual ghostly presence might be at work, he could begin at last to get down to the crux of the matter. 'If a spectre is at work here, there has

51

to be a reason the dead are feeling restless,' he added, careful to keep his face sombre.

Amy tossed her head. 'Certainly not. As you know, there are not that many of us Phelpses around any longer, and I feel the responsibility of safeguarding our family name and inheritance quite keenly. I have done nothing to which Wilbur Phelps could take exception.' Then she paused, very perceptibly gave a little start as if just remembering something and sniffed a bit. 'I may have had to rebuke a . . . family member . . . recently, but it was no more than he, I mean, than they deserved, I'm sure.'

Val and Arbie wisely said nothing, but even so the woman gave herself a shake and rose to her feet. 'Well, I've kept you from your duties long enough. I should be getting back to my bed.'

'I'll come with you and see you safely there,' Val said, and was as good as her word.

Arbie thoughtfully watched the two women ascend the stairs then took up his old place in his chair in the hall. He was feeling just a little worried, and only hoped he hadn't inadvertently made matters worse.

When Val came back a bit later and sat beside him in her own chair, she was visibly bristling with excitement. 'So, what did you make of all that?'

Arbie yawned hugely. 'Well, apart from the fact that she's worried sick that that nephew of hers is behind it all, not much.'

'Oh,' Val said, her face falling. 'You'd figured that out too?' She was unable to keep the disappointment from her voice. She'd been rather looking forward to expounding her new theories to a suitably impressed Arbie Swift, and now she felt distinctly deflated.

Arbie, oblivious to the sudden cooling in the atmosphere, yawned again. 'She did rather make a point of mentioning that, around the time of both incidents occurring, Murray was visiting and was present here in the house. And then there was the slip of the tongue when she said that the member of the family she'd had to "rebuke" was male. It hardly takes a Dr Watson to figure it out that she's worried that he's behind it all, does it?'

Val, still feeling cross at having her thunder stolen, having reached all the same conclusions herself, said sulkily, 'You mean Sherlock Holmes.'

'What? No, I meant Dr . . . ' Arbie paused and then subsided. He'd been about to explain that he'd made a quip – that the events at the Old Forge were so plain that even the notoriously slow sidekick of the great detective could figure them out without the aid of the master detective for once. But something told him Val wouldn't appreciate his literary wit. 'Oh, never mind,' he said instead.

In the corner, the old grandfather clock chimed the half-hour after midnight. 'And you can shut up, clock,' Val muttered at it viciously, 'or I'll remove your pendulum.'

*

The next morning, Val returned home stiff in limb and bored in mind. Luckily, in the summer, dawn arrived early and she was able to get away by five. In the old vicarage, not even the maids were stirring yet, and Val made her way to the kitchen, in dire need of a cup of tea. She lit the fire in the stove and filled the kettle and slumped despondently in the nearest kitchen chair as she waited for the water to boil.

It was here that her father found her, morosely sipping tea. 'See any spooks then?' he asked her mildly.

'I'm afraid not,' Val responded gloomily.

Her father checked the progress of the kettle and set about slicing two pieces of bread from a rather stale loaf and seeking out the toasting fork so that he might begin his breakfast. He hovered over the stove, toasting fork waving a little in the air, as he expounded. 'I can't imagine what Miss Phelps is thinking of – ghosts of all things! I'd always thought of her as a very sensible, shrewd sort of person.'

'Oh, don't worry, I think she still is. I'm not sure that she believes in her ghostly smithy either.'

'No? Then why the appeal to our young Mr Swift?'

'Oh, Arbie was no use,' Val said scornfully. 'All he did was sit in the hall waiting for something to happen. Which of course, it didn't.'

'And how is our celebrity?'

Val shrugged but remained eloquently silent on the subject.

Her father looked at his pretty daughter for a moment, noting her bowed, fair head and slightly drooping mouth, and was careful not to smile. He'd long since harboured vague suspicions that his offspring might be far more taken with a certain man of letters than she would ever let on.

He said gently, 'And how is that beau of yours? Are you seeing him at the Andersons' dance next week?'

Val scowled. Her parents, desperate to see her safely married off before she gained the too-humiliating reputation of being a confirmed old maid (she was now twenty-two years old after all), had recently taken to inviting Gerald Handley-Forbes, the younger son of a local landowner over to tea and tennis parties, hoping to foster an 'understanding' between them. Val, however, was not impressed by this latest, and to her mind rather lacklustre, offering. He couldn't play tennis for toffee and had a chin that was almost non-existent. And trying to have an interesting conversation with him was like trying to fill a bath one thimbleful of water at a time.

The vicar of Maybury-in-the-Marsh sighed slightly as he speared his second slice of bread and held it over the stove's embers, watching it slowly turn brown. His dear wife was set on seeing Valentina married before the year was out but believed her hopes would prove to be in vain.

54

Whilst Val made tea in the silent vicarage, Arbie had already turned into the grounds of his home, tiredly contemplating his uncle's birthday, which was less than a month away, and the present he'd finally decided to get him.

Normal people wouldn't regard either event with much trepidation, but Arbie and his uncle had something of a history when it came to misfires regarding gifts, so he'd had to think long and hard about what he would get the old sausage this year. It had to be something that he didn't already own and would be of use to him but also please him, whilst at the same time being something which couldn't possibly cause mayhem or bring shame down on their heads.

His uncle, much as Arbie loved him, had an unfortunate knack of creating chaos out of the most innocuous of things. He still shuddered when he thought about the use his uncle had made of a splendid box kite that Arbie had bought for him four years ago. But who'd have thought you could paint such a realistically nude figure on such an oddly shaped collection of materials? Let alone fly it so accurately. (The verger still hadn't recovered and refused to speak to either of them.)

But this year, Arbie thought that he might have cracked it. The Old Chapel grounds were bounded on the southern side by the river, so he had put some of his royalties from his book to good use and had purchased a small but jaunty little river cruiser, ideal for spending some time messing about on the river. He knew Uncle had read *Three Men in a Boat* many years before and had loved it and had always said he would one day follow their journey up the Thames.

But Arbie had bought the one-room craft mainly to be used as a travelling outdoor studio for his uncle's painting. He was currently in negotiations with the boatyard people to spruce it up a bit to his specifications and add a skylight to allow more natural light inside, and once it was complete, he was pretty sure his uncle would be delighted with it. Now he would be able to paint al fresco without having to worry about sudden gusts of wind or rain, and putter about finding the perfect riverside landscapes to paint. And what harm could he come to in a small river craft?

As he let himself into the cavernous main room of his unusual home, Basket, their lazy mongrel, lifted his shaggy head from his favourite spot – his basket – and looked at him incuriously through big brown eyes. His plumy tail wagged once or twice to show willing, then he put his head back down and closed his eyes.

Arbie eyed the animal with a mixture of fondness and irritation and left him to his slumbers. Then he made his own way wearily to bed, contemplating the wasted night he'd just spent. Dropping down on top of the blankets without bothering to get undressed, within moments he was fast asleep.

One thing he was confident of. There was no ghost at the Old Forge and Miss Phelps had no reason to worry. It was probably just someone playing tricks on her, and now that they'd seen how seriously she had taken it, would conclude that it had gone on long enough, and would cease and desist.

She was in no danger at all.

CHAPTER FIVE

The following night, Amy Phelps woke suddenly sometime in the early hours, aware that some sound or other must have disturbed her. She knew all the usual creaks and groans of the house, and they never bothered her, so it must have been something unusual that had stirred her. Outside, low cloud had covered the moon, and her room felt uncomfortably dark. Sitting up in bed, she strained her ears, but could hear nothing further.

Certainly there was no sound of a tiny, tinkling bell.

She had retired early, as had her nephew, both of them leaving Cora and Reggie downstairs playing cards (it was so nice to be able to be so informal with such lifelong friends), and had dozed off almost at once. She hadn't been sleeping well lately and had been enjoying her first deep sleep for some time. For a moment she sat on the edge of her bed, contemplating just slipping back under the blankets and trying to get back to sleep again, but she knew she wouldn't be able to do so. She would simply lie awake all night, tense and growing more and more agitated as she listened out for . . . something.

With a cross sigh, she reached for the box of matches on her bedside table, and after years of practice, lit the wick of the candle that had lighted her to bed hours before. It annoyed her to see the flame wavering, mute testimony to her nervousness, as she picked up the candlestick in a shaking hand and then looked about her for her slippers and housecoat. Then she walked to the door of her bedroom and opened it cautiously, peering out of a gap of only a few inches or so.

If someone was lurking about in this wing of the house, she wanted to catch the culprit unawares. But there was no sound and no sense of movement in the narrow corridor. She stepped fully outside, careful to make no sound as she closed the door behind her and slowly made her way to the top of the nearest flight of stairs.

There she paused and moving closer to the rail that protected her from the drop into the hall below, she lifted the candle higher and peered about her. Then almost let out a shrill yelp of terror as she saw the face of her dead ancestor, the infamous Wilbur Phelps, the ghostly smithy himself, looking up at her. But then, within the next moment, she slapped a grateful hand over her fast-beating heart as her boggling brain finally interpreted correctly what it was that she was actually seeing.

It was only the portrait of him, which hung on the wall above the small landing at the bend in the stairs. She told herself not to be so silly – the portrait had been there for years, but she had long since ceased to pay attention to it. It was just her luck to have noticed it now, when she was feeling as jumpy as a cat!

Smiling to herself now that all had become so prosaically clear and feeling mildly ashamed of herself for her attack of nerves (really, what would Nanny have said?), she started to turn to go back to bed.

But as she did so, she felt a shiver go through her, and the hairs rise in the back of her neck. And suddenly she was convinced that someone was watching her – maybe even gloating over her fear.

She cast a quick glance over her shoulder, but her meagre candlelight illuminated only a small portion of her surroundings. If someone had been observing her from the depths of the dark corridor, she had no hope of seeing even a vague outline of the person. She really was going to have to get more gas lights fitted in her part of the house if this carried on. For almost a full minute she stood absolutely still, staring over her shoulder until her eyes adjusted to the candlelight and she was sure that nobody else was behind her.

Then she checked that the small window, looking out over the roofs, was firmly shut.

She told herself not to be silly.

And it was then that she heard it. The faint ring of the bell – was it coming from outside? Or from somewhere in one of the far rooms in the house down below? Wherever it was coming from, the sound of it not only frightened her further, but also succeeded in making her very, very angry. It was intolerable, she fumed, to be toyed with like this, in some outrageous cat-and-mouse game in her own home! She was going to put a stop to this at once.

With an out-thrust chin and determination in her heart, she took another step down. And that was when she felt it. Something light, unseen, but definitely *there* touched her forehead and the side of her temple. And yet – there was nobody but herself there! It was then that Amy Phelps finally let out a cry of fear and shock. Instinctively, and in a state of total panic now, she clawed at the air in front of her, half-expecting to feel a ghostly cold hand reaching out to her.

Not surprisingly, at this wild treatment, the candle was jettisoned from the candlestick and snuffed itself out as it landed on the stairs, leaving her in darkness. The slipper on her left foot slid out from under her as she danced precariously on the edge of the next step. Her hands windmilled desperately as she attempted to maintain her balance, but it was no good. The next instant, Amy Phelps was falling . . .

*

Seven hours later, Cora Delaney watched from her bedroom window as her friend limped out to a waiting taxi and was borne off to the railway station in the next village. Amy looked as if she was carrying her own thundercloud with her, but at least she was still mobile and feeling fit enough – if a little stiff and sore – to attend to her sudden but urgent business in town. And this business, she had announced boldly at the breakfast table, was to make some changes to her will.

And hadn't that put the cat amongst the pigeons. Since she'd refused to be drawn on the specifics of these changes, speculation was running rife. Although everyone was being too polite to mention it of course.

When Cora had been woken by a cry and a thumping noise in the night, she hadn't given a thought to silly ghosts or any other such nonsense but had simply donned her housecoat and gone out to investigate. Her mind had been more on potential burglars or Empress Maud knocking over some vase or other on one of her nightly feline wanderings than on ghostly goings-on. Luckily, when she found her friend sitting indignantly on the floor at the bend in the staircase, Murray had quickly joined her there, for she doubted if she'd have been able to get Amy to her feet and help support her back to her room. Although Murray had originally planned to leave the day before, his friend had sent a message to say that he couldn't give Murray a lift until the next day. So at least poor Amy hadn't been left in the dark for long.

Happily for Cora, Murray had now also left the house, so she felt perfectly safe to go about her business. And her business that morning was to have a good snoop around – her first chance since she'd arrived for her little holiday.

Throughout their lifelong friendship, Amy had always been close-mouthed about herself and her feelings, which had always made Cora very curious indeed. She knew that her need to ferret out information no matter its relevance was one of her few weaknesses but found herself unable to conquer it. During her student days this had been an advantage, but she was aware that it was not a trait that would endear her to her acquaintances. Which meant, over the years, that Cora had found circumspect ways and means of discovering what her friends were doing, and the more intimate details of their lives, and having Amy's house to herself now was too good an opportunity to miss.

Besides, Cora thought, salving her conscience somewhat, unless she was very much mistaken, there was something more behind all this 'ghost' business than met the eye, and she was bubbling over with curiosity to find out what it was. Because one thing Cora was sure of – Amy was far too sensible and stubbornly logical to *believe* in her ghostly, vengeful ancestor. And yet she'd invited over that charming Mr Swift to sit up on a ghost-watch. Begging the question – what was her friend up to?

When they'd all been young gels together, Amy had prided herself on being the leader of their small coterie of debutants. Not the most beautiful – that had been poor Clementine D'Abry, who'd died so tragically young. Nor the wealthiest – that had been Bertha Young-Smith, who'd married an earl. But Amy had been the boldest and the most determined to get her own way. And right now, her old friend was showing all the signs of being 'up to something'.

And Cora couldn't wait to find out what it was!

Making sure that the housekeeper was safely installed in her kitchen downstairs, Cora walked quietly to Amy's bedroom door and slowly pushed it open. Once inside, she closed the door firmly behind her, and looked around in satisfaction. This was the first time she'd managed to infiltrate her friend's most private room, and she was not surprised to discover that Amy had an enormous feather bed, for Amy had always been serious when it came to her physical comforts. Nor did the lack of any pink ruffles or frou-frou touches surprise her either. Amy, although as

61

vain about her appearance as any woman of quality, had never gone overboard about advertising her femininity.

For all that, she'd had admirers aplenty, although she'd never taken the same trip down the aisle as had Cora and so many of their contemporaries. Cora had often wondered if Amy had been afraid that her beaus were more interested in the Phelps family's newly acquired (by county standards!) wealth. Or whether it had been because she'd simply never wanted to be at the beck and call of some man.

Cora first indulged herself by exploring Amy's wardrobe and envying her slightly delicious coat that bore a famous Parisian label. Her shoes, however, Cora could dismiss with a satisfactory sense of disdain. Cora was known for her collection of shoes (since she was inordinately proud of her small dainty feet) and Amy, predictably, had nothing to match those that currently resided in her own wardrobe back in Yorkshire.

She next went to the small dressing table where she sat down and absently picked up a bottle of scent and sniffed it thoughtfully. No, she didn't know it, but it was probably something expensive and rather exclusive. She debated dabbing a bit on her wrist but decided against it. Shaken up by her recent fall though she may be, there was nothing wrong with her friend's nose! And if Amy realised she'd been snooping in her room, there would be the devil to pay.

She glanced outside the window and saw Reggie come out of his studio and set off with his awkward and bulky camera equipment, heading towards the river. Dear Reggie, with his menagerie of animal waifs and strays, his rather dreadful daubs, and transient hobbies. She knew why he still came here so often, of course. He and Francis had been so very close, the Old Forge probably helped keep the memory of him vibrant.

She remembered the look of worry on his face when she'd told him of Amy's nocturnal tumble, followed by his obvious relief when he'd been assured that it hadn't resulted in any serious injury. Amy herself had roughly brushed off his concern for her, telling him gruffly to sit down and eat his breakfast, which Reggie had taken in his usual good part.

Cora shrugged. Safely ensconced in Amy's private inner sanctum, she reached for the handle on one of the set of small drawers that framed each side of the vanity mirror. In the first were some minor jewels, and Cora was interested to see that, for all the Phelpses' money, she had just as good pieces – if not better – in the drawers of her own vanity dresser back home. The next drawer produced some stamps and unused pen nibs and ink, and some spare mother-of-pearl buttons.

The next drawer instantly intrigued her, for it seemed subtly different from the others. For a moment she couldn't quite think what it was – and then, with a grin of nostalgia – realised that it was the dimensions that seemed off. Which could only mean that it hid a secret drawer! Her own dear mama had had a drawer similar to this one in her writing bureau, and Cora could clearly remember her childish delight when, at the age of seven or so, she had been shown how it worked. 'A lady must always have places to hide her most precious secrets, Cora,' her mother had whispered, guiding her tiny fingers to the little wooden catch hidden beneath the draw's keyhole.

This dresser of Amy's wasn't the same, of course, but it didn't take Cora long to explore and find the tiny catch needed to spring open the secret hidey-hole. And when she did, her heart did a little leap of excitement to see the ageing, yellowing stash of papers that lay inside.

For here was treasure indeed! Bringing out the small bundle of letters tied up in pink ribbon, she hesitated regretfully. She couldn't really read them, of course, even given her overwhelming need to know what they contained. Already, she could feel the weight of reproof from her long dead parents, nanny, governesses and many others, who would be shocked to the core at the idea of a lady reading a friend's private correspondence.

No, it must be enough for her to know that she'd pierced the veil of her friend's secretive nature enough to discover that Amy was only human after all. Who'd have thought that the sceptical, cynical Amy had kept love letters? It made her glad to think that Amy, stern, old-maid Amy, had had at least some . . .

Her somewhat condescending thoughts crashed to a sudden halt, for her eye had fallen on one envelope in particular and her hand began to shake uncontrollably as she recognised the dear, familiar handwriting. And for a moment, Cora Delaney, respectable widow and upright society matron, was eighteen once again. And so dreadfully, completely, dangerously and totally in love. Back in time and in another world far away from this somewhat severe bedroom.

Gone, now, were all the taboos against reading private correspondence. Gone was any thought about right or wrong, or the dues owed to decades of friendship. Only one thought now flooded Cora's mind.

Why had *he* of all people written to Amy Phelps? What could possibly have passed between her best friend and her first love, all those years ago?

With fingers that trembled slightly, Cora took out the single sheet of paper and began to read.

CHAPTER SIX

Four days later, Arbie was surprised to find a note from Miss Phelps inviting him and Val to dinner at the Old Forge on the following Saturday night.

He was enjoying a rather late breakfast with his uncle, who took the missive from him when Arbie offered it, and read it thoughtfully.

'I wonder what the old bat wants,' Uncle said irreverently.

Arbie asked himself if his relative would dare call Miss Phelps that to her face and decided, uneasily, that he just might. He sighed heavily and speared a piece of sausage. 'I have no idea. Maybe she wants to thank me for laying her ghost to rest, so to speak.'

'Humph,' Uncle said, reaching for a piece of toast and lavishly coating it with butter. 'If I were you, I'd be careful there, lad.'

Surprised, Arbie paused, fork in mid-air, one eyebrow raised. 'Oh?'

'I've never known the Phelpses to do anything without a reason, and the reason usually involves the making of money somehow,' Uncle said, thoughtfully eyeing the apricot preserve. 'Never known a family like it for being so money-grabbing. Not that it's done them much good, mind. The family has all but died out. Unless that nephew of hers marries soon and produces an heir, the old girl will find she's got nobody to leave the family fortunes to, if she's not careful. You take my advice and stay away. That woman wants something from you, you mark my words. And she usually gets her own way. You only have to look at how she handled that poor brother of hers.'

'Which one?' Arbie asked curiously.

'Frankie, we all called him, but the family insisted on using "Francis". Poor chap couldn't call his life his own. No wonder he travelled so much. It was a good way to get free of them all. Mind you, that didn't always work.'

'What do you mean?' Arbie asked.

'Well, for a start, the poor lad wasn't allowed to leave his money where he wanted. There was this clerk in the family solicitor's office who knew a thing or two. We used to meet up at the turf accountant, and I'd give him the odd tip now and then. Poor chap, bored witless half the time. No wonder, out of office hours, he was always sozzled and spilling various beans that he shouldn't have. If his bosses had been aware of how indiscreet he was he'd have been out on his ear and no mistake! Mind you, he used to tell me some corking tales of what the upper classes got up to. Hair-raising some of them,' he added with ghoulish relish.

Arbie blinked, not at all sure that he wanted to have his hair raised. 'But what was this, about Francis Phelps?' He tried to keep his uncle to specifics.

'Oh, he made a will leaving a lot of his money to that great chum of his, Reggie what's-his-name. But Amy got wind of it, and bullied him into changing it, so that the family got it all instead. Which, eventually, meant *she* got it all, when she became the last of them.'

'Oh my,' Arbie said. 'Reggie couldn't have liked that. I suppose he knew about it?'

'Oh yes, he knew apparently.'

'And yet he's still good friends with Miss Phelps it seems,' Arbie mused. 'Goes to her every summer, and whatnot.'

Uncle shrugged. 'Folks are strange. But it just goes to show what I said. You be careful of them Phelpses. They're a sly lot.'

Arbie shrugged. 'Well, it's only a dinner invitation,' he pointed out. 'What harm can it do to go? Besides, I can't see how my going or not will affect the Phelps family coffers. It's not as if she's likely to ask me to invest in her garages or forges, or what have you, is it? Everyone knows I can't touch my money until I'm thirty.'

Which was true. On the death of his parents, Uncle had asked the family solicitors to put Arbie's inheritance into an unbreakable trust until he'd reached his thirtieth birthday. And in the almost magical way of things, that snippet had somehow become common knowledge in the village.

Sometimes Arbie wondered if his uncle had done this in a moment of clear-headed self-knowledge. Concerned that, if left unprotected, he might just be tempted to dip his fingers into his young nephew's legacy, when times were tight and his paintings failed to sell, or one of his madcap inventions failed to fly.

Or, on the other hand, he might have considered the possibility that his young nephew might well grow up to be a feckless so-and-so who'd blow the whole lot on gambling, wine, women and song before he was twenty-five!

Somehow, Arbie had never quite worked up the courage to ask him which it was.

Not that it worried him much these days. He knew that his uncle was very proud of the success of his first literary venture, and since Arbie now seemed to have a legitimate, if not particularly wanted, career ahead of him as an author, what was the point of rocking the old boat by asking silly bally questions of one's nearest and dearest?

One thing was for certain – there was no way Miss Phelps could be asking him to dine in order to sell him some stocks and shares in her family empire, and he'd simply tell her that all his royalties for *The Gentleman's Guide* had already been spent if she tried!

'I wonder if Val will come,' he said thoughtfully, polishing off the last of the black pudding on his plate, and snaffling a piece of toast from the silver toast rack before his uncle could eat it all.

'A nice girl, that Val,' his uncle said amiably.

'Is she?' Arbie said, sounding a little astonished.

*

Val, who'd received her own written invitation to dine at the Old Forge, agonised long and hard over her meagre wardrobe that Saturday evening. Having an enormous family to support, her father's stipend didn't stretch to too many posh frocks, so her choice was wretchedly limited. If only she could get a paying job, she might have money to spend for herself – but of course, that was out of the question. Even if she could take typing lessons and find a job as a typist in some respectable office, her mother would still have a fit of the vapours, and her dear papa would receive a very stiff note from his Bishop.

Although all but four of the siblings had now married and moved out of the family home, that left her in the precarious position of being the eldest child still at home. Her two younger brothers and the youngest of them all, her sister Abigail, had first call on the family purse, which was as it should be, she thought staunchly.

It was just so beastly to feel as if she was letting the side down and taking the food out of the mouths of babes by not having found herself a husband yet. But for some reason, she just couldn't bring herself to set her cap at any of her suitors so far. And whilst her parents were, so far, being patient with her, she sometimes felt on the edge of panic, terrified that she might find herself sleepwalking down the aisle in a daze someday. And that a near-stranger would be waiting to receive her in front of the altar, and demand that she love, honour and obey him.

She gave a shudder and told herself sternly to concentrate on the task in hand.

Thus she regarded one outdated ivory-coloured dress with disfavour and sighed heavily. The trouble with living in a small village was that one's neighbours had invariably seen you in every stitch that you owned! Wouldn't it be lovely, just for once, to turn up at the Old Forge in a new Parisian mint-green silk evening gown, with a deliciously floating silver scarf and . . .

But what was the use of daydreaming? Unless she bowed to her parents' pressure to marry well and soon, she'd never have such luxuries.

With a sigh, she reached for her least-ancient gown – a pale forget-me-not-blue muslin – and donned it. At least with her hair done up in a complicated chignon with the help of her youngest sister (who had an eye for such things), and with a pair of her mother's long, dangling pearl earrings, she would look reasonably elegant.

Not that she expected Arbie to notice, she mused crossly. *He* never seemed to notice whatever she wore. As she dabbed on a small amount of her precious perfume, she wondered what the dinner invitation could be all about. It seemed odd that Miss Phelps should be summoning her and Arbie back to the Old Forge again. Could something else have happened? Perhaps the troublesome ghostly smithy would make an appearance between the soup and the fish courses? Or would there be another threatening message left somewhere, presaged by the ghostly ringing of a dreaded bell?

Val gave a slightly nervous little giggle. Well, whatever the reason for the invitation, it broke up the monotony of the routine of her life. And for all her wild speculations, it was only dinner with a neighbour, after all. The evening would probably end up being as dull as ditch water, and the best she could hope for was that the wine would be good.

*

It was a lovely evening, and as Val walked the short distance to the Old Forge, she spotted Arbie's figure a little ahead of her and called out his name. Dressed in impeccable evening dress he turned at her hail and waited for her to catch up.

'Hello, old thing. Once more into the fray, eh?' he said cheerfully by way of greeting.

Val nodded. 'I suppose so. Any idea what it's all about?'

'None, I'm afraid,' Arbie admitted. They walked on in amiable silence for a while, and then, as they approached the entrance to the Phelps family residence, heard voices in the garden. By mutual consent, they veered off the front path and followed another route around the side, where they found a small party sitting in the garden, underneath an old apple tree.

The roses were out, scenting the air, and on one bench, Reggie and Cora sat together, watching the antics of a thrush trying to pull a worm from the lawn. A few yards away, sitting on wrought-iron chairs placed either side of a wrought-iron garden table, were Phyllis Thomas and her cousin Murray. Neither were speaking to each other, and they watched the new arrivals with an intensity that made Val, for one, feel a little uneasy.

Arbie, of course, didn't seem to notice the constrained atmosphere. Instead, he ambled over towards the two older people and sat down on a bench that was set at right angles to them, and Val was happy to follow his lead.

'Ah, our famous author,' Reggie looked across at them with a smile, 'and the delightful Miss Valentina. I do hope I can call you that, my dear?' He barely waited for Val's smiling nod before

70

turning to Arbie once more. 'Drink, old boy?' he offered, and it was only then that Arbie noticed a jug of something cold and probably non-alcoholic resting on the grass beside him, along with some empty glasses.

'Think I'll wait a bit,' Arbie said hastily. He'd never been fond of non-alcoholic drinks. Val, however, accepted a glass and Reggie gallantly poured it out for her.

'I had no idea you were going to join us tonight, Mr Swift, Miss Coulton-James,' Cora said with a refined smile. 'But I'm glad that you are. Our hostess has been a bit morose lately, hasn't she, Reggie? It'll be nice to have some younger people around to cheer her up a bit.'

'Oh? I hope she's not unwell,' Val said politely.

'No, she's fit as a flea, I'm glad to say,' Reggie said cheerfully. 'Still a bit stiff and sore after her tumble, but she never complains. Amy never has been one to make a fuss, has she, Cora?'

'Oh no,' Cora said quietly.

'A tumble?' Val asked sharply.

'Yes. Took a header down the stairs, apparently, last week,' Reggie said. 'Could have been really nasty, but luckily she only had a few bumps and bruises.'

'Down the *stairs*?' Arbie said, looking from Reggie and Cora to Val and then back to the older man again. 'I say, that sounds a bit worrying. What happened?'

'She just lost her balance, apparently, or so she said,' Reggie recounted, jigging the ice in his glass and staring at it thoughtfully. Cora took a sip from her own glass and said nothing.

'Ah,' Arbie said vaguely. He didn't like the sound of this. An accident coming so soon after the other curious incidents that had been happening around their hostess felt decidedly suspicious to him.

What's more, he was fairly sure that he'd just learned the reason behind this dinner invitation tonight.

71

The thing was though, if Amy Phelps *were* to take him aside some time tonight and tell him that a ghostly hand had pushed her down the stairs, just what was he supposed to do about it? *The Gentleman's Guide to Ghost-Hunting* had been written as nothing more than a bit of fun, and should be read in the same spirit (pardon the pun). It most certainly did *not* make Arbie a bona fide expert in all things supernatural!

Uneasily, he began to wonder who he could call on to relieve him of the burden? Perhaps a professor at Oxford would be interested enough to take it on? Now, did he know one daft enough to . . .

'Being told all the latest about Aunt's adventures in the night, hmmm?' Murray Phelps, who'd wandered over from the table and chairs, interrupted Arbie's inner musings to smile down at Val with what he imagined to be a charming smile. Her mass of upswept blonde hair, revealing her pale neck and pretty ears, hadn't gone unnoticed by him, at least.

'It all sounds most upsetting,' Val said. And then, remembering the conclusions that she and Arbie had come to that Amy herself suspected this man of being the prankster, added coolly, 'Women shouldn't fall down the stairs.'

'Oh, I quite agree,' Murray said lightly. 'I told her so myself, in fact. Luckily, she only fell down one or two, so wasn't badly hurt. Isn't that so?' He tossed the question vaguely towards the two older members of the party.

Reggie nodded, but it was Cora who spoke. 'Oh, it'll take much more than a fall down some stairs to kill our Amy,' she said simply, her voice and face perfectly expressionless.

'Isn't it time to go in?' Phyllis called restlessly from over by the table, where her cousin had left her without so much as a by-your-leave. 'Aunty will begin to wonder where everyone is,' she chided in afterthought.

At this, everyone rose obediently and began to walk to the house, where dinner awaited them.

*

Mrs Brockhurst had prepared the dinner very carefully that evening, giving each dish considerable thought beforehand. Her employer, she knew, liked 'good simple fare' which she felt was a nod to her ancestor's humble beginnings, but insisted on the best of ingredients combined with that little bit of 'flair' necessary to give her guests the feeling that they were being pampered and treated to something of an occasion.

Accordingly, the first course was a simple but exquisite Oxford herb soup, made with the greenest leaves from the house's square-walled kitchen gardens. This was served with chunks of bread ripped from a perfectly baked loaf just out of the oven, made to an old family recipe that Mrs Brockhurst had inherited from her granny, and butter from the nearby farm, churned that morning.

To follow, the fish course was a whole baked turbot, from which portions were to be served with tarragon or dill sauces, according to individual taste. The fish had been delivered specially that afternoon from the best fishmonger in Cheltenham and was so fresh it had practically still been swimming.

The main was a roasted leg of lamb, served with minted new potatoes and the first of the garden peas, and a gravy that was, once again, a secret Brockhurst concoction. The housekeeper had noted early on in her career that nearly all gentlemen seemed to have a favourable predisposition towards gravy.

Pudding was a concoction of many summer berries presented in a splendid cut-glass dish with home-made elderflower and white chocolate ice cream in a smaller but matching bowl. Cheeses and biscuits and coffee would then be served. Since Amy Phelps disliked mints, no after-dinner mints or chocolates would be offered, but Mrs Brockhurst was sure that nobody would mind that after such a feast.

With the help of the usual girl from the village, she had no worries that her employer or her guests would have cause to complain about the service or the food.

As she stood in her kitchen, patiently waiting for the bell that would indicate the diners were ready to begin their meal, the cook-cum-housekeeper glanced wearily out of the window, which overlooked the back garden. She'd been working like a Trojan all day, and since her supply of nervous energy seemed to be all but spent, she would be happy when this night was over. As her eyes wandered around the attractive garden, she saw that the door leading into the lane behind it was beginning to open.

And from behind it, a pretty young woman looked in and glanced across at the house. She had a sly smile on her face.

Jane Brockhurst's lips tightened into a firm line, and she stepped outside. The girl hesitated, clearly put out to have been discovered, and frowned angrily as the housekeeper marched towards her.

Doreen Capstan was a petite little thing, with auburn hair and big blue eyes. The housekeeper knew she must be at least twenty-four, but she looked barely out of her teens. Jane Brockhurst had known from the moment that Amy Phelps had hired her on as a maid that she would cause nothing but trouble.

And how right she'd been! Miss Phelps had had to dismiss her, without references, within less than a year. And how that had shocked little Miss Capstan, who thought her pretty ways and sly cunning would let her get away with murder.

Now the young madam's chin came up pugnaciously and she stood her ground firmly as the older woman reached her. 'Hello, Mrs Brockhurst,' she said jauntily, determined to get in the first word. 'I was just here to . . . '

But the housekeeper was having none of this little chit's nonsense. 'I can guess only too well what you were just here to do, young lady. And you can think again. The family is going to sit down to dinner soon, and—'

'Oh yes, I know all about that,' Doreen interrupted her rudely, and with some glee. 'Murray told me all about it. He said I could call around, as he wanted a chat with me.' She loved lording it over this woman and making it clear that whilst she, Mrs Brockhurst, was still a lowly servant here, the same could not be said of herself any longer. And placing herself in the role of a legitimate caller with a right to be there gave her even more of a sense of one-upmanship.

But the housekeeper merely put her hands on her hips and shook her head. 'One of these days, young lady, your tongue will turn black and fall out, the amount of lies you tell. Mr Murray would do no such thing.' He knew it would enrage his aunt for one thing, the older woman thought grimly, and besides, Mr Murray was not such a fool as to flaunt his dallying ways under Amy Phelps's nose.

'Now be off with you. If you think I'm letting you into the house, well then, you're just plain deluded. Now then!' she concluded implacably.

At this, Doreen tossed her head cheekily and a sly smirk crossed her face as she turned and flounced away. If the sour old bat thought that Doreen needed her permission to enter the Old Forge, then it was *she* who was the deluded one. During her time as a maid in the house, Doreen had come across an old missing key to a disused coal cellar. Access to this were some overgrown steps leading down to a sunken wooden door at the back of the house, which let out into the lower back scullery inside the house itself. It meant she could come and go as she pleased, if she was careful. Something that Murray had found sometimes amusing, and sometimes annoying. He'd warned her that if his aunt found her sneaking in to meet him, the fat would be in the fire.

But Doreen had never been caught yet going about her secret business, and she wasn't about to be now. She would just wait until she saw her chance – probably after dark – and then slip inside and rendezvous with her lover.

*

Sometime later, Arbie watched with pleasure as a huge fish was brought in, served on a fine platter, and the housekeeper and the slightly awed teenage girl who was helping her began to 'flake' the fish apart and hand around individual serving plates.

'Smells delicious,' Reggie said, giving the housekeeper a beaming smile. 'I must say, Amy dear, apart from your wonderful company, I have to admit that Mrs Brockhurst's cooking is one of the highlights of my little holidays here. How your brother would have loved this,' he added wistfully.

Amy's eyes softened, as they always did, when contemplating her late sibling, and she nodded. Then, turning to her niece, said, 'Phyllis, dear, you should have some of the sauce. Which do you prefer?' She indicated the prettily decorated Spode sauce boats, and the younger woman smiled but shook her head. 'Murray?' Amy next turned to her nephew, who helped himself lavishly to the dill.

'My dear cousin is probably watching her figure, Aunt,' he said mildly. 'Isn't that the lament of most ladies nowadays? Thoroughly modern things need to be stick-thin to wear the latest fashions, or so I've heard.' It was an innocuous enough comment, but for some reason it made Phyllis flush angrily.

Val, sensing that an old argument of some kind was in danger of rearing its ugly head once more, tried to step in before Phyllis could be baited into a reply she might regret. 'Oh, you mean those shift-like things, which have to be worn with loops and loops of long string beads? Yes, I saw a fashion magazine from London the other day at the dentist and I have to say, they do look rather splendid. As do all those lovely headbands with feathers and things. I'd never have the nerve to wear them myself.'

'Ah, but you'd look spectacular if you did, my dear, I'm sure,' Reggie put in gallantly.

'Murray's just being his usual beastly self, Reggie dear, just ignore him,' Phyllis said lightly. 'He just likes to tease me,' she added with a brittle smile.

'Not guilty.' Murray grinned, defending himself robustly. 'It's just that I happened to see you emerging from *Madame Fifi's* in Oxford the other day, bearing a rather large and bulging shopping bag. And since I have it from the wife of a good friend of mine that Madame only sells the latest fads and trends, I was sure you must have an ulterior motive for cutting back on the old feedbag.'

Val, who would love to shop in the super-expensive establishment under discussion but would never be able to afford to do so, fought a battle against the green-eyed monster and almost won.

'Murray, don't be vulgar,' Amy rebuked him mildly. 'I don't like all this modern way of talking nowadays. I dare say it's all very clever and meant to be amusing and all that, but please refrain from it at the table. Your cousin is not a horse! Feedbag indeed.'

'Sorry, Aunt,' Murray said contritely and gave her a mocking smile, but he didn't look pleased by the censure, and nobody missed the tiny smirk that crossed his cousin's face at this example of their aunt's displeasure with him.

How tiring it must be, Arbie mused, to have to be in thrall to a rich relative. Sucking up to someone so as not to lose out when the old last will and testament was read and all that must be a crushing bore. Although if village gossip had it right – and it usually did! – Miss Phelps had recently visited her solicitor to alter her will. Arbie quickly rescued them all from a minor but uncomfortable silence with an anecdote from a well-known watering spa where he'd spotted a certain politician of some note attempting – and failing – to learn to swim, which saw them safely through to the meat dish. At this point, Murray was asked to carve the joint, as befit his position as nominal head of the family, a task he clearly enjoyed performing. He laid the meat on a silver salver, which was then passed around by Mrs Brockhurst, allowing everyone to have as much or as little as they desired.

Val, happy to find that the wine was indeed excellent, turned to Cora and tried to start a conversation with her which she found surprisingly hard work. The normally intelligent and pleasant woman seemed to be subdued for some reason, and so she turned to Reggie on her other side, who was only too happy to engage in a light and playful flirtation with her, explaining his latest passion for landscape and wildlife photography.

Arbie, whilst happily tucking into lamb and potatoes, was primarily watching his hostess, however. Apart from a fading and slight bruise on one side of her face, she seemed to be showing no signs of distress from her recent mishap. Indeed, she looked, if anything, relaxed and largely entertained by her guests. And when the pudding was served, amid much ooh-ing and delighted aah-ing from her guests, Amy watched attentively as the house-keeper scooped individual portions from the bowl of berries and helped herself to a scoop of the ice cream with every evidence of benign pleasure, before tucking in heartily.

The conversation, as it was wont to do, casually drifted from such diverse topics as politics, to the King's opening of the British Empire Exhibition at Wembley Stadium, to the more scandalous Russell case, discussion of which Amy quickly put to an end, saying that it was unfit for such innocent ears as those of Miss Coulton-James. Which, naturally, annoyed Val considerably, as she'd not been allowed to read the papers about it at the vicar-age and was dying to know why Mrs Russell's being cleared of adultery could be so scandalous!

Finally, coffee and tea were served in the drawing room, and

Amy rose, leading Cora, Val and Phyllis from the room, leaving the gentlemen to their cigars and brandy.

*

It was nearly midnight when the party finally broke up. Both Phyllis and Murray were spending the night at the Old Forge, and it wasn't until Arbie was in the hall and just about to walk Val home that Miss Phelps made her move.

Nodding a polite apology at Val, she pulled Arbie to one side and murmured something quietly in his ear. Val, watching Arbie's face like a hawk, thought she saw a slightly puzzled look cross his affable features, followed by one of resignation. He smiled, nodded, and bowed good night to his hostess and then re-joined her at the door.

Outside, a pair of tawny owls gave voice from the oak tree near the village pub. 'Well, that was nice,' Val said as they made the short walk down Old Mill Lane towards their neighbouring residences. 'The food was super, wasn't it?'

'Top hole,' Arbie agreed distractedly. Val said nothing as they turned into Church Lane and he left her with a brief 'Nighty-night, Val,' at the entrance to the vicarage.

'Good night, Arbie,' she responded casually, walked a few paces up the gravel path and then carefully stepped off onto the lawn and crept behind the nearest shrub. Silently, she waited. The full moon watched her without curiosity. A hedgehog, noisily snuffling about in some leaves, made her almost miss the sound of soft footsteps, but not quite.

When they'd passed, Val tiptoed out of her garden and peered down the lane. Just as she thought! She could make out, several yards ahead of her and making his way back towards the Old Forge no doubt, the tall, elegant figure of one Mr Arbuthnot Swift.

She always knew when he was up to something – and in this case, it wasn't hard to guess what. Amy Phelps had asked him to do another ghost-watch tonight.

Well, she wasn't going to miss out on any of the fun! She nipped back into the house and left a note saying where she would be and why – being careful to point out that it was at the request of Miss Phelps, which was technically true – and changed into a simple skirt and blouse and sensible shoes, then left the silent building.

By this time, Arbie had made it back to the Old Forge and had been admitted through the French windows by his hostess.

'Thank you for doing this for me, Mr Swift,' Amy Phelps said briskly, not liking being beholden to anyone, and trying to hide that fact behind a no-nonsense manner. 'I have reason to believe . . . er . . . that the ghost might walk tonight.'

Do you indeed? Arbie thought sceptically. But it was a small price to pay for her peace of mind, he supposed. And if her nephew – or someone else in the house – *had* been responsible for her recent fall down the stairs, he supposed it was just possible that he might catch someone out in the act of setting up another such incident. Which, unless he was an utter fool – and contrary to popular opinion, he most definitely wasn't – was precisely what Miss Phelps suspected was going to happen.

He watched his hostess climb the stairs, a lone and lonely figure. For all her wealth and position, it struck him suddenly what a tragic figure she made. A woman beset by problems, now climbing a dark staircase all alone in the night.

At the top, where the gas lamps on the walls ended, he saw her pick up a candlestick from a small side table and light it, no doubt a nightly ritual which allowed her to find her way to her bedroom in the unlit wing of the house where she slept.

He only hoped that Miss Phelps had warned the housekeeper that he was standing guard in the hall, otherwise he might just be responsible for some female hysterics of his own, when it came time for her to dim the oil lamps and lock up!

As before, he took a chair and sat down wearily. He could hear the murmur of female voices somewhere far away and wondered how long it would take Mrs Brockhurst and her helper to finish tidying up, and if he should offer to walk the village girl back home.

He was still pondering that when he heard a sly step somewhere in the shadows off to his right. He turned his head sharply and the next instant drew his breath in abruptly. In the moonlight filtering in from the lead pane window, he saw a silvery human shape move.

It came forward slowly and carefully. 'Hello. I thought I'd join you,' Val said. She'd been lucky enough to find the French windows still unlocked and had unknowingly followed his own route into the house. 'Did I scare you?' she asked hopefully.

Arbie ignored the hard knocking of his heartbeat and said vaguely, 'Hmm? Oh, no, not at all. Draw up a pew, old thing. Something tells me it's going to be a queer sort of a night.'

Feeling a little put out (after all, it would have been such a hoot putting the frighteners on such a famous ghost specialist and she could have dined out on it for years), Val sat down. 'Why? Do you sense especially ghostly vibrations or something?'

'Or something,' Arbie said flatly. 'I think our Miss Phelps is expecting her ghostly ancestor to be up to some shenanigans tonight.'

But it turned out that Amy Phelps was wrong. Nothing at all disturbed the peace of the Old Forge that night, and Val and Arbie took turns dozing and keeping watch to no avail.

CHAPTER SEVEN

Mrs Brockhurst put the tray on the small table that habitually sat just outside Miss Phelps's door and knocked once, then reached for the handle. Unusually, it didn't turn.

For a moment, the housekeeper hesitated, then knocked again. Although the lady of the house had never locked her door before, somehow Jane Brockhurst wasn't particularly surprised to find it locked now. Ever since Miss Phelps had fallen down the stairs, she'd been acting in a very marked manner. She'd become far more wary, and not her usual assertive self. It was as if she'd been expecting something to happen – something unpleasant – and had been determined to safeguard herself against it, and the locked door now was just more evidence of that. As had been her asking Mr Swift to spend the night 'ghost-watching' again.

'Miss Phelps, it's only me,' she said loudly. 'I have your morning tea,' she called through the door and waited. In normal circumstances, she would now expect to hear the turning of a key in the lock, or maybe Miss Phelps's voice calling out for her to wait.

Neither event occurred.

She rapped harder and called out more loudly. So sharply, in fact, that in a few minutes she found herself joined at the door by Arbie, with Val close on his heels.

'Trouble?' Arbie asked, feeling a shade foolish asking such a silly question. It was clear that some sort of trouble was in the offing. 'Can't wake Miss Phelps up, eh?' he asked nervously.

'No, Mr Swift, I can't,' the housekeeper said, beginning to look a little pale. 'And she's always been a light sleeper.'

Arbie nodded and hammered a bit harder on the door, but after waiting for a few seconds longer, and hearing nothing, he shook his head. 'Do you have a spare key to this door?'

'No, sir, I don't. It's never usually kept locked. In fact, this is the first time I've ever found it so,' the housekeeper said, trying to keep her voice steady and mostly succeeding.

Arbie shot Val a quick look and saw that she was as uneasy as he was. He quickly turned back to the housekeeper. 'Isn't there a general pass key or anything that you keep somewhere safe for emergencies and things?'

'No, sir, and I don't believe someone else's door key will fit this lock either. I know in some houses, internal keys are all the same and interchangeable, but the Old Forge is so higgledy-piggledy I imagine each door would have come with its own lock. The Phelpses, as you can imagine, created and forged all their own ironwork in the house on an individual basis. They'd never have bought standard goods from an ironmonger, such as keys.'

Arbie could well imagine that such a thing would amount to treason in a family of smithies, and he sighed gloomily.

'And Miss Phelps was always careful about keys – she didn't hand them out willy-nilly as some like to do. She and I are the only two to have keys to the external doors to the house for instance,' the housekeeper swept on, made more loquacious than usual by her evident nervousness.

'Then there's nothing else for it – you'll have to break the door down, Arbie,' Val said urgently. 'Put your shoulder to it!'

Arbie eyed the stout oak door, with its even stouter, hand-forged (of course!) iron hinges and sighed. 'My dear Val, if I did that, I should no doubt dislocate every bone in my upper torso. But there must be an axe or something I can use. In the old tool shed?'

Jane Brockhurst coughed drily and ventured, 'Wouldn't it be easier to climb a ladder to her window and crawl in that way?'

Arbie blinked and mumbled humbly, 'I imagine it would, yes. Do you know if there's a ladder about?'

'There's sure to be one in the shed, sir,' she said helpfully and with admirable patience.

Arbie nodded. 'You stay here and wait, Mrs Brockhurst. I'll let you in once I gain admittance. Val . . . ' But before he could finish, Val was already headed off towards the stairs.

'I'm coming with you,' she said, unnecessarily.

They rushed down the stairs and across the hall and found a ladder eventually in one of the gardener's outhouses. It was one of the extendable types, and once they'd fixed it to its full height, Arbie rammed the two sturdy legs into the earth of the pristine flowerbed beneath what he thought must be the right window and began to climb.

'Hold her steady, old thing,' he said, clambering up with the nimbleness of a monkey. He'd been too lazy to do any real rowing at Oxford, but he'd played cricket all his life, and made short work of the climb to the window. Once there, however, he found it firmly shut and locked, which was a bit of a facer. A quick peek inside showed him a large bed, with a slight bump in it that must be the inhabitant. She was not moving.

'Blast,' he muttered, then gave a little yelp as right below him a voice said, 'What?'

He looked down to see Val, her face about level with the bend in his knees. It had, he thought resignedly, been too much to expect Val to have stayed safely on the ground, anchoring the ladder. Oh well, if the ladder began to list and they both took a header into the rhododendrons she'd have only herself to blame!

'The window's not only shut, it's locked from the inside,' he said flatly. 'I'd have thought it being summer they'd be wide open.'

'Not everyone is a fresh air freak,' Val said tensely. 'And older women feel the cold. It still does get chilly around dawn, you know.'

Arbie sighed. 'We'll have to break a pane of the glass,' he said, eyeing the sash window without much pleasure. 'Don't suppose you thought to bring a rock up with you or anything, did you?'

'Funnily enough, no,' Val said icily. 'Just pull your shirtsleeve over your fist and smash the glass, man.'

Arbie eyed the glass with even less pleasure. 'Thanks, but people only do that in books and in the cinema and things,' he informed her with lofty distaste. 'In real life, a boddo knows that if you do something so bally silly, you're likely to get your hands shredded for your trouble.' He thought for a few seconds, then lifted his right foot. 'Just slip off my old shoe, will you, and hand it up to me, do you mind? It's got a good stout heel on it.'

Muttering something about 'babies' and 'lily-livered something-or-others', which Arbie pretended not to hear, Val did as he asked, and a moment later, he was poised to strike.

'Turn your head down and well away, Val, there might be some falling glass,' he warned her. But when he tapped a pane, strategically placed just over the catch on the inside, most of the glass fell helpfully inside. He carefully smashed out the whole pane with his shoe heel, then gingerly reached inside to slip the catch, congratulating himself on not getting so much as a scratch from the shards of glass remaining in the opening. That done, he used his shoe to brush the glass off the sill, where it fell on the floor inside the bedroom, then slid the window up to the extent of its reach. That gave them plenty of room to clamber in.

It wasn't until they were fully inside, and Arbie was hastily slipping his shoe back on, that he took a more detailed look around the room. It was large and pleasantly furnished, with a small skylight in the roof at the far end allowing in a little more daylight. A woman's bedroom was not his usual habitat, but he was surprised by the lack of feminine fripperies. He was about to walk to the door to allow the waiting housekeeper into the room, but then saw that Val was already making her way to the bed.

'Miss Phelps,' she called as she approached, but there was no movement of her head lying on the pillow. She reached out and tentatively touched the woman on the shoulder. If she really was only sleeping very soundly, she didn't want to frighten her by being too abrupt. But the lady's shoulder felt so stiff and unnatural that she quickly took her hand away. She put one knee lightly on the mattress and with one hand steadying herself on the night table beside the bed, leaned over to get a better look at her face.

What she saw made her freeze in shock. She must have made some little sound of distress for Arbie, who was halfway to the door, suddenly diverted and dashed over to her. As he did so, he saw Val go very pale and begin to sway. Her eyelids fluttered.

'Val!' he called out in warning and was just in time to pull her away from the bed before she fell on top of its current resident. He carried her, half-fainting, away from the bed and over towards the window where there was sunlight and cool fresh air. There he sat her down on a delightful Queen Anne chair and left her bent forward with her head between her knees and fighting back tears of shock.

'You all right, old thing?' he asked anxiously.

It wasn't like Val to get all wibbly-wobbly on him, as she usually prided herself on her stiff upper lip and fortitude, and he was therefore very much reassured when she waved an imperious hand in the air and a moment later said groggily, 'I'll be fine in a minute. Just went a bit light-headed for some reason. I'm already feeling much better. Oh Arbie, she's dead!'

'Yes, I guessed as much,' he muttered glumly.

Unwillingly, he went towards the bed himself, looking anywhere at first rather than at Amy Phelps. He saw that the bedclothes weren't in much disarray, and beside the bed that her slippers stood waiting patiently on the floor, ready to provide their usual service. Arbie turned his attention to the bedside table. It was a large, walnut pie-crust table, and on it was a burnt-down candle in a brass candlestick, a hairbrush and a pair of spectacles with its arms unfolded. A book also lay facedown on its opened pages, as if its last reader had just put it down temporarily, intending to pick it up again and continue reading. Underneath was a washbasin set in an attractive blue-and-white willow pattern. Nothing else.

Unable to put it off any longer, he glanced at the woman's blue face and swallowed hard. There was something ghastly in the open, horror-filled eyes and the gaping mouth that made him quickly turn away.

As he moved he felt his head begin to swim, and his throat seemed to close up, leaving him feeling as if he was battling for air. Before the sensation could get any worse he got up and walked towards Val, desperate for the fresh air of the open window. Not for anything short of torture would he admit to having a fit of 'the vapours' as well!

'You feeling better now, old thing?' he said, hoping his voice wasn't as shaky as he felt.

Val groaned but nodded gamely. 'I didn't make a mistake. She *is* dead, isn't she?'

'As the proverbial door nail, I'm afraid.'

'Oh Arbie, I have a bad feeling about this. What with everything that's been going on – I'm sure she must have been murdered!' Val wailed.

At this, Arbie shied away from her like a startled horse. 'I say, Val old girl, that's putting the cart before the horse, isn't it?'

Val shot him one of 'those' looks. 'You think so too,' she accused him shrewdly. 'I know you do. I can tell.'

Arbie bridled. 'Fat lot you know then,' he responded weakly. 'I wasn't thinking any such thing,' he lied. 'The most obvious answer is that she had a weak heart or something. She was getting older, after all. Old folks die blamelessly in their bed all the time.' But even as he spoke, he couldn't quite convince himself – let alone Val – that this was one of those times.

'You just want to brush it all under the carpet and bury your head in the sand like an ostrich,' Val said furiously, 'and don't tell me I'm mixing my metaphors or what have you,' she put in as Arbie opened his mouth to do just that. 'As ever, you just want to take the easy way out. But for once, I'm not going to let you.'

'For *once*?' Arbie squeaked. When had Val ever let him off the hook?

'You and I, Arbuthnot Swift, are going to get to the bottom of this,' Val said firmly. 'We owe it to poor Miss Phelps. Didn't she ask for our help? *Your* help, specifically,' she corrected, fixing him with a glare.

Feeling like a butterfly specimen pinned firmly to a piece of card, Arbie could only nod miserably. She was right, of course. If someone had helped Miss Phelps into the great hereafter they couldn't let it slide.

'Righty-oh then.' He sighed. 'We'll just have to join the ranks of amateur sleuths, like that Belgian chap with spats.'

'Who?' Val asked, momentarily sidetracked.

'You know, the one in the books. With his grey cells.'

Val sighed. 'Arbie, do stop waffling. Just give me your solemn word, we're going to get to the bottom of this, no matter what people say, and no matter what we have got to do.'

Arbie solemnly crossed his heart with a finger, and as he did this, there was a firm knock at the door. He had forgotten all about Jane Brockhurst waiting outside. She must have been able to hear their voices and knew they'd gained entry minutes ago. Feeling contrite at leaving it so long, he moved quickly over to the door, and saw with relief that the key was firmly in the lock. If it hadn't been, and he'd had to search for it, he wasn't sure his nerves would thank him! He turned the key and heard it unlock the mechanism and opened the door, allowing the housekeeper inside.

She looked at his face intently for a moment, then said hesitantly, 'Is she . . . gone?' She glanced quickly at the bed and then away again.

'Yes, I'm afraid she is, Mrs Brockhurst,' Arbie said gently.

'It must have been her heart then,' the housekeeper said firmly. 'I'll see about getting the doctor.'

Arbie nodded vaguely and watched her leave with a thoughtful look on his face. Had it been his imagination or had the housekeeper been rather overemphatic about the probable cause of the death of her mistress?

Val, showing no signs of moving from her chair, remained ominously quiet.

Arbie wandered vaguely over to the far side of the room and looked up at the skylight. It was small and square and shut. He doubted that anyone except a very small child could have fit through it anyway. And even then, it would have first had to clamber over the roof and . . .

He wondered, abruptly, why he was thinking of an intruder. An older woman, one who'd been under some stress and strain lately, had died in her bed. The door was locked from the inside. The windows the same. The only other means of entry was a skylight in a roof that would have been useless even to Raffles, that famous cat-burglar and jewel thief. Surely Miss Phelps had simply died in her sleep, and most likely from heart failure, as the housekeeper had said.

Slowly he wandered over to Val. 'You know, old girl, if we

start poking and prying into this, we might, er, get more than we bargain for. There's something really nasty about this setup.'

'I feel like that too,' Val whispered. 'Oh Arbie, did you see her face?'

'Yes. I saw it.'

'Didn't she look . . . terrified to you? As if she'd seen a . . . ' Val couldn't quite bring herself to say it. But then, she didn't need to.

'Yes. But look here, Val, nobody really believes in ghosts and things. Not really. Not even my readers,' Arbie said, then sighed. He shook his head. 'We'll just have to wait and see what the doctor has to say. You ready to go home, old thing?' he asked softly, looking down at her woebegone, bent fair head.

Val lifted her pale face to him. 'Oh yes, Arbie. Please take me home. I thought it would be fun, a bit of a lark, this nonsense of Miss Phelps's,' she said, gulping a little. 'But it's all turned beastly. And I hate this room. It's as if I can't breathe in it!'

Arbie knew what she meant. His own chest still felt tight with tension and nerves. With more haste than dignity they left the room and made their way back to the hall. There they met the housekeeper just turning away from the door.

'I've sent the kitchen maid to fetch Dr Beamish,' she said simply.

Arbie nodded in relief. The village doctor, at least, could be relied upon to be here within minutes, he knew. 'I'm going to take Miss Coulton-James home,' he said. And then, seeing the mute look of appeal in the older woman's eyes, smiled tiredly and added, 'And then I'll come back, of course. Anything I can do to help.'

'Thank you, Mr Swift,' the housekeeper said.

Arbie nodded and along with Val, passed on out of the house.

*

90

Val's parents weren't happy to find their daughter being brought home in a state of some distress after spending an unexpected and unscheduled night away from her home, but once they heard Arbie and Val's slightly stammering explanation, things changed quickly.

Val's mother agreed to go at once to 'help' Mrs Brockhurst with the laying out and the arrangements. The vicar agreed to come along a little later to give succour to the poor lady's relations and friends, who had yet to be told of the tragedy. One thing about the Old Forge's rambling layout and feet-thick stone walls was that it had meant that everyone had slept through the morning's events, which was a blessing of sorts.

Arbie popped next door to his own place to tell Uncle of the latest events and missed the worried and speculative look his relation gave him as he left.

Making his way back to the Phelps residence, his thoughts turned rather dire. His sense of self-preservation (which was always reassuringly robust) was telling him to do the bare minimum required and then make a graceful exit. The less involved he was, the better. That had always been one of the mottos that he lived by. Unfortunately for Arbie, he had somehow or other acquired along the way both a conscience and a healthy sense of fair play, which, frankly, were nothing but a damned nuisance.

Right now, for instance, they were insisting that he couldn't let the death of Amy Phelps pass by without being thoroughly investigated. Which meant interfering in a family's private business, and no doubt incurring the wrath of all concerned. And Arbie was a man who liked to avoid incurring wrath wherever he could.

Moreover, if the worst came to the worst, and the police had to be called in and something untoward was discovered, resulting in a scandal of some kind, he was miserably aware that that would be the last thing the lady herself would want. She'd always been fiercely protective of the family name – especially now there were so very few Phelpses remaining.

Perhaps he was worrying about nothing though?

The doctor, Arbie surmised a few minutes later, must have hotfooted over from his own place, for though he had arrived at the Old Forge, his car was absent from the drive. He was talking quietly to Mrs Brockhurst in the hall, and from the open door to the kitchen, Arbie could hear the reassuring voice of the vicar's wife speaking gently but firmly to the daily girl, who was prone to tearful outbursts.

Dr Beamish greeted Arbie with his usual warmth mixed with the solemnity that the occasion called for. A man in his early forties, the village physician was a plump, pleasant man with a brisk but competent air that greatly reassured his many patients. He saw these patients either at his house, a portion of which had been dedicated to a surgery, or in their own homes. Visits to the local hospital, both doctor and patients agreed, were best avoided.

It was clear he'd only just arrived, for he now set off upstairs to perform his last sad service for one of his oldest and most respected patients, whilst Arbie and Mrs Brockhurst looked at one another a bit blankly.

'I suppose we should tell everyone,' Arbie said at last. 'I take it nobody's up and about yet? Ready for breakfast and that sort of thing?'

'No, Miss Phelps was always an early riser, and I always took her morning tea long before most people wanted to be disturbed. Miss Phyllis is usually a late riser, as is her cousin. Miss Cora is usually up and about by now though, and Mr Bickersworth will soon be coming over from the studio for his breakfast.'

'The studio's separate from the house?'

'Oh yes, it's a separate annexe. Miss Phelps's mother had it converted into a sort of studio flat.'

'Does Mr Bickersworth have a front door key to the house itself?'

'Oh no. He usually leaves the house after playing bridge or what have you and then only comes over in the morning when he's sure everyone else is up and about.' If the housekeeper wondered why Mr Swift was so curious about the arrangements of her household, she didn't show it.

'And Mr Phelps and Miss Thomas – the nephew and niece. Do they often stay the night?' Arbie pressed on.

'They're regular visitors, but they only stay overnight on occasion.'

Arbie nodded. 'And they definitely don't have a key to the house?'

'No,' Mrs Brockhurst said carefully. 'Miss Phelps liked to ensure her privacy,' she added. 'She wouldn't have liked it if she knew that Miss Phyllis used to—' She stopped abruptly and then blushed. 'Oh sir, please forget I said that,' she begged him. 'I'm that upset, I don't know what I'm saying.'

Arbie wasn't as slow on the uptake as most people assumed. So for some reason, the niece wasn't above going into her aunt's room on the sly. He wondered why. Then gave a mental shrug. It was probably for totally innocent reasons – to borrow some stockings if she'd found a ladder in her own perhaps, or to indulge in a dab of expensive perfume or some other feminine requirement like that. No, he mustn't let himself be distracted.

Arbie rocked back a bit on his heels and stuffed his hands into the pockets of his Oxford bags. 'Mum's the word, Mrs Brockhurst. I won't say a thing,' he reassured her. 'So Miss Cora . . . ?'

'Has no key either,' Mrs Brockhurst confirmed firmly.

Arbie nodded. 'Well, I suppose we'd better get on with telling everyone then?' he muttered without enthusiasm. 'I suggest I tell the men, and you inform the ladies?'

Mrs Brockhurst nodded acquiescence, and together they

mounted the stairs, separating on the first of the landings and going their separate ways, after the housekeeper had given him directions to the location of the gentleman's room.

Murray Phelps answered the knock at his door half-dressed and looking impatient. He was surprised to see Arbie at his door, as well he might, and his face went totally slack when Arbie rather stutteringly, broke the news of his aunt's demise. For a moment or two after that, Murray neither moved nor said anything, then he seemed to give himself a little shake and pull himself together. Avowing that he'd be down once he'd finished dressing, he started to shut the door. Arbie nodded and turned away before he could get the door actually slammed in his face.

Outside in the cobbled courtyard, the haphazard collection of outbuildings was being visited by a few white doves, courtesy of the nearby dovecote. Arbie followed the sound of a wireless to track down the 'studio' and saw that this had once been a two-up two-down building, probably used for forge workers back in the old days. It was built of ironstone, with grey slate roofing, and when he knocked on the door, a window above opened and Reginald stuck his head out. His hair stood out in tufts and the top buttons of his shirt were undone. Clearly, he'd not long risen and hadn't set about his personal toilette yet.

'Oh, hallo there, young Arbie Swift! I wondered who could be knocking on my door at this hour. Not seen the ghost at last, have you?' he asked with a grin.

'No, sir. I'm afraid it's bad news,' he said solemnly. 'About Miss Amy Phelps.'

'Not taken another fall, has she? It's often the way, you know, when you get to our age in life. The first fall you have seems to set off a whole lot of others. I had a great-uncle once who—'

'I'm afraid it's more serious than that, old man,' Arbie said regretfully, cutting into what seemed likely to be a long-winded reminiscence. Looking up at the cheerful face above him, he was sorry to have to see the grin falter and fade. 'I'm afraid Miss Phelps passed away in the night,' he said gently. 'We found her dead in bed a little while ago.'

He knew he'd made it sound more peaceful and natural than it all felt, and he hastily supressed an image of the woman's blue, frightened face as it tried to force its way to the forefront of his mind. But he felt it would be far kinder to the man to leave him with a false but comforting impression than regale him with a more factual account. When you'd just lost someone that you'd known all your life, it was bound to take it out of you, and you needed it broken to you with a little kindness.

As it was he saw the other man's lower lip begin to tremble, before he had time to pull himself together. Then the thin shoulders showing through the window frame visibly straightened, and he coughed slightly. 'I see. Oh my. That's terrible. I'll . . . er . . . I'll be down in a jiffy.' As he spoke and turned and looked across the way to the main house, Arbie, following his gaze, realised that the annexe was connected to the original forge itself, which, in turn, abutted the smallest side of the main house. But Reggie had no direct line of sight with Miss Phelps's bedroom, which was a mercy.

The last thing the poor chap needed was to look on at the place where his old friend now lay lifeless.

Arbie tactfully turned away and wandered up and down a little, kicking the odd stone about and waiting for him to appear. Reggie emerged about five minutes later looking pale and shaken and even a little shrunken. Something of Arbie's shock must have shown in his eyes, for Reggie managed a small smile. 'Sorry, but this has rocked me a bit. One somehow thought of the Amys of this world as indestructible, do you know?'

But Arbie didn't, not really. Reggie could see that at once. Which was only right, he supposed. The young have no idea about mortality. Why would they? 'I remember her when she was your age, you see. My word, she was a sight to see in those days,' Reggie muttered as they walked slowly and reluctantly back to the house. 'Spirited and full of life and determined to take the world by the horns and master it. That was Amy.'

When they stepped back into the hall, it was just in time to hear Dr Beamish finish saying something. In the hall, Phyllis Thomas now sat in a chair, silently weeping. Cora, sat beside her, kept patting her hand somewhat half-heartedly. Murray Phelps was on his feet, standing beside the doctor and listening intently.

'It was her heart I take it then, doctor?' Murray said.

'Like I just said, Mr Phelps, I think it must have been sudden. The bedclothes were in very little disarray, so I don't think she suffered unduly.'

Arbie, thinking of that blue face, thought that the good doctor was sparing the family's feelings.

'So a heart attack then? Or a stroke?' Murray pressed.

The doctor, however, did not seem to want to be pressed. 'Most likely,' he contented himself with saying.

Arbie, hearing his cue and not liking it, was just building himself up to approaching the doctor, and privately informing him that he thought a little more investigation was warranted, and was astounded – but very pleased – to find himself forestalled.

'I think you should do an autopsy.'

It was, astonishingly enough, Reggie – dear, bumbling, mild-mannered Reggie – who spoke, and spoke with a, for him, surprising firmness. It was not only Arbie who looked at him in some consternation. Dr Beamish stared at him intently but didn't appear particularly startled by the request. Perhaps the canny doctor had already had some medical doubts about the cause of death? Mrs Brockhurst blinked and said nothing. Phyllis was shocked into taking a short break from her weeping, then commenced again. Murray made some vague exclamation and appeared the most likely to rain angry words down on the older man's defiant head.

But it was none of these who reacted first.

It was Cora who shot to her feet, her face flushed in outrage. 'Oh no! No! Amy would have hated that!' she said fiercely. 'To be cut up by strangers and inspected on some cold slab like a piece of cod. No!'

As this vivid piece of imagery floated ethereally in the morning air of the Old Forge's hall, it was perhaps only to be expected that Phyllis Thomas fainted. It was not a spectacular faint; she simply made a little sound and slipped from the chair, landing in a ladylike puddle on the floor.

The housekeeper went to her at once, as did the doctor. Reggie tut-tutted and flapped helplessly on the fringes.

Arbie alone kept his face fixed on that of Murray Phelps, who looked . . . surprised. Which in turn surprised Arbie, who'd been expecting to see a totally different emotion on the other man's face.

CHAPTER EIGHT

Dr Beamish stayed until the body was taken to the local hospital where 'further examinations' would be made. Phyllis and Cora said nothing as they stood by the door watching the vehicle depart, but both were looking very pale. Mrs Brockhurst seemed to Arbie to be rather pensive or distracted, and after making a few scoffing remarks about how unnecessary all the fuss was, Murray Phelps made no further comment and took himself off into the depths of the house.

If the nephew of the dead woman was unduly worried about what the medical men might find, he certainly wasn't showing it.

With the sad departure of the lady of the house, the others drifted listlessly into the morning room, where Murray was already ensconced and reading the morning papers. Phyllis sat down in a chair opposite him and pretended to do the same. But every now and then she cast her cousin quick, troubled glances.

Arbie, not quite sure what was expected of him now, hovered uneasily on the fringes. It had been Miss Phelps who'd asked him to stay, and with her absence, he was feeling distinctly de trop and was thinking up the best way to withdraw tactfully from the scene.

'Do you think I should leave?'

Again it was Reggie who spoke, making Arbie wonder for a moment if the man could possibly have psychic abilities with which to read his very thoughts. Then he realised that Reggie was addressing his fellow summer house guest, Cora Delaney. 'I mean, this is a house of mourning now, and . . . ' He broke off and gave a wry smile. 'My own place is rented out until September, but there are plenty of guest houses, one supposes, where I could lay my head. Perhaps one of those Mr Swift recommended in his splendid book will have a vacancy,' he added, suddenly catching sight of Arbie and managing a brave smile.

At this, Phyllis stirred herself. 'Oh, I'm sure Aunty Amy wouldn't have wanted that, Reggie. You're practically our honorary uncle and you've always spent your summers here. I'm sure we have no objection to you staying on, do we, Murray?' she asked, a shade sharply.

Murray looked across the top of his newspaper and gave a brief smile. 'Of course you must stay, old fellow. You as well, Cora, if you like,' he said indifferently.

'Oh, I'm not sure . . . ' Cora murmured. Unlike Reggie, she *could* go back to her own home anytime, but she was not so sure that she wanted to. Not yet, anyway. 'If you're certain that you don't mind, dear?' she asked Phyllis. 'I mean, there'll be the funeral and everything and you might need help . . . er . . . with things,' she added vaguely. 'So I'd be happy to stay, if I'm needed. But I don't like to intrude and with Amy not here . . . '

Suddenly it became clear to Arbie why everybody was feeling a bit nervy. It was because nobody was totally sure of the terms of Miss Phelps's will and who, now, was legally owner of the house. Who had the right to say who could stay or had to leave? Presumably, as the last male heir, Murray Phelps would come into the lion's share, if not everything? He could see from the self-satisfied smile that played around that gentleman's mouth that he was confident that that was so. And probably with some justification, Arbie mused unhappily. A lady with Amy Phelps's sense of family responsibilities and the inalienable rights of male

99

primogeniture would hardly be likely to have left a contentious will behind.

And yet . . . Arbie wondered. It was now common knowledge that Miss Phelps had stated she was going to make some changes to her will. That could have been the removal of a codicil, or the addition of a small benefice to someone or other. On the other hand, it could have involved major re-writing.

'Thank you, Cora, that would be most kind.' Phyllis accepted Cora's offer with a smile. 'It's horrible to think of such things now, but at some point we'll have to sort out Aunty's things. Not that she kept many trinkets and such like,' she added casually. 'She wasn't a trinket sort of person. And Reggie, it's always nice to have a man about the house at times like this, so please don't feel you're imposing.'

Reggie sighed with not very-well concealed relief. 'Well, if everybody's sure. I'll stay then too.'

'Well, I think if nobody needs *me* . . . ' Arbie took this golden opportunity to extricate himself, and was already turning to the door in anticipation of his freedom when it was rudely snatched from underneath him.

'You'll be coming back tonight though, old man, I'm sure?' It was Murray who spoke, and when Arbie met his mocking gaze with one of genuine puzzlement, the other man's grin widened. 'I mean you'll want to hold another vigil, won't you? For your next book? That was what Amy wanted, after all. And from your point of view, it could hardly be a better time, could it? I mean, won't the emanations or whatever you call them be extra strong or something now?'

Phyllis gasped, and Cora gave a shocked exclamation. Reggie turned angry eyes on him. 'That's an atrociously disrespectful thing to say, young man. Your aunt would be appalled.'

Murray Phelps regarded them all without any evidence of shame. 'It was my aunt who believed in all that bunkum, if you'll recall,' he pointed out coolly. 'And I think it would be very remiss of us not to let the old girl have the chance to get her message across from the "other side" to Mr Swift here. And if she's going to do it, surely tonight would be the ideal time? Or perhaps it's all a bit too "real" for our illustrious author now?'

Well, there was obviously nothing Arbie could do after having the gauntlet thrown down like that. Besides, he knew that Val would never forgive him if he didn't take this chance to potentially help forward their own investigation into Amy's death. He met the older man's sardonic gaze and gave a stiff bow. 'I'll be here just before dark. Which means I really must get off now and catch up on some sleep.' He caught Phyllis's eye and bowed again. 'My deepest condolences on your loss.' He let his gaze include Reggie and Cora, and without looking at the insufferable nephew again, let himself out of the house, in high dudgeon.

*

Jane Brockhurst saw Arbie leave and sighed loudly. The shocks of the day's events had left her feeling heavy-limbed and inclined to be tearful, and she was fighting off a sense of lethargy when she went to the stove to brew up a much-needed cup of tea.

As the kettle began to heat, she stared vacantly out of the window into the garden beyond. And when she saw the outer door that let into the garden open, felt a distinct sense of déjà vu as the familiar female figure slipped inside. Anger and alarm rose swiftly inside her, and in an instant, the housekeeper was out of the door and walking swiftly and firmly across the lawn to intercept the interloper.

The girl, who had been making her way towards the side of the house, spotted her and stopped dead, a flush of annoyance, perhaps tinged with shame, rising in her face. As well it might, the little madam, the housekeeper thought savagely. And today of all days too, creeping about, and up to no good.

'Hello, Doreen, I'm afraid now's not a good time. You may not have heard, but this is a house of mourning,' she said stiffly. If the young minx thought that she was going to be able to have one of her little trysts with Mr Murray, the girl could think again. Her poor dead employer would have a fit if she'd known about what that pair got up to behind her back. And now she was dead and gone, it only made the girl's presence here even more outrageous.

'So it's true then?' Doreen said, her chin coming up defiantly as the housekeeper stood firmly in front of her, blocking her way to the house. 'I heard in the village that the old cow had finally popped her clogs. I couldn't believe it when Ma told me. But she got it from the milkman.' She added the afterthought with a toss of her head.

The housekeeper ignored the crass language, guessing – quite rightly – that it had only been used to get under her skin. Not that she could expect anything better from a common little baggage such as this one. The Capstan family lived crammed into a tiny cottage, the father doing seasonal farm work, whilst the mother was a char for several of the more prominent families. The rest of their vast brood scraped a living as best they could. And although none of the family had ever gone so far as to fall actual foul of the law, everybody knew that they were poachers and probably petty thieves as well. The village constable was always trying to lay one or other of them by the heels, but they were one and all far too wily.

Doreen, however, was too clever to do anything that might risk imprisonment. Losing her job at the house meant that she'd been reduced to having to accept the drudgery of work at a hot, smelly biscuit factory in the nearest town, and she'd been spitting mad about it ever since. Not only about the fall such a move had made to her wages, but also about the reduction it meant to her social status. Doreen, Jane Brockhurst knew only too well, had always had ideas above her station, and was intent on using her beauty to make a better life for herself.

But the housekeeper, who knew much more about the ways of the world than silly Doreen Capstan ever would, could have told the little chit that luring Murray Phelps into matrimony was as likely as one of old Sid Cooper's sows suddenly taking flight over the church steeple. Whilst Miss Phelps's no-good nephew might enjoy dallying with a pretty girl, when it came to marriage, he was going to choose a bride with both money and breeding.

'I told you last night, and I'm telling you now,' the housekeeper said flatly. 'For your own good, you keep away from this house.'

'You can't tell me what to do anymore, I don't work here,' Doreen shot back angrily, and tossed her magnificent Titian locks provocatively. 'I've come to give my condolences to Murray.'

'*Mr* Murray is busy,' the housekeeper said flatly. 'His aunt has just died. He has family obligations to see to, and arrangements to be made. He'll not have time for the likes of you now. Better get along.'

Doreen cast her a nasty smile, but seeing that the housekeeper was not for moving, reluctantly turned on her heel. 'Fine, but I'll be back later,' she warned, determined to have the final word.

She probably would be too, the housekeeper thought, with a mixture of anger and pity that left her feeling tired all over again. She trudged back to her kitchen where she had to rescue the boiling kettle from the stove and sat down heavily on a chair, her thoughts turning to the woman who'd just died.

Jane had worked in her service for nearly all her adult life.

And had never much liked her.

*

Arbie returned home to find a stranger loitering with intent just outside his uncle's studio door. Although his relative regularly sold 'tourist' pieces at several local galleries, they were hardly likely to attract the attention of a private buyer – or thieves. At least, he hoped not.

Right now, the last thing he wanted to do was to have to act the hero and defend the family seat from marauders. He was feeling dog tired and limp lettuce leaves had nothing on him. In fact, he was feeling far more inclined to simply let the stranger help himself to whatever loot he thought he could find in his uncle's shed! But therein, of course, was the problem in a nutshell. Who could say what Uncle kept locked and secured in there? Knowing him, it could be anything from illegally produced bottles of booze to precious metals he was using in some experiment or other.

One thing was for certain – the very shifty-looking customer was making all his worries re-surface. One of these days, he couldn't help but worry, his uncle was going to come a proper cropper. Although the village bobby was hardly the brain of Britain, he wasn't as green as people in Maybury sometimes supposed. And whilst Arbie was very careful to make sure that he knew nothing about the mad money-making schemes his guardian occasionally got up to, he didn't want to have to visit the silly duffer in the clink!

But he was not the only one less than pleased by the unexpected encounter. If anything, the stranger looked more uncomfortable and discombobulated by it than Arbie.

Arbie was just about to bite the bullet and ask the man his business, when his uncle stepped out of the studio door behind him and draped a friendly arm around his shoulder. At this sign of friendship, Arbie relaxed. Uncle spotted him watching and raised one eyebrow in query. This economical gesture was the older man's way of asking if he needed anything.

Arbie hastily shook his head and dragged himself off into the house. His bed was calling to him with all the vigour of a siren luring a sailor to his doom on the rocks, and he really did *not* want to know what his uncle's business was with the stranger.

Uncle watched his nephew slump away into the house and turned back to his friend. 'Right then, Peter my old mucker,' he said, addressing the Rt Hon. Peter Forbes-Bowright with all the easy familiarity of old school chums. 'Like I said, I'll have that Stubbs ready for you in a month or so.'

'You've really pulled my fat out of the bacon this time, Streaky,' he responded, using Uncle's schoolboy nickname. Uncle couldn't now quite remember how he'd come by it – unless it was for his ability to leg it so fast that the geography master could never lay a hand on him when he failed to come up with the proper name for a fjord or mountain. Not even if he chucked the cane at him, instead of his usual trick of trying to wop it across the back seat of his trousers.

'If my wife ever found out I've had to sell it . . . ' His friend, who was a decent enough cove but with the backbone of a jellyfish, mopped his forehead with a handkerchief and shook his head.

Uncle sighed in sympathy. 'A fine gel, but a bit of a dragon, your good lady,' he said, leaving his friend unsure whether his spouse had just been complimented or traduced.

But the honourable gentleman was so happy to have found a way out of his recent fix that he couldn't be bothered to work it out. 'If only Dog's Breakfast had got his nose just a few inches further in front, I'd have won enough to settle the bill for the roof,' he lamented, letting his old friend lead him gently down the gravel path towards the gate.

Uncle, who'd won enough pocket money off the Rt Hon. Peter in his youth to keep him in minor luxuries all through his public-school education, shrugged with genuine sympathy. Even as a child, his pal had been bitten by the gambling bug, willing to bet his last sherbet lemon on the outcome of a snail race, or who was the last down to breakfast on any given morning. Alas, he'd never been any good at it. So it hadn't come as any surprise when his pal, whom he hadn't seen in a good twenty years or so, had suddenly turned up on his doorstep with a painting, a tale of woe and a sheepish expression on his face.

'Still, I suppose Stubbs would have approved,' Uncle said, slapping him on the back and nodding to his studio, where that artist's minor work of a minor racehorse was now safely ensconced.

'Eh?' said the Rt Hon.

Uncle grinned. His pal had never been the brightest of academic sparks in the minor public school where they'd passed their time learning, it seemed, very little about anything remotely useful. 'Having to flog one of his paintings because of the leaden footedness of one of his subjects,' Uncle explained.

'Oh. Yes! Hah!' His companion let out a humorous snort, but then subsided back into misery again. 'I say, Streaky, nobody will notice it's not the original, will they?' he asked nervously.

'Of course not,' Uncle said, trying not to feel offended. 'Nobody's ever complained yet, have they?' he asked, a little askance.

His friend's worried brow cleared at this and he nodded. Streaky was right. He'd got it off Lord Horace Cough-Brough why and how Streaky was the fellow to go to when you got in a tight spot and needed to generate some cash, and he should know! And nobody in the Cough-Brough household had ever questioned the veracity of any of *his* Reynoldses and whatnots.

'Well, once again, thanks a lot, old boy,' Peter Forbes-Bowright said, vigorously pumping Uncle's hand. 'Oh, by the way, is that lad of yours I saw just now the author of that ghost book thingy? Old Buffers at the club told me you'd taken a relative under your wing, and that he'd come up trumps with that jolly useful little book.'

'*The Gentleman's Guide to Ghost-Hunting*, you mean? Yes, he is,' Uncle said, his chest swelling with pride.

'Jolly good read that. Made me laugh out loud a couple of times, I can tell you. And my butler, apparently, stayed at one of his recommended spots in Margate. Or was it Minehead? Well, somewhere anyway,' he added vaguely. 'And very happy with the place he was too.'

Uncle beamed, and with that, both men were left feeling very happy with their morning's work.

As his friend toddled off to his chauffeur-driven Bentley, Uncle heard the postman's bicycle wheels coming along behind him on the gravel, and he hung around to wait for his post. But it was clear from the look of glee on the postie's face that he had more news to impart, and of better quality than whatever might be contained in the envelopes he handed over.

'Mornin', Uncle,' Fred said cheerfully. If the postman had ever once addressed Uncle by his given surname he could not now remember what it was. 'Have you heard? About the goings-on up at the Old Forge?'

Uncle nodded, his cheerfulness over Peter's commission abruptly fading. 'Yes. Bad news. She was a bit of an institution around the place.'

The postie sighed. 'I can't say she was the easiest of people to get on with, but you're right – there's been Phelpses at the Old Forge for centuries. Who's to say if they'll still be there next year?'

'You don't think the nephew will move in then?' Uncle asked, generally curious about the mood and the latest speculation in the village.

'Not him!' Fred said scornfully. 'He's practically a townie now. And too interested in building up the garage side of things and expanding. He only ever comes to the village in the first place to keep the old girl sweet. He never had no feeling for the old days.'

Uncle nodded. 'Still, horses will always want shoeing, and people will always want ironwork mended. He'd be a fool to let that side of the business go. His aunt, for all her faults, was adamant that all the forges stay in business.' Apart from the first and original one right beside the family home, of course! After all, nobody wanted all the noise and heat where they resided.

'Ah, she was a hard-headed woman, God bless her,' the postie said reverently.

Clearly, it hadn't got around the village yet that she had called in his nephew to deal with a pesky ghost, Uncle mused, but he was sure it wouldn't take long. Still, it would be good publicity for his second book.

'She'll be missed in the village,' Uncle said piously. He'd never had anything to do with Amy Phelps on a personal level, and wouldn't miss her in the slightest, but you had to pay lip service to things in a small community, or you'd never hear the end of it. 'A fine woman. But a bit of a tartar,' he couldn't help but add.

The postman grinned. 'True. You'd never have thought she'd been a bit of a goer in her day, would you?'

Uncle turned truly astonished eyes on him, making the other man all but glow with pride. If there was one thing the post office worker really liked, apart from winning at darts, it was being privy to knowledge that no one else had. And imparting it. 'Really?' Uncle enticed.

'According to old man Verney, and he should know.' The postman nodded emphatically. 'Back in the Old Queen's time, she cut a bit of a figure, so they say. Oh, nothing truly scandalous – you know what the Victorians were like. But there were rumours that she was a bit of a one, for all that. Knew what she wanted and made sure she got it, if you know what I mean?' And he knowingly tapped the side of his nose. 'Mind you, according to old man Verney, she came a cropper somewhere along the way. There were definite rumours in the county about one of her promising romances going sour on her for some reason or other.'

'Well I never,' Uncle said, wishing he hadn't dismissed Miss Amy Phelps so thoroughly.

The two men gossiped happily for a while longer, then the postman had to get off on his rounds to spread the news in the next village, and Uncle retired to his studio to study Peter's minor Stubbs with a clinical eye.

Finding an old canvas of just the right age would present him with no problem. He regularly attended country-house sales and bought up dire amateur works of the right vintage for such purposes as this. But he'd have to be careful when it came to the paints. Although his old school pal would quietly sell the original abroad, the copy Uncle would make for him to hang back on his wall would have to be as flawless as possible. You just never knew when some arty type with more knowledge than was good for him might be invited to a house party and want to show off his skills!

*

The local hospital was not the largest in the county, nor did it attract the cream of the crop when it came to its surgeons and physicians. Likewise, its pathologist was now approaching retirement age, and hadn't kept up with all the latest medical advancements. Moreover, pathology was a thankless job with no kudos attached to it at all, which meant that very few doctors went into that field. And those that did found themselves in the role because they'd been 'gently encouraged' by the rest of the medical establishment who deemed that their attentions were probably best spent on those already safely dead.

But not even the greenest tyro could fail to spot the signs of an unexpected substance in the corpse of Amy Phelps. It wasn't a rare substance and finding traces of it wasn't that complicated. In its many forms it had been known to man for many years. Widely used to exterminate pests and vermin in houses and ships, it also had many other uses.

It was cyanide. And somebody had used it to help Miss Amy Phelps leave this mortal realm.

The pathologist had a little skip in his step as he set about making up his report for the police. Having little work on that morning, he'd made his initial examinations of the woman's body his first and top priority and was proud of his speed in finding results so quickly, and was expecting high praise for it. At any rate, it made a very nice change from his usual diet of mundane coronaries, accidental deaths due to falls or industrial mishaps, and the occasional drowning.

And when this report landed on the desk of Cheltenham-based Inspector Bernard Gorringe, and he was told by his superintendent to 'sort this out, will you?' the first thing he did was get out his maps and find the tiny dot in the middle of the Cotswolds that was the little village of Maybury-in-the-Marsh.

The second thing he did was hope that it had a decent pub.

*

When Arbie awoke from his much-needed six hours of sleep, it was still barely three o'clock. Knowing that Mrs Privett, the daily woman who looked after them, would probably have finished her morning's work and wouldn't be back until later to cook their supper, he foraged for scraps in the kitchen, finding a cold chicken leg and a hunk of cheese, to which he added a slice off the loaf. He then set off in his trusty (for the most part) black Alvis saloon and made his way to the nearby boatyard, where his uncle's birthday present was currently being overhauled.

The boatyard consisted of a wet and dry dock, a large, corrugated iron building and three old men and one boy who looked bored to death. The young boy eyed him pityingly when Arbie introduced himself and told him that he'd just bought a small craft which was being 'geed-up a bit' here, but he led him obligingly enough to the dry dock. There Marcus Finch was busy scraping something unspeakable off the hull of the small white craft that Arbie recognised as his recent purchase.

'Ah, hello there, Mr Finch? I'm Mr Swift. We've been cor-responding over this.' He nodded at the boat in question. 'I've come to see how things are progressing.'

'Eh?' the old man said, but clambered down off the craft obligingly, wiping his hands on a rag. Again Arbie introduced himself, quickly realising that the old man was hard of hearing, and during the next ten minutes, found himself quite literally shouting to make himself understood.

Nevertheless, when the two men had finished their consulta-tion, Arbie was pleased enough about how things were going. He might have a sore throat from all the bellowing, but he was happy with his colour choice for the new paintwork and was satisfied that the small river craft's extra windows allowed in plenty of light to suit his uncle's painterly needs. Shaking hands, and promising that he'd be in touch when he'd thought of a new name for the vessel (he didn't think his uncle would want to keep the rather twee name of *Rambling Rosie* somehow), Arbie took off, feeling pleased with himself.

For once, when it came to thinking up a present that his guardian would appreciate, he was confident that he'd come up trumps. Consequently, when he got back home he was whistling happily to himself. That is, until he saw the identity of the visitor waiting for him in the front garden.

'Hello, Val,' he said with forced cheerfulness as he climbed out of the car. 'Feeling better now?'

Val shook her head. 'Not really,' she said shortly. 'I can see you haven't heard.'

'Heard what?'

'It was murder after all. So we are going to have to find a killer.'

'Huh?'

'Miss Phelps. Oh, Arbie, there's a police inspector come already, and he wants to see us all. Isn't it terrible?'

'Huh?'

111

'Miss Phelps – they're saying she was poisoned!' Val wailed.

'Huh?'

'Oh, Arbie, can't you do anything else but stand there looking like a stunned mullet?' Val said crossly, all but stamping her foot. 'And can't you say anything else but "huh" like a . . . like a . . . like some idiot who just stands there saying "huh" all the time?'

Arbie swallowed hard. 'I say, Val. This is all getting rather serious, isn't it?' he managed feebly. Although he'd let Val persuade him they needed to investigate and all that sort of thing, the thought that someone really *had* killed the old girl after all made him feel slightly sick.

Val looked at him resignedly and gave a heavy sigh. 'Come on. You'd better come over to the vicarage. Father wants a word with you,' she added ominously.

At this, Arbie swallowed. Hard. But at least he managed not to say 'huh?' again.

CHAPTER NINE

The vicar of Maybury-in-the-Marsh sternly regarded his daughter and Arbie Swift from behind the desk in his study. Val started off holding his gaze determinedly, but after a few moments of the parental silent treatment, her head began to droop and she eventually began to shift her feet.

The vicarly gaze was then transferred to Arbie, which was totally unnecessary, since he'd been shifting his feet right from the start.

'I say, sir, I'm most awfully sorry about all this,' he began, having once been told by his uncle that, when you found yourself in the soup, it was a good idea to start off on the defensive. And the fact that he was now taking his uncle's advice was a good indication of just how desperate he was feeling. 'I had no idea any of this would, er . . . get so . . . well . . . I mean . . . I didn't really want to do a ghost-hunt in the first place,' he found himself saying hotly, beginning to feel more than a little put upon. 'If Miss Phelps hadn't asked me, I wouldn't have dreamed of getting mixed up in it all. And, well . . . Val was there when she asked me to do one of my ghost-watches, so . . . ' He trailed off miserably, realising that erudition had well and truly deserted him.

At this last statement, however, the vicar sighed heavily and with a vague nod of defeat. He, who knew his daughter only too well, had no trouble at all in picturing the scene. Val would have been fascinated by the older woman's entreaties and the thought of ghosts and a bit of harmless adventure would have meant that even someone with far more gumption than young Mr Swift wouldn't have been able to rein her in. Well, the situation was harmless no longer.

'Cyanide,' he said flatly.

Arbie, with a heroic effort, just managed to stop himself from saying 'huh?' and contented himself with a mere blink or two instead. Yet whatever he'd expected the vicar's first words to him to be, it certainly wasn't that.

As usual, it was Val who was quicker off the mark. 'Is that what was used to poison her, Papa? And how do you know?' she added curiously.

'I got it off Miss Perkins. Who shares a lady that does with the wife of the Chief Constable,' her father responded dryly.

'Ah,' Val said, which was all that was needed. In the way of the village, what one person knew, the rest of the village knew about ten seconds later. And when the source was so impeccable . . . 'Oh but that's horrid. Vile!'

The vicar agreed. Having a parishioner poisoned was horrid indeed. But having one of his children involved, even on the periphery, was beyond the pale. 'There'll be talk in the village,' he said, in massive understatement. It took Val – who knew her father as well as he knew her – only a second to realise he wasn't referring to the murder so much as to the fact that she and Arbie had been up at the house in the days beforehand. Which meant that their 'ghost-watching' was bound to come out sooner or later. And wouldn't the village goggle at that!

'Sorry, Papa,' Val said miserably and looked across at Arbie, expecting him to echo her sentiments. But she was subsequently astonished to see that he was deep in thought. It wasn't an expression she saw often on his face. In fact, it was so unusual that before she could think about it, she said instantly, 'What's biting you, old bean?'

'Cyanide,' Arbie repeated her father's earlier quote. 'I've read the odd murder mystery or two – haven't we all? And Mrs Christie is well up on poisons and stuff. And in the books people are always being bumped off with the stuff.'

'So?' Val and her father said together with matching impatience.

'Well, according to all the writers, it's supposed to be quick-acting stuff. Sometimes, really quick acting, depending on what was used and how, and the dose and whatnot. Which means . . . if Miss Phelps really was poisoned with the stuff it must have been very shortly before she died, mustn't it?'

Val suddenly gulped as she twigged to what he was thinking. 'You mean it must have happened when we were all at dinner!'

At this, her parent went rigid with shock. 'Then it could have been you who was killed, if the killer made a mistake,' he said, appalled. He half-rose from his chair and then slumped back, eyeing his daughter keenly. 'Have you been feeling quite well, Valentina?' he asked anxiously, the use of her full first name a clear indication of how upset he was.

'Oh, we must be all right, sir, otherwise we'd have turned up our toes by now,' Arbie said, with a cheery lack of tact. 'The stuff's deadly, apparently.'

Val shot him a fulminating look, which didn't bode well for when she got him on her own, but her father was far more inclined to be lenient, simply because Arbie had put his mind at rest – albeit without much finesse.

'Now look here, Val,' her father began; having got over his sudden fright he was fully intending to lay down the law and forbid her to have anything more to do with the Phelpses and all this murder business.

But before he could do so, Arbie shook his head vigorously

and let out a sharp exclamation. 'Poppycock! It's no good,' he all but yelled. And when Val and the vicar gaped at him, he shook his head again. 'Don't you see? She *couldn't* have been poisoned at the dinner. It's simply not possible.' He appeared almost cross.

Father and daughter exchanged surprised looks. It was not often the always-affable, anything-for-a-quiet-life Mr Arbuthnot Swift was roused to anything like this sort of animation.

'Something troubling you, young man?' the vicar asked mildly, and with a hint of amusement. Just a few minutes ago, he'd been intending to read this young fella a lecture that would make his ears burn for leading his daughter into a scandal. Now he was as curious as Val to hear what sort of bee the lad had in his bonnet. 'If what you say about the quick-acting nature of the poison is true, surely the most logical explanation is that the poor unfortunate lady ingested something with her last meal?'

'But that's just it, sir, it can't have happened that way!' Arbie said, then turned to Val. 'Think, Val, back to that night. We arrived at the house. We met up with the others in the garden. Miss Phelps didn't have a drink in her hand when we arrived, did she?'

'No,' Val agreed. 'But then we all went in to eat. Like Papa said, it must have happened then, right under our nose!'

'But, Val, it couldn't have,' Arbie insisted. 'Think – what was the first course?'

'Soup, some clear vegetable thing or other.'

Arbie, who was rather fond of Oxford herb soup, especially when it had been prepared properly, as it had that night, tried not to shudder at her derogatory description. 'Yes, and Mrs Brockhurst brought it in a large tureen and ladled it out into our bowls individually.'

'So if the poison had been in the soup, you'd all have ingested it,' her father said, nodding, then suddenly perked up. 'Unless the poison was already in the ladle!' the vicar said, pleased with himself. 'Tell me, was the lady of the house served first?'

'I'm afraid not, sir,' Arbie let him down sadly. 'I noticed Murray Phelps, as the "man of the house" sitting at the head of the table, was always served first. I imagine it was some standing order or something from Miss Phelps herself.' He sighed. 'She was a Victorian, after all.'

'Oh,' the vicar said, deflated. 'Still, if I'd been right, it would mean that the housekeeper must have done it, because she'd be the only one who could have put the poison in the ladle beforehand. And I rather like Mrs Brockhurst. A very nice lady, I've always thought her.'

'Besides, Papa, even if the poison had been in the ladle,' Val felt compelled to point out, 'the moment she dipped the ladle into the tureen to serve the first person, the poison would have leaked out in the soup and we'd all have been ill.'

'Oh. Yes, of course,' the vicar said, now utterly deflated. He too had read his fair share of murder mysteries and had fancied himself as a bit of a Sherlock Holmes too. It was coming as quite a blow to his ego to realise that these things were a bit more complicated in real life.

'So what was served next?' he asked, shaking off his self-doubts and turning an eager eye back to his daughter.

'Fish,' Val said succinctly.

'Hah, then . . . ' the vicar began, but Val was feated to disoblige him yet again.

'I'm afraid not, Papa, it was one large piece of turbot that came in on a platter, and we all had flakes taken from it and transferred onto individual plates. We all watched it being done.'

'Exactly,' Arbie chipped in. 'No individual portions were served. So again, no would-be killer could be sure of poisoning only one portion.'

'Then we had lamb for the mains, which was carved off the same joint by Murray,' Val swept the recital along.

'And the side dishes all came in big bowls from which we

helped ourselves to the vegetables and potatoes and things,' Arbie said. 'And the sauce.'

'Sauce?' the vicar asked hopefully.

'Two kinds, I think, served in two sauce boats, leaving us to pick which one we preferred,' Val added. 'No way a killer could guess which Miss Phelps would choose.'

'Besides, even if the killer *did* know Miss Phelps well enough to guess which she'd pick, anyone else could have helped themselves to the same sauce subsequently,' Arbie put in. 'And unless the killer was willing to poison anyone else unlucky enough to choose it, willy-nilly, I can't see how that could be the culprit. Which it wasn't, because I seem to remember I had the same sauce as Miss Phelps did, and I'm fit as a fiddle.' As he said it, though, he felt a slight twinge in his solar plexus, but this he put down to his imagination running away with him.

'Which leaves the dessert then,' the vicar said brightly. 'Surely that was served in individual dishes. What was it – ices – sorbet? Slices of gateau?'

'Summer berries and ice cream,' Arbie said glumly.

'Served from one big cut-glass bowl,' Val added, even more glumly.

'Oh, gingernuts,' the vicar said, which for him was very strong language indeed. 'But wait a minute – what about drinks?' he asked, brightening visibly.

'Wine was opened and poured from the same bottle,' Val said, remembering how pleased she'd been by its quality, but careful not to let that show in front of her father.

'Coffee?' the vicar asked hopefully.

'Served in the drawing room I think,' Arbie said, shooting Val a questioning look. 'Like the rest of the male party, I stayed on at the table for brandy and cigars. But when we joined the ladies, I think I remember seeing a large coffee pot on the table?'

'Yes. The housekeeper brought it in and poured out cups right in front of us,' Val said, beginning to look as puzzled as Arbie had been earlier.

'I say, Val, is it possible Miss Phelps had milk or something, and nobody else did? Or sugar, and nobody else did?' Arbie asked, but without much hope.

Val screwed up her eyes in thought for a moment, and both men, who were watching her like hawks, saw her shoulders slowly slump. 'It's no good. Miss Phelps had it with milk and sugar. I didn't have sugar but did have milk. And Cora, I think, had sugar but not milk. But Phyllis had both milk and sugar, like her aunt.'

'So it couldn't have been in the coffee,' the vicar said. 'But what about afterwards? Did you have after-dinner drinks?' he persisted.

'No,' Val said. 'I don't think they were offered, were they?'

Arbie shook his head. 'No, I rather got the feeling Miss Phelps wasn't much of an imbiber. I don't think Murray was altogether pleased at the lack of a nightcap, but he didn't make any comment about it. He was probably used to his aunt's ways.'

For a moment there was total silence in the room. 'Could she have taken some cocoa or a glass of milk or something up to bed with her?' the vicar asked.

But Arbie shook his head, remembering the moment he'd watched his hostess climb up the stairs on the last night of her life. 'When she went upstairs to bed, she had one hand on the banister rail, and the other was hanging at her side,' he said morosely. 'The only thing she picked up was her night-light.'

'Perhaps the housekeeper was in the habit of taking her something up later?' the vicar asked desperately.

'There wasn't a cup or a glass or anything like that left on her bedside table,' Arbie said flatly, and when Val gave him a surprised look, he flushed a little. 'I noticed what was there when we found her,' he explained defensively.

119

'That doesn't mean the housekeeper couldn't have taken her something up later though. And then, after her mistress had drunk it, taken away the evidence and washed it up,' Val said reluctantly. 'It's the only thing that makes sense, isn't it?' she added pensively as both men looked at her thoughtfully.

'But why would Mrs Brockhurst want to kill her employer? She'd lose her job and her home all in one fell swoop,' Arbie pointed out.

'Unless she knew she was mentioned in the will?' Val proffered uncertainly.

The vicar sighed. 'The only thing you can do is ask her if Miss Phelps was in the habit of having a drink taken to her room,' he added, his gaze fixed firmly on Arbie.

At this, Arbie nearly jumped out of his skin. 'Eh? Who? Me?'

'Yes you, young man,' the vicar announced imperiously. 'Since you've got yourself and my daughter mixed up in this, you can jolly well help in sorting the mess out. The sooner someone's been arrested for this horrible crime, the sooner the gossip will die out.'

'But I can't ask Mrs Brockhurst about her employer's drinking habits!' Arbie yelped, appalled at the very idea. 'She's sure to realise why I want to know and what it is I'm getting at!'

'What's this about drinking habits?'

They all turned at the sound of the mild, feminine voice that interrupted them, and saw Val's mother hovering in the doorway. She was an older, faintly more faded version of Val, but with none of her daughter's astringency. 'I've come to tell you I'm off, and there's seed cake in the pantry,' she said comfortably.

'We were discussing Amy Phelps, my dear, and whether or not she was in the habit of having a drink brought up to her bedroom at night,' the vicar explained.

'Oh, I can tell you that,' Mrs Coulton-James said serenely, unaware of the bombshell she'd just dropped. 'She didn't. Wouldn't hear of it, apparently. Said hot drinks in bed were for the lower classes. Quite how she came to that conclusion I have no idea.'

She looked at the three sets of eyes staring at her in consternation and raised an eyebrow. 'What on earth's the matter? What have I said?' she demanded.

'Mother, how do you know that?' Val asked.

'My dear girl, the flower roster. Miss Phelps ruled it with a rod of iron. All us ladies were often lectured on what was, and wasn't proper, and on a great deal of subjects other than the best time to use Michaelmas daisies, and why gladioli must never be seen in a church. I can't remember when or how she came to tell us about her night-time habits. I think she said something like "no real lady has breakfast in bed" or "the proper place for eating is at the dining table" or something like that. Eating and drinking in one's bedroom leads to terrible indigestion or a corrosion of the moral spirit or some such, apparently. Anyway,' that veritable lady said with an elegant shrug, 'there you are. She was a funny old stick in many ways. Now, I'd better see to the WI ladies before there's an uproar.'

And with that intriguing statement, she was off.

Leaving all three of them looking at one another and at a total loss.

*

Arbie was reluctant to go back to the Old Forge so soon, but Val was having none of it. 'I thought we decided that we owed it to Miss Phelps to find out what happened?' she began to argue forcefully as they set off from the vicarage.

'Yes, but I dare say the police will do a lot of the . . . ' Arbie tried to interrupt the flow with a reasonable counterattack of his own, but typically didn't even get to finish the sentence. If there was one thing he'd learned before he could even walk properly, it was that there was no point in trying to divert Val once she'd made up her mind. Yet it had never stopped him from trying.

'What's more, Papa is right about the village gossiping about our ghost-hunting,' she swept on ruthlessly. 'And we need to stand up for ourselves. Show the village we've got nothing to hide. Otherwise, you know how they are! They'll have us down as prime suspects if we're not careful.'

'What do you mean, *our* ghost-hunting?' Arbie put in dryly. That was the thing with Val – let her have an inch, and she'd take a country mile! 'And I still think we should keep our noses out of this mess, Val,' he pleaded. 'I know Uncle would advise us to have nothing to do with it.'

She turned to face him, hands on her hips. 'Your uncle,' Val began ominously, but before she could continue to say something that would probably be extremely disparaging (and true, and would amuse his uncle no end), they were distracted.

For as they turned out onto Old Mill Lane, a familiar voice rang out. 'Ahoy there, Arbie old chap! Wait half a mo'!' They both turned to see Walter Greenstreet hurrying towards them, waving a frantic hand in greeting.

Arbie's old friend and representative of his publishing house was panting slightly as he jogged up to them, but there was no denying the glint of happiness in his gaze. 'I say, is it true? Has one of your ghosts up and made itself famous? When old Petherington told me there'd been murder done in your neck of the woods, I couldn't believe it. So I caught the Bampton Flier and hotfooted it down here as fast as I could. I must say, this will boost the sales of book two of *The Gentleman's Guide*, no end!'

Arbie eyed his friend with displeasure. 'Who said anything about a second book?' he asked petulantly.

'Oh, Arbie, don't you see? It would be ideal for us,' Val said happily. 'Everyone will be expecting another volume and it gives us the perfect excuse to hang around the Phelps house and find out what's going on. Not even the villagers will object to you making Maybury-in-the-Marsh famous for having a ghost!'

'I say, Arbie, do listen to your lovely friend,' Walter butted in, eyeing Val with pleasure. 'She clearly knows what's good for us. I mean *you*,' he corrected himself hastily.

Arbie sighed, knowing when he was defeated, then all three of them had to step onto the side as a covered van, bearing groceries for the village shop, went past them. The old grey horse pulling it plodded along patiently, head down, but the man with the reins eyed them keenly, especially Walter, who was a stranger to the village.

Arbie knew that as soon as the man reached the village shop, Walter's presence would be doing the rounds, and he wondered in which role his old chum would be cast by the village. A newspaper reporter? A witness? A suspect? A long-lost son of Amy Phelps, come back to demand his inheritance? He wouldn't put any nonsense past some of his more woolly-minded neighbours.

Somehow or other, he found the three of them ambling inexorably towards the Old Forge, with Walter flirting like a moonstruck goose with Val, and the vicar's daughter shamelessly playing up to him. Arbie knew that the vicar was keen to marry off all his daughters (and his sons, come to that) and encouraged them endlessly to find suitable mates, and he half hoped, rather vindictively, that Mr Walter Greenstreet would be ensnared by Val's husband-hunting charms.

That would serve him right, coming here, demanding that Arbie do some actual work again.

When they reached the Old Forge, however, they hit an unexpected obstacle, in the form of a police constable posted at the garden gate and blocking the ingress.

Arbie brightened at this example of being turned away by officialdom. However, when Val rather imperiously gave them their names, the Constable perked up considerably. 'Miss Coulton-James and Mr Swift, you say? That's lucky, the Inspector's been wanting to have a word with both of you. If you'll just wait here, I'll tell him that you've turned up.' Unspoken seemed to lay the threat that if they hadn't done so soon, they'd have been rootled out of their house and home and brought before the law in handcuffs.

Arbie's gloom deepened.

'I say, Arbie, what *have* you been up to, old man?' Walter asked nervously. Whilst publicity might be good – and a juicy murder was the absolute tops – having your author too much embroiled in a cause célèbre could prove embarrassing.

'Nothing!' Arbie squeaked, giving his fair-weather friend a baleful look. 'I expect it's just routine.'

'Well, I don't suppose the Inspector will have any use for me,' Walter said, cravenly backing away. 'I was miles from here, blamelessly asleep in my own bed last night. I'll just pop off and say hello to your uncle and wait for you back at your place, hmm?'

'Don't bother on my account,' Arbie said grimly and watched his chum slink off with a disgusted sigh.

Beside him, Val snorted. 'What a lily-livered specimen, Arbie. Are all publishers like that?'

'Oh yes, I expect so,' Arbie said glumly. Then he nearly jumped out of his skin as the long arm of the law descended on his shoulder in the form of a firm pat. The Constable beamed at him. 'You're to go on up to the house. Inspector Gorringe is in the morning room with the family.'

Arbie swallowed hard, gave a feeble grin and reluctantly set off up the path, with Val jauntily striding along beside him. She seemed to be totally undaunted by the thought of what lay ahead, and Arbie mused bitterly on what it must be like to have such a clear conscience and an innocent view of the world.

For himself, he was busy trying to think of ways and means of ensuring that this Inspector chappie and his uncle never crossed paths.

'Cheer up, this will be interesting,' Val said, a shade impatiently. 'Just think – we'll be like the characters in one of those murder mystery books that you seem so keen on.'

'Most of them end up horribly murdered,' he informed her bitterly.

She looked at him closely. 'Arbie, you haven't been keeping things from me, have you?' she accused. 'You know, to try and keep me out of this?'

Arbie bridled. 'As if I would!' he said stoutly. 'I promise you, everything I know, you know,' he insisted. Then felt a little niggle at the back of his mind, and in an instant the cause of his unease popped up obligingly. 'Oh, er, did I mention that Mrs Brockhurst let it slip that Phyllis, the niece, was in the habit of going into her aunt's room uninvited?' he asked diffidently.

Val scowled at him. 'No, you did not. Have you tackled her about this?' she demanded.

'Who, me?' Arbie squeaked. 'Certainly not. A chap can't go about asking delicate questions like that!'

'Oh, Arbie! I could throttle you sometimes,' Val wailed. 'If we're going to find out who killed poor Miss Phelps we need to follow up *every* clue.'

Val, in contrast to her set face, was dressed demurely today, and with her long blonde hair caught back in a becoming French pleat, she looked the picture of fresh-faced innocence. Arbie could only hope the Inspector would get her measure quickly and instantly ban her from his investigation. He certainly would if he knew what was good for him. And that way, Arbie could continue to investigate quietly away without worrying about what mischief Val was getting into!

CHAPTER TEN

Inside the Old Forge, in a rarely used drawing room, the Inspector had just finished interviewing the dead woman's niece, who insisted she had seen nothing, heard nothing and knew nothing.

Now it was the turn of the nephew. Murray Phelps entered, looking competent and at ease. The Inspector watched him take a seat with a bland smile, and then began.

As he had with his cousin just minutes before, the Inspector took Murray through the events of the previous evening, the dinner, his aunt's movements and behaviour, and filled his notebook almost to capacity. By the time they were finished, the Inspector felt as if he'd got a reasonably good idea of the events of last night.

It was only when he said mildly, 'And now, can you tell me your movements after your aunt retired to bed?' that the Inspector sensed the other man become warier.

'Me? Well, as I'm sure the others will have told you, we stayed up for a bit, chatting, playing some cards for a while, you know, how you do. Then I went to bed.'

As he said these words, his eyes left the Inspector's and vaguely inspected a bookcase. The Inspector coughed gently. 'I see, sir. Did you sleep the whole night through?'

At this, the other man's leg jerked a little and, catching the

Inspector's eye, he scowled and uncomfortably pulled at the collar of his jacket. 'Oh yes, out like a light,' he assured Gorringe. Who abruptly put a big question mark in his notebook next to his name.

As the policeman moved on to ask him whether he knew if his aunt had fallen out with anyone recently, he began to relax once more and became again his confident self, as he assured Gorringe that his aunt was respected by one and all and that he couldn't conceive of anyone who would have wanted her dead.

At this, the Inspector nodded placidly. But Murray Phelps wasn't fooled. He could see that the Inspector wasn't totally convinced by his performance. Which meant that he was mightily relieved once the Inspector said they were finished and he could go and join his cousin in another part of the house.

'Oh, would you mind sending in the kitchen maid, please?' Gorringe asked.

Murray condescended to do just that.

*

The kitchen maid – who looked all of fourteen years old – was the nervous, tearful sort, who vowed she hardly ever left the kitchen or the protection of Mrs Brockhurst's skirts. And since she didn't even live in, she was almost certainly correct in her fearful avowals that she didn't have anything to do with the family, and that she'd never dream of speaking to the gentry, let alone know anything about their doings. So it was, that Inspector Gorringe spent very little time on her, and when the house received its new visitors, he had re-joined the cousins in the morning room.

Everyone glanced up curiously as Arbie and Val were shown in by the tight-lipped housekeeper. But it was the man who rose from the sofa in front of them that commanded Arbie's instant attention.

Somewhere in his early fifties, he was heavy-set and beginning to lose his hair, which was a mousey shade of brown/grey. He had a competent but not driven air about him that spoke of many years of solid if undistinguished service. Dressed in an old but well-cut brown suit, he had matching brown eyes which turned to regard Val with a soft look. Arbie's heart instantly sank. Just his luck if the Inspector turned out to be the doting and indulgent father of any number of daughters. Val would twist him around her little finger in no time, and then there would be no holding her back.

The gaze the Inspector then turned on him was much more razor-like in its appraisal.

'So this is the famous author,' he said. They were not, it had to be admitted, the most comforting words Arbie could have wished for on first meeting the officer in charge of the case. 'Mr Phelps here has just been telling me how you spent the night in the hall watching for ghosts. Apparently.'

Arbie didn't like that last word. It smacked alarmingly of judiciary scepticism. Exactly what had that blackguard Murray Phelps been saying about him? And what did this Inspector Gorringe think he, Arbie, had been doing, whilst the lady of the house was killed? All his uncle's dire warnings about the constabulary and their nasty, suspicious natures flooded his mind, and a mental image of himself being led away in handcuffs and charged with murder made his mouth go horribly dry.

Definitely time, Arbie thought, to efface himself. He coughed a little and shuffled pathetically. 'Well, er, what's a fellow to do, eh, Inspector?' he appealed. 'I mean, when a lady asks for your help, you're obliged to set off on your white steed, waving your sword aloft, and all that. What?'

Val shot him a disgusted look at this pitiful sally, which Arbie totally ignored. It was all very well for *her*, Arbie mused mood-ily. Nobody would ever think of accusing a vicar's daughter of committing murder. But if this police inspector could be made to regard him as a bit of a buffoon, he'd be happy enough.

'Yes,' Inspector Gorringe said, eyeing Arbie thoughtfully. 'Mr Phelps here was just telling me how his aunt seemed convinced that the family ghost was trying to tell her something.' His voice couldn't have been more deadpan and disbelieving. 'And did you, by any chance, run across this spook in the wee small hours?'

Murray Phelps turned away to hide a grin, but Phyllis looked on disapprovingly.

'Can't say I did, no,' Arbie said vaguely. 'But then, you so often don't. Ghosts can be remarkably disobliging, you know. I noticed that when I was writing my book. I could be all set up with a camera ready to capture the formation of ectoplasm or what have you and poof, nothing.' He spread his hands eloquently. 'But two days after you leave a place, your host will write to you telling you that he's being bothered by manifestations galore.'

'Very annoying I'm sure, sir,' the Inspector said, lips twitching.

'Mr Swift is very good at what he does, Inspector, I assure you.' Val did her best to spoil all Arbie's good work, by asserting stoutly, 'He really is the authority on such things. In fact, his publishers have just this second commissioned him to write a follow-up to *The Gentleman's Guide* with the Phelps ghost being his first investigation. Isn't that right, Arbie?'

Arbie groaned.

'Yes, Inspector, I meant to warn you about that.' Murray, of all people, chose that moment to come to his rescue. 'I'm rather afraid I've kind of given Mr Swift permission to ghost-watch here whenever he wants.'

The Inspector's sharp eyes turned to Murray. 'Indeed, sir? I must say I find that rather surprising.' Inspector Gorringe, who thought he'd got the measure of his man, wouldn't have bet a bent brass farthing that the new master of the Old Forge was the kind to be all that free-handed with his largesse.

'It came about as something of a bet. Or a bit of a dare, if you like,' Murray muttered in explanation.

'Ah. I see,' the Inspector said. Well, boys would be boys, his expression clearly said, raising both Murray and Arbie's hackles. 'Well, your, er, ghost-hunting will have to wait for a few days or so, Mr Swift. We'll be here at the house for some time, questioning people and making our investigations. And we can't be having you underfoot.'

'Oh, right-ho,' Arbie said, with such evident relief that this time it was the Inspector who had to turn his head sharply to hide his grin. 'In that case, we'd best be off then, Val.'

'Just a moment, sir, not so fast,' the Inspector said. 'Whilst I have you here, I'd like to take your statement about what happened here at the relevant time.'

'Mine as well then?' Val put in. 'I was ghost-watching too.'

'Yes, miss, yours as well,' the Inspector agreed indulgently. 'Miss Thomas,' he turned to Phyllis, 'may I commandeer a room again, in order to conduct my interviews?'

'Oh yes, of course. I think the drawing room again . . . ?' She raised an eyebrow at her cousin, who merely shrugged. 'This way,' she added, rising from her chair and leading the way back out into the hall and into the small but pleasant drawing room.

'Thank you, Miss Thomas, this is ideal,' Inspector Gorringe said. 'I'll call you and Mr Phelps as and when I need you. It's nothing to be alarmed about,' he added as Phyllis gave a little squeak of alarm. 'We don't bite, miss,' he added with an avuncular smile. 'But we have to know the whereabouts and movements of everyone who was here last night and this morning. I'm sure you'll appreciate that.'

Phyllis gave a brief but terrified smile. 'I still can't believe that

Aunty didn't just have heart failure or something like that. I'm sure there must have been some mistake about all this. Who on earth would want to hurt her?' she said, and with that shot out of the room, sniffling.

As the door closed behind her, Arbie sent Val a quick, nervous look.

Val, of course, was watching the Inspector with wide, fascinated eyes and a look of intense concentration on her face. She was so evidently enjoying all this, that Arbie, for two pins, could have kicked her.

'Now then, you two,' Inspector Gorringe said, turning to face them. 'Have a seat, and let's get down to it, shall we?'

*

Arbie and Val answered the questions Inspector Gorringe put to them as best they could. But really, what did it boil down to? They had dinner – and Arbie was sure the Inspector didn't miss the significance of all the shared dishes – and afterwards, when he'd come back, Arbie had watched Amy Phelps climb the stairs, empty-handed, as she went off to bed. And to her death. Val and he had then spent the night in the hall and heard and seen nothing out of the ordinary – either ghostly or otherwise.

'And you heard no odd sounds in the night? No one crying out for instance?' the Inspector persisted.

'No, I didn't,' Arbie said. 'And believe me, on a ghost-watch I'm always alert for any noises.'

'Ghosts?' the Inspector said with a smile.

'More likely someone playing the fool and trying to trick me,' Arbie responded with a grin.

'But not this time?'

'No,' Arbie said sombrely. 'At least, I didn't hear anything. Did you, Val?'

But Val shook her head. 'No, I'd have told you if I did. But it was all quiet.'

Inspector Gorringe sighed. 'But you must have heard some of the people moving about at the start of the night, when everyone had just retired? The sound of people going to and from the bathrooms for instance? Doors opening and shutting? Running water for a bath perhaps?' the policeman pressed. When he'd been given the startling information that on the night of the murder two independent witnesses had been ensconced right in the hall all night, he'd thought his luck must surely be in. Now he was not so sure.

Arbie shrugged helplessly. 'I don't know if you've had time yet to inspect the house at all, sir, but it's solidly built, let me tell you, and straggles about all over the place. And even if any of the floorboards *do* creak, it would probably be impossible to tell where the sound comes from. It's like a maze everywhere – staircases here, there and everywhere, different levels, and dog-leg corners in the corridors at every turn.'

'Yes, it's a bit of a mish-mash in styles,' Val agreed loyally.

'Now, about this ghost business.' The Inspector sighed, fixing Arbie with a stern eye. 'It all sounds a bit pie in the sky to me. Do you really take it seriously?' he asked the good-looking young man curiously. 'You went to Oxford, I understand, so you're an educated fellow. Come on, now, just between you and me?'

But Arbie could only shrug. 'A lot of people take the occult seriously, Inspector. And not just men of letters, but men of science too.' He wasn't about to be caught out quoting something that his publishers might take exception to!

'I thought a lot of the so-called mediums had been debunked and proved to be frauds many years ago. All that table-tapping and smoke-and-mirrors stuff. We're not living in the Victorian era now,' the Inspector said stolidly. 'Surely, we're not so gullible nowadays? Your book is all very amusing, I grant you, and the

132

holiday-making aspects of it are, so I've been told, genuinely helpful. But just between you and me, when Miss Phelps asked you to help her with her family ghost, you couldn't have taken her seriously?'

The Inspector looked at his witness carefully and saw him hesitate. He wasn't surprised when, a moment later, a swift, questioning glance passed between the two young people that made him sit up and take notice.

'Well, Inspector, to be honest, no, I didn't,' Arbie said. 'But only because I, that is we, Val and I, I mean, well, we sort of came to the conclusion that Miss Phelps probably didn't believe in the ghost either. Didn't we, Val?'

As Val nodded, the Inspector frowned, sitting forward a little on his chair. 'I'm not sure I follow you, sir,' he said. 'Can you elaborate on that?'

Arbie nodded and wearily took the Inspector through the times when he and Miss Phelps had talked, explaining about the Phelps family legend, the ghostly smithy and his bell, the so-called warnings that had been left where she could find them, and trying to convey the woman's vacillating attitude to it all. By the time he'd finished, the Inspector was looking troubled.

'I didn't realise it was anything as substantial as all that,' the older man said grimly. 'I thought maybe Miss Phelps was simply hearing mice in the wainscotting or what have you, and letting her imagination do the rest. But that sounds rather nasty. Someone was obviously trying to frighten the poor lady.'

Arbie nodded. 'Yes, that's what we thought too,' he agreed. 'Not that Miss Phelps was the sort to scare easily.'

'But then there came her accident,' Val put in.

'Ah yes. The tumble down the stairs.' The Inspector nodded. 'Her niece told us about that. Luckily, her aunt suffered no more than a few bruises. Do you think that she was pushed?' he shot out.

Arbie jumped in his chair. 'No,' he said at once, caught off guard by the suddenness of the question. Then he paused and said, more thoughtfully, 'No, I don't see how she could have been. Miss Phelps never said anything about there being a second party involved, anyway,' he added.

And then he had to wonder. If she had seen her attacker, would she have spoken out? Certainly she would, and most loudly and indignantly, if it had been one of the household staff. But if it had been a member of her family?

Then he had a thought. 'I say, Inspector, what if someone tied a piece of string or something across . . . '

'The top of the stairs? So that it would catch her at ankle level and trip her forward, sir?' the Inspector asked, eyes twinkling as the young man's shoulders slumped a little. 'Yes, I did wonder if that old chestnut might have been used when I was told about it. So I inspected the woodwork at ground level on the stairs very thoroughly, sir.'

'And?' Val asked eagerly.

'I found a lot of woodworm holes,' the Inspector said flatly. 'That notwithstanding, I don't think any cord could have been used. A good solid screw would have had to have been put in place either side of the stairs in order to trip someone over and would have created a bigger hole than woodworm.'

'Also, whoever had set it up would have had to remove the evidence pretty smartly. And we know that although Miss Phelps was shaken up, she didn't actually lose consciousness. So she'd have seen anyone acting suspiciously at the site of her accident when she was discovered,' Arbie pointed out. He could have kicked himself when the policeman turned thoughtful eyes his way.

'Indeed, sir. That was well thought out,' the Inspector complimented.

Arbie affected a surprised air. 'Was it?' But he sensed it was now too late to play the dunce to any good effect. 'It was Murray Phelps who was first on the scene, wasn't it?' he asked innocently.

The Inspector slowly nodded.

'That's one of the reasons we think the nephew must have been behind it all, Inspector,' he heard Val say clearly, and he shot her a quick, appalled look. 'Don't we, Arbie?' Val said determinedly, meeting his look with a level one of her own.

Arbie ran a harassed hand through his dark hair. One of these days, this girl was going to land them in a mess that not even he could get them out of! 'Yes, Val, I agree, but you can't go around making accusations like that! There are such things as slander laws and what have you! And we have absolutely no proof that Murray Phelps, or anyone else for that matter, was involved in Miss Phelps's death.'

'I never said he's the *murderer*,' Val responded, a shade sulkily. 'I mean, Inspector, that we think all the "ghost" stuff was her nephew's doing. The silly ringing of the bell and leaving the forge's equipment lying about and all that.'

'And why do you think that it was Mr Phelps?' the policeman asked, genuinely curious now.

Val and Arbie exchanged looks again, and Arbie sighed, seeing that Val, after putting them in the soup, was now leaving it to him to explain. 'Mainly, Inspector, because we think that Miss Phelps herself suspected him,' he said reluctantly. And went on to explain how she had been careful to mention that the 'ghostly' warnings only seemed to happen when her nephew came to visit.

'Ah,' the Inspector said. 'And you think Miss Phelps was right in her deductions?' he asked, looking from the successful author to his pretty companion with a slightly amused eye.

Arbie shrugged. 'Well, let's face it, the other candidates for the role of practical joker don't look all that promising, do they?' he challenged. 'Why would her housekeeper of umpteen years suddenly take to playing the fool? And I can't see Phyllis lugging around heavy pieces of metal. Cora, I think, is only here for a summer holiday, and Reggie, it seems, has always come here for the summer to live and work in the studio. Why should such old and long-standing friends of Miss Phelps suddenly take to resurrecting the family ghost?'

'Why should her nephew?' the Inspector asked inevitably – and reasonably.

To this, Arbie could only offer a shrug. 'If you're asking for cut and dried proof, I can't give it to you, I'm afraid,' he admitted. 'Only . . . ' he hesitated.

'Yes?'

It was Val who came to the rescue. 'It's just that sometimes Miss Phelps seemed to hint . . . I don't know . . . that there had been some sort of . . . friction, or a little falling-out with her nephew. A difference of opinion perhaps? Oh, it's hard to put it into words.'

The Inspector nodded and glanced at the handsome youth in his Oxford bags and his misleadingly vacant expression. 'Was that your impression too, Mr Swift?'

'Hmmm? Oh yes, rather,' he agreed, and gave the Inspector a very vague smile. The pretty girl beside him, the policeman noted with amusement, shot him an angry glance.

'All right. Well, that's all been very interesting. Now, let's get down to the nitty-gritty and go through what happened when the housekeeper came back down from trying to raise Miss Phelps, and getting no response to her knocking . . . '

With a sigh, Val and Arbie settled down to a thorough grilling.

CHAPTER ELEVEN

As Arbie and Val relived the events of that unpleasant morning, Mrs Brockhurst stepped outside the village shop, her wicker basket packed with that day's food shopping. She wasn't in the least surprised to find herself accosted almost at once by a curious villager.

Enid Richardson was an old acquaintance of some years' standing, so Jane had no choice but to stop to chat. She knew the news about her late employer was all over the village by now, and as a resident of the Old Forge, she had to expect that everybody was keen to know first-hand the latest doings. As such, she doubted she would get home before being stopped at least half a dozen more times by her neighbours wanting to 'pass the time'.

But at least Enid would be kind about it, Jane supposed, and it would certainly give her kudos to be the one with the latest gossip.

'Oh, Jane, I was hoping to see you. How are you, dear? It must have all been such a shock for you? The doings up at the Forge?'

Jane put down her basket on the street (no point in having to bear its weight whilst having her brain picked, she thought) and turned to sigh at her friend.

'I'm all right, Enid. It's all come out of the blue, as you can imagine. And as you said, such a terrible shock too.' She spoke the platitudes expected of her with weary patience.

'And you found her, they say?' Enid asked avidly. A few years older than Jane, she was wearing her usual skirt with the sagging hemline, and a starched white blouse with a rounded collar. Her long iron-grey hair was in a massive bun held somewhat insecurely at the back of her head with copious amounts of hairpins. It always seemed in danger of collapsing down her back, but somehow never did. A widow of some years, she vied with the shopkeeper for position of village sage.

'Not quite,' Jane corrected her wearily. 'Technically, that was young Mr Swift. Of course, I had to lay her out afterwards. We had no idea then that there was anything wrong, you see. We just thought the poor thing had an episode of some kind in the night, and died in her sleep,' she added, trying to hide her impatience. She had to get back and set about preparing lunch. It was very well for the likes of Enid to spend all day gossiping, but she had a house full of people who needed watching.

'Ah yes, your last sad service for her,' Enid said portentously. 'I hope she looked . . . peaceful?'

Seeing the avid expression in her friend's face made Jane inwardly shake her head. People! They were all the same. Sensation-mongers all of them. Well, there was nothing for it but to give the old gossip what she wanted in the hopes of getting away sooner.

'Y-yes,' she said uncertainly. 'The poor lady would be appalled at all this trouble though. You know Miss Phelps, she was always such a private person. She'd hate being the subject of so much scandal.'

'Oh yes,' Enid said, with a sniff. 'You'd think she had some-thing to hide, the way she was so close-mouthed all the time. Mind you, she probably had, come to think of it. She was no saint, was she?' Enid looked over her shoulder to make sure that nobody could hear her speaking ill of the dead. 'Just look at the way she treated you after that little bit of trouble you had. My mother said it was a downright shame the way she . . . '

Jane felt herself go hot, then cold, and knew she had to shut this silly woman up before anyone else *did* overhear them. 'Oh, that old story isn't *still* doing the rounds, is it?' she asked with what she hoped was just the right amount of world-weary amusement. And then, putting a gentle hand on the other woman's forearm, she added softly, 'Besides, that was all so long ago now. Why, it must be nearly thirty years if not more. And I always think the past should stay in the past, don't you?'

Enid nodded slowly. 'Yes, I suppose so,' she said, but she was looking at Jane oddly now. 'Do the police have any idea who might have . . . ?' She trailed off delicately. 'It was poison, they say?' she added avidly.

Jane had immediately been aware of the danger she was in, once the method of death had been established. Overseeing the kitchen from whence all the food and drink was served at the Old Forge, who was in a more dangerous position than herself? The police had already taken away every scrap they could find of the remains of that last dinner party. She had also been thoroughly questioned about the preparation of the food. So far though, she had the impression that the police didn't suspect her more than anyone else who'd been in the house at the time, but how long would it be before the villagers started to say there was no smoke without fire, and began whispering about her behind her back?

Not long, if she knew village life. And Jane Brockhurst did. Knowing the residents of the village could make her life very uncomfortable if they put their mind to it, she quickly cast around for a sacrificial lamb and didn't have to think very hard. As she moved a little closer to Enid and lowered her voice, the other woman's eyes lit up with the expectation of something juicy.

'Yes, the police have already asked me if I saw anyone hanging around in the vicinity around dinner time that shouldn't have been there, and I had to tell them that I had.'

'No! Who was it?' the woman asked, practically clinging onto the housekeeper's arm.

'Who do you think?' Jane asked, looking around quickly. 'Who do you know who's been coming to the house when she shouldn't, having no legitimate business there anymore, save for making trouble?'

Enid screwed up her eyes for a moment, then gasped and nodded as understanding dawned. 'Oh! You mean that little madam, Doreen Capstan? I can't say I'm surprised,' she said, with a judicial sniff. 'Not maid material, I'd have thought. Those Capstans are a disgrace. I'm surprised at you for hiring her, Jane.'

'Nothing to do with me, Enid, I assure you,' Jane said. 'It was Miss Phelps who had the final decision. I could have told her, with Mr Murray visiting so often, there was bound to be trouble. Say what you like, Doreen is a pretty little thing, and always happy to turn a man's head.'

Enid sighed and nodded a woman-of-the-world nod. 'Men,' she said. 'At least Miss Phelps had the sense to fire her when she saw which way the wind was blowing. And you're saying she was still sneaking in and seeing him?'

'Yes, I've caught her once or twice sneaking into the garden when Mr Murray was up. Including the time I was in the kitchen cooking for the dinner party,' Jane said. 'Oh, I quickly went out and shooed her off. But I was in and out of the kitchen, as you can imagine, seeing to a dinner party like that. And the kitchen door isn't locked until bedtime.' She nodded wisely.

'Fancy!' Enid said, wide-eyed. 'Did you tell the police this?'

'Oh yes,' Jane said flatly. She'd told them all right. And now hoped that she could rely on Enid to spread the word around the village. And the fact that nobody much liked or trusted the Capstans would help.

But she should probably sow some more seeds of doubt around, and to this end, she pretended to look around worriedly, then lowered her voice to a mere whisper. This had the effect of making Enid stand even closer and instilled in her mind that she was about to receive even more pearls of wisdom worth knowing. 'But the police always say, don't they, in cases like this, that you should think of the money first. Who benefits the most? And I suppose that makes sense. Most of the horrible crimes you read about in the papers come down to money, don't they?'

'Yes, that's true. So did they ask you about the will then?' Enid asked, breathing a little heavily now.

'They did.' Jane nodded solemnly. 'Not that I could tell them anything mind. I never talked about Miss Phelps's business when she was alive and I won't do it now she's dead,' she added firmly. 'But you know as well as I do about Miss Phelps being such a stickler for tradition. And, what with the Great War, and the flu epidemic, she only had one close male relation left, didn't she?'

And she felt more of her fear melt away as Enid's face suddenly lit up with a knowing look. 'Oh, you mean . . . *he* gets it all, I suppose? Her nephew?'

But Jane took the opportunity to pick up her basket and bring the distasteful conversation to a close. 'I shouldn't say any more,' she said. 'The police have asked me not to talk about things,' she added, giving the false impression that the police trusted her and that she had their confidence. Seeing the other woman's respectful look, she nodded and bid the gleeful woman a brisk good morning.

Before long, it would be all over the village that the nephew had killed the lady of the house to inherit her estate – perhaps with the connivance of the dismissed maid, Doreen. And people would be only too willing to believe it, Jane thought cynically. But at least, *she* would be left in peace.

*

Reggie had set up his ancient camera in a patch of gloriously flowering thistles in the hopes of getting a good photograph of some bees and butterflies. He was hoping to write and get published a modest but comprehensive volume of the fauna and flora of the Cotswolds (if he could find a publisher) with his own plates for illustration. Right now, he was glad to have something to take his mind off recent events.

With the thick black cover over his head, shoulders and the camera lens, he peered at the upside-down image of a gatekeeper butterfly and clicked the switch, counting down the exposure time. When he emerged from under the black-out material, however, he found himself face to face with an interested Arbie Swift and perked up. Just the man he wanted! An author like this was bound to know a publisher who might be interested in his natural-history project.

But before he could ask, Arbie spoke first. 'I say, Mr Bickersworth, I had no idea you had a camera with you – and such a . . . er . . . beauty too,' he said, looking at the Victorian contraption with a determined smile. It looked as if it came out of the ark and was nowhere near as good as his own Sico. Swiss made and only one year old, the camera's unusual wooden casing had attracted him first, though he had quickly come to value it for its relatively compact form and reliability. It took 30 x 40 millimetre exposures with a 1-300 shutter speed, and he'd used it extensively to illustrate *The Gentleman's Guide*.

'It's a total relic of course, but I've found it does produce marvellous plates,' Reggie said, feeling a little ashamed of the horror. The truth was, the camera had been given to him by a friend clearing out his attic, and he was in no position to look the proverbial gift horse in the mouth. And at least he was of the generation that could still remember how to use one. Just!

Arbie was not, as some might suspect, totally insensitive, and saw that the old fellow was a little ashamed of his equipment and sought a way to be kind. And, as so often happened to Arbie – who had always had more than his fair share of luck – he came up with something that was also to his benefit. 'I don't suppose I could persuade you take some photographs of the Old Forge for me, could I?' he asked craftily. For if he *had* to get on with writing another book (and it was beginning to look as if circumstances were so much against him that he just might), then why not farm out as much of the actual work as possible?

'I'd be delighted, old chap, absolutely delighted,' the older man said, for a moment forgetting his sorrows and actually beaming. 'I say, does this mean you're writing another *Gentleman's Guide*? How exciting!'

'Yes. I was thinking of concentrating on other tourist spots inland this time. The Peak District and the Lakes. And of course, right here in the Cotswolds. Oxford too has lots of ghosts, so I might go back to my old stomping grounds, what?' In fact, as Arbie spoke, he was, almost, looking forward to it. 'And I've just bought this rather super cine-camera too. A Hewit-Beaufort, an absolute pip, with a little folding frame finder. It even has an adjustable shutter. Who knows, if I'm lucky, I might actually catch something interesting on film, and give a little moving picture show. I might even branch out into giving lectures and things,' he added vaguely, having no intention of doing any such thing. It would interfere with his fishing trips for one thing. And for another, it didn't do to encourage Walter and his publishers, who would probably demand that he did such a lecture and tour as a way to boost book sales.

'Splendid,' Reggie said, manfully hiding his jealousy of such fabulous objects. 'A man needs to be up and doing things, I say. Always trying new things. Take me,' he nodded happily at his contraption on the tripod, 'I'm going to write an illustrated natural history of the area. That'll keep me busy.'

Arbie sensed that he was about to be asked if he could possibly persuade his publisher to take a look at the finished article when the time came. And knowing that Walter would definitely have something pithy to say to him should he bring Reggie's no doubt worthy, but hardly gripping, manuscript to his attention, he sought a way to forestall him. 'Sounds like a top-hole idea. But since you're an artist too, why not sketch and paint your subjects yourself?'

As he'd hoped, the other man was duly distracted. 'Oh, I'm not sure my little daubs are worthy of mass publication,' he said sadly. 'They're more by way of a hobby of mine. A man must fill his days, that's what I say, Mr Swift. Of course, when I was *your* age, my days were filled with much more physical and interesting pursuits. Believe it or not, I used to lead a troop of Boy Scouts!'

Arbie could well believe it, but of course was far too polite to say so. He himself, he recalled now, had been kicked out of the village troop in disgrace by his scout master for some minor piffling matter that had made his uncle roar with laughter and treat him to a chocolate cake in celebration.

'And before that, I did a bit of mountaineering,' Reggie went on, perking up as he saw that he'd managed to genuinely surprise the younger man. 'Oh, not on any of the big mountains, you understand,' he felt compelled to add truthfully. 'But the cliffs and smaller peaks here in Great Britain – oh yes. Wouldn't think of it to look at me now, would you?' Reggie smiled. 'It's all right, you can admit it. I'm a bit of an old duffer these days.'

'Not a bit of it,' Arbie said gallantly. 'I imagine you were a proper rip when you were my age, sir,' he cajoled.

Reggie chuckled at the compliment, and Arbie, his good deed done for the day, nodded, bade him an amiable good day and went on his way. At least he'd managed to cheer the old soul up a bit.

As Reggie got back to trying to capture the buzzing and flying things that visited the thistle patch, Arbie headed back towards the village, his mind on other things. Although he'd taken quite a few photographs in his time, he was the first to admit that he was no expert and had always had his plates developed by a man he knew in town.

But didn't photographers use poison during the process of developing? He seemed to have a vague memory that mercury and . . . yes . . . cyanide played a part in it somewhere. And he wondered – did Reggie too send out his photographs to a professional? Or did he do his own work in his artist's studio? Did he have a dark room there? Because, if he did, it would certainly give him unlimited access to poison.

Was it possible Reggie had waited all this time to get his revenge on Amy for persuading her brother Francis to change his mind about leaving Reggie a comfortable nest egg for his old age? But if so, why wait until now? Francis had been dead for some years, after all. And Amy and Reggie *seemed* to have been mutually fond of each other.

Arbie sighed. It was almost impossible to see the lackadaisical Reggie bothering to lock up the place every time he went out. And since every member of the Phelps household probably knew all about Reggie and his hobbies – which the whole village would know as well – it was odds on that *any* member of the household could just have helped themselves to something lethal whenever the fancy took them.

Even a relative stranger could have picked up via the village grapevine that an amateur photographer had set up shop (as it were) in the artist's studio, thus advertising the fact that there were likely to be poisons there, just begging to be pinched and used.

It was not, on the whole, a pleasant thought.

CHAPTER TWELVE

The next morning Arbie rose, late as usual, and was just sitting down to the scrambled eggs and bacon that Mrs Privett had placed wordlessly in front of him when he heard the telephone bell. Ignoring Basket's soulful brown eyes directed at the table, and admonishing the dog that he hadn't better try to help himself to Arbie's breakfast or there'd be trouble, he pushed back his chair.

The installation of this, as Mrs Privett put it, 'new-fangled contraption' had been at his uncle's instigation, and for once, with Arbie's total approval. He hastily forked up some more eggs and trotted to the hall, knowing that Mrs Privett would have nothing to do with the appliance, and still masticating his breakfast, he scooped up the speaking tube and mumbled somewhat inaudibly, 'Yes? The Swift residence. Arbie speaking.'

There came a confused rumbling sound in the background, and then a voice he vaguely recognised, but which did not belong to any of his many friends. 'That you, then, Mr Swift?' the voice asked tentatively.

Realising that he was probably dealing with a novice on the telephone, Arbie patiently admitted that it was indeed he, still struggling to place the voice. It had the rounded country vowels of a local, rather than one of the smarter set that he'd met up at Oxford, and suddenly he placed it. The old man at the boatyard.

146

'Oh, is that you, Mr . . . er . . . ' Arbie, not at his best in the mornings, scrambled (like his eggs) for a memory of his name. And thankfully came up with it. 'Mr Finch, is it?'

'Eh?'

Arbie sighed, remembering the old man's deafness. 'Mr Finch?' he bellowed. As he did so, he glanced anxiously out of the window and was relieved to see that his uncle was safely at work on repairing a motorbike some distance away. He might have been terrified at the sight of this, if he hadn't seen some youth bring it in last night, with the usual tale of woe, and ask his uncle if he could 'fix' it.

Everyone in the village knew that Uncle could probably fix most things. Otherwise, Arbie might have worried his guardian was contemplating life on the open road atop a Clyno or a two-strike Enfield! In which case, no pedestrian or cyclist would be safe.

'Is my boat ready?' Arbie shouted, thinking that this could be the only reason for the boatyard owner to be ringing him.

'Tomorrow, I reckon,' the voice came back faintly. Hearing someone in the background order a pint, Arbie realised – and with a certain amount of envy – that Marcus Finch was probably using the telephone in the public house in his village. 'But I've got the sign-painter in now, and he needs to know what you want to call the vessel. Have you made up your mind yet, sir?'

'Ah yes, I have, as a matter of fact,' Arbie said.

'Eh?'

Arbie sighed, and with a quick glance to make sure that his uncle was still safely out of earshot, bellowed the name he'd come up with.

There was a momentary pause on the end of the line, and then the boatman said, 'Sounds like an odd name to me, Mr Swift. Are you sure you don't want to call it *Maid of the River* or something?'

Arbie bristled at this lacklustre and unoriginal offering. *Maid of the River* indeed. 'No, I don't think so.'

'Eh?'

Arbie sighed, and bellowed the preferred name again. And for good measure yelled, 'My uncle is an artist, you see, so that name fits perfectly.'

'Oh, arr, that explains it then,' Marcus Finch said glumly. 'I had heard that artist gentlemen are different from the rest of us.' And with this somewhat obscure statement, he sighed heavily. 'Right you are then, Mr Swift, I'll tell the sign writer to get started. He won't like it, mind. Are you sure you wouldn't like something more pretty, sir? A girl's name – now those are popular. What about the name of your uncle's wife?'

'My uncle doesn't have a wife,' Arbie said.

'Eh?'

'Never mind! Will you deliver the boat to our address when it's finished?' he yelled instead. 'We're on the river and have a dock.'

'Yes, sir, I can do that,' Marcus said, and abruptly hung up. Arbie might have thought that rather rude had he not already decided that the call might have been the first experience of a telephone the boatman had experienced and so didn't realise that you were at least supposed to give the other fellah fair warning you were signing off with a 'cheerio' or something.

Thinking no more of it, he hung up and went back to his cooling breakfast. Basket still waited hopefully by his chair and was finally rewarded with some bacon rind.

*

Breakfast finished, Arbie then wandered into the village. The farm workers were busy about the land, and the fact that a flock of sheep had just been herded into a field from the other side of the village was much evident in the many odorous black droppings that they'd left behind on the lane.

Neatly sidestepping his way through this potentially

shoe-ruining minefield, Arbie eventually found himself outside the village shop. He was just about to go inside to buy the paper and replenish his cigarette supply when he was abruptly hailed.

'Mr Swift. Just the man I wanted to see.'

Arbie shot around to see Inspector Gorringe eyeing him thoughtfully.

'Oh? Really?' Arbie asked feebly.

'Yes. I've just been up at the house.'

Arbie didn't doubt he meant the Old Forge, and again, said, 'Oh, really?' just as feebly as before.

'Yes. The housekeeper there was hoping to have a word with you.' He relayed the message with a deadpan face and voice, wondering if the young man would make it three 'oh reallys' in a row.

Arbie, perhaps sensing this, gave his best puzzled smile instead. 'I can't think why.'

The policeman, tiring of playing with him, simply jerked his head sideways to indicate that Arbie was to follow him, and set off in the direction of Amy Phelps's one-time residence with a no-nonsense stride. He seemed, after his initial greeting, to be in no further mood for conversation, and after walking in silence for a while, Arbie began to feel uncomfortable.

'You know, Inspector, it's probably just as well we bumped into each other,' Arbie began, deciding he might as well take the bull by the horns and get it over with. 'I was wondering if you were aware that, apart from being an amateur artist, Mr Bickersworth is also a photographer?' And, after considering the Victorian monstrosity he'd looked over yesterday, felt compelled to add, 'Well, of a sort.'

'No, I can't say that was mentioned by anyone,' the Inspector admitted.

Arbie waited for more, and not receiving it, was forced to continue unhappily. 'The thing is, er, I've taken the odd photograph or two myself . . . '

'For your ghost book? Yes, sir, I'm sure you have,' the Inspector agreed.

Arbie wondered if it was a trick of the light, or were the other man's lips twitching slightly? Nevertheless, now that he'd started, he supposed he'd better press on.

'Thing is, I send my plates out to be developed, don't you know, but I often chat to the chap I use, being the curious sort – me, I mean, not the chap – so I can't help but pick the odd things up here and there, and . . . er . . . '

'Such as that there are a lot of poisonous materials used in the industry?' the Inspector butted in mildly.

'Ah,' Arbie said, a little deflated. There he was, working himself up to drop poor old Reggie in the soup, and all the time he'd been wasting his nervous energy. 'You know all about that then?'

They were now approaching the main gate into the garden of the Phelps house, and as the Inspector opened it for him, allowing him to go in first, he nodded and said dryly, 'We in the police do try and keep up, sir.'

Arbie felt himself flush. 'Sorry I mentioned it, Inspector,' he said stiffly.

But at this, the older man softened somewhat. 'I'd rather you *did* keep right on mentioning things, sir, as a matter of fact. Now that I know about Mr Bickersworth's hobby, I'll have a discreet word and just see what, if any, chemicals he has about his studio.'

'Righty-ho,' Arbie said, unenthusiastically. The last thing he'd wanted was to let Reggie in for a bit of a grilling, but it sounded as if the Inspector wasn't going to give him too much of a hard time, given the circumstances. He could only hope that the killer of Amy Phelps had brought their own beastly poison with them. But if, as he suspected would be the case, it turned out that some dangerous stuff had been hanging around behind Reggie's unlocked studio doors, then the police needed to know about it.

Once inside the house, the Inspector led him to the kitchen

and the waiting Jane Brockhurst, then excused himself to go across the courtyard and beard Reggie in his studio.

'A cup of tea, Mr Swift?' the housekeeper asked. 'And thank you for coming. When I mentioned to the Inspector that I was hoping to bump into you at some point, I certainly didn't intend for him to fetch you here right away. Really, I can't imagine what he was thinking! I do hope nobody saw him and jumped to the wrong conclusions!'

'Oh, don't you worry about that, Mrs Brockhurst,' Arbie said gallantly. 'I'm sure nobody thought I was being arrested.'

The housekeeper winced a little at this bold response, then abruptly sat down. 'Oh dear. It's all so ghastly, isn't it? I still can't believe she's dead. And *murdered*? I never thought . . . ' She broke off and shook her head. 'I'm sorry, Mr Swift, we must bear up, mustn't we?' and with this, got up and saw to the singing kettle.

With bracing cups of tea in front of them, they drank in decorous silence for a while, and then the housekeeper came to the point. 'Mr Swift, I understand you're going to, er, carry on investigating the, er, hauntings here for your next book?' she began cautiously.

At this, Arbie blinked and bridled a little. 'So that's already going the rounds of the village, is it?' he asked despondently, his shoulders slumping a little. 'Oh well, between my publisher and the vicar demanding action and Mr Phelps giving me permission to carry on here, I suppose I shall just have to,' he conceded.

The housekeeper looked at him with a certain amount of sympathy mixed with perhaps just a little surprise. 'I can see that you don't much care for the idea, Mr Swift?'

'I don't, Mrs B, and that's a fact. But . . . ' He shrugged eloquently.

The housekeeper nodded, then leaned forward a little on her chair. 'In some ways, Mr Swift, I have to say I'm rather glad that you *are* doing so.'

'Really?' Arbie asked, genuinely startled now. He'd have thought that the various inhabitants of the Old Forge couldn't wait to see the back of him.

'Yes. You see, Miss Phyllis has returned home this morning, and who can blame her? Having the police in the house . . . Well. It's not nice for a young lady, is it?'

'No,' Arbie said promptly. It wasn't nice for him to be waylaid by them in the village either!

'And Mr Murray has returned to the office and his own residence in town. Which leaves just myself and Miss Cora here in the house. And well . . . I have to say, Mr Swift, if we knew there was a man about the place, it would settle our nerves a bit. I know Mr Bickersworth is only over in the studio, but he's not here, in the main house *at night*. You see?'

'Oh. I see. Yes. Right,' Arbie said miserably. 'Well, I'll probably do another vigil sometime soon. But I'm not sure that the Inspector will be happy about it. He might veto it altogether in fact,' he added hopefully.

'Oh, he and his men have been gathering evidence ever since it happened. He told me this morning they were almost through and would be leaving shortly, so we can carry on as normal,' the housekeeper said.

'Ah,' Arbie said.

'And Miss Val has been around,' the housekeeper went on, and this time Arbie was almost sure that *her* lips *were* twitching. 'She said that she'd come around and sit with you when you were ready to do another vigil.'

'Oh, *did* she?' Arbie said ominously. Although their investigation into Miss Phelps's death wasn't exactly coming on in leaps and bounds, he still felt nervous about Val's involvement with it all. What if they were getting closer to the truth than he thought? And the killer knew it? And suppose they did actually manage to run the murderer to ground, what then?

Would he be in a position to protect her if the murderer of Amy Phelps decided to add more victims to his or her tally?

'Yes, so that's all right then, isn't it?' Mrs Brockhurst said with satisfaction.

*

Arbie, tea drunk and sensing that his presence was no longer required in the kitchen, wandered out into the hall, intent on leaving, but eyeing the staircase his pace slowly slackened and then he paused altogether.

Something had been tickling away at the back of his mind ever since the Inspector had informed him that no piece of string or cord had been placed at the top of the stairs in order to trip Amy Phelps on the night of her accident.

Seeing and hearing nobody about, he took the opportunity to lightly climb the stairs, and there he paused on the short second half-landing to look around. Above him were the six stairs that finished the climb to the main landing itself. On the wall beside him was an uninspiring painting of an uninspiring individual and not much else.

The stairs were carpeted to within two inches of the wall and banisters, and the brass stair rods were in perfect order. But it was not the possibility that a ruck in the carpet might have been the cause of Amy's tumble that was bothering him.

Slowly, he climbed the six stairs, eyes not on floor level, but on the ceiling. Here, it was relatively low, the plaster work bulging out in places, as plaster in centuries-old buildings tended to do. He wished he had a bright torch with him, but with the aid of a single landing window and by standing on tiptoe, he was able to see quite well the state of the ceiling above him.

It took him some time, but eventually he spotted what he'd

half-expected to see. A small tack-sized hole in the ceiling, just above the first stair of the six.

Arbie nodded thoughtfully. So that's how it was done, he mused. Without conscious thought, he sank down onto the top stair and stared down thoughtfully. Below him, the carpeted stairs ran down to the turn in the stairs, and the subsequent half landing, and he wasn't surprised that Miss Phelps hadn't been seriously injured. Now, had the stairs run in a straight line from top to bottom, and the poor lady had fallen the entire amount, well then, just *possibly*, the fall might have proved to be fatal. And had the stairs been stone, it most certainly would have been. Even uncarpeted wood would have increased the likelihood of injury. And an older woman with brittle bones . . .

But just six stairs? And carpeted stairs at that? Surely, if someone had seriously intended to kill Miss Phelps, they wouldn't have set the booby trap at the top of the half landing, when there were far more stairs for the victim to fall down *after* the bend and that terminated, what's more, in the hard tiles of the hall.

What kind of murderer were they dealing with here? A total fool? Or someone very, very clever?

'Just what in the blue blazes has been going on here?' he muttered to himself.

*

As Arbie scratched his head on Amy Phelps's staircase, her nephew, Murray Phelps, walked into a tea shop in Cheltenham, and swept the room for a familiar face. He quickly located it and, bracing his shoulders for a tricky interview, moved forward.

Doreen Capstan, one-time maid to his aunt, was dressed in her prettiest Sunday best and had her hair done specially that morning, spending her precious coins on a trim and shampoo. She smiled at him coquettishly as he sat down in front of her and listened with greedy satisfaction as he ordered a large lunch for them both. That done, she looked around with pleasure. It wasn't often she ate out and she was determined to enjoy it.

'This is nice, isn't it?' she said, eyeing the chintz and gingham and stacks of mouth-watering cakes on the counter.

Murray shrugged uninterestedly at the aspidistras placed by the windows in big majolica pots and little posies of flowers set in the middle of the tables. The place was full of old cats drinking tea and observing him and his pretty companion with knowing looks, and quite frankly, the whole place gave him the horrors. But he knew that nobody of his acquaintance would be seen dead in such a tea shop, which was the sole reason he'd chosen it to meet Doreen. That, and the fact that it was also well away from Maybury-in-the-Marsh, and the eyes of curious policemen. And nosy neighbours.

Deciding to leap right in, he cleared his throat and leaned confidingly forward across the table. 'Look, Doreen, you can see that the death of my aunt has put us in an awkward situation,' he began, using that soothing, reasonable voice he adopted whenever he had to deal with troublesome women.

'Has it?' Doreen interrupted him flatly.

Murray sighed. Damn the little chit – he could see by the stubborn set of her lips and the defiant angle of her chin that she was determined not to make this easy. No doubt she already suspected what he was going to say, and naturally enough, didn't like it. But she'd have to be made to see sense. It was imperative.

'Yes. We've got . . . ' he leaned forward even further and lowered his voice yet another decibel, ' . . . the police in the house, for pity's sake. Snooping about the village and asking questions. And who knows what my aunt's dreary neighbours might be telling them.'

'About us, you mean?' Doreen said, tossing her pretty head. 'Well, what of it? It's nothing that need worry us, is it? After all, the whole bloomin' village will know about us when we get engaged,' she pointed out triumphantly.

Murray drew in his breath impatiently at this, but the hiss of it made her eyes narrow ominously. 'We *are* getting engaged now, right?' she pressed urgently. 'You said we would, as soon as that old cow was dead. You promised – the only reason we agreed to keep it secret at all was because she would have cut you out of her will otherwise. The old biddy had no cause sacking me like she did,' she whined resentfully. 'And don't you dare forget, Mr Murray high-and-mighty Phelps, *why* I was doing what I was doing in the first place! Because you asked me to!'

And if he thought he could now toss her aside after doing his bidding, Doreen thought grimly, he could just bloomin' well think again! Now that he was free and clear and rich, she was not letting him wriggle out of her grasp, no matter what he might say.

Murray fought back the urge to throttle her and took a deep, calming breath. There was no doubt in his mind that, things being as they were, he would have to play along with her for a while yet, and the last thing he needed was for her to start making waves now. 'Yes, darling, I know, and don't think I'm not grateful. But it's not as easy as you make it sound.'

'Oh? I don't see why not,' Doreen shot back suspiciously.

A pair of middle-aged women at an adjoining table were leaning a little closer, sensing a fascinating lovers' tiff, and Doreen gave them a furious look. Indignantly, they leaned back the other way.

Seeing this by-play, Murray lowered his voice even more. 'If she'd had a heart attack or died of the influenza or something like that, it would be different for us now, surely you can see that?' he whispered. Seeing her mouth set stubbornly, he tried again. 'As her main heir the police are bound to have me down on their list of suspects. Do have some sense, Doreen! Right now, it's imperative that we lie low until all the fuss dies down. The last thing we can afford to do is draw attention to ourselves at this point. We were lucky that nobody saw you in the house the night she died, so we don't want to waste that luck by drawing attention to you now. Tell me you understand that?'

Doreen frowned. She knew when a man was trying to back out of his promises all right, and she was not about to let Mr Murray Phelps get away with it. On the other hand, Doreen's acute sense of self-survival was telling her that what he was saying was fair enough.

'You mean, we don't want the coppers looking too hard at *us*. Not now,' she said flatly. 'Yes, of course I can see that,' she agreed, watching with some inner amusement as his tense shoulders relaxed a little. 'Mind you, if things start to get a bit tight, we could always tell them what that little butter-wouldn't-melt-in-her-mouth cousin of yours has been up to. That would give them something else to think about, besides us.'

'Yes. Maybe,' Murray said thoughtfully. 'But we'll hold that in reserve, in case we really need it. So don't go saying anything to anybody about it,' he warned her.

'Don't worry, I won't,' she conceded. 'But don't *you* go forgetting what *I've* done for you, Murray,' she warned, leaning across the table to lay her hand on top of his. And digging her fingernails painfully into his knuckles. 'You were happy enough to have my help when it suited you.'

Murray gently but firmly removed his hand from under hers. 'I remember,' he said quietly.

'And don't you go forgetting what I could tell the police, if I had a mind to. You think they're looking at you funny now, think how they'd look at you if I told them all I know.'

'Don't be such a fool!' he hissed. 'You won't come out of it smelling of roses either. And don't forget, my girl, you have a motive for getting rid of my dear old aunty too. You were acting like a wet cat when she fired you, saying how you'd get even with her! And your reputation isn't exactly lily white, is it? The police would be only too delighted to nab one of you Capstans for once, wouldn't they?'

Doreen leaned angrily back in her chair. 'All right, all right, no need to get nasty,' she muttered. Then sighed and gave him a melting look. 'Oh, Murray, let's not fight,' she cajoled, abruptly changing tactics. 'All we have to do is wait, like you said, and then after a bit, we can move away from this dreary backwater and set up together in London, like you always wanted. We could start living then, couldn't we, just like we always planned. Theatres and restaurants, cruises and holidays abroad. Won't that be wonderful?'

Murray smiled, careful to keep his contempt for her from his eyes. 'Yes, it will be marvellous. But we've got to stop seeing each other just for now. Agreed?'

Doreen watched him like a cat at a mousehole. 'Just as you say, Murray,' she said demurely. 'But once the will is read this afternoon, and the old lady buried and things have cooled off, we'll get married. Don't think I'll let you get out of your promises, because I won't.'

Murray Phelps looked at the pretty, greedy, cunning little creature in front of him and his smile widened into a rather menacing grin. 'What a nice piece of work you are, my dear.'

'And don't forget it,' Doreen warned him sharply, brazenly unaffected by the unspoken threat in his face. She was no milk-and-water miss, to be scared by a gentleman like Murray Phelps. Besides, she had a father and several brothers who'd stick up for her, if need be.

So she felt safe enough.

*

Cora Delaney had wandered sedately down the main village road and over the bridge and was now sitting on the bench overlooking the river. She was desultorily feeding the ducks and a pair of importunate swans, but looked up as Val and Reggie approached her.

'Hello, see who I ran across whilst looking for a cinnabar moth,' Reggie said, indicating a smiling Val.

'Hello, Miss Coulton-James,' Cora said pleasantly, 'please, have a seat beside me.' She patted the wooden slats of the bench seat invitingly. 'Reggie, my dear, I'm afraid you'll have to sit on the grass.'

Reggie gallantly, if a little stiffly, obeyed the command, and after arranging his gangling limbs to his satisfaction, absently plucked a daisy and regarded it. Val eyed the stretching neck of the male swan with a wary eye, but Cora held out a crust to it without fear.

'I was just telling Miss Coulton-James that I wasn't certain what to do about this afternoon,' Reggie remarked lazily. 'About the solicitor coming over, and the family being here for the reading of the will and everything,' he added, when his old friend looked at him blankly.

'Oh yes, I'd forgotten about that,' Cora said, nodding.

'Do you think we should, you know, be discreet and take ourselves off to Oxford or Cheltenham or somewhere?' Reggie asked anxiously. 'One doesn't want to intrude at times like this.'

Cora looked at him fondly. 'I think not, Reggie. I know Amy has left me a little something in her will because she did delight in telling me so. Often,' she added with something of a bite. 'And I daresay she's remembered you too, Reggie. It would be very unlike Amy if you weren't in for a little windfall too. She liked to spread her largesse around, didn't she?' she said, with a little more sourness than she'd meant to reveal. Hastily, she swept on. 'So I suspect the solicitor would prefer us to be present. It'll save him the trouble of writing to us at any rate,' she added prosaically.

Reggie sighed. 'Yes, I suppose so. And you're right. Now you mention it, Francis and I always admired that painting of the church tower in the stand of elms that their mother painted back in '98. And Amy always said I was to have that, and that she

159

was going to leave it to me. I've got just the right place to hang it back home too,' he added, giving Val a smile.

Cora reached out and placed a hand on his shoulder. 'You still miss Francis so much, don't you?' she said softly.

Reggie nodded, looking suspiciously teary-eyed. 'Yes. I wish every day that he was still with me.'

Val, catching a knowing look in Cora's eye, felt herself blush a little in sudden comprehension. So that was the way of it, was it? Of course, as a vicar's daughter she was not supposed to know about such things as 'special friendships' between men, but she'd had brothers who'd attended public school, and they had been more than happy to shock her with what went on in the world! And at least it solved the puzzle of why Reggie had remained a bachelor all his life.

'Oh, don't mind me, Miss Coulton-James, I'm just getting maudlin,' Reggie said, seeing the look on Val's face and straightening his shoulders visibly. 'When you get to our age, you find yourself getting more and more sentimental, and memories of departed friends become more and more precious.'

Val nodded and smiled warmly at him. 'I'm sure they do, Mr Bickersworth. And I'm sure that Miss Phelps would expect you to be there this afternoon. She was clearly very fond of you,' she added reassuringly.

Reggie nodded. 'Well, that's settled then. I wonder if the solicitor chappie will know when the family might have the funeral? It's so awkward, I imagine, in the circumstances, but I hope it won't be too long.'

'I think, in cases of mur . . . like these, it can take a long time,' Val tried to warn him gently. 'Months sometimes, or so I believe.'

'No! Really? That long?' Reggie said, appalled. Then he sighed. 'But there – whenever it is, I'll attend. I couldn't miss Amy's funeral. Will you come too, Cora?' he asked absently.

Cora Delaney tossed the bravest mallard her last piece of bread and stood up. 'Oh yes,' she said firmly. 'I wouldn't miss Amy's funeral for all the world.' She looked around and took a deep breath. 'Well, I think I'll get back to the house before the sun gets too hot. Goodbye, Reggie dear. Miss Coulton-James.'

Val nodded and Reggie waved a languid hand at her, knowing that etiquette demanded that he should scramble to his feet until she'd gone, but knowing just as well that dear old Cora wouldn't care a tuppence if he let his old bones rest comfortably where they were.

'Miss Delaney seems to be taking her friend's death very well,' Val said thoughtfully.

'Hmmm? Cora?' Reggie said, who'd just spotted a speckled wood butterfly and wondered if it would be worth his while to take his cumbersome camera for a foray into the trees. 'Oh, yes, but don't let that fool you. She feels the loss as much as anyone. But Cora is of the old school. Stiff upper lip and all that. Mind you, she always was very self-possessed.' He surprised Val by tapping his temple with a knowing finger. 'She always had brains, you see. She was easily the cleverest one in our set. Studied at Oxford – Somerville, you know.'

Val's lips twisted sardonically, knowing that Cora wouldn't, as a woman, have been allowed an actual degree. 'Oh? What did she study?' she asked casually.

'Oh, maths, I think,' Reggie said, tossing aside the daisy onto the village green. 'No, I'm wrong. Chemistry. Her heroine was Marie Curie.'

CHAPTER THIRTEEN

Cora hadn't got far when she heard someone walking behind her and turned, without surprise, to see the vicar's daughter hurrying after her. Once she saw that she'd been spotted, Val slowed down to a more decorous pace, and hailed her cheerfully.

'Hello again. I just heard from Reggie that you went to university,' Val said, opening her eyes and giving the other woman her most admiring look. 'I do wish I were clever enough to have gone too.' But she knew that her parents wouldn't have been able to afford to send her, if she were. 'He said you studied chemistry?' she began determinedly.

'Yes,' Cora said. 'What would you have liked to study?'

'Oh, nothing so highbrow as that,' Val said self-effacingly. 'Literature perhaps. Or art. But chemistry now, that sounds fascinating.'

Cora nodded vaguely. 'Is there no way you can apply?' She liked to see young women forging a path for themselves in the world and she rather liked this strapping competent lady. And if she could offer her encouragement to improve her life, then so be it.

Val sighed. 'No, I'm afraid not. My parents are anxious that I should find a suitable man and settle down,' she added, unable to keep a trace of resentment from creeping into her voice.

'Ah,' Cora said, diplomatically refusing to be drawn into a family skirmish. 'But I dare say, you are looking forward to having a husband and children of your own?'

'I suppose so,' Val said doubtfully. 'Mother says children are a blessing.'

'Not always,' Cora found herself saying dryly. 'Just ask Mrs Brockhurst.' And then told herself off for mischief-making. But she couldn't help herself. Sometimes, whenever she met ignorance and innocence, especially if they were combined, she felt the urge to drop a little firework of experience or knowledge into the mix and watch the fun.

'The housekeeper? Oh, but I thought her "Mrs" title was strictly honorary,' Val said, much surprised.

'Oh, it is,' Cora agreed. 'But you'd be surprised how often unlucky or foolish young girls have to "go away" from their home for five months or so, in order to stop the tongues wagging. Usually with the excuse of visiting a sick relative, I believe.'

For a moment, Val looked at Cora blankly. Then her eyes widened, and a blush stained her cheeks as she caught on. 'Oh! You mean,' Val looked around, and then lowered her voice to a whisper, 'you mean, she had a baby? Out of wedlock?'

Cora, perhaps regretting her impulse, said severely, 'Now don't go brandishing that around, young lady. I'm sure Jane Brockhurst has already paid for her sins over and over during the years. Although Amy was a Christian soul and kept her on in employment when most would have turned her out of the house once and for all, she was not always the easiest woman to live with. Mind, she had to insist Jane give the baby up for adoption. Which couldn't have been easy. So don't go ruining the poor woman's reputation.'

'Oh, I won't breathe a word,' Val promised and meant it. Well, except to tell Arbie, of course, she mentally added. But that didn't count, as she'd only be doing it because it was pertinent to their investigation. Because now they had found someone else at the Old Forge who might have had a reason to kill Miss Phelps.

Cora nodded approvingly, and then bid the young girl a brief farewell. Some would have chided her for shocking the vicar's daughter, she knew, but in her opinion, the innocent and ignorant needed to be taught a salutary lesson in life now and then.

Val watched Cora Delaney disappear out of sight and then rushed off to find Arbie to tell him about her latest discovery. It was only much later in the day that she realised that she had initially caught up to Cora to try to squeeze more information out of her about how much, as a chemist, she might know about poisons. But the older woman had so quickly and completely distracted her, that she'd never asked a single thing about noxious substances.

*

Mr Alfred Mulligan was punctual. As one of the more senior partners in Ramsbottom, Mulligan, Mulligan and Trent, Solicitors, it was a point of pride with him that he set a good example to all the juniors. Moreover in over thirty years of service to his clients, he could never recall giving them cause for complaint.

Well, not much.

As he parked his modest but respectable Morris car in a shady spot on the gravelled drive and gathered up his briefcase, he was thinking of one of his clients right now – the late Amy Phelps, naturally.

He had been shocked to his conservative core to be informed by the police that her death had not been natural and had readily agreed to the reading of the will in their presence today. He only hoped that their sobering presence might prevent any fireworks and unseemly displays from the family, but he had to admit to himself that he was not particularly sanguine about this. No indeed.

In his years as a solicitor, Mr Mulligan had overseen many a will-reading, and the behaviour displayed at some of them had been shocking. And it was sad to say, more often than not, the more socially superior the family, and the more money there was at stake, the more uncivilised their behaviour could be.

He climbed a little stiffly from the car, a sombre black-suited, lean figure, with his bowler hat firmly fixed on his head. The afternoon was a scorcher, and with an equally firm grip on the handle of his briefcase, he set off towards the house, not looking forward to the next half an hour or so at all. He most definitely did *not* like having a murder victim for a client – which alone was so sordid a circumstance that he had no idea what the late Mr Ramsbottom would have said about it all. Even worse, he mused unhappily, he had to face the fact that in talking to the inhabitants of the house, the odds were that he was probably going to have to converse with a murderer too.

It really was intolerable.

Of course, he thought judiciously, it was *just* possible that someone outside the Phelps family and its immediate social circle was to blame for the lady's abrupt passing, but Mr Mulligan, who prided himself on being a man of the world, didn't think so. Not when it was poison. And not when the woman had such a fortune to leave. Poison intimated that somebody must have been close enough to the victim to administer it, and had, at the very least, a good knowledge of his client's habits and movements. And money – well. People simply went mad when a fortune was at stake. And Miss Phelps had left behind her just that.

As Mr Mulligan neared the front door, he looked about him at the pleasant garden under the benign summer sun and wished that he was trout fishing somewhere far away. But there – a man had to do his duty.

Grimly, he reached out and tugged on the heavy wrought-iron bell pull. The door was opened almost instantly, not by the housekeeper, but by a man he knew immediately to be a police officer.

Inspector Gorringe further surprised him by stepping out, instead of inviting him into the relative coolness beyond, and firmly closing the door behind him. 'Ah, you must be Mr Ramsbottom?' he asked, and introduced himself. It was his sergeant who had dealt with arranging this afternoon's activities with Amy Phelps's solicitor, and that worthy individual had left him a note with the name of the firm.

'Mr Ramsbottom died several years ago, Inspector,' the solicitor informed him somewhat stiffly. 'I am Alfred Mulligan. At your service.' He gave a stiff bow.

Meanwhile Val, after her meeting with Cora and Reggie earlier, had lost no time in seeking out Arbie and spilling the beans, and both of them (well, more Val than Arbie, it has to be said) had decided that if they should just happen to be passing by around the time of the solicitor's visit, and by sheer coincidence also just happened to bump into any member of the household afterwards, that it would be only polite to stop and chat. And perhaps learn an interesting fact or two.

So it was that they came to be loitering, most definitely with intent, in the vicinity. But the unexpected sound of male voices coming from the porch had frozen them in their tracks, just behind the hedge that bordered the main gate. Both recognised the forceful voice of the Inspector, and by unspoken consent agreed that it wouldn't be much fun if he found them lurking there. Thus, they proceeded to make like mice and tried to melt unobtrusively into the shrubbery.

Blissfully unaware of his audience, the policeman faced the bristling solicitor with a placatory smile. He'd met this sort before, and the last thing he wanted to do now was to get the legal man's hackles up. He'd be there all day else! 'I'm so sorry, Mr Mulligan. I hope you don't mind me waylaying you in this manner,' he began, not sounding, it had to be said, particularly sorry. 'But you see, I was hoping to have a word with you before you begin the, er, formal proceedings.'

'That's somewhat irregular, Inspector,' Alfred Mulligan said, eyeing him warily. In his opinion, the rules of etiquette were there for a reason.

'It's a somewhat irregular situation, Mr Mulligan, as I'm sure you'll have to admit,' the Inspector parried neatly. 'I have, as you know, the family's permission to sit in on the reading, but I'd rather know the conditions of Miss Phelps's dispositions before I enter the library where they are gathered.' He didn't elaborate further, but he suspected that, for all his seemingly demure appearance, this dry legal specimen could probably guess his reasons why he wanted things done this way easily enough. If there were any surprises in the will about to be read, he wanted to keep an eye on the expression of those nearest and dearest to the murdered woman. And not to be distracted himself by any bombshells that might be in the offing.

'I see,' Alfred said, and put down his briefcase neatly beside his well-shod feet in a mute gesture of acquiescence. 'What exactly is it you wish to know?'

'First, I'd like an overview of the family history. I understand it's somewhat complicated?' the Inspector said.

In their hiding places, Val and Arbie held their collective breath and hoped that no nosy passer-by would spot them and spoil their chances of learning what the solicitor had to say. Luckily, the sheer force of the heat meant that most people seemed to be staying indoors during the worst of it.

'It is and it isn't, Inspector,' Alfred said patiently, glad that the shadow cast by the porch roof was preventing him from beginning to perspire. 'The Phelps family, like many of our prominent families, suffered big losses in the Great War, and the Spanish influenza that followed it. They were never a very prolific family anyway, which meant that Miss Phelps was one of the last of the line.' He paused, removed a handkerchief from his jacket pocket and proceeded to clean his pince-nez.

'Her own father, Clive, inherited the company from *his* father, Cuthbert, who was in turn the eldest son of the original founder, and as such, had already inherited the bulk of the estate. However, Cuthbert had a major falling-out with his only brother, Victor, and so took steps to see to it that although the company assets were divided equally among the few male heirs, as he had little choice but to do, the majority of the actual cash and valuables – that is to say, the considerable liquid assets and so forth – passed down only to his favoured son Clive, and thus on to *his* descendants.'

'And not to Victor or his descendants?' Gorringe said a little uncertainly. 'Yes . . . but . . . I'm sorry, sir, I'm not quite sure I'm following this,' the Inspector said, and he wasn't alone in that. Arbie couldn't make much sense of it either. 'As I understand it from talking to the family, Mr Murray is head of the company. Yes?'

'Quite correct. As a descendant of Victor, and now the only close *male* heir to the original founder, he, to all intents and purposes, runs the Phelpses' commercial businesses. That is, he is the major stockholder. But you must bear in mind that all his holdings relate to the business itself. The plants themselves, the business premises, the machinery, etc. The nuts and bolts, if you will, of their ironmongery and related companies. However,' the solicitor went on, in best lecturing mode, 'a lot of these assets aren't as substantial as an outsider might think. The majority of the plants were obtained with mortgages that are not yet paid off, for instance. The machinery is hired. The business premises, their garages, ironmongery shops and so on are all rented. And so on, and so forth. The company itself actually owns very little. For tax purposes, you understand?' he added delicately.

'You're not telling me that the Phelpses aren't as wealthy as people think?' the Inspector asked, sounding surprised. 'Is the company in danger of going bust then?'

'No, no, Inspector, you fail to understand me,' Alfred said patiently if a little wearily. 'The business is as hale and hearty as it always was. And Mr Murray Phelps is a very respected man of business. He's run it well, and I can assure you, neither he nor it is in any difficulties with the bank manager. But Mr Phelps's *personal* fortune is minor, compared to that of Miss Amy Phelps. It consists, I would imagine, almost entirely of his salary, in fact. Which, although I would imagine is substantial enough, is nowhere near the fortune possessed by his aunt. She, if you remember, was directly descended from Clive, and as such, inherited the bulk of his, er . . . actual cash. Both Cuthbert and his son Clive were very generous with their wives and children. Just the combined inheritance of all their furs and jewellery alone would stagger the average man on the street. Not to mention the private residences, paintings, etc, etc, etc.'

'Oh, I get you now,' Gorringe said, his brow unfurrowing. 'Whilst Mr Murray inherited the business, Miss Amy was the one with the real wealth.'

'Exactly,' the solicitor said with relief, and bent down to pick up his briefcase. 'Is that all?'

'Not quite, sir,' the Inspector said politely but firmly.

The moment Gorringe had been handed the case, he'd set his subordinates all the usual jobs, but no trace of poison had been found in any of the remains of the victim's last meal, and nobody had yet come up with a feasible explanation for how the dose of poison actually got in the woman's system, since everyone had stated that Miss Phelps never took a drink or food after dining. Even the promising lead given to him by that interesting young man, Arbuthnot Swift, about a possible source of poison amongst Mr Bickersworth's photographic paraphernalia hadn't been of much help.

After going extremely pale and admitting that he had chemicals in his studio, Reggie had been useless as a witness. He couldn't recall how much, if any of the alarming substances, were missing. Worst still, he admitted almost tearfully that he never locked the doors of his little home-away-from-home, even at night. Why would he? Which meant that literally anyone could have helped themselves to whatever had been there.

The routine questioning of the villagers was still on-going, but so far nothing startling had come to light. Which left the policeman sure that if he was going to find the answer to this crime, it would have to be done the old-fashioned way. That is, by listening and using his old noggin.

And someone like the family solicitor was too good a source to let go without wringing him dry.

'The impression I've got from the family over the last few days is that Miss Phelps was an old-fashioned sort of lady, and a stickler for upholding the family's good name and traditions. And they were unanimous in their belief that the nephew is likely to be the main beneficiary. Indeed, it seems that the lady herself made no secret of the fact that Mr Murray Phelps was to be her main heir.'

'I can see how they would have formed that opinion,' the solicitor said slowly and cautiously.

'Can you confirm, then, that she'd made out her will under those conditions?' the Inspector asked, almost perfunctorily, certain of an affirmative answer.

'I can confirm that the will she made when Mr Murray Phelps reached his twenty-first birthday named him as her primary beneficiary, yes,' the solicitor confirmed, even more slowly and cautiously.

By the hedge, Val reached out and grabbed Arbie's arm in excitement. They didn't need to be standing as close to the man as the Inspector was to tell that he was choosing his words very carefully indeed.

Inspector Gorringe stiffened, like a pointer spotting a pheasant falling from the sky. 'And does that will still stand, Mr Mulligan?' he asked sharply.

'Indeed it does not,' Alfred Mulligan admitted primly. And with a little pardonable satisfaction. He wouldn't be human if he didn't enjoy having the spotlight to himself occasionally, and there was no doubt that he now had the Inspector's undivided attention.

'Ah,' the Inspector said softly, nodding. Now they were getting to it! 'So, she made out a new will?'

'Yes, Inspector, she did.'

'When?'

'A few days before her death,' Alfred said, careful to keep his voice free from any inflection.

'Indeed,' the Inspector said, breathing out fulsomely. After thinking that this case was in danger of becoming bogged down, he now sensed that things were about to get moving at last. 'Can you give me the gist of those changes before we go inside and make it formal?'

Alfred Mulligan proceeded to do so.

And behind the hedge, Arbie and Val each drew in a sharp breath.

*

Inside the house it was several degrees cooler. Mrs Brockhurst, hearing the door, emerged from the kitchen and greeted them formally. 'Good afternoon, sir, Inspector,' she said. 'The family are in the library. As are Miss Cora and Mr Bickersworth. I've

171

just served some iced lemonade. There will be plenty if you would like some also?'

'That sounds delightful,' Alfred said, meaning it, then caught the housekeeper's eye. 'Since you have been left a legacy by your former employer, it would be as well if you were to be present also, Mrs Brockhurst.'

Jane Brockhurst's mouth opened slightly, either in surprise or maybe to protest, but after a moment, she simply nodded and wordlessly proceeded them to the library, from whence muted voices could be heard.

The moment they walked in, several sets of eyes swivelled towards them. Murray, dressed in a formal dark suit, was standing in front of the unlit fireplace, leaning one arm nonchalantly along the mantelpiece. He was smoking a cheroot and his eyes narrowed on the Inspector, but he said nothing.

On one end of the sofa, Phyllis Thomas sat neatly, her hair severely swept back in a chignon, and wearing a light-weight twin-set in a becoming peach colour. On the other end of the sofa, Cora Delaney regarded them with interest. The older lady was wearing a long summer skirt of sprigged muslin and a neat, plain white blouse with a rounded collar.

Reggie was sitting in a chair near the piano, gazing out of the window, and was the last to notice the arrival of the newcomers.

The housekeeper took a chair at some distance from them all, which was set against the wall, and tried to pretend that she was invisible.

The Inspector moved to one side of the door and leaned against the wall, where he had a clear view of all the room's inhabitants.

The solicitor, feeling as he sometimes did at times like this, rather like an actor upon a small stage, cleared his throat, walked to a large walnut table and deposited his briefcase on it. He pulled out a chair and in the suddenly tense and expectant silence, the slight scraping noise it made on the wooden floor sounded unnaturally loud and unwarranted.

'Good afternoon, ladies and gentlemen,' he said, smiling briefly around to encompass them all before opening his briefcase and pulling out a document bound with the usual judicial pink ribbon. 'As you know, we're here for the reading of the last will and testament of Amy Elizabeth Eleanor Phelps.' Here he gave the usual preliminary little speech about the validity of the document, it being witnessed by such and such, and with the usual disclaimer that this latest document invalidated all previous wills and such like, then briskly got down to the nitty-gritty.

It didn't take long for the first of the shocks to penetrate the minds of those present. Indeed, it began with almost his first words, when he read out the date of the will.

Instantly, a little stir spread around the room. So it was true. Amy Phelps *had* altered her will in some way.

Alfred took a steadying breath and plunged in. Taking a firm grip on the paperwork, he kept his eyes on the print, refusing to look up at those in the room.

'I, Amy Elizabeth Eleanor Phelps—'

It was Murray, not surprisingly, who interrupted. 'If you don't mind, Mr Mulligan, I think I can speak for all of us if I ask you to spare us all the legal language and whatnot. Most of us here wouldn't understand it anyway,' he added snidely, making his cousin shoot him a withering glance, suspecting his jibe was aimed at her. 'If you could just tell us the main gist of it, it would speed things up no end. And again, I think I can speak for all of us when I say we'd rather not prolong things unnecessarily.'

Of all those present, everyone knew that he, most of all, had the biggest vested interest in whatever changes had been made to Amy's legatees. And although he still felt confident that he was the main heir, he did wonder if his aunt, who liked to have things her own way, mayn't have added some conditions to his inheritance. Wouldn't it be a hoot, he thought absently, if the old girl had stipulated that he inherited only on the condition that he didn't marry Doreen? The thought of his paramour's fury if that was the case almost made him laugh out loud.

Cora regarded Murray curiously, as she might an ugly centipede that had just crawled across her shoe. Reggie looked away embarrassed. Neither the housekeeper nor the Inspector's face showed any expression at all. Phyllis merely sighed heavily.

Alfred Mulligan, still with his eyes on his paperwork, said dryly, 'Very well, if that's the consensus?' There was a small silence which he took for acquiescence, and then he nodded. 'Then I'll begin with the legacies.'

He could picture his client now, coming into his office, limping a bit from her recent fall, and stating her business. He'd been a little surprised, since her old will had stood for many years, and was slightly perturbed by her request. She was not the sort of person who was constantly swapping and changing her bequests, unlike some he could mention, who seemed to delight in keeping their relations on tenterhooks.

But when she'd stated her wishes, he'd felt most of his unease fade away. Usually when rich older ladies started fiddling unexpectedly with their wills, he suspected the influence of some good-looking, young, or sometimes *not* so young, man. But when Amy Phelps had informed him of what she had in mind, he was happy that that was not the case here.

Hastily, he pushed his musings aside and got down with the job at hand.

'To my housekeeper of many years, Jane Brockhurst,' he began with all due solemnity, 'I bequeath Tithe Cottage, three hundred pounds, and a lifelong pension, to be administered by my designated executors. I would also like to take this opportunity to thank her for her many years of faithful service.'

Here he broke off and finally looked up, seeking out the

housekeeper. 'Miss Phelps led me to believe that you are familiar with the cottage, I understand, and would have no objection to either living there yourself, or renting it out and living elsewhere?' He asked this with just a little trepidation, for quite often, he'd found, what the deceased believed to be the case and what the living thought about it could be poles apart.

'Oh yes, sir,' the housekeeper said promptly. She looked both relieved and happy, as well she might, having just heard that her future was secure, and the looming spectre of an impoverished old age was forever banished.

The solicitor gave a little sigh of relief and Jane Brockhurst a small, friendly nod and returned his eyes to the document in his hand. 'To my dear friend, Reginald Bickersworth, I bequeath the painting entitled *Church at Evening*, currently hanging in the front parlour, my collection of first-edition Thackerays and the sum of five hundred pounds, in the hopes that he will enjoy it thoroughly.'

At this Reggie swallowed hard, and murmured, to no one in particular, 'Oh, what a dear lady.'

By the fireplace, Murray gave a heavy sigh of impatience and glanced at the clock on the wall opposite. Taking the hint, but in no way hurrying, Alfred returned to the next clause.

'To my old schoolfriend, Cora Delaney, I leave my peridot suite of bracelet, necklace, earrings and tiara, my garnet and lapis lazuli necklace, and the sapphire and diamond cluster ring she so admired. I know she will wear all the jewellery with far more élan than I, myself, ever managed to do.'

On the end of the sofa, Cora gave a small bark of reluctant spontaneous laughter, shook her head slightly and then relapsed back into a rather brooding silence.

Alfred then sped through the number of charitable donations that she had left to the village church, the Salvation Army and several missionary endeavours in Africa, and some more keepsakes left to servants that no longer served her but had not been forgotten.

He then cleared his throat portentously and took a swift breath.

'The residue of my estate, including the Old Forge and all my other real estate, all monies currently residing in my various bank accounts along with all my stocks and shares and various investments, the rest of my jewellery, furs and all other personal possessions, I leave in their entirety to my niece, Phyllis Thomas.'

Here Alfred lifted his head to hastily explain that this concluded the last will and testament of Amy Phelps. He turned the last page and began to return the document back into his briefcase.

In the room there was absolute silence.

Inspector Gorringe did his best to look at both Phyllis and Murray at the same time.

Phyllis looked stunned. Her mouth dropped open, her eyes widened a little, and after the shock of the words was assimilated, a huge and happy smile spread spontaneously across her face, as well it might. She was now a very rich woman indeed, and the happiness and glee were unmistakable. The Inspector didn't blame her for it one bit. It was not every day you learned that your life had changed – for the better – for ever.

That she had also been totally surprised by this, he was reasonably sure. Unless she was an outstanding actress, which was always possible, she had not known about the change to her aunt's will.

An instant later, the Inspector was watching Murray's face like a hawk. To begin with, his expressions had almost eerily imitated that of his cousin, in that his mouth dropped open and his eyes widened. But, not surprisingly, what followed was neither glee nor happiness but yet more shock, followed by fury and puzzlement. He straightened up with a jerk and glared disbelievingly at the solicitor.

'What?' he all but shouted. 'That can't be right. I don't believe it.'

Over by the piano Reggie shifted uneasily on his chair. Cora too, for the first time, began to look less amused and more disdainful. 'I think, Reggie, you and I should take a turn in the garden. It's such a lovely day,' she said carefully. She hadn't even finished the sentence before Reggie was eagerly on his feet, his face a picture of dismay. Family ructions and unpleasantness of any sort were things he abhorred.

'Oh yes, I think so too. Shall we use the French windows?' he suggested. They were not only the nearest means of exit but using them meant that they didn't have to tiptoe across the room and out of the door like naughty children caught trying to gate-crash a party.

The housekeeper, seeing them leave and realising that this was also her best moment to escape, simply got up and walked to the door and left.

Alfred continued packing away his briefcase, and the sound of it snapping shut seemed to galvanise Murray.

'Not so fast, if you please! I want to see that document,' he said flatly, walking across, hand held out imperiously, staring white-faced at the solicitor, who stiffened.

'I can assure you, Mr Phelps, that it's all in order, and . . . '

'Let me see it. Now!' he roared.

Alfred drew his shoulders back. It was abominable that his professional reputation should be traduced in this way, but one look at the irate face in front of him convinced him that discretion was probably the better part of valour.

With a sigh, he reopened his case and extracted the document, which was instantly snatched out of his hand. Murray rifled through it to the last page and stared at the signature.

Then at the signatures of the witnesses.

Then he read it through, from top to bottom.

As he was doing this, the Inspector alternated his gaze from Phyllis to that of her cousin. Phyllis was glowing. Murray was glowering. And that about said it all.

'I can't believe she'd do this,' Murray finally said bitterly, and by doing so, conceding that the document was genuine. 'When she came to your office, did she give you any reason for her change of heart?' he demanded, waving the detested document in the air, and turning a now distraught face to the legal man.

'No, Mr Phelps, she did not,' Alfred said stiffly, prising the document back from him. Although he felt a certain amount of pity for the man, who had, after all, just received a very nasty shock, he didn't feel it was his place to offer him false words of comfort.

'But surely you must have asked her, man?' Murray huffed. 'Isn't it your job to see to the family's welfare? Your firm has been the family solicitors for long enough! Didn't you tell her that, as the eldest and only male heir, it was her duty to keep the family fortune together and in my hands?'

Alfred regarded the handsome, irate man in front of him, and summoned up all his patience and forbearance. 'No, Mr Phelps, I did no such thing,' he responded stiffly. 'It is my duty to oversee the wishes of my *client*. And she was perfectly clear and lucid about those. Now, had she proposed leaving her estate entirely away from the family . . . ' he paused delicately and gave the slightest of shrugs, 'then indeed, I might have, er, tried to gently persuade her to reconsider. But since that wasn't the case . . . '

Suddenly, behind him, Phyllis rose to her feet. 'Indeed, it was *not* the case, cousin, since I'm as closely related to her by blood as you are. A fact you seem to have forgotten,' she said softly. 'And it seems that you were not her favourite after all.'

Murray turned on her savagely, but whatever words he meant to fling at her, he strangled them at birth. Instead, he fought for control and won, his quick and clever mind finally beginning to recover from its shock and starting to work ferociously. As he thought, he stared at her long and hard, almost as if seeing her – properly *seeing* her – for the first time.

And under that stare, Phyllis's momentary courage seemed to falter.

'So it would seem,' he said slowly. 'And I'm just now starting to wonder, dearest cousin, exactly why that is?'

Inspector Gorringe looked from cousin to cousin with the concentration of a scientist watching a particularly intriguing petri dish. Phyllis, approaching middle age, no great beauty but handsome enough in her way, conservatively dressed, a little flushed, her chin tilted upwards in a probably hitherto unused tilt of defiance. Clearly, this usually unobtrusive member of the Phelps family had hidden depths to her.

And Murray – the businessman, undeniably handsome, dressed in a Savile Row suit and clearly a man used to wielding power and influence – now very much on the back foot. And not liking it one little bit.

Phyllis's head tilted back even more, but the canny Inspector noted that her hands were clenched into tense fists. For all her bravado, he had the feeling that she was, at that moment, rather afraid of her cousin. 'You would know that better than I, Murray, surely?' she said coolly. 'Just what did you do to upset her so? Whatever it was, it was a bad miscalculation on your part, wasn't it?' she said sweetly.

At this ominous parry, Alfred muttered a very hasty farewell and decided to show himself out.

The cousins, totally ignoring his abrupt departure, continued to face each other, like wary, warring cats.

'Oh, I'm not the only one capable of making miscalculations, cousin of mine,' Murray warned her softly. 'I might have been a little slow off the mark but believe me I'm catching up fast. And don't think for one minute that you're going to get away with this.'

Phyllis's gaze faltered a little under Murray's inimical stare. She might be newly wealthy and already beginning to feel that wonderfully liberating sense of being inoculated from the worst of the world's slings and arrows by the power that that wealth gave her, but she was by no means immune to bullying.

'I don't know what you're talking about,' she said quietly, her mockingly sweet tone of earlier totally deserting her now. She swallowed hard. 'And I think it's time you left,' she added nervously.

'Oh yes. It's *your* house now, isn't it?' Murray blazed, making a mocking show of looking around the library. 'Mistress of all you survey. *Or so you think.*' Utterly ignoring the Inspector, he turned and stalked to the door. But once he'd opened it, he turned and looked over his shoulder at her. 'I can only suggest you enjoy it while you can. Because that will won't be worth the paper it's written on by the time I'm through proving just what you've been up to.'

A tiny frown of puzzlement marred the otherwise smooth brow of Phyllis Thomas. 'What on earth are you talking about, Murray?' she asked anxiously, and Gorringe wasn't sure if it was anger or fear that ruled her now.

But her cousin merely shook his head. 'You know, right enough, Phyllis my dear. *Ghost* my foot!' he snapped. And with that rather startling – and apparently utterly irrelevant – statement, he walked out, slamming the door mightily behind him.

Phyllis jumped nervously at the sharp sound it made. And only then did she herself seem to recall the presence of the policeman. She looked at him, hands spread out in that universal gesture of helplessness.

'I really don't know what he was talking about,' she said quietly.

The Inspector smiled at her politely. 'No? Well, I shouldn't let it worry you. Your cousin was obviously upset. Understandable, under the circumstances, don't you think?' he added.

'Hmmm? Circ— Oh, yes. Yes, of course,' she muttered. She sank back down weakly onto the sofa, looking thoroughly washed out. Elated but worried. Happy and yet uneasy.

And who could blame her for the turmoil of her emotional state, the Inspector mused. Although those two attractive youngsters had told him all about the legend of the family ghost, even he couldn't help but wonder why Mr Murray Phelps had dragged that into the proceedings now, or what he meant by those last few words either, except that the threat they held was unmistakable. But what, exactly, had that furious and thwarted individual meant by bringing the Phelps family ghost into the proceedings?

One thing was for certain – the person who had most benefitted by the death of Amy Phelps was her niece, Phyllis Thomas. And for that reason alone, she was now at the top of his list of suspects.

CHAPTER FOURTEEN

The Inspector didn't have far to look for Murray. He found him standing in the shade of a large horse chestnut tree in the west garden, furiously smoking a cigarette. When he saw the Inspector approach, the younger man scowled at him horribly.

Nor did the Inspector's first words do anything to modify his basilisk stare. 'I take it that you were unaware that you had been cut off without a penny, sir?' the Inspector remarked pleasantly.

Murray snorted, which made him cough and then throw down his cigarette and stamp it out viciously, taking pleasure in grinding the item into shreds under his heel. 'Couldn't wait to kick me when I'm down, eh? Hoping I might let something slip? I'm not a fool, Inspector,' Murray snapped. 'I know full well that you and everyone else have me down as suspect number one in my aunt's death. And this will business only makes it worse. Can't wait to slap on the irons, hmm?' he accused, eyeing the Inspector with disdain.

'Well, sir, if you look at it from my point of view,' Gorringe began mildly, but Murray wasn't in any mood to see things from any point of view other than his own.

'Oh, be damned to you!' Murray exploded. 'Well, for your information, I happen to have an alibi for my aunt's murder. Now then! What do you say to that?'

The Inspector, much surprised, said that he found that information very interesting indeed, and that he'd be obliged if Murray would tell him more.

Murray, lighting another cigarette, sighed heavily and then shrugged. 'Oh, what's the point. You wouldn't believe me anyway. In fact, with the way my luck's going, it would only make things worse.' For, try as he might, he couldn't help but believe that were he to confess that he and Doreen had in fact spent almost the entire night in his room, the Inspector would only be more suspicious of him still, and say that he and his paramour had connived to commit the crime together.

'Oh, just forget it,' he snarled, and rudely turned his back. And with a thoughtful look, Inspector Gorringe duly drifted away.

*

Meanwhile, elsewhere in the garden, it was, of course, Reggie who inevitably spilled the beans to Arbie and Val.

Having spotted Cora and Reggie coming out into the garden, Val very nonchalantly called out a greeting and, much to Arbie's embarrassment, all but invited herself, and perforce him, to join the elder couple under the shade of the tree where they were now sitting, conversing quietly.

After a short but polite period, Cora had excused herself with a vague murmur about having letters to write, and thus stripped of what would surely have been her restraining presence, Reggie let himself be delicately and expertly grilled by the vicar's daughter.

In truth, Arbie couldn't blame the fellow for being bamboozled by his companion. In honour of the weather, even he had to admit that Val was looking particularly fetching today. In a becoming white cotton frock and with her long blonde hair swept away from her face and tied back with a mint-green-and-white ribbon, she looked the quintessential English rose.

Reggie, obviously, was sheer putty in her hands. In no time at all, the old boy was regaling them with the news that Phyllis, not Murray, had inherited Amy's fortune, and giving them a scene-by-scene account of the drama in the library.

'And so, at that point, we lit out and headed for the hills,' Reggie concluded. 'Well, one doesn't want to be de trop when a family fight is about to break out, does one? And poor Murray did look fit to blow his top like a volcano.'

'I can imagine,' Arbie said dryly. He wasn't sure why it was, but the misfortunes of others always seemed to buck people up, and for the life of him, he couldn't feel the littlest bit sorry for the imperious Murray. And yet . . . he was worried.

For years, Murray had been firmly and openly ensconced as the main heir, much to nearly everyone's mutual satisfaction. And in Amy's original will, he was confident that Phyllis would have been adequately provided for by her aunt, so even *she* would probably have had no real cause for complaint at being only a residuary legatee. And yet, immediately after her fall down the stairs, Amy changed her will.

The inference was obvious, of course. She had done so because she suspected Murray of playing the 'ghostly' tricks on her. And, presumably, held him responsible for her 'accident' as well, and hadn't found *that* very funny at all.

All that, Arbie could follow perfectly well.

But what was bothering Arbie was – *why* would Murray, who had only to wait for his Aunt to shuffle off the mortal coil and all that, suddenly get it into his head to make her life a misery? The accident on the stairs had been carefully set up only to hurt her, not to kill her. It made no sense – if he was rumbled, there was bound to be a price to pay. Surely he'd be careful to keep on her good side?

Which meant . . . Well, the inescapable conclusion was that he *hadn't* been responsible for either his aunt's tumble on the

stairs, or the pranks about the ghost at all. Which meant . . .
Well, again, it only left Phyllis, didn't it? She was the one who
ended up with all the lolly, after all.

'Oh dear, there he goes,' Reggie said unhappily, interrupting
Arbie's mental sleuthing, and he looked across the garden just
in time to see Murray striding angrily away down the drive.
'I daresay he's in a frightful rage. I do hope he's going back to
town. The atmosphere in the house will be unbearable if he stays
on. He won't do that, though, will he?' Reggie asked nervously.

'Oh, I'm sure he wouldn't want to,' Val surmised reassuringly.
'I wonder if . . . '

But before she could finish whatever she'd been about to say,
the French doors opened and Inspector Gorringe stepped out.
Reggie took one look at him and turned rather pale.

'I think, you know, I'd best get back to my studio,' he said
hastily. 'I'm afraid the sight of the Inspector gives me the jitters
nowadays. Ever since he came and took away my photography
chemicals for testing, I've been feeling awful. I can only hope
and pray that whatever killed poor Amy it wasn't anything that
I brought with me.'

'Oh, Reggie, poor you!' Val said, reaching over and patting his
hand. 'I'm sure it wasn't. And even if it was, you mustn't blame
yourself. Anyone could have taken it. Nobody locks their doors
or things in Maybury – why would we?'

Reggie nodded and managed a rather wan smile, but when
the Inspector, looking around, spotted them in the shade of the
tree and started to come over, the older man got to his feet and
all but bolted.

Arbie and Val watched him go, giving each other amused
glances mixed with a little concern, then girded their loins as
the majesty of the law sat himself down on the garden chair
nearest their bench and stuck out his size twelve feet, encased
in well-buffed brown leather, and regarded them thoughtfully.

'Mr Swift. Miss Coulton-James,' the Inspector said, with just a hint of a smile. 'Just passing, were you?'

Val flushed guiltily. She couldn't help it. She was the vicar's daughter.

Arbie merely sighed. Unlike Val, he'd been raised by his uncle, whose respect for authority – any authority – was virtually nil. 'As a matter of fact, I was hoping to have a word with Miss Thomas,' he lied amiably. 'You may have heard – the family have asked me to continue my investigation into the hauntings here? For my next book?'

'Ah yes. The family ghost,' Gorringe said thoughtfully, and with a certain gravitas that made Arbie look at him more closely. Ever since Murray Phelps's intriguing words to his cousin after the reading of the will, the Phelps's family ghost had become of much more interest to him.

When it had first been mentioned, he'd thought Miss Phelps's obsession with her dead ancestor had been just that – nothing more than one of those harmless bees-in-the-bonnet that ladies sometimes fell prey to. But until now, he'd never seriously considered the fact that it could have anything to do with her murder.

You didn't expect a spook to go about administering cyanide, after all.

'Whilst I have you here, Mr Swift, I was wondering,' he began urbanely, 'have you come to any conclusions about the ghostly blacksmith? I mean, do you think he's, er, genuine, so to speak?'

Arbie regarded the older man with a disapproving eye. 'Oh, do come off it, Inspector,' he said firmly, unknowingly impressing Val for perhaps the first time in his life. 'You no more believe in ghosts than you do in fairies at the end of the garden.'

Gorringe smiled. He couldn't help it – he was beginning to like this young chap. 'It's not a question of what *I* believe, sir. It's a question of what Miss Amy Phelps believed. Or any member of her inner circle, come to that.'

186

At the mention of the dead woman, Arbie's challenging gaze instantly faltered. When all was said and done, her last weeks hadn't been the happiest, and that, really, was quite horrible, when one thought about it. And certainly nothing to be taken lightly. 'Yes. Yes, I know. I was wondering much the same thing just now. It doesn't make sense, does it?'

The Inspector's eyes sharpened. 'What doesn't?'

'That Murray was behind the pranks and ghostly goings-on and whatnot. Even though I think Miss Phelps was convinced that he was,' Arbie elaborated.

'And do you have a better candidate?' Gorringe asked, genuinely curious.

'Well, yes, since you ask, given recent—'

'Oh, Arbie, look there's Phyllis,' Val interrupted him swiftly and rather too loudly, correctly guessing that the silly muggins was just about to admit they already knew that Murray had been cut out of the will, and that the niece had got the lion's share instead. And the last thing she wanted was for the police to call on her father, demanding that he keep his daughter's nose out of police affairs! 'Didn't you want to ask her about the ghost-watch tonight?' she said, glaring a warning at him.

Arbie, who'd had no such intention, blinked back at her. Then he looked over his shoulder and saw that Phyllis was indeed standing on the terrace just outside the open French windows and looking over at them uncertainly.

'Well, I have no objections to you carrying on with your, er, ghost-watches, sir,' Gorringe said magnanimously. 'My men have finished taking fingerprints and what have you.' And much good *that* had done them. The housekeeper had thoroughly cleaned the lady's bedroom before they knew it was a case of murder. And nothing suspicious so far had been found in the house at all. No signs of a break-in, no signs of a small bottle that might have contained poison in the rubbish bins. Nothing, in fact, of any use to him at all.

Ah well, a policeman's lot, and all that. He rose to go, but then added mildly, 'Oh, and if you should run into the ghostly blacksmith during your tour of duty, sir, you might like to ask him from me, just what the blazes he thinks he's been playing at, will you?'

'I shall make a point of it, Inspector,' Arbie responded, totally unfazed. 'And if Miss Phelps decides to put in an appearance as well, I'll be sure to pass on your best wishes to her too.'

At this neat little parry, Gorringe grinned widely and, nodding at the pretty girl who was again looking admiringly at her handsome young companion, wished them both a good day.

'I say, Arbie old boy, that was a rather splendid little sally,' Val was forced to admit. 'That'll teach the Inspector to mind his p's and q's from now on. But what was that about there being a better candidate? I didn't quite follow it,' she admitted plaintively.

Arbie shrugged. 'I was just about to say that the reason that Miss Thomas is now a rich woman is because Miss Phelps suspected Murray was behind all her woes. Which has worked out very conveniently for our Phyllis, hasn't it?'

Val's eyes widened as she realised what he was getting at.

'You mean . . . you think *she's* the one behind the ghostly goings-on and whatnot?' she asked, her eyes narrowing as she thought about it. 'You know, that would make sense, in a way, wouldn't it?' she continued, in growing excitement. 'She invents the ghost to rile Miss Phelps up, and then drops hints or something that Murray must be behind it all. That way, she undermines him in her aunt's eye.'

'I don't think she'd have needed to do much hint-dropping,' Arbie said thoughtfully. 'I imagine Murray was already in her bad books over his flirting with the maid and all that. The whole village knew he was gadding about with Doreen.'

Val nodded. 'Yes, that's true,' she said. 'But, Arbie, if Phyllis did all that, then does that mean she was responsible for her aunt's death?'

Arbie shifted uncomfortably. 'Well, logically, I suppose it could follow. Although she might only have done it to get her cousin disinherited. She might not have thought further ahead than that.'

Val eyed him with a disapproving eye. 'But that's a bit lame, old thing, isn't it?' she said staunchly. She knew how much Arbie hated to confront the nastier side of life, and she was determined not to let him get away with it now. 'Suppose Murray weaselled his way back into his aunt's good books? She'd be back where she started. You know it only makes sense, if Phyllis is behind the ghost, that she must be behind the murder as well. And don't forget, she knew her aunt had been to her solicitors to make a change in her will. She'd have no choice but to strike while the iron was hot.'

Then she swallowed hard as her eyes drifted past his and to a spot over his shoulder and she went a bit pale. 'Oh, Arbie!' she said, clutching his arm as most of her brave face crumpled away. 'She's beckoning us over. What should we do?' she hissed.

Arbie looked across the lawns and saw indeed that the new mistress of the Old Forge was waving at them. 'We go and say hello, old thing, what else?' he said amiably. And only wished that he actually felt as nonchalant and sanguine about it as he had managed to sound.

And so he and Val set off across the lawn, each of them unsure what, exactly, you were supposed to say to a woman who'd just inherited the fortune of a murder victim, and whom you now suspected of having committed the crime.

*

Phyllis looked pale but composed as they met by the French doors. 'Hello again. My word, isn't it hot?' she said, instantly setting the tone. 'Won't you please come in and have some lemonade?'

Arbie and Val accepted gratefully, and once seated, accepted the iced liquid. Arbie tried not to think about poison at all, but still almost choked on his first mouthful. Val and Phyllis sipped their own libations with apparent enjoyment.

'I'm sorry to bother you, Miss Thomas,' Arbie began timidly, 'but I was wondering if you still wanted me to, er, see if there are any further disturbances here in the house? I can, of course, forget all about it if you would prefer?' he proffered hopefully.

'Oh no, that's perfectly all right,' she said, dashing his last chance to duck out from under. 'In fact, you can begin right away if you like. Murray has left and gone back to his own place, and I'm catching the next train myself. I have so many arrangements to make. It won't take me long to pack. So apart from Mrs Brockhurst, the house will be empty, which should be ideal for your experiments, I imagine? I have to say, the villagers would be rather thrilled if dear old Maybury-in-the-Marsh made it into the pages of your next book, and I'd hate to be the one accused of disappointing them.'

Here, she looked at him pointedly. 'Of course, you will only be concerned with, er, Wilbur Phelps. The blacksmith. And not . . . I mean – oh, this wretched business about Aunty Amy! It's got me all in such a muddle. I don't know how to say this without sounding . . . Oh dear, you won't . . . ' She trailed off helplessly.

Arbie, able to translate this garbled appeal with ease, looked equally as horrified as his hostess. 'Oh no! Of course, I wouldn't dream of mentioning . . . I mean, there'll be nothing salacious or scandalous about the next volume, I assure you. Just the usual mix of holiday guide and *ancient* ghosts and legends, that sort of thing,' he muttered. 'Current events won't be mentioned at all,' he promised rashly.

And then added mentally – *well, not by me at any rate*. He had no idea what atrocities his publicity-hungry publishers might get up to in order to ensure more huge sales.

'Oh, then I'm sure that will be all right then,' Phyllis said, looking vastly relieved. 'In that case, perhaps you'd like to seek out Mrs Brockhurst in the kitchen and let her know you'll be here tonight?'

'Yes, of course,' Arbie agreed, shooting to his feet as Phyllis also rose. He wondered if the lady of the house knew that her newly acquired servant was also eager for him to continue his activities.

'Now, if you don't mind, it's been a rather taxing day, and I must get on,' Phyllis said somewhat wearily.

Val and Arbie watched her leave in relieved silence, then went to the kitchen to confirm their itinerary with the housekeeper.

Once outside, Arbie moodily kicked a stone out of his way as they made their way back to Church Lane, and their respective dwellings. 'You know, Val, the first thing I want to do when we get back to that house is have a good snoop in Amy Phelps's bedroom.'

'Arbie!' Val said, pretending to be shocked.

'Well, you don't have to come with me, you know,' he pointed out, rather wickedly.

'Oh, wild horses wouldn't stop me from being there,' Val informed him promptly.

'No, I don't suppose they would,' he concurred sadly.

*

When Arbie returned home, he took a detour into his uncle's studio. He wanted to borrow the electric battery lamp that Uncle had invented last year. It looked like an old-fashioned traditional glass lantern but produced an almost blindingly bright light when you flicked a hidden switch. Uncle had done something clever to the bulb he invented to go with it, but what exactly this was had, naturally, gone right over Arbie's head. Alas, to create this luminous device, Uncle had had to construct a large battery that he concealed in its base, which made it too heavy to be of interest to manufacturers. People, they had pointed out politely, wanted a portable lamp to be just that – portable. Not something that only Atlas could successfully carry around for any length of time. Therefore, it had remained to date, a single prototype, but it was just what Arbie needed right now.

Although he wouldn't admit it to Val for all the world, having a light that he could rely on, and that would illuminate every corner of a room – and probably for miles around outside whilst it was at it – was just what he wanted. Hunting a ghost was one thing – but hunting a killer was something else. And Arbie didn't fancy being in the inadequately lit Old Forge without knowing that he could throw a light on at any time he chose. And if he gave himself a hernia carrying the wretched thing, well, so be it!

He found the studio unlocked but empty, which meant that his relative was somewhere nearby. He was tempted to yell for him and ask where the lamp was, because the studio was not the easiest place in the world to find anything. But as he looked around, he spied the pyramidical black iron top of the lantern peeking out from a pile of what looked like former automotive parts. He was just heading for it when he glanced up and saw, on his relative's painting platform, a canvas on an easel which literally stopped him in his tracks.

Even from that distance the quality of it hit him squarely in the eye, and its form was so well-known that he abruptly detoured from his mission, headed up the few steps needed to put him on the dais and gravitated towards the glowing siren of painted horseflesh. A Stubbs! He was sure of it. Who hadn't, at some point, seen one of these beauties either in the flesh in a gallery, or reproduced in the pages of a magazine? He moved reverently closer and eyed the painted equine with breath that caught in his throat. What a beauty – an absolute stunner.

He leaned closer and bathed in it. Then he took a step back and frowned. Had Uncle hit the jackpot with one of his inventions and hadn't told him? Otherwise, how could he afford to buy such a gem as this? And why on earth was it in here and not in a bank vault where it belonged?

Then he saw the second easel next to it, covered with a cloth, his uncle's paints and brushes on the table next to it. With his heartbeat doing a rapid Charleston, he moved very reluctantly over to it and gingerly lifted up one corner, taking a tiny peek underneath. And saw four, now very familiar, fetlocks looking back at him. Hastily he let the cloth drop and backed away, swallowing hard.

Feeling just a bit light-headed, he went back down to collect his lamp, grunting a little at the weight of it as he hefted it outside. But the fine sweat that had broken out on his forehead and on the palms of his hands had nothing to do with his physical labours.

Had his uncle finally lost his mind? If he was caught forging a Stubbs, it would mean utter disaster. And with an Inspector like Gorringe lurking around the village . . . What was the silly old reprobate thinking?

As if his nerves weren't stretched enough as it was!

CHAPTER FIFTEEN

The sun was just beginning to set when they returned to the house. Luckily, Val was far too excited to comment on Arbie's new acquisition, even though he did keep shifting its cumbersome bulk from hand to hand to try to ease the ache in his straining arms. Mrs Brockhurst let them in, for the first time looking rather uncertain of the protocol. After all, none of the family were in residence, and exactly what did you do with visitors who were going to do a ghost vigil? They were not guests, as such, nor were they tradespeople.

In the end, Arbie reassured her that they wouldn't need looking after, and that she should just continue with her normal routine as usual.

Thus with the only witness to their upcoming misdeeds safely ensconced in the kitchen, Arbie put the lamp out of the way against the back wall under the stairs, and then quickly scampered after Val who was already upstairs, and onto the landing.

There Arbie paused.

Val, suspecting him of funking it and wanting to put off going to the scene of the crime, regarded him with her usual mixture of impatience and fondness.

Of course, he was just standing there with a slightly vacant look on his annoyingly handsome face and doing nothing useful that she could see. It was, however, Arbie's misfortune – or good luck, depending on the circumstances of the moment – that he always looked at his most vacuous when he was doing his best thinking.

'I can go first if you like,' she prompted. Most of her friends, when *The Gentleman's Guide* had first come out, had been envious of her lifelong friendship with the suddenly famous author. And those who met him saw only his good looks and succumbed all too readily to his rather off-hand charm, and envied her even more. Val found this state of affairs, naturally, most annoying. If only they knew what a chump he was, generally! Someone really needed to take him in hand, otherwise he'd just spend the rest of his life loafing and doing not much at all. Like he was doing now!

He roused himself at her words and looked across at her, as if in some surprise to see her standing there. 'What? Oh, no, we'll go in a minute. I was just making sure that I remembered that night properly. That when I said goodnight to her, Miss Phelps walked up these stairs with nothing in her hands.'

Val looked down the stairs. 'And are you sure?'

'Yes, I am. Then, once she got to about here, where we are now, she picked up a candle from, presumably, this table.' He pointed to a small cherrywood pie-crust table placed under a pleasant but not outstanding watercolour of sheep grazing in a field. One of Miss Phelps's late mother's, presumably.

'She did?'

'Then she walked along the corridor . . . ' Suiting his action to his words, Arbie began to walk along the corridor, which looked dark and menacing. Here, the twist and turns of the corridor allowed little light to penetrate from the nearest window and Val began to wish they had a candle of their own right now. Or that the gas lighting extended this far.

'So she walks to her door,' Arbie muttered, reaching for the door handle, 'opens it and enters.'

They were now back in the room where they had found Amy

Phelps dead, and Val's eyes went straight to the big bed, relieved to find that it had been stripped and covered with a dustsheet. The curtains were drawn, and Arbie went over to open them, wanting as much light as possible whilst it lasted.

'All right now, let's try and work this out,' he began briskly. 'Miss Phelps comes to bed, following her usual routine. I think we can feel it's safe to assume that much – most people do the same things when they turn in at night. Now, what would hers have been, do you think? I noticed a wash basin under the table, but don't most ladies wash in the morning?'

Val, with a smile, admitted that they did.

'All right. So, she comes in and, what? I know the first thing I'd do is go to the window and have a breath of fresh air and open them wide. But when we climbed in that morning and found her, the curtains weren't drawn and the windows were all shut.'

Val, getting caught up in the reconstruction, frowned. 'Yes, but Arbie, you're a young and fit man,' she pointed out. 'Miss Phelps was an older lady, and I seem to recall that that particular night was more chilly than usual.'

'Yes, you're right, it was,' Arbie said, snapping his fingers. Hard to believe that he'd sat in the hall almost wishing he'd brought a coat, when the weather, with typical capriciousness, had now turned so blazingly hot. 'And older folks feel the chill more than we do,' he conceded. 'So, that explains *that* little mystery,' he continued. 'Miss Phelps didn't bother to open the windows but kept them closed. Or they were open during the day, and she then closed them.'

Val nodded. 'All right. But I don't quite see where this is getting us, Arbie.'

But Arbie held up a hand, still thinking. Beside the bed, the table was now denuded of its former contents, and, like the bed, had been draped in a dustsheet. Mrs Brockhurst had certainly been busy, he thought uneasily. And wondered – what else might she have obliterated in pursuit of her domestic chores?

'On that table were . . . let me see . . . ' Arbie cast his mind back and listed all that he could remember being there. 'The thing that stands out most is that there was a book lying there open and facing downwards, the way you put a book down when you want to keep the place for a moment, and a pair of glasses, presumably reading glasses, beside it, which were also unfolded. Which suggest to me that she'd been reading in bed.'

Val was beginning to feel just a little impatient with all this evidence of a dead woman's final minutes. After all, how could it possibly matter? Besides, it was giving her the shivers. 'Yes, that all sounds very feasible,' she agreed, wishing he'd get on with it and do whatever it was he wanted to do, so that they could leave before it got fully dark. Sitting vigil for a mythical ghostly ancestor in the hall was one thing. Actually being in the room where someone had been murdered just a little while ago was another thing altogether.

Reluctant to stay by the bed, she wandered off and started poking around. The older woman's vanity dresser was also covered by a dustsheet, but she pulled it back, looking thoughtfully over its contents. Here, the smell of lavender lingered, and she noticed some talcum powder had been spilt. A pretty mother-of-pearl jewellery box caught her eye and, feeling very guilty but unable to resist the temptation, she lifted the lid and peered inside. What her father would say, she couldn't imagine, but her mother might forgive her. There was always something irresistible about looking at someone else's jewellery!

Amy Phelps didn't have anything really fancy – those had probably been kept in the family vaults – but she still had some nice pieces. With a sigh that Val told herself was not at all envious, envy being one of the seven deadly sins, she picked up a ruby drop pendant and held it up against her throat, peering at herself in the vanity mirror.

As she did so, a ray of the setting sun caught it, making it look like a drop of blood on her throat. The thought gave her the horrors, and she was just about to hastily thrust it back in the box, when the sunlight exposed something else about it. Something rather unexpected.

Oblivious to the fact that Val had left his side, Arbie was still thinking – and talking – furiously.

'So, we have Miss Phelps retiring to her room for the night, leaving the windows shut because it had turned cooler and then climbing into bed, and reading a book for a little while before blowing out the candle and settling down to sleep.'

Val rubbing her upper arms, returned to his side, beginning to feel distinctly chilly herself. 'Arbie, I think you should know . . .' she began, but he was already off again.

'But in that case, why didn't she close the book, after putting in a bookmark or turning down one corner of the page, or whatever it was she usually did? And why didn't she fold up her spectacles? Isn't that what we all do, automatically, when we've finished reading for a while?'

Val shrugged. 'Perhaps she was just in the habit of leaving the book that way?' she asked, momentarily distracted from telling him what she'd discovered.

Arbie looked at her sceptically. 'Would you leave a book that way? It would be sure to break or ruin the spine eventually.'

'Well, no, *I* wouldn't,' Val was forced to admit. 'Mother would spank me, if I did. We were brought up to respect books.'

'And Miss Phelps would no doubt have been brought up by a similarly minded governess,' Arbie vouchsafed firmly. 'No . . . I think she was still reading in bed when someone . . . or some-*thing* disturbed her.'

At this mention of something potentially supernatural, Val felt a definite shiver ripple through her. 'Oh, Arbie, don't! You're just being a rotter, trying to frighten me on purpose. Well, it won't work,' she said crossly.

Arbie, much maligned, eyed her with displeasure. 'I'm doing no such thing,' he denied righteously. 'I'm just trying to work it all out in my mind. If it's really giving you the horrors, you can always go home,' he added hopefully. Val looked at him scornfully. 'Right. Well then,' he muttered. 'Miss Phelps is in bed reading. She hears a noise . . . '

'The ghostly rattling of chains?' Val couldn't help but snipe nervously.

'Perhaps.' Arbie raised a dark eyebrow mockingly. 'I was thinking more along the lines of something much more prosaic – a knock at the door, perhaps.'

'Oh.'

'So she calls out to whoever it is to come in—'

'Wait a minute, we were in the hall. Don't you think we'd have heard?' Val interrupted his theorising with a slightly triumphant air. To her surprise, he didn't rally with a cutting reply of his own but instead thought about it carefully.

'I'm not sure,' he said. 'On the one hand the hall isn't that far away and we were being quiet. On the other hand, this dratted house is so thick-walled and topsy-turvy, I'm not sure if the sound of a human voice behind a closed door would have carried to us.'

Val had never seen Arbie Swift so invested in something before. He was almost . . . well . . . impressive.

'We'll do an experiment later – I can stay in here and call out, and you can stand in the hall and tell me if you can hear me,' he swept on.

Arbie finally noticed that she was giving him a look that he'd never seen in her repertoire before, and instantly got a bad case of the jitters.

'What?' he demanded uneasily.

Val shook her head. 'Oh, nothing. It's just . . . I've never seen you like this. I rather like it,' she muttered.

199

Intrigued, Arbie regarded her with his head a little cocked to one side. 'Like what, exactly?'

'I don't know. Animated. Interesting. Doing something other than just jaunting around and having a good time.'

Arbie shook his head. Really, the things Val came out with sometimes. 'Whatever you say, old bean. Now . . . where was I?'

'Someone distracting Miss Phelps from her bedtime reading,' Val prompted.

'Right. So she calls out for someone to enter. Or gets up and goes to open the door . . . ' Arbie says. 'And someone – let's call them X . . . '

'Why do we have to call them X?' Val objected. 'They're always doing that in thrillers and books and so on. It's just silly.'

'Well, we could just call them "the murderer" if you prefer.'

Val most definitely *didn't* prefer and frowned crossly. 'Oh, let's just stick with X then,' she conceded huffily.

Arbie's lips twitched, but he knew better than to laugh out-right. Hastily, he got back to his theorising. 'So X comes in. X has a mug of cocoa, or a plate of biscuits, or something. And some reason for needing a chat.'

'Oh, come on, Arbie, that's a bit thick, isn't it?' Val interrupted him yet again. 'Miss Phelps was as sharp as a tack! Someone's been playing tricks on her in this house and sent her tumbling somehow down the stairs, and she's already changed her will because of it. She's not likely to entertain late-night visitors on the sly and not be on her guard, surely?'

Arbie sighed. 'No. I don't much like it either, Val. But we can't get around the fact that she *was* poisoned, and we all seem to agree that it couldn't have happened at dinner. And since she came up here empty-handed, ipso facto, she must have eaten or drunk something at some point after dinner and before we found her.'

Not even Val could dispute the logic of this and nodded. 'So,

X comes in with some poisonous offering of some kind,' she conceded. 'And Miss Phelps just eats or drinks it?'

'Unless it was forced down her,' Arbie proffered, but without much enthusiasm.

'Oh, Arbie, she'd have kicked up an unholy fuss! We'd surely have heard her.'

'She was getting older,' he said, but again without any real belief in the proposition.

'But not all that feeble!' Val objected. 'And if you're going to force-feed somebody, you have to let them open their mouth, at which point she'd simply shriek the place down. And when we found her, it didn't look as if there'd been a struggle,' she continued, remorselessly hammering holes in the theory.

'The killer could have made things look normal before leaving. No, all right, I don't think much of it either,' he said hastily as she began to roll her eyes. 'I agree that X would have had to be desperate to try something that risky when he or she knew we were just down in the hall. Which leaves us with . . . ?' He raised an enquiring eyebrow.

'Miss Phelps eating and drinking with someone, like you said,' she admitted resignedly. 'Which means it must have been someone she would have trusted.'

'Which lets out Murray right away.' Arbie sighed. 'The last thing she'd do is accept a cup of tea from *his* fair hands in the middle of the night. Especially after she'd just disinherited him! He was hardly her flavour of the month, was he?'

'So it had to be Cora then,' Val said, 'or Phyllis, or Mrs Brockhurst. Reggie sleeps in his studio and doesn't have a key to the house. Remember the housekeeper said Miss Phelps was always careful about keys?'

'Hmm. And which, of that lot, do you fancy as a prime candidate for X?' Arbie asked.

Val thought about it and bit her lip. 'Well, I suppose . . . it has to be Phyllis, doesn't it?' she said reluctantly. 'I mean, she *was* the one who benefits the most.'

'But according to everyone we've spoken to, it was no secret that *Murray* was the heir,' Arbie pointed out. 'And according to what Reggie said about what happened at the will-reading, nobody knew about the sudden switch to Phyllis – *including* Phyllis. So unless she'd found out somehow – and I don't see how she could have – she wouldn't know that bumping the old girl off would leave her in clover.'

'Unless Miss Phelps had confided in her that she was now the heir, and she was play-acting at the reading of the will,' Val agreed. 'Oh, Arbie, this is getting more and more confusing,' she complained.

Arbie grunted. 'And we haven't even got properly started yet,' he prophesied gloomily. 'Let's just say for now that *someone* comes in, and for whatever reason, Miss Phelps trusts them enough to eat or drink in their company. So . . . the poison starts to work . . . '

Val shuddered.

'And X waits until it's done its beastly work, and then leaves. And that's when it really starts to get complicated, my girl,' Arbie said. 'Because when we got in here the next morning, the windows were firmly shut and the door had been locked from the inside. With the key still in it. So how the Dickens did the killer manage that? And even more importantly, perhaps, *why*?'

Val gave it a little thought. 'The obvious explanation is that Miss Phelps locked the door herself after X had left. And after the nasty tricks that had been played on her, and the fall down the stairs and all that, who can blame her? I'd sleep with my bedroom door locked too, if I'd been her.'

'Yes, yes, I'd already considered that,' Arbie said, not noticing her sceptical look. 'But look here, Val, that doesn't really make sense either, does it?' he appealed. 'Look at things from X's point of view. You've been playing ghostly pranks – for whatever reason – and sent the woman tumbling down the stairs, and now you've decided it's time for the grand finale. You're going to actually kill the old girl. You come here, with your poisoned chalice, and she drinks the stuff. You don't just then leave. What if she starts to feel the effects and cries out for help? We're just downstairs in the hall, remember? What if we come running, and she manages to gasp out X's name with her dying breath or whatever? It's too much of a risk. No. You'd wait, wouldn't you, to make sure the stuff's done its job.'

Val shuddered. 'Arbie, that's horrible,' she protested.

'Yes, it is,' he agreed grimly. 'Very horrible. But it makes sense. So, the woman dies. X puts her into bed – if she isn't there already. By the way, Val, did you know that a big enough dose could have killed her in seconds? Or so Uncle told me.'

'Arbie!' Val said crossly, stamping her foot. 'You really are doing this on purpose! Do get on with it. Poor Miss Phelps is dead, so the killer is safe to leave. That's where we'd got to.'

'Yes, yes, so X leaves,' Arbie swept on hastily. When Val got in this mood, experience had taught him that it paid to pacify her. 'But that's when we run smack up against it again. How, and why, did X take the time and effort to finagle with the lock with a pair of wires, or a string-through-the-keyhole or whatever mechanism was used, in order to lock the door behind him or her? I mean, why bother?' he asked helplessly, looking around the room. 'It's almost as if he or she was determined to make a mystery of it. And yet – that makes no sense either. I've thought and thought and thought about it, and I tell you, Val, I'm stumped,' he finished, looking despondent.

At this, Val felt herself softening. Really, Arbie wasn't such a bad old stick. At least he seemed to genuinely care about what had been done to Miss Phelps and wanted to try to put it right.

'Well,' she said, determined to help him if she could. It was the Christian thing to do, after all. 'If X *did* lock the door – and that's hardly set in stone – but if he or she did, then it must have been *necessary* for some reason. Does it give somebody an alibi or rule them out or something?'

'Not that I can see,' Arbie said, after agitating his brain cells for a bit. 'We're still left with the same set of suspects. Whoever was here in the house on the night she died.'

'Yes,' Val said thoughtfully, then suddenly went wide-eyed. 'But Arbie, *you* and *I* were in the house as well,' she gulped noisily. 'Do you think the Inspector suspects *us*?'

'Oh yes, I imagine so,' Arbie said casually. 'That might be one of the reasons he's not kicking up a fuss about us hanging around, doing ghost-hunts and things. It keeps us under his eye, where he can keep a watch on us.'

At this, Val went a little pale, but when Arbie began to wander around, checking the windows, the door lock and such, she pulled herself together. If it didn't ruffle Arbie's feathers to be a murder suspect, then she could be just as insouciant. She was, after all, a modern young woman, not some silly Victorian miss from a gothic novel!

She followed him to the back of the room and watched with interest as he pulled up a chair and stood on it to inspect the small skylight. Standing underneath and looking up at it, she watched him open it and close it, jiggling with the latch.

'A cat could barely fit through there,' she said dismissively. 'In fact, I doubt if that humongous moggy of Reggie's, Empress Maud, could even manage it. She's far too fat.'

'Hmmm,' Arbie murmured. 'This latch is a bit loose. I think the spring's gone in it. It would be easy enough, I think, to open it from the outside.' He stood on tiptoe and peered through the skylight but had only a prosaic view of undulating tiled roofs and a series of oddly shaped chimneys for his trouble.

Frowning, he got down and sighed. 'Well, I suppose we'd

better set up in the hall. Mrs Brockhurst might retire early and we don't want to be found out snooping in here. If she told the Inspector about it, we might go right to the top of his list of suspects,' he teased.

Val tossed her head as if to say what she thought about that and sauntered out. But Arbie noticed that she sauntered rather quickly, and again his lips twitched.

'Oh yes, I meant to say before,' Val called back casually over her shoulder, determined to have the last word. 'It might or might not be relevant, but quite a number of the stones in Miss Phelps's jewellery are paste.'

*

Whilst Arbie and Val had been theorising in Amy Phelps's bedroom, Inspector Gorringe had called in at his office, where some startling news from the home office pathologist awaited him.

Although he understood very little about the technicalities of the latest test results, the pathologist's summing up in layman's language was at least short and to the point. Amy Phelps had died quickly indeed. Within minutes, in fact, of the poison getting into her system. Any chance that she had ingested poison at the dinner held that night was definitely out.

He lit up his pipe and sat smoking it for some time, frowning thoughtfully. Had he but known it, his thought processes were following, almost exactly, those already discussed between Arbie and Val.

CHAPTER SIXTEEN

Mrs Brockhurst had gone to bed. The house was locked up tight. It was hot. The clock had struck midnight, and then one. Val was gently dozing in her chair and Arbie was fighting not to do the same.

He undid the top two buttons on his shirt and got up to take a quiet stroll around the hall, having discovered on previous such occasions that getting a case of cramp was no fun at all. Although he knew that, strictly speaking, you were supposed to keep quiet and still on vigils, Arbie had never taken the 'rules' on these matters all that seriously. As far as he was concerned, if a spook was so sensitive it objected to a chap stretching his legs, then the bally thing could forget it.

He yawned and studied yet another painting of the late Amy Phelps's mother that was bathed, for the time being, in bright moonlight. Having learned a little about art from his uncle, he found her amateur but well-painted country scenes pleasant and inoffensive. Of course he . . .

Suddenly, Arbie froze. Not only did he become totally still and his thought process utterly stall, but he felt his blood run cold, and icy shivers began to crawl up his back. And all because he could hear, faintly but unmistakably from somewhere in the house, the tinkle of a tiny bell.

Arbie swallowed hard as his heartbeat accelerated like a bolting hare. Moreover, he was inclined to make like a hare himself and head for the hills at a considerable rate of knots.

Although, as a boy, he'd had little doubts that his chapel home was haunted by an organ-playing spook, probably the spirit of some disobliging organist or a reluctantly deceased pastor, that belief had gradually dimmed and mellowed as he matured. So that by the time he'd come to write his *Gentleman's Guide* he, along with the majority of his hosts, took the family spooks under investigation with a pinch of salt, so to speak. But since others firmly believed in their existence, he had always been scrupulous (up to a point, vis-à-vis getting the cramp) when researching and ghost-hunting, otherwise he felt that he hadn't earned his daily bread. But he'd never been surprised when he'd seen and heard nothing at all. Apart from the times when some of the younger members of his family, or residents of the holiday hotels, had thought it amusing to play tricks on him, naturally.

But now he felt the hairs rise on the back of his neck, and his skin began to crawl. The grandfather clock ticked ponderously, and in her chair, Val gave a small, ladylike snore. Arbie ignored both, his ears just attuned to listening out for one specific thing, and tried to get his breathing under control. When he'd managed to stop snorting like a man who'd just run a marathon, he could hear nothing alarming.

Perhaps he had imagined that tiny sound? But no sooner had he given the thought voice in his head than he heard it again. As if it were mocking him, and his pathetic attempts to explain or will it away. It was faint – but it was still a thread of sound that was unmistakably the musical tinkle of a small bell.

And now that he had his wits about him and was actively listening out for it, it sounded to him as if it was coming from somewhere above him. Reluctantly, and dry-mouthed, he turned his head slowly and forced himself to look up the stairs.

It was a full moon, and plenty of light was streaming in through the high hall windows. Enough light anyway, so that he could see clearly that there was nothing to be seen. Not with the human eye, anyway.

All right, Arbie old son, he told himself firmly. Don't get a case of the old collywobbles now. Just think what a chump you'd make of yourself! He needed to be logical about this. So, what had experience taught him? Well, every time he'd thought he'd seen or heard something specific it had turned out to be a hoax. And with Val in plain sight, snoring obliviously and happily away on her chair, blast her, the only person who *could* be ringing that little bell was the housekeeper, Jane Brockhurst.

Which seemed, on the face of it, very unlikely. Still, he knew Reggie was away in dreamland over in his studio, and besides which, he didn't have a key to the Old Forge itself. And he'd seen for himself both Murray and Phyllis leave for their own residences.

So – the housekeeper it had to be. Perhaps she'd invented 'the ghost' to torment Amy Phelps for making her give up her baby all those years ago? But in that case – why was she keeping the legend of the ghost alive (so to speak!) now that Amy Phelps was dead? Tiptoeing past Val, Arbie headed for the stairs, congratulating himself that he'd had the forethought to get from Miss Phelps a layout of the house before he began his vigils. A layout which had included the allocation of bedrooms, so that he knew where the housekeeper slept.

His knees felt just a little bit rubbery as he put his foot on the first stair. He paused and listened nervously. No bell.

He climbed silently up to the small half landing, where Amy Phelps had taken her tumble a week or so earlier. No bell.

He reached the top of the now less moon-lit corridor and looked towards the room where the lady had died, trembling a little and half-bracing himself to see some ghostly human figure watching him. But there was nothing, and better yet, still no sound of any bell.

Beginning to feel less like a human jellyfish, he turned and headed away down a small offshoot of the main landing, towards the room where he expected to find the empty bed of the house-keeper. Although he still couldn't for the life of him think why she should have taken to tormenting her mistress with 'warnings' from her dead ancestor and pretending to be his restless spirit. Or why she was now trying to put the wind up a certain inoffensive author of holiday guides! The only thing he could think of was that Mrs Brockhurst had been quietly going doolally over the years and no one had noticed.

Somewhere, at the back of his mind, a little voice was warning him that he'd forgotten something. He tried to chase what it could be back to its lair, but it was having none of it, and remained stubbornly elusive. Probably because he was too distracted by the need not to get nabbed by a ghost or a madwoman to give it the concentration it needed!

He shook off the nagging of his subconscious and approached the door that he was fairly confident belonged to the housekeeper and was just reaching out to the handle to turn it when he heard a sound. No spine-chilling ring of a bell, but a far more human and comical sound altogether. The sound of a snort, and a deep resonating snore, coming from behind the wood. This was followed by the unmistakable 'twang' of bedsprings as the occupant of the bed rolled over, no doubt in search of a more comfortable position.

So, Jane Brockhurst must have finished her bell-ringing trick and was back in bed, pretending to be innocently slumbering. Coward that he was, he felt nothing but relief, since he hadn't really wanted to catch the poor demented woman red-handed ringing a . . .

Bell!

Arbie, his heart shooting up somewhere past his tonsils, heard it again. That faint but unmistakable tiny tinkle of a bell. Somewhere not too far away now. But definitely *not* coming from the room in front of him.

Now he broke out into a real sweat. He swallowed hard. It was at times like this, or so he'd been informed, that a chap found out if he was a man or a mouse.

He promptly ran swiftly away from the sound and back down the stairs. He had the front door firmly in his sights, and almost screamed blue murder when he sensed movement from something pale stirring close by.

'Arbie? Did I fall asleep?' a soft voice asked.

Val! By the almighty cringe, he'd forgotten all about Val being there! A chap couldn't be seen acting like a sensibly fleeing rodent in front of a lady. He hastily came to a halt, straightened his shoulders and ran a shaky hand through his hair. 'Oh hello, Val. Did I wake you?' His voice was somewhat on the squeaky side, and he cleared his throat and tried again. 'I was trying not to.'

'Aren't we supposed to be qui . . . ' She began to ask, then stopped talking abruptly as the sound of the tiny tinkling bell once again sounded faintly from upstairs. She shot up off her chair and was by his side in a few seconds, and he felt at once the steely strength of her fingers as she gripped his forearm in alarm. No wonder, he thought with a wince, Val's forehand on the tennis court was such a winner.

'Arbie, did you hear that?' she hissed, excitement and fear battling it out for supremacy in her tone.

'Oh yes, I heard it a few minutes ago,' he said, nonchalantly. 'Naturally, my first thought was to check on Mrs Brockhurst.'

'Was it?' Val asked, sounding far too sceptical for Arbie's liking.

'Naturally. Since you were sitting in the chair snoring your head off, and she was the only other person in the house, it had to be her ringing that blasted bell.' But as he spoke, that annoying little voice in his head insisted once again that he was forgetting something. Or was it someone?

'I don't snore!' Val's accusing hiss cut across his speculations. 'And was it?'

'Was it what?' Arbie asked, confused.

'Was it Mrs Brockhurst ringing the bell?'

As if in response to being mentioned, the bell sounded again. And was it his imagination, he thought frantically, or was it just a little bit louder than before? He cast the front door another adoring glance.

'Hmm? Oh, no. She was in bed, snoring too,' he said distractedly.

'I *don't* snore!' Val insisted angrily, then her fingers dug even more painfully into his arm as the bell sounded again. 'Arbie, isn't it getting louder?' she whispered.

'Oh yes, I think so,' Arbie said, determined to sound casual. In fact, he was having so much trouble controlling his breathing and heart rate, that he didn't have it in him to be more animated. He eyed again the front door, mentally mapping the distance, and estimating that he could be through it within six or so strides. And then he wondered what the chances were that he could persuade Val to bolt for it with him.

'Well, shouldn't we track it down?' Val demanded. Her voice, too, sounded suspiciously wavering, but if she had the horrors as badly as he did, experience told him that she'd never acknowledge as much in a thousand years. A more stubborn specimen of womanhood than Valentina Coulton-James probably never existed, he thought gloomily.

'It's etiquette to let the ghost come to you,' he tried. He knew that this was not at all true – and that every famous ghost-hunter had their own methods – most actively pursuing 'phenomenon' wherever they found it. But since Val hadn't read his book, no matter how much she protested that she had, she was unlikely to know this, not having read his short and potted history of the subject that prefaced *The Gentleman's Guide*.

The bell sounded insistently again, as if getting annoyed at being ignored.

'Well, that might be just as well, because it's definitely getting louder,' Val gulped. 'Which means it's coming our way.'

Beginning to feel light-headed, Arbie took a deep breath and thrust his trembling hands into the pockets of his Oxford bags so that Val wouldn't notice them. 'Yes, it is. Pity I haven't got a camera set up. It would be just my luck to have a fantastic phantom appear and not get a photograph of it. I'll be drummed out of the whatchamacallit society. I can see the chairman now—'

'Arbie, you're waffling,' Val cut across him ruthlessly. 'You always waffle when you're terrified. You were the same at school, when Mr Bunce called you up to his desk.'

'Everyone was terrified of Bunce,' Arbie protested.

'I wasn't,' Val lied.

'Oh, come off it, Val, even you . . . '

TINKLE, TINKLE.

Arbie and Val both spun around, staring in petrified fascination at the stairs. For the sound of the bell was now so close it could only be coming from the landing above them. 'Arbie, the ghost is coming,' Val whispered. 'What do we do?'

Run, Arbie thought. What else did any sensible person do? He looked again at the front door, and Val, catching the movement of his head, dug her fingers even harder into his forearm.

'Ouch, Val, that hurts!' he complained, freeing his hands from his pockets. 'Let go.'

'No. I want to see what happens,' Val said, her voice now distinctly on the edge of hysteria.

And she probably did, too, Arbie's feverish mind informed him bitterly. Trust Val to be stubborn, even in the face of her own fear and the spectre of a ghostly blacksmith with a bell on his toe!

'It's coming down the first set of stairs,' Arbie whispered, now unable to move at all. His feet felt as if someone had glued them to the tiles on the hall floor, whilst his eyes seemed similarly glued to watching the stairs. But with the aid of the moonlight, he should be able to see whoever – or whatever – was coming down the stairs but he could see no movement at all.

And then he knew what it was he had forgotten.

Cora Delaney! *Petite* Cora Delaney. The unobtrusive house guest and lifelong friend of Amy Phelps was also resident in the house. She was so self-effacing that she had totally slipped his mind. So it could be she who was now playing tricks on them, for some unfathomable reason.

But if so, despite her small posture, she must be crouched down almost double behind the concealing banisters, and somehow the thought of that dignified lady duck-walking down the stairs whilst gleefully ringing a tiny bell just wouldn't form in his mind's eye.

Beside him, Val swallowed noisily. Arbie was right – her ears could follow the now almost continuous tinkling noise as it approached the bend in the half landing, and she'd never felt so frightened in all her life.

Together they stood in the hall, clinging to one another like petrified children, their eyes fixed on the level of the stairs where a human figure would naturally be as it walked down. Yet the moonlight, coming in through the high windows, illuminated the top half of the walls, ruthlessly confirming that no such human figure was there.

Now the bell sounded with an almost merry twinkle at the top of the first set of stairs, right in front of their eyeline, as they stared up, transfixed.

Nothing appeared.

But the bell kept on tinkling away merrily, as if mocking them.

'I don't believe it,' Arbie breathed. He was now, right this instant, experiencing his first, genuine ghostly goings-on! Oh, there was no actual ghost to be seen, but the sound of the bell was undeniably coming down the stairs towards them! 'It's not manifesting!' he whispered in awe. 'It's more like the cases where ghostly footsteps are heard, but the ghost is never seen.'

Val gave a little whimper.

And it was then that Arbie finally saw it. Perhaps his experience of ghost-hunting had given him better night vision, or perhaps, during his writing of *The Gentleman's Guide* he had simply become more used to processing shapes and things in half-light, but he spotted the culprit about halfway up the stairs in the darker bottom half of the illuminated area.

Instantly, the terror drained away and he felt almost giddy with relief. But in the next second, he recovered and acted quickly. He was not his uncle's nephew for nothing! And if there was one thing his disreputable relative had taught him, it was to think quickly on your feet, and where possible, turn any situation to your advantage.

'Here, Val, get behind me,' he said manfully, taking the excuse to prise her painful grip from his arm once and for all, and thrusting her gallantly behind him. 'I'm going to go forward and see if I can communicate with it. But if I say run, then, Val, I want you to run out the front door as fast as you can, and don't come back. Not for anything. Do you understand?'

'What?' Val said dazed, and watched, open-mouthed, as Arbie Swift moved bravely forward.

'I can't see anything yet,' Arbie said, trying his best to hide his relief and glee behind a solemn tone. 'There's no evidence of ectoplasm or luminescence. The temperature isn't dropping yet either . . . Val, I need you to remember what I'm saying, in case you need to repeat it later.' He wondered how much longer he could go on before Val, too, spotted the source of the tinkling bell, and decided, regretfully, that it wouldn't be for much longer. Still, he'd done enough, he hoped, to give her pause for thought.

The next time she looked at him with that withering gaze of hers, he could jolly well remind her of this night, when he'd taken his life in his hands and . . .

'Is that a cat?' Val asked.

'What? Oh . . . ' Arbie crouched down and peered. 'By Jove, Val, well-spotted! Yes. It's Reggie's precious Empress Maud. Here, puss puss.' He made a squeaking noise through his lips and rubbed his thumb and fingers together in invitation. The friendly feline, needing no further encouragement, quickened its pace and ran to him, setting the little bell on its collar ringing out musically.

'She must have got in somehow, and has been busy mousing,' Arbie said, reaching down to pick up the cat and bury his face thankfully in her lush fur.

He became aware of Val by his side and removed his face from the purring feline's ribs. 'Well, that's one mystery solved. If I'd known the silly cat had one of these bird-scaring thingummyjigs on her collar,' he tinkled the bell deliberately as the cat pushed her furry cheeks against his face and purred loudly, 'we wouldn't have been fooled.' Or nearly been given a heart attack! But the only time he'd been introduced to the cat was when they'd first come to the house for tea, and then the feline had been mostly stationary on Reggie's lap.

'Arbie, did you know it was the cat all along?' Val accused, watching him with blue-eyed suspicion.

'What? No, of course I didn't,' he said huffily and feeling mortally offended. 'Did you think of the blasted cat yourself?' he challenged her flatly.

And at this, Val was forced to admit – very grudgingly – that no, she hadn't.

After that, neither one of them fell asleep in their chair, and when dawn finally came, Arbie opened the front door and Empress Maud sped off with her tail flickering in the air, in search of her master and breakfast.

Which, Arbie thought, was a jolly good idea. He could eat the odd kipper or two himself. Nothing like a good fright, overcome, to give a fellow a hearty appetite!

CHAPTER SEVENTEEN

It wasn't until two days later that Val and Arbie were once more roped into the Phelps affair. During that time, Arbie had been informed by the boatyard that his uncle's boat was now ready, and he'd arranged with Marcus Finch that one of his employees would deliver the boat to the jetty at the bottom of their garden on the morning of his uncle's birthday.

He'd also reluctantly signed a contract with a jubilant Wally Greenstreet for a second volume of *The Gentleman's Guide* and had (even more reluctantly) started to make some notes on his travel itinerary for the tail end of the summer.

The heat had now broken, and a far more bearable summer day awaited Arbie when he awoke, so he and Basket took a short walk across the fields. Basket, as usual, was too lazy to go any farther than a mile or so, and unless he wanted to end up carrying the stubborn animal home, Arbie had no other option but to keep his ramble down to a modest one.

Even so, he was in a good mood when he returned to the chapel, but that changed the instant he heard noises coming from his uncle's studio, and thought that he recognised the voice of the visitor. He felt a nasty jolt rocket through him and all but sprinted for the entrance to the outbuilding. As he pushed open the door and almost fell in, he discovered, to his dismay, that he was indeed not mistaken. The less-than-dulcet tones of Inspector Gorringe greeted him immediately.

'That's an interesting object, sir, if you don't mind my saying so.' He was speaking to Uncle, and eyeing something warily on the nearest workbench.

His uncle saw Arbie first and – to his nephew's practised eye – was clearly not at ease. But then, Uncle was never easy when the constabulary were within spitting distance. 'Yes, it's an idea I have for a portable battery-operated fan,' he was saying calmly enough. But Arbie, who knew him well, had no trouble interpreting the look Uncle shot at him. He wanted Gorringe out of his studio. And with the Stubbs canvas not ten feet away on the painting platform, Arbie could well understand why. He was feeling a bit queasy about it himself.

At his uncle's look, he forced himself to stroll casually up, hands in his pockets, and, assuming a nonchalance that would have made an actor at the Palladium applaud him, drawled, 'Oh, hello there, Inspector, was it me you wanted?' manfully putting himself forward as a distraction.

'Ah yes, our famous man of letters,' the Inspector said, turning slightly amused eyes onto the younger man. 'I thought I'd call in whilst I was passing. I've heard so much about your uncle from the local magistrate that I couldn't resist meeting this notorious relative of yours.' If this young rapscallion thought that there were any flies on him, Gorringe mused, it would do well that he should think again.

Uncle bit back a groan. The local magistrate was the bane of his life and would insist on regarding him as something of a crook. The cheek of the jumped-up little jackanapes. Uncle had never been convicted of anything in his life.

He was far too clever.

'Ah, ha-ha,' Arbie laughed feebly. 'Hear that Uncle? You're notorious! You mustn't believe all you hear, Inspector,' he pleaded. 'Uncle has the reputation of being a bit of an eccentric, that's all. Take the Old Chapel, for instance,' he said, indicating the converted building visible through the open door. 'Only my uncle had the vision for creating a residence out of it. Would you like a tour?' he offered desperately. 'It's remarkable what he did with the floating gallery.'

But the Inspector was not going to be lured from the studio so easily. 'Thank you, Mr Swift, but I'm not much interested in architecture. Now what's this curious object?' He pointed to something that looked like a cross between a cheese grater and a kite.

As his uncle launched into a convoluted explanation of his latest project, Arbie chanced a swift glance upwards, and saw at once that the tops of the two easels were exposed.

He broke out in a cold sweat, and when he glanced nervously back and saw the Inspector watching him with hawk-like interest, he felt even worse. 'So, what was it you wanted to see me about, Inspector?'

'All in good time, Mr Swift. Is that where you do your painting, sir?' He turned to Uncle again, nodding towards the short set of steps leading to the painting platform.

'I rather think he's just at a delicate stage with his watercolour landscape, isn't that right, Uncle?' Arbie interrupted rudely, aware by the way that the older men looked at him with bemusement that his voice was probably climbing higher than an operatic diva's. What's more, he was pretty sure that he'd just gone as pale as an under-baked meringue. 'Mustn't keep you, Uncle. If his colours dry out before he's finished, he's apt to be like a bear with a sore head all day. So, better leave him to it, eh?'

He did everything but take the policeman by the arm and march him out.

'So, what can I do for you, Inspector?' Arbie asked, feeling a little weak with relief after averting disaster.

219

'Hmmm?' the Inspector murmured, still looking thoughtfully over his shoulder at his uncle's domain. 'Oh, yes. I wondered if you had made any interesting discoveries on the ghost front, Mr Swift. I saw Miss Coulton-James in the village earlier and she told me you'd held another ghost vigil?'

'Oh, no, nothing out of the ordinary, you know. Well, we heard a bell ringing in the early hours,' he added casually, feeling inordinately pleased to see the look of astonishment cross the older man's face, 'but it only turned out to be Empress Maud.'

'Empress Maud?' Gorringe echoed faintly. 'Would that be a ghost or living person, Mr Swift? And either way, is there gentry staying at the Old Forge now?'

'Of a sort.' Arbie grinned. 'A queen, in fact, but only of the feline variety. And one who wears a bell on her collar.' Arbie went on to explain, all the while oh-so-casually leading the forces of law and order further and further away from the site of a Stubbs of dubious origin and towards the garden gate.

'Ah.' The Inspector was openly grinning by the time Arbie's tale was finished. 'I dare say that must have given you a bit of a fright, sir?'

'Me? Nothing of the kind. Of course, Miss Coulton-James was alarmed, but Val's made of stern stuff.'

'Yes, that was the impression I have of Miss Coulton-James,' the Inspector agreed blandly. 'Well, I must be getting on, sir. Oh, by the way, I understand that Miss Thomas is now back in residence at the Old Forge. I daresay, now that she's inherited the place, she's deciding what to do with it. Live in it, or sell it, or maybe let it?'

Arbie nodded, suspecting that the niece of the dead woman was now the Inspector's number one suspect. Or was the disinherited Murray still the frontrunner? He himself was beginning to wonder.

'I say, Inspector, you *do* know that the whole village is just waiting for you to arrest Murray Phelps, don't you?' he asked artlessly.

The Inspector, not fooled for a minute by this piece of fishing, decided to take the opportunity to make a little mischief. He had long since suspected that the author and the vicar's daughter were trying to solve the case as well, fancying themselves, no doubt, as modern-day versions of Sherlock Holmes and Dr Watson – with both of the youngsters assuming they were taking the leading role as the sleuth with the deerstalker hat!

Now he smiled amiably. 'Are they indeed? Rather hard on him, don't you think, when he was the only one in the house to have an alibi. Or so he claimed,' Gorringe added casually, gratified to see the author's jaw drop comically. In truth, the Inspector, after investigating Murray's movements, wasn't altogether sanguine that that young man's movements were quite as cut and dried as he had made out. But that was the trouble with police work – you very rarely could be sure of anything!

When the Inspector then instantly bade him an amiable good day, Arbie was too relieved to see him go even to try to worm more information out of him. Mind you, what Val would say to him when she realised that he'd let such a golden opportunity slip didn't bear thinking about. No doubt she would have pumped the Inspector mercilessly for more information!

Instead, he sped back to his uncle's workshop and rushed inside. Seeing that Uncle was now upstairs on the painting platform, he hurried up the few steps and erupted onto the stage. 'Where is it?' he hissed. 'I hope you've hidden it somewhere safe.'

His uncle, standing contemplating his half-finished horse, looked up from the canvas, clearly puzzled. 'Where's what?'

'The Stubbs!' Arbie walked forward and groaned when he saw the canvas his uncle was working on. 'For pity's sake, Uncle, if Gorringe comes back he's going to see what you're up to! Can't you hide these pieces somewhere away from the village until the bobbies are no longer swarming all over the place?'

'Stubbs?' Uncle repeated, baffled. 'You're not making sense, boy. Are you coming down with something?'

'Don't give me that innocent look,' Arbie advised him. 'I stopped falling for that when I was ten, and you conned me out of my last bar of Christmas chocolate. I saw the Stubbs myself, right here, not so long ago. And I'm not such a muffin that I can't tell a genuine Stubbs from a packet of lard. And look – look at that!' He waved a demented hand at the canvas in front of them. 'You're obviously painting a copy! Do you know how many years you can get for art forgery?' he demanded. 'Not to say aiding and abetting the theft of a major artwork?'

'No. Do you?' Uncle asked, genuinely curious.

Arbie didn't. Not off-hand. But that was not the point! *'Uncle!'*

'Oh relax, boy. You didn't really think I'd nicked a Stubbs from somewhere, did you? Who do you think I am – some kind of geriatric Raffles?'

Since Arbie *did* think it, he naturally began to look huffy. 'No, of course not. It's just that . . . er . . . just that . . . With the Inspector lurking about I er . . . ' He pulled his collar away from his throat and began to shuffle his feet.

His uncle took one astonished look at him, and then smiled affectionately. 'You're a good lad, young Arbie, looking out for your aged relative and all.' He reached out and patted the lad on his shoulder. 'Daft as a brush, mind, but a decent enough cove.' He gave a sudden bark of delighted laughter. 'So you thought I was about to be nabbed, did you?' He shook his head at the absurdity of it. 'As a matter of fact, the Stubbs belongs to an old pal of mine, and he's got to sell it because he's found himself embarrassingly short of cash and has commissioned me to make a copy so that his nearest and dearest don't find out he's had to sell off a family heirloom. It's all above board, and quite legal, I assure you.'

'Oh,' Arbie said faintly, slumping down on the nearest shabby armchair. His relief was so great that he even ignored the importunate jab of the chair spring which had just introduced itself to his posterior.

Chuckling, his uncle took up his paintbrush again, and contemplated a troublesome fetlock.

CHAPTER EIGHTEEN

Val was not particularly surprised to run into Phyllis Thomas in the village shop.

The rumour mill had already done its round, and the paperboy had informed her earlier that Phyllis was back in the village. Curious, Val had questioned the lad about the state of the latest gossip, and was confidently informed that the majority of her neighbours were simply waiting for Murray Phelps to be arrested and duly hanged for the murder of his aunt.

Val was not so sure that it was so cut and dried, so when she bumped into Phyllis over the meat paste and jars of Bovril, she was extra-friendly towards her, and was consequently invited back to the Old Forge for morning coffee. It wasn't hard to get the invitation, and Val was left with the feeling that Miss Phelps's niece was upset about something and wasn't averse to having some company.

She was proved right, for after a few minutes of polite conversation over the teacups, Phyllis plucked up the courage to talk about what was worrying her.

'I saw the Inspector about the village just now,' Phyllis began, trying to be casual and not quite succeeding. 'He's such a nice man, but, well, as you can imagine, everything's just so awkward right now. What with Aunty and everything,' she added helplessly.

Val nodded. She could well imagine that having a murdered aunt – not to mention finding yourself her main legatee – could well be awkward. 'I'm sure Inspector Gorringe will find out what happened,' she said encouragingly – or threateningly, depending on how Phyllis stood in the matter. 'Do you have any ideas about this terrible business yourself?' she added delicately. It wasn't something she would normally have asked, but she could sense that Phyllis herself was desperate to discuss the issue, or else why bring up the Inspector's name at all?

Nevertheless, Val was relieved when she saw the other woman lean forward in her chair eagerly. It meant she hadn't caused offence, which, as a vicar's daughter, was perhaps the ultimate sin.

'Well, yes, I do.' Phyllis looked around nervously, but of course, they were alone in the morning room, Mrs Brockhurst and the village girl being busy preparing lunch in the kitchen. 'I know it's an awful thing to think, but, well, really, I can't help it.' She looked at her pretty companion with anxious eyes, obviously in need of a prompt to continue.

'I'm sure nobody could blame you for worrying the matter over.' Val gave the prompt to her willingly enough and, just to leave the field wide open for her, leapt nobly into the role of co-conspirator in the gossip and speculation. 'Arbie – Mr Swift and I – for instance, have been questioned by the police also, and we can't help but wonder what happened that awful night. So you're not alone, Miss Thomas, I assure you. And, you're right, it *is* awful, but we've been wondering . . . well . . . about Mr Phelps? Murray Phelps, that is?' she proffered delicately, her voice rising at the end to make it just enough of a question so as not to cause offence. As she spoke, however, she kept a close eye on her hostess, and knew she'd hit the nail on the head when she saw the look of relief cross her face.

'Oh, you're thinking along those lines too?' Phyllis all but whispered.

'And so is half the village,' Val assured her, rather more coarsely.

'I mean, I know it's ghastly, but it all seems to make a terrible kind of sense, doesn't it? He thought he was the heir. And then there was all this ghost business with the "warnings", and bell ringing and things. And then your poor aunt's tumble down the stairs. All that happened only when Murray was here, didn't it?' And if she could hear her father's lecturing voice in the back of her head telling her that only naughty girls cast aspersions, she salved her conscience by reminding herself that if she could get more information out of Phyllis, she was only serving the course of law and justice.

Phyllis let out a long, trembling sigh of relief. 'Oh, I'm so glad he isn't getting away with it. Miss Coulton-James, I can't tell you just how frightened I am,' she said, her eyes getting that shining look that indicated that tears couldn't be far away.

At this, Val goggled a bit. She was getting more of a reaction from Phyllis than she had bargained for and now felt a little out of her depth. Phyllis was beginning to look genuinely distraught. 'Oh? Miss Thomas, my dear, please, is there anything I can do?' she asked, reaching across to put a hand on her hostess's knee in a gesture of support and wishing that her mother was here. The wife of a vicar knew how to cope with emotional crisis all right. 'What on earth has scared you so?' she found herself asking simply.

Phyllis sat back, trembling just a little. 'My cousin, of course,' she said bitterly. 'He paid me a visit at my house, the evening after the reading of the will. He . . . well, not to put too fine a point on it – he *threatened* me.'

For a moment, Val thought that somewhere at the back of Phyllis Thomas's stricken eyes, there was a more calculating look peeking back out at her, as if assessing her reaction to these words. But then it was gone, and Val saw that Phyllis was as pale as any ghost. There were also dark rings under her eyes that she felt sure weren't due to clever make-up or artifice.

'He *threatened* you?' she repeated, numbly. 'What? *To kill you?* Did he admit to killing his *aunt*?' The words tumbled out of her mouth in a rush, she was so shocked.

But already, Phyllis was shaking her head. 'Oh, no. Nothing so straightforward as that,' she said bitterly, her voice sounding tired and strained. 'Murray is far too clever to be caught out so easily. No, it was much more . . . sly and sinister than that. He intimated all sorts of things, horrible, ugly things. Amongst them . . . well, he said that he could go to the police and tell them things which would ensure that they'd arrest me! For poisoning Aunty, I mean.'

Val, aware that her mouth had dropped open, closed her jaw with an almost audible snap. With some effort she pulled her scattered wits together, trying to make sense of it all. 'I'm sorry, but why should the police arrest *you*?' This, of course, was a little ingenuous on her part, as she and Arbie had also wondered if this woman could be the killer. But she was hardly about to admit as much now!

Phyllis gave a small, helpless shake of her head. 'Well, Aunty did change her will in my favour. And Murray said that that gave me a motive. I was there that night, so I had opportunity. And he said, if he wanted to, he could tell the police some things that would make it look even worse for me.'

'Like what?' Val scoffed, somewhat inelegantly. To her surprise, Phyllis looked shiftily away, and shrugged her shoulders.

'Oh, he wouldn't say. Not in so many words. It was so beastly – he just prowled about my room, dropping vague hints and threats. Did you hear that the police are now sure that the poison that was used on Aunty came from Reggie's photography bits and bobs? Which means that any one of us could have got hold of the murder weapon. And he went on and on about how evidence could be "discovered" and "witnesses could come forward" and how things could be made to look so black for me that by the time he'd finished, I could practically feel a noose around my neck.' At this, Phyllis held up a hand to her throat as if she could feel the rope already there.

Val swallowed hard, imagining she could feel its heavy weight around *her* neck too.

'And then he suggested a way out for me,' Phyllis said despairingly. 'I asked him what he meant, and he said that if I shared the inheritance with him, he would "keep quiet" about what he knew. Of course, I demanded he tell me what it was he thought he knew, but he seemed amused by that. He kept telling me that I knew very well what it was. He said the money should be his by right anyway, and that Aunty had gone batty about ghosts and things, and if there was any justice in the world, he'd still be inheriting it all, instead of just the business side of things. But then . . . then he really frightened me.'

At this, Val all but gaped. As if threatening to get you arrested somehow and hanged for murder wasn't frightening enough – there was something *worse*?

'What?' she whispered, by now as pale and almost trembling as much as Phyllis herself.

'He said . . . that is, no, he didn't *say* anything outright. He never did.' Phyllis shook her head in evident frustration. 'That was what was so devilishly cunning about it. He just intimated that what had happened to Aunty could happen again. He seemed to find it amusing, somehow, blaming it all on the ghost. He kept looking at me in a queer way, as if I should be sharing the joke somehow, but I couldn't make head nor tails of it. He just kept on in that mocking way, about how "the ghost" had punished Aunty for breaking up the family fortune and leaving most of it to me. About how "the ghost" would now be angry with me. How "the ghost" could come after me next. And all the time he was watching me and smiling. I tell you, Miss Coulton-James, my blood ran cold!'

'I'm not surprised,' Val said faintly. Hers was running pretty chilly just hearing about it second-hand.

'And the worst of it is,' Phyllis concluded miserably, 'Murray always was the clever one. I don't know how he means to do it but I'm sure that he *can* and I'm worried – so desperately worried – that something *will* happen, and the Inspector *will* arrest me. Or else something awful will happen to me. And, you see, if either of those things happen, as my closest living relative now, Murray will inherit the money after all. And I just don't know what to do!' Phyllis finished, almost on a wail.

At this, Val bristled, and angrily straightened her shoulders. It was time they both stopped acting like wilting wallflowers and stuck up for themselves! Her chin came up and her blue eyes flashed. 'Well, I know what *I'd* do if I were you,' she said forcefully. 'I'd march straight down to my solicitors this instant and make out a will leaving everything I have to some charity or other. That would spike your beastly cousin's guns all right.'

Phyllis stared at Val wonderingly. 'Oh, Miss Coulton-James, of course, you're right. And I should have thought of that myself,' she added, sounding genuinely annoyed with herself. 'And I'm sure that I hope I would have done, eventually. It's just that I've felt so frozen, ever since it happened. It's as if I've been acting like a mouse, frozen stiff under the gaze of a cat and unable to think or move to save myself! But you're right – if he knows he won't get my money, he'll have no reason to . . . well . . . '

But here, she couldn't seem to say the actual words.

Val, however, had no such trouble. 'He won't have any reason to bump you off,' she said bluntly. 'No, quite. And what's more, if I were you, I'd go to the Inspector right now and tell him what your cousin has been up to! Threatening you, the swine! That will give your cousin something to think about when the Inspector asks him what he thinks he's up to.'

229

But at this, Phyllis turned even paler. 'Oh no, I couldn't do that,' she said nervously. And once again her eyes shifted away.

'But why not?' Val demanded. 'You owe your cousin no loyalty,' she pointed out hotly.

But still, Phyllis shook her head stubbornly. 'Oh no. I couldn't possibly . . . It's family . . . But I will take your advice about making out a new will. I'll call my solicitor right away in fact and leave it all to charity. In fact, I know just the good cause to leave the money to as well! Aunty would have approved of it, I'm sure.' At this she smiled and seemed to revive.

She even poured out another cup of coffee and drank it.

And whilst Val was glad to see her get back some of her fighting spirit, she still felt vaguely dissatisfied when she left the Old Forge some little time later. Whilst the morning had provided shocks and revelations aplenty, she was still not convinced that she had been given the whole picture. Oh, she didn't doubt that Murray Phelps had been bullying his cousin, with the aim of muscling in on the inheritance he had lost. And she didn't doubt that he'd be ruthless enough to try to pin the murder of Amy Phelps onto Phyllis if he thought it could help him achieve this aim. Especially if he was the murderer himself – which was beginning to look more and more likely.

But she was also convinced that Phyllis hadn't told her *everything*. There had been those moments when she'd looked shifty and guilty. And why was she so reluctant to tell the Inspector about Murray's behaviour?

It wasn't until she was turning into Church Lane and was almost home that it suddenly hit her what it might be that Phyllis was being so cagey about. She stopped dead in the middle of the lane, her eyes widening. Of course!

Running past the entrance of the vicarage, she sped on instead to the lane's end and into the grounds of the Old Chapel. She needed to tell Arbie all that had happened and was looking forward to bathing in his admiration as she presented him with the solution to the conundrum.

*

'And that's when it all fell into place,' she said, half an hour later.

After finding Arbie sitting loafing about in the garden as usual, with a sleeping Basket at his feet, she'd launched into her morning's adventures. Arbie had listened, with satisfyingly more and more attention, as her tale went on.

'When what fell into place?' Arbie demanded now, sitting forward on the garden bench, hands dangling between his slightly open knees, his handsome features rapt on her face.

Val preened herself. 'What it was that Phyllis had been up to, and that Murray knew about, of course,' she said, happily revelling in the situation for all it was worth.

'And what's that, do you think?' Arbie was forced to ask.

'The *jewellery*, Arbie,' Val said complacently. 'Don't you remember? When we were looking over Amy Phelps's bedroom that time, I told you that some of the stones in her pieces were paste? Well, the lady herself wouldn't have had any reason to sell off some stones, would she? She was rolling in it, as were her ancestors before her. But *Phyllis* wasn't – as a relative of the less favoured branch of the family, she was always something of the poor relation. And she had access to the house. Oh, yes,' Val hugged her knees under her chin, and grinned beatifically, 'I just bet she's been supplementing her income for years! All she had to do was take a small piece of jewellery away with her to a jewellers – say a brooch or something small – and get one or two of the stones replaced. Then simply put it back the next time she visited her aunt.'

'But wouldn't Amy Phelps notice?' Arbie objected.

'Why should she? Women have favourite pieces of jewellery,

just as they do favourite hats or gloves. And Phyllis would know which items of jewellery her aunt preferred and was likely to wear at any major social event. She'd just have to be careful to select only a brooch or bracelet or whatever that wasn't a particular favourite of her aunt. And the lady's eyesight couldn't be what it once was, so she'd be unlikely to notice the fake stones – not without examining them with a magnifying glass or something, and why should she do that? No, I don't think Phyllis would have been running all that much of a risk.'

'But how could Murray have worked all this out?' he wondered. 'According to your theory, he must have known what she was up to, or he'd have nothing incriminating to threaten her with. But he's a man like me, and I'd have no idea what was diamond and what was glass.'

Val frowned at him. 'You always have to rain on my parade,' she accused crossly. But then she snapped her fingers as the solution presented itself to her. 'The maid!'

Arbie blinked. 'Eh?'

'The maid, Arbie, the one who was dismissed! Do keep up!' she admonished him impatiently. 'The one who, according to village gossip, is so sweet on Murray – and he on her! She could have stumbled onto it. She was the type to snoop, all right, and just the sort of clever hussy who might spy and catch Phyllis out pinching the gems. I bet the housekeeper probably knew about it as well. Poor old Phyllis isn't exactly anyone's idea of a clever criminal mastermind, is she?'

'And this dastardly maid would have spilled the beans to Murray, naturally,' Arbie said, nodding. 'Come to think of it, she probably kept Murray informed every time Phyllis visited anyway, just in case she managed to sweet-talk Miss Phelps into giving her more of the family loot. Which would be the last thing he'd want.'

'Or he put her up to it, more likely,' Val snorted. 'Either way, if he tells the Inspector about the thefts, he knows the police will have to investigate it, and it wouldn't take them long to find out which jeweller Phyllis had been using. None of which would look good for her at a subsequent murder trial, would it?' she said uneasily. 'And with Phyllis inheriting all the money after all and being at that awful dinner . . . No wonder she got into such a state. Any jury might well convict her of killing her aunt, given all that!'

'And she couldn't confess to you the hold Murray had over her without admitting to being a thief.' Arbie nodded. It all hung together all right. 'You know, Val, I really don't like all this,' he said slowly. 'I mean, if we say, just for the sake of it, that Phyllis had nothing to do with killing her aunt, but Murray *did*, then poor old Phyllis's position is looking bleak. What's to stop him doing the same to her? Murdering her, I mean.'

'Oh, I forgot to mention that bit. Arbie, I did something rather clever,' Val preened.

At this, Arbie began to look really alarmed. 'I say, Val! What on earth have you done? I know you and your clever ideas. They usually end in calamity!'

'They do not!' she instantly denied. Although, looking back on their childhood, one or two of her ideas hadn't exactly worked out quite as she'd thought, like that affair about making a natural dye from beetroot and colouring Miss Wilkinson's silly standard poodle pink . . . 'Oh, but this is different. I really came up with the goods this time, and no mistake, Arbie,' she said confidently. 'I told her that if she was that worried that her beastly cousin might kill her and inherit her new fortune, that she should change her will immediately, leaving it all to charity!'

Val got up to smell a carnation, a triumphant look on her face. 'You know, I've always thought, when reading murder mysteries and thrillers and what have you, that the silly heroine in question would only be out of danger if she made it clear to her nearest and dearest that it would do them no good at all to bump her off if they didn't get a bean.'

Arbie, after some thought, had to concede that as far as Val's ideas went, there was probably nothing objectionable in this one. For a change! If Murry *was* the killer, it would certainly give him pause for thought, if nothing else. And if it turned out that Phyllis was being very clever and playing some subtle game that they hadn't got to the bottom of yet, he couldn't see how it would do any harm either.

He said as much to Val, who smirked happily. 'You see, I was right. Now that she's made out a will leaving it all to charity, she'll be as right as rain. You wait and see.'

*

The body of Phyllis Thomas was discovered at the Old Forge four days after making out her new will, and one day before the scheduled funeral of her aunt, Amy Phelps.

Inspector Gorringe was called to the residence by a shaken housekeeper, who had found Phyllis insensible in bed, and cold to the touch. This time there was no locked door or window to complicate things, and beside Phyllis's bed on a small table were a glass containing water and a bottle of sleeping pills that had recently been prescribed by her own doctor.

Her cousin Murray, who had also stayed the night at his aunt's house in preparation for her funeral the next day, had given his evidence, along with those of Cora Delaney, Reggie Bickersworth and the housekeeper. They had all agreed that Phyllis had seemed her usual self, if a little distracted by the idea of the funeral the following day, and had dined well. Reggie had played the piano after dinner, and then the four of them had sat down to a few, somewhat desultory, rubbers of bridge.

The only odd thing that anyone had remarked upon was that

Phyllis had asked Reggie earlier in the day if he wouldn't prefer to sleep in the house that night instead of his quarters in the studio, a request that had surprised him, but one to which he had, naturally, agreed. As he'd confessed to the Inspector later, when it was his turn to be questioned, he'd felt as if he couldn't possibly say no. 'She seemed rather nervy, Inspector, and who could blame her? And as she and her cousin, unfortunately, have never been what one might call close, I was happy to take on the role of honorary uncle and sleep under the same roof, if it would put her mind at rest. She was having enough trouble sleeping as it was.'

Murray, as far as Gorringe could make out, had found the idea of Reggie as Phyllis's knight in shining armour amusing but hadn't made any comment on it otherwise.

Cora Delaney was upset by the latest tragedy to befall the Phelps family, but being a lady, was keeping her emotions very much under control. She had asked though, if, after her friend's funeral, she could leave the Old Forge and go back to her own home, and under the circumstances, the Inspector had agreed. For all that she was holding up well, he could tell that she was tired and beginning to feel the strain. And the last thing he needed was for another woman to breathe her last.

The housekeeper knew nothing about Miss Phyllis's sleeping pills or her night-time regimen, and hadn't observed her retire for the night, so couldn't possibly say if she carried the glass of water with her or not.

There had been no suicide note found in the dead woman's room. There were no signs of violence. Of course, he had to wait for the post-mortem to be performed, but the Inspector had little doubt that the evidence would show that Phyllis Thomas had died as a result of an overdose of her sleeping medication.

But had she taken it herself? That was the question! And if so, had she simply made a mistake in the dosage? Her doctor, when contacted, had confirmed that she hadn't been taking them long, only since the affair of her aunt. The subsequent murder investigation, it seemed, had led to a bout of insomnia in his patient. He thought it *possible* that she hadn't understood his instructions, but not *probable*.

So had she taken them deliberately? And if so, the Inspector mused, was it because she had a guilty conscience? Had she murdered her aunt and then found herself unable to live with it?

Or had she been tricked or forced somehow into taking an overdose? In which case, he had another case of murder on his hands.

Either way, that morning, as he stood outside in the garden taking a much-needed break whilst his team continued working diligently away at the routine surrounding a suspicious death, it was safe to say that Inspector Bernard Gorringe was not a happy man.

He was gloomily watching a blackbird rootling about under some shrubbery when he heard himself hailed.

'Hello, Inspector?'

He looked up to find the vicar's daughter and her usual handsome escort approaching him. Neither Arbie Swift nor Miss Coulton-James looked their usual happy selves, however, and for that he was rather sorry. He'd become almost fond of the pair of youngsters, in his way.

'Is it true, what they're saying in the village?' Val asked anxiously, so forgetting herself that she didn't even begin with a formal and polite greeting. 'About poor Phyllis Thomas?'

'That she's dead? Oh yes, that's true enough,' the Inspector said rather savagely. He regretted taking out his ill-humour on the visitors immediately though as the pretty blonde girl went very pale and shot Arbie Swift an agonised, appealing look.

Sensing developments, he stiffened.

'Er, in that case, Inspector, I think there's something you should know,' Arbie said slowly. 'Perhaps we could sit down in the garden and have a word?'

CHAPTER NINETEEN

The funeral of Amy Phelps was an odd event. Normally, the death of a well-respected villager would have resulted in a formal, properly conducted affair, with the whole village turning out to make the most of it. The farm labourers would have been given time off to pay their respects, the shop would have closed for a half-day, and everyone would have turned out in their most sombre dark clothes to sing hymns reverently, and see the dear departed interred with all the pomp and circumstances she would have expected. Then everyone would have gallivanted off to the deceased's home to consume large amounts of free food and alcohol.

And although that was all still happening, it was not *all* that was happening. Reporters had descended like a flock of carrion crows, as the latest death in the 'house of tragedy' had finally awakened them to the fact that they were now on to a major story. Likewise, an inordinate number of members of the public who had hitherto never heard of Maybury-in-the-Marsh found themselves – totally by chance, naturally – walking or picnicking nearby, or visiting the church strictly for brass-rubbing purposes, only to be amazed to stumble upon a funeral.

The police were also in the church, watching everyone, but most ardently, those in the front pew, where the nearest and dearest to the deceased were seated. These included an irate and now visibly worried Murray Phelps, who'd been invited to Inspector Gorringe's police station yesterday for a 'bit of a chat' which had lasted almost all night.

Val, sitting next to Arbie and his uncle somewhere in the centre of the rows of pews, right in the midst of the crush, leaned even closer to Arbie and whispered in his ear, 'What on earth is Murray doing here? I thought the Inspector was going to arrest him?'

'Apparently not,' Arbie said laconically.

He and his uncle were dressed in the suits they always wore for this occasion, and he was very much aware that his uncle was wrestling, as usual, with his starched collar. His relative didn't often go to church, and Arbie knew that he was merely passing the time, as it were, until they could get on to the baked meats. These were being provided – contrary to tradition – by The Dun Cow Inn, apparently on the orders of Murray Phelps, after a hasty consultation with Jane Brockhurst. Somehow, the thought of the whole village, agog with curiosity, descending on the Old Forge, where another woman had died less than forty-eight hours earlier, was simply too bizarre to countenance.

'But why not?' Val hissed at him, earning a speculative look from the wife of the local milkman, who was sitting in front of them, nursing a grizzling infant.

Arbie lowered his voice even more. 'How should I know?' he whispered. 'Buck up, your father's giving you the eye.'

At this Val instantly straightened up, a guilty flush crossing her face as she saw that, sure enough, her father, now in the pulpit, was watching her disapprovingly. If she'd been able to, she'd have nudged a little further away from Arbie, but such was the crush in the church, that this was impossible.

They were packed in like sardines.

The Reverend Coulton-James had never had to bury a murder

victim before, let alone bury one in a village almost febrile with scandal and fright over the death of yet another member of one of their most prominent families. Under the circumstances, he did his best.

In the front pew, Cora Delaney listened to the eulogy with her back ramrod straight and her gloved hands resting neatly in her lap. She had had her funeral outfit sent from home, making sure that her maid had included a rather fine black lace veil. From behind this, she was able to smile grimly and with satisfaction whenever she wanted, secure in the knowledge that nobody could tell how much she was enjoying herself.

To hear the vicar talk, she mused sardonically, you'd have thought that Amy was a cross between an army general and a latter-day saint. Aware that everyone – reporters and sightseers exempted – knew the deceased well, The Reverend gentleman did his best to portray her rigid personality and sometimes upper-handedness as a whimsical and endearing trait. He took great pains to point out all her many – and genuine – charitable contributions over the years. He emphasised how much employment and prosperity the various enterprises of her family business provided for people not just locally but nationwide, and how the village had lost 'a distinct and much-liked member under such sorrowful circumstances'.

Cora let all this wash over her. She, for one, was not in the least sorry that Amy Phelps was dead, and she suspected that a number of people nearby her were not sorry either. And as the vicar's attempt at soothing words for his parishioners in these 'trying times' echoed around the cool stone interior of the church, Cora went back over the days to that moment she'd found *his* letter in Amy's secret drawer.

His name had been Bartholomew Carmichael – but everyone simply called him Bartie. When they'd first met, he had been twenty-three, whilst she and Amy had both been eighteen. In those far-off days, her life had seemed so idyllic – a seemingly never-ending round of house parties and holidays, balls and dances, with light-hearted flirting being the order of the day after 'coming out' at court. The Great War hadn't blighted everyone and life was fun and gay for the young, beautiful and wealthy. Which was nearly everyone in Cora's and Amy's world.

Bartie had caught Cora's eye the moment she'd seen him at old Colonel Fitzhugh's London fancy-dress ball, just before Christmas, too many years ago now for Cora even to want to calculate. He'd dressed as Lord Byron and had the dark good looks to carry it off. But his personality had been far removed from that famous brooding poet, being bright, uncomplicated and sunny – as why should it not? As the eldest son of a minor lord who, nevertheless, possessed so much land that he could almost have declared it as his own county, he had the world at his feet. And, naturally, his choice of debutants on the lookout for a husband.

And she had caught his eye too, without doubt, Cora thought with satisfaction. Oh, how they'd danced that night! All the wilting wallflowers and maiden aunts had noticed, naturally, and had gossiped spitefully. As if she and Bartie had cared! It wasn't long before he was regularly picking her up to take her to the theatre or punting on the Cherwell. Bartie had always been fond of Oxford, having taken a minor degree in Literature at Wadham, and they often visited the 'city of dreaming spires'. She, too, had come to love it, and it was one of the reasons she'd went on to study there herself, a year later, after things had all gone so horribly wrong.

But even Cora, smitten though she was at the time, had had to admit that her wonderful Bartie wasn't intellectually gifted (unlike herself) but what did that matter? He had a fine seat on a horse, estate managers perfectly capable of overseeing the family farms and a laugh that could brighten up any room.

She, his parents (who had liked and approved of her) and all their friends, not to mention the society pages, awaited the inevitable engagement announcement with some anticipation. Instead, out of the blue, Bartie departed one day on an unscheduled tour of Europe, leaving her a letter that wished her well. Just that, nothing more. But then, nothing more had been needed to be said.

Her parents hadn't been best pleased and had blamed her for whatever it was that she'd done to lose a very desirable match indeed. In vain did she try to explain that she had no idea what the 'it' was that she'd done!

Of course, she'd had her pride, and when he returned from Europe about six months later, made no contact with him. Indeed, she was already in Oxford, studying, and pretending all was right with her world. She even acted 'vaguely pleased' for him when friends showed her the announcement in *The Times* of his upcoming marriage to a minor earl's buck-toothed daughter later that same year.

After a while, she had resigned herself to settling down to find another match, and of course, being pretty and well-connected, found one soon enough. She had married a good, if somewhat dry and pedantic man, and had children and been content enough, in a way. But the haunting feeling that she had lost out on a golden future had never completely left her. She'd adored Bartie and had been convinced that her marriage to him would have been a happy one. Good-natured, good-looking, amiable Bartie would have suited her very well indeed.

And until the day, many decades later, when she'd snooped in Amy Phelps's bedroom, she'd never discovered why Bartie had suddenly cooled on her.

But all that changed when she'd found his letter to Amy.

When she'd first recognised his handwriting, the green-eyed monster had reared its head and she'd suspected the worst – that

Amy had seduced him away from her. But she soon realised that she hadn't got that right. Not *quite* right. For once she'd read the actual lines of his letter – or rather, *between* the lines – she realised that the betrayal hadn't been as simple or unoriginal as all that.

That Amy had wanted him for herself and had tried to get him, Cora didn't doubt. But Bartie evidently hadn't fallen for her after all, which meant that Amy had been forced to change tactics. So it turned out that the letter from Bartie hadn't contained the sweet whisperings of one secret lover to another. No. It had been something far more insidious.

On that afternoon not long before Amy's death, Cora had read the long-ago written words of her dear Bartie thanking Amy for 'opening his eyes' to what, she, Cora had been doing. Which, apparently, had been pursuing a titled earl, having set her heart on becoming a countess. That the earl in question was thirty years older than her, and widely ridiculed for the extraordinary amount of hair in his ears and growing out of his nose, seemed to have aroused no alarm bells in her admittedly dim-witted beloved.

Suddenly the sound of organ music made her jump a little, and all around her people were rising to sing 'Rock of Ages' and Cora was once more dragged back to the present.

Which was the funeral of her so-called friend.

Of course, Cora knew why Amy had done it. Unable to win the man herself, she'd determined that she, Cora, would not have him either. Amy had always been like that. It was not enough for her that she should win, but that others must lose. For that reason alone, she was not at all surprised that Amy had ended up almost the sole owner of the Phelps family fortune. It seemed now, in retrospect, almost inevitable.

Cora's slight but pleasant voice rose with the rest as the hymn was sung. And under her veil, her smile never wavered as she eyed the flower-bedecked coffin a few feet away from her. For it was indeed true, what they all said. Revenge really was sweet. And surely, outliving your enemy was the best revenge of them all?

*

At The Dun Cow, the Inspector munched thoughtfully on a ham sandwich and watched, wearily amused, the antics of the press, who were busy interviewing anyone and everyone silly enough to speak to them. And since they were plying the yokels with beer and spirits, that was quite a few. Although what the more bucolic types could tell them about the life and times of Amy Phelps and her poor niece was moot.

None of the immediate family or closest friends would give them the time of day, naturally.

His eye fell presently on Arbie Swift's extraordinary uncle. He was currently eating like a Trojan and had already managed to dispose of his shirt collar. But despite the man being a known eccentric who sometimes flew close to the wind, the Inspector was not interested in Uncle. Gorringe had met people like him before. Whilst he might enjoy playing up to his louche and disreputable reputation, there was no real harm or malice in him.

His eye then sought out Murray Phelps, who was at the bar, drinking steadily. Now the same, he was sure, could not be said for that particular gentleman.

He did not doubt the vicar's daughter's account of what Phyllis Thomas had told her. But as Mr Murray Phelps had repeatedly pointed out during the mutually unsatisfactory night that they had both spent at the police station, second-hand hearsay meant nothing.

He had simply denied, and carried on denying, that he had ever done any such thing. He, bully and threaten his cousin? Perish the thought! Perhaps, he'd suggested snidely, his dear cousin Phyllis had been feeling guilty about stealing his inheritance, and

243

spreading lies about him was her way of salving her conscience, and paving the way to make her own life more bearable? After all, if people came to believe that he was the devil incarnate, she could enjoy her ill-gotten gains in peace, could she not?

Pressed to explain this reference to her ill-gotten gains further, Murray Phelps, finally beginning to lose his temper, had asked him just what he was using for brains. Surely, he'd expostulated angrily, the Inspector must have realised by now that his dear cousin was behind all those puerile 'ghostly' hauntings and such? Who else had a motive for alarming his aunt by playing tricks on her and oh-so-subtly laying the blame at his, Murray's door? After all, it had worked, hadn't it? His dear aunt had come to believe that he was behind all that falling-down-the-stairs business too and had written him out of the will, and dear cousin Phyllis in.

And, of course, the Inspector had to admit that the man was making sense. So much so, he'd pressed craftily, that the thought of it must have made him hopping mad. So mad that he was determined to bully his cousin into sharing the money with him, perhaps?

Prove it, Murray had challenged.

And there, of course, was the sticking point. Because Miss Valentina Coulton-James's word about what Phyllis had told her was all but useless in a court of law without more solid evidence to back it up. And what solid evidence did he have? None. That was how much.

So far, neither he nor the best brains in the county police could even work out *how* the poison had been administered to Miss Phelps, let alone who had done it. For if the killer had simply gone to Amy's room and somehow inveigled her into drinking something containing the poison, how and why had they then gone to all that trouble to leave their victim in a room locked from the inside?

The Inspector sighed heavily, feeling the onset of a headache, and valiantly ignoring it, tried to concentrate. *If* Murray's theory about the crime was to be believed, Phyllis Thomas must have been the killer of her aunt. Why set up all that ghost business, leading successfully to Murray's downfall, and then not follow through with killing the woman after the will had been changed in her favour? But even if that were so, it still left him with the same problem – what had it gained her to set up such an elaborate locked-room mystery?

Putting that aside for the moment, Gorringe turned to the latest death. Here, surely, there could be little mystery. Murray had killed Phyllis – who else had a motive? Except, according to his two young amateur sleuths, that made no real sense either, for Phyllis had sworn that she was going to alter her will, leaving it all to charity. Unless, of course, her cousin had killed her out of sheer pique or spite!

Naturally, the first thing Gorringe had done was to get someone on to that business of Phyllis Thomas's will, but here, yet again, this frustrating and convoluted case continued to do its best to drive him to distraction. For the solicitor Phyllis had gone to had already left on his holidays, choosing a walking tour of Aberdeenshire of all places for his annual bout of relaxation. His whereabouts was being sought, but he'd left no set itinerary and the chances of tracking him down to a small inn or hostel weren't good.

Just to further set the Inspector's nerves twanging, it was a small firm, and alas, the very junior partner who was the only other member of it didn't have the keys to the senior partner's lock-boxes. So getting a peep at the actual document was also out of the question.

The clerk could tell them, though, that Miss Thomas had indeed called in prior to her death, and that the senior partner had subsequently worked on making out a will for her. Moreover, he could confirm that Miss Thomas had called in just two days later to sign the will, for he himself had been one of the witnesses to the signature. But, alas, he had no details as to the deposition of this document, and until the senior partner returned, therefore, could not confirm how the deceased had left her property.

But for all that, the Inspector was confident that Phyllis's will, once read, would provide nothing that would contradict the idea that she had left her detested cousin penniless.

He'd had more luck with Val's idea that Phyllis had been fiddling about with the lady's jewellery though. Experts had quickly been called in and discovered that, yes indeed, several gems within the various suites of jewellery belonging to Miss Amy Phelps were in fact duds. What's more, a trawl of the jewellers within a twenty-mile radius of Phyllis Thomas's home had soon traced the respectable firm who'd been only too happy to remove the gems for the nice gentlewoman, and sell them on, replacing the stones with good quality fakes.

His sergeant had questioned the jeweller closely, and was confident that the man, a thoroughly respectable member of a thoroughly respectable firm, which had never fallen foul of the law or even been suspected of fencing, had carried out the requests in all good faith. As the nervous and unhappy gem smith had pointed out, a lot of genteel families, in these days of rising taxes and dwindling private incomes, had found themselves in 'embarrassed' and reduced circumstances, and had thus been forced to realise some of their assets. In fact, the jeweller had informed his sergeant earnestly, Miss Thomas was by no means the only gentlewoman who had come to him over the past few years with jewellery that needed to be 'discreetly rearranged'.

All of which was interesting but put him no further forward. So, the unfortunate Miss Thomas had been reduced to pilfering her aunt's jewellery. Did that make her less or more likely to have been the killer of her aunt?

Either way – that lady was now dead herself, and so couldn't be asked to explain herself.

And so, like a weary tennis ball, the Inspector found himself once more being knocked back into Murray's side of the court again. During their long night of fruitless questioning, Murray had admitted that Phyllis had already told him that he was not mentioned anywhere in her last will and testament. So, he'd demanded, why would he have had anything to do with her overdose? 'I gained nothing from her death. It's as plain as a pikestaff that my silly chump of a cousin just mucked up the dosage of her new and unfamiliar sleeping pills and died accidentally. Nothing else makes sense.'

Of course, it was in his best interests to say all this, and they only had his word for it that such a conversation had taken place. But much as the Inspector might like to see the worst in the man, even he had to admit that it was unlikely that Phyllis Thomas would have kept the change to her will a secret. Surely, the whole point of her making out a new will in the first place was to ensure that Murray would have nothing to gain by killing her? Which meant that she would have gone out of her way to tell him so!

All of which was making his headache worse and bringing him no closer to making an arrest in either case!

Later, he would bring in and question the recently dismissed maid, Doreen Capstan, who seemed by all accounts to have developed a very close relationship with the man of the moment. Putting a scare into her might shake things loose a bit!

He was contemplating this possibility with some pleasure when he spotted young Arbie Swift trying to detach his now somewhat inebriated uncle from the bar, much to a nearby newspaperman's amusement. The Inspector stepped in to offer his assistance, and between them they managed to manoeuvre a placid, slightly over-affectionate Uncle out into the garden and deposit him under a spreading elm. There he happily contemplated a duck, which was on the lookout for scraps.

'Thanks, old man,' Arbie said gratefully. 'I say, you're looking rather gloomy and worn out. Bad night?' he added.

The Inspector knew that the young pup was only fishing for information and smiled grimly, but was nevertheless inclined to indulge him a little. Just a little. After all, he had proved useful so far.

'I dare say you're surprised to see Mr Phelps at his aunt's funeral?' Ignoring Arbie's vague and unconvincing denials, he swept on. 'The trouble is, we have nothing concrete to go on. He might very well have threatened his cousin, but as he so carefully pointed out, we can't prove it. And it's not as if he's the only one with a motive to kill his aunt. By the way, we know now that Miss Phelps would have died very quickly after being poisoned. Not that that helps us much, does it? And as far as motive goes – even the housekeeper has come under suspicion.'

'Eh?' Arbie said, opening his eyes wide enough to resemble an owl. 'Mrs Brockhurst? By Jove, that's a turn up for the books! What on earth could she have had against the poor lady?'

The Inspector sighed wearily. 'Oh, my men have been out and about talking to everyone and anyone about the residents of the Old Forge. And one of them unearthed an old scandal going back nearly thirty years. Apparently, the housekeeper, who was a maid at the time for Miss Amy's mother, had to leave the village for a while to have an illegitimate baby.'

Arbie swallowed hard, not wanting to admit that he'd known that for some time, due to Val's sleuthing. The less the police knew about what you'd been up to, the better. So his uncle maintained, anyway, and for once Arbie was inclined to agree with him. 'You don't say!' he managed to mumble, conspicuously avoiding meeting the policeman's eye.

'It happens more than you'd think,' the Inspector said,

misconstruing his unease and taking pity on him. 'They get into trouble and go away for a bit to have the babe and put it up for adoption. Or give it to the nuns, poor little blighters.'

'And one of your foraging constables wormed this out of one of the villagers, I suppose?'

'Yes. Naturally, we then wondered if the housekeeper might not have secretly resented Amy Phelps and her mother for all these years. In her own mind, she might have convinced herself that they could have let her stay on as maid and keep and raise the child herself. Impossible of course – no respectable family could have kept on a maid in those circumstances. But Jane Brockhurst might not have thought so. In the end, though, we tracked it all down and found out that the poor babe didn't survive the birth. So she had no reason to resent the Phelpses after all.'

Arbie wasn't so sure. If he'd been Jane Brockhurst, he might not have felt so kindly towards them, even so.

'No, I think you and your pretty Miss Val are probably right, and Murray is our man – at least for his cousin's death. It's just proving it that's going to be the bugbear. And as for who was responsible for the death of their aunt – I think it's a toss-up between Phyllis or Murray. And again, I have no idea how we're going to prove it either way.'

'Ye-es,' Arbie said, but slowly and uncertainly. And if the Inspector had been less aggrieved and sleep-deprived, he might have recognised the doubt in the younger man's tone. But right then, he had other things on his mind.

'Well, I must get back to the fray,' he said, nodding towards the noisy pub, and with a last yawn, set off back into the thick of it.

Arbie watched him go with an anxious eye. He'd been doing a lot of thinking since the shock of Phyllis's death, and his thoughts had been leading him down some very dark and startling places. Now he thoughtfully regarded his uncle, who was watching the duck with a silly smile on his face. He sighed heavily. 'Come on,

Uncle, let's get you home and get some coffee into you. I want to pick your brains about something.'

'Hmmm? Perpetual motion, eh? Leonardo couldn't crack it, but I think I might. Yes, that latest little idea of mine . . . '

Arbie, who had no idea what he was talking about, hauled him to his feet and began guiding him determinedly towards home. 'No, Uncle, come on, buck up. I really *do* need to ask you about something. How are you on chemistry?'

CHAPTER TWENTY

The Inspector was back in the village first thing the next morning, set on tackling Doreen Capstan before she left her family's cottage for her job at the factory.

Before he set off to find Polecat Lane, however, he was neatly waylaid by Arbie Swift again. Feeling a little more impatient than he had on other such occasions, he loitered under a lonely horse chestnut tree for the young man to catch up and once he had, glanced tellingly at his watch.

'Mr Swift. I don't have much time I'm afraid,' he began firmly.

Arbie nodded. 'Oh, quite, quite,' he conceded hastily. 'I don't have much either, as it happens. It's my uncle's birthday tomorrow and although I've got a big surprise lined up for him, I want to go off into town and get him a few bits and bobs to open on the day, as it were. It's just that I've been thinking about this murder business . . . ' He took a deep breath, looking slightly terrified, and said, 'And I have to say, I'm beginning to think that you're on the wrong track altogether. About Amy Phelps and Phyllis's death and whatnot.'

Having got that out, he took a long, shuddering breath and looked at the policeman with a mixture of alarm and despair. Rather, the Inspector thought, secretly amused, like his spaniel looked at him whenever a trip to the vet was required.

Since the youth was obviously expecting to get a kick in his trouser seat for such presumption, the Inspector smiled amiably instead. 'I see. And do you have any evidence for this thinking?' he asked mildly.

'Well yes. And no.'

'Very nice,' Gorringe said sardonically.

Arbie felt himself flush. 'I mean, I think the evidence is there – or that you'd find it – if you only knew where to look.'

The policeman looked at Arbie shuffling his feet and sighed. 'All right.' He settled his back more comfortably against the trunk of the tree. 'Let's hear it then, Mr Swift.'

Arbie gulped then shrugged. No doubt his ideas would be shot down in flames, for anyone less qualified to be an amateur sleuth than himself he couldn't imagine, and the expert beside him was sure to find no end of holes in his neatly constructed theories. But he wouldn't be able to rest until he'd shared them with someone.

At least Val wasn't around to hear him make an ass of himself, he consoled himself.

'All right. Shall I just . . . er . . . go through what I've been thinking, and you can just listen and smile, and then when I've finished, you can have a good laugh and let me get on my merry way?' he asked.

'I'm all ears, Mr Swift,' the Inspector assured him.

'Right,' Arbie mumbled, not looking him in the eye. 'Well then, here goes.' He took a massive breath. 'As you know, I was dragged into this when Miss Amy Phelps asked me to sort out her ghost business. Well, to be honest, I wasn't keen. I only wrote *The Gentleman's Guide* as a bit of a laugh, and it hardly makes me a bona fide ghost-hunter. But she was insistent, and then Val egged me on and . . . ' Seeing the policeman's eye was beginning to glaze over already he got himself in hand.

'Yes, sorry.' He cleared his throat. 'Well, right from the first,

252

I was pretty sure that Miss Phelps wasn't a believer in the supernatural and, as you know, it didn't take me and Val long to realise that she was worried that someone in her family was playing tricks on her. And that she believed her nephew to be the culprit. Then she died, after changing her will. So far, so simple. But then comes the complication of how on earth she was poisoned in a room that had been locked and bolted from the inside. Not so simple. And then Phyllis dies, also after changing her will. Now it seems to be a right muddle.'

'On that we can agree,' the Inspector said dryly.

'Yes. Quite. So, as one of my Oxford dons was fond of saying, think logically, boy! Fair do's, I say to myself, begin to think logically, Arbie old son. Well, not very logically if I'm honest . . . ' Catching the warning glance the Inspector cast him, Arbie hastily swept on. 'All-righty-then, to cut a long story short, I told myself that since I couldn't come up with any answers looking at things the way I had been, then I had to be looking at things from the wrong angle. And what I needed to do was wash away all previous ideas and start again, this time taking nothing for granted. And when I began to really put my mind to that locked-room and poisoning business, and how that might have been managed – well, after I'd done all that . . . then I began to see the light. And once I'd realised to my satisfaction who *really* benefits from the first murder and almost certainly from the second too – there really was only one person, to my mind, who *could* be the killer.'

Now we're coming to it, the Inspector thought, highly entertained. It was going to be interesting to see which name this engaging rascal was going to pull out of the hat. 'And have you come up with someone who fits the bill, sir?' he said encouragingly.

'Yes, I'm afraid I have,' Arbie said unhappily. 'And I'm afraid it's Reggie Bickersworth. And it's a bit of a facer, sir, I can tell you, because I like the old sausage and the thought of landing him right in it . . . But then, murder is murder and . . . well . . . '

Arbie trailed off as he watched the play of emotions pass across the Inspector's face. He saw surprise first, obviously. This was then quickly followed by amusement, and puzzlement. Now he was left with only a waiting thoughtfulness on the Inspector's features.

'And why have you alighted on that particular gentleman, may I ask?' the Inspector asked mildly. 'And by the way, we do have slander laws in this country.'

At this Arbie blanched a little. 'You know, Inspector, you're quite right.' He kicked at the earth by his feet for a few moments, and then heaved a massive sigh. 'Inspector, do you mind if we call on Reggie right now? I think I should say what I have to say to you in front of him as well. It's only right he has the chance to defend himself, and then, well, if I've got things massively wrong both you and he can call me all kinds of a fool.'

The Inspector looked at the young man beside him. Clearly, the young chap was determined to say his piece, and he didn't see what harm it could do. And if he made a fool of himself – well, he thought Reggie Bickersworth would probably be lenient with him. After all, the young were apt to come a cropper now and then, and their elders usually let them off lightly.

'Very well, sir. If you're really determined to get things off your chest, let's go see if he's in then,' the Inspector said comfortably.

*

Reggie was indeed in and looked surprised but willing enough when the Inspector asked if he could spare them a few minutes of his time.

Arbie, feeling deeply uncomfortable, followed the two men into the main room of the house that was a combined living space, painting space and kitchenette. A mezzanine level presumably housed the older man's sleeping quarters, and could be accessed by a wide set of rough but sturdy-looking wooden stairs. The exposed rafters and dust motes dancing in the sunlight coming in through the windows gave the building a sleepy, timeless air, and the Inspector could well understand how an artist would feel at home here.

'Please, sit down,' Reggie invited them eagerly. 'The armchairs are, I think, discarded relics of the old house, but are quite comfortable nonetheless, I assure you. Can I get you some tea?'

'No, sir, not for me, thank you,' Arbie said quickly. He wasn't quite sure of the etiquette in such circumstances, but he was pretty sure that accepting the hospitality of a man you were about to accuse of murder was definitely not the done thing.

'Nor for me, sir,' the Inspector echoed.

'In that case . . . ' Reggie's affable smiling face turned from one to the other of his unexpected visitors, with only a slight frown of perplexity pulling at his grey eyebrows. 'I must say, I'm rather intrigued.'

'Mr Swift here has been doing some amateur sleuthing, it seems,' the Inspector began blandly, 'and he thinks he's come up with the answers to our recent tragedies.' The policeman thought the other man paled a little at this, but he couldn't be sure. 'And, as men of the world, he'd like our opinions on his theory.'

'Ah, been reading Mrs Christie, have we?' Reggie said, grinning. 'I don't blame you. I read her books too. They're almost addictive, aren't they? Alas, I can never guess who did it though.'

Arbie managed a wan smile. He wished the older man wasn't being so nice and looking so . . . well . . . like everyone's idea of a favourite uncle. Dressed in old tweeds and comfortable brogues, he looked as harmless as yesterday's leftover rice pudding. It was most disconcerting.

'Ah, but perhaps Mr Swift always does manage to identify the murderer.' The Inspector, no fan of crime thrillers himself, took the bull by the horns. 'So I, for one, am anxious to know what he's made of our very own murder mystery.'

'Oh, indeed,' Reggie said, sitting up a bit straighter and looking encouragingly at the young man. 'So am I.' He reached for his briar pipe and waved it vaguely in the air in enquiry. 'Do you mind if . . . ?'

Nobody minded, it seemed, and as he began the process of lighting up, Arbie took a deep, steadying breath. Well, he was committed now, and no mistake. Not wanting to look either the representative of law and order or the man placidly lighting his pipe in the eye, he leaned back in his ancient armchair and stared resolutely at a slightly dirty window just beyond the Inspector's shoulder.

'All right, well, I see it like this. Reggie, you first met Francis, Amy Phelps's beloved brother, at school, and as a schoolboy you spent all your holidays here, since your own parents were abroad. Is that right?'

'Yes, indeed,' Reggie said, puffing industriously at his pipe.

'And, er, Val thinks . . . er . . . that is, she believes that as you grew older, you and Francis developed a rather . . . er . . . *particularly close* relationship, if you understand me?' He hoped he sounded more like a man of the world than a tongue-tied schoolboy right then, and hastily swept on as he saw from his peripheral vision that Reggie had flushed painfully. 'Neither of you married, and throughout your adulthood you spent much of your time together. Long holidays abroad in out-of-the-way places and such. And even after Francis died, you continued to come to Maybury all the time, even living here in the studio in the summers so that you could rent out your own place to earn some extra lolly.'

Reggie swallowed hard. 'I don't think my private life, or that of my dead friend, is anyone's business,' he said stiffly.

Arbie felt himself flush and cleared his throat. Never, in his whole life, had he felt so awkward with himself or the circumstances in which he now found himself. 'I'm sorry, Mr Bickersworth, you're quite right. I can only assure you I believe it to be relevant or wouldn't dream of mentioning it. But there's certainly no need to dwell on it and I think we should pass on swiftly.'

'Yes, sir, I agree, and I think we can take all that as read,' Gorringe put in gently. 'But that does rather beg the question – why then do you think Mr Bickersworth killed Amy, who must have been like a sister to him, and his own goddaughter? Did you know that he was Phyllis's godfather?'

Reggie dropped his pipe in his lap and gaped at Arbie. 'What?' he yelped. 'What's all this?' he spluttered.

'No, Inspector, I didn't but I'm not surprised,' Arbie said grimly. 'And the answer, of course, is probably what it always is. Money.'

'Now just wait a minute,' Reggie said, rescuing his pipe and placing it on the table beside him, where, neglected, it quickly went out. He was now sitting up straight in his chair and staring from the Inspector to Arbie and back again, his mouth gaping open and closing again, reminding the policeman, unhappily, of a guppy. 'Am I to take it that *I'm* the one being accused of killing Amy?'

'Yes, sir, I rather think Mr Swift believes so.'

'But that's, that's . . . that's *preposterous*!' the man gasped. 'You're not taking him seriously? Please, Inspector, tell me this is a joke?' he appealed to the policeman. 'You're just ragging me, aren't you? Both of you?'

The Inspector looked solemn. 'I think, sir, it would be best if we just listened to what Mr Swift has to say, and then afterwards, you can take your turn. That, I think, is the best way to deal with this, don't you?'

Under Gorringe's mild but firm eye, the older man wilted a little. 'Well, I don't know, I'm sure . . . ' Reggie muttered feebly.

'It's . . . well . . . it's extraordinary, that's what it is. But . . . if you insist, I suppose . . . Yes, all right, I'll listen to what the young whippersnapper has to say. But afterwards I'll probably blister his ears for him,' he warned.

But the Inspector could see Reggie had begun to sweat.

'Indeed, sir, you may very well be entitled to do that, and maybe much more. In the meantime, thank you for your forbearance. Now, Mr Swift, where were you?'

'The motive,' Arbie said miserably. 'Being money.'

'Ah,' the Inspector said. 'Here, I can probably help you out a bit, sir. As a matter of routine, we run background checks on all our suspects, and it's true enough that Mr Bickersworth's fortunes have, alas, dwindled over the years. In fact, he's very close to being destitute.' At this, Reggie shuffled in his chair and looked about to protest, but the Inspector held up a conciliatory hand, and carried on swiftly. 'Like a lot of minor gentry, his source of income was wiped out in the Great War, and his family never had much land to speak of. But if all of our so-called betters who have been forced to tighten their belts resorted to murder, we'd be up to our necks in corpses.'

With this welcome disclaimer, Reggie subsided back in his chair, but the Inspector could tell that the extent of the constabulary's knowledge about his own personal finances had come as a nasty shock to the older man. No doubt, he thought, the police had no right digging out embarrassing skeletons from respectable family's cupboards.

'Oh yes. I dare say,' said Arbie. 'But you see, I think Reggie had not only come to depend rather heavily on the Phelpses – but probably came to feel as if he was *entitled* to their largesse as well. I think he sees himself as an honorary member of the family and decided to take his "share" as a matter of course. After all, if Francis was still alive, he'd be in clover, for I think you'll find that it was Francis who always paid all their bills.'

At this, Gorringe saw Reggie give a little annoyed start, but he made no effort to refute the claim. Which Gorringe found rather interesting.

'But Francis was gone now, and even though Miss Phelps continued to indulge him, she wouldn't live forever. The cold wind of reality must have been blowing about his old ankles for some time now,' Arbie said sombrely, still keeping his gaze resolutely on the window. 'And he knew that when she went, Murray would get the lot. And can you see Murray Phelps letting Reggie continue to rely financially on the family in the same way that his aunt did?'

'I cannot,' the Inspector said flatly. 'But this is still a long way from him committing double murder, sir,' he pointed out respectfully.

'I'm so glad one of you is keeping your feet firmly on the ground,' Reggie, despite his promise to remain silent, couldn't resist putting in bitterly. 'I'm beginning to suspect that Mr Swift has had some sort of brainstorm. All of this is sheer poppycock and the most lurid kind of speculation, you know.'

'Yes. I know, and I'm sorry about that, but please bear with me,' Arbie said stiffly. 'You see, sir, I think you came to the Old Forge this year with a very clever plan.' He addressed the older man directly now, and finally managed to look him in the eye. 'A plan that might seem barmy to me and the Inspector but to yourself – who knew the family so well – not so barmy at all. After all, you've known these people all your life, enough so that you felt confident that you could predict their behaviour in any given circumstance.'

Here he paused for a much-needed breath and plunged on.

'I think, Mr Bickersworth, that you came to Maybury well prepared. With your old-fashioned photography equipment you had all you needed to kill Miss Phelps. But first, you had to set the scene and create the "ghost".'

Here he turned to Inspector Gorringe. 'You'll note, Inspector, that Miss Phelps had no trouble with her hammer-wielding ancestor before Reggie arrived for his usual summer stay.'

He turned back to Reggie, who was now looking at him wide-eyed and pale as milk. 'And so you go about ringing a little bell and leaving various "warning signs" for Miss Phelps that succeed in getting her all riled up, even going so far as to cleverly engineer her tumble down the stairs.'

'Ah yes, and just how did I manage that, may I ask, when I was tucked away in this studio, and by everyone's admission, had no access to the house?' Reggie demanded defiantly. But if he hoped to see signs of panic on Arbie's face, he was disappointed.

Arbie merely waved a hand in the air. 'I'll come to all that in good time. Let me first deal with motive, otherwise it'll all get hopelessly muddled. I'm sorry, Mr Bickersworth, really I am, but I've got all the angles worked out – I just need to come at them in the right order.'

The Inspector watched this by-play with considerable interest, but he wasn't looking, or feeling, quite as entertained as before. Was it possible that this outwardly seeming indolent young lad was, in fact, on to something?

'Now,' Arbie swept on. 'You knew that Miss Phelps, who was always exceptionally strong-willed and not the most forgiving of people, wouldn't take kindly to this sort of treatment, and that once she comes to believe that her nephew is the one playing tricks on her, she'll do exactly what you want and expect her to do. Namely, change her will in favour of her niece. Now whether Miss Phelps intended that will to stand, or whether she intended to change it back, once she'd informed Murray of what she'd done and given him a good fright, we'll never know. Because once the will had been changed, you had to act. And quickly. And you did. And so – exit Amy Phelps.'

Here he paused and took a deep breath. 'And I know what

you're going to say to that, Mr Bickersworth,' he said quietly, looking at the older man sadly.

'Oh, do you now?' Reggie growled angrily. 'And what is that, pray tell?'

'That if all this is true, then the death of Amy Phelps didn't benefit you in any way at all,' Arbie said. 'So why would you kill her? And you'd be quite right – on the face of it, it doesn't. Which means that nobody is likely to suspect you of it. Which, if you're a murderer, is quite a bonus, I'd say.'

'Indeed,' the policeman put in mildly.

'But in many ways, you see, it *does* benefit him – and enormously,' Arbie said, turning back to the Inspector. 'Because now Murray is cut out of the will, and Phyllis is left in charge of the money. Phyllis, the little girl he saw grow up – and that you now tell me is his actual goddaughter. Phyllis, who thinks of him as her honorary uncle. Phyllis, who's clearly very fond of him and would be much more amenable to dear old Reggie continuing to use the Phelps fortune as his little nest egg when times become hard.'

The Inspector had been closely watching the various emotions flickering over Reggie's face as Arbie had talked. Some were obvious – surprise, anger, disbelief. But above all, a growing consternation that was slowly but remorselessly transforming into real fear. But was that because he was guilty, and felt the trap closing around him? Or because he was innocent, and feared being wrongly accused?

'Well, it's a theory, sir,' Gorringe said at last. 'And perhaps now you would oblige me and tell me how, exactly, this rather elderly gentleman managed the murder of his lifelong friend?'

'Do you mean this elderly gentleman who is as fit as a flea and used to be a mountaineer in his youth?' Arbie asked, waving a hand at the suddenly very still and alert Reggie Bickersworth. 'This gentleman who's had a splendid education and has indulged in many mind-improving "hobbies" over the years? Yes, it's a bit of a facer, isn't it?' Arbie said unhappily. 'All right, sir. This is how I see it,' he began.

'Now this is where you come unstuck, young man,' Reggie said in warning. But he didn't sound quite as confident as he might have wished, and he darted a quick, worried look at the bland-faced Inspector.

'Let's begin with the simple trick behind that staircase tumble,' Arbie began, once more addressing the blank glass panes of the window. 'Forget all that rot about a piece of cord or what have you tied across the top stair and tripping her up at the ankles. No, the only cord used there was a short length of extremely fine black embroidery silk or something similar, and it was attached to the *ceiling* just on the top stair of the short landing. At the end of it would have been something like a bit of brown or black feather-down – or maybe a length of fluffy wool? Miss Phelps was a tall woman, nearly six feet tall, I'd say, whilst her housekeeper is rather on the short side. Which meant that all Mr Bickersworth had to do was make sure the length of silk was positioned just right, so that when Miss Phelps passed beneath it, it would have reached her, whereas anyone else in the house would have passed underneath it without it touching them. Then he just had to wait and later lure her out of her bed by ringing his little bell somewhere close to the house. She'd hear it and, being a forceful woman, would refuse to be frightened and come out to explore the source of the sound, probably hoping to catch her nephew in the act. Instead, she walks to the top of the stairs, with only a candle for light, remember, since she didn't have gas lighting in that part of the house, and steps off. She immediately feels something that she *can't see* touch her face, and being in a heightened state of agitation already, it's no wonder it startles her so much that she loses her footing.'

Here Arbie paused to see how this had gone down and was relieved to see the Inspector nodding.

'Very plausible, sir.'

Thus encouraged, Arbie battled on. 'Now, all along, that fall of Miss Phelps's struck me as odd. If someone really wanted to hurt her, maybe even kill her, why set up the booby trap just there? It meant that poor Miss Phelps only tumbled down five or six stairs before she'd come to rest on the half landing. Now unless she was very unlucky and landed on her head or something, it was unlikely to *kill* her or even do her that much harm. Far better to set the booby trap at the start of the longest flight of stairs that ended on the hard tiled floor of the hall.'

'But, according to you, killing her or seriously injuring her was the last thing Mr Bickersworth here would have wanted,' Gorringe said, easily following his logic. 'He'd want to upset and anger her, but not cause her too much actual physical harm. Also, he must have made sure to set it up only when Murray was in the house again, thus reinforcing Miss Phelps's assumption that he was to blame.'

'Yes!' Arbie said, pleased the Inspector wasn't knocking his exercise in logical thinking out of bounds. 'Of course, once acti-vated, the booby trap would virtually disappear,' Arbie swept on. 'The piece of thread and the feather or wool or whatever would have been wrenched out of place by the fall and onto the stairs somewhere, where the village girl who did the housework would simply have swept it up with her dustpan and brush as part of the usual detritus when doing the household cleaning. Mr Bickersworth didn't need to be in the house at all! In fact, the only thing he needed to do, at some point after the affair, was remove the small pin or tack he'd put in the ceiling to hold the booby trap in place. And in fact, I spotted a tiny pin-hole in the plaster where it had been when I looked it over. It would have been child's play to do, Inspector, I assure you. Mr Bickersworth is quite tall, as you can see, and the ceiling in that part of the house is low. I could reach up and do it, so could you.'

'Hmmm. Intriguing, I grant you. But how in the world did he do the actual murder itself?' Gorringe asked. He was now genuinely interested. And if this young feller-me-lad had actually come up with a way of explaining that, he would shake the man's hand!

'Yes, I'd rather like to know that too,' Reggie put in with biting sarcasm. But his voice was a little shaky now, and the Inspector noticed that he was surreptitiously wiping his sweating palms on the knees of his trousers.

'Yes, that stumped me too for ages,' Arbie admitted candidly. 'Until, practically by a process of elimination, I finally came up with it. I had to ask Uncle a bit about the chemistry aspect of it, but—'

'Chemistry?' the Inspector couldn't help but interject. 'Did you know that Miss Cora Delaney studied chemistry in her youth?'

'Did she?' Arbie asked, considerably startled. But then, after a moment's thought, firmly shook his head. 'No, no good, Inspector. What motive could that nice lady have for killing her friend?'

'Hmm, you're right there,' the Inspector agreed complacently. He might as well suspect Father Christmas himself as a nice lady like Cora Delaney of being a potential murder suspect. 'Go on then, let's hear it,' he said fatalistically. 'I can see you're dying to tell me how the murder of Amy Phelps was done.' And *he* was certainly dying to *hear* it.

Especially since he had not missed the way that Reggie had jumped like a startled goose when the young author had brought chemistry into the conversation.

'Right. Well, here it is,' Arbie mumbled, finding it harder to hold his nerve now that they'd come to the crux of the matter. What if he'd got it all drastically wrong and ended up with egg on his face? Nobody would let him live it down!

'We know that Miss Phelps wasn't poisoned at the dinner

that night, yes? A fact that relieves me mightily, I have to say,' Arbie added with feeling. If her killer had done it at dinner, and a mistake had been made, he might have ingested some of the stuff himself! 'And we know that Miss Phelps didn't partake of anything after retiring for the night. And I've gone over it, and gone over it, and I just can't for the life of me see how or *why* it advanced the cause of the killer to engineer that locked-room mystery anyway. It just didn't make sense at all. Until, that is, I looked at it from a different angle.'

At this the Inspector glanced across at his companion and saw that the young man was regarding his shoes thoughtfully. Reggie, the Inspector noted, was now staring at Arbie like a rabbit would stare at an approaching snake.

'What if, I asked myself,' Arbie said gently, 'the locked-room mystery wasn't designed to throw us off the scent or provide the killer with an alibi or any of those usual things? What if the locked-room aspect of it was totally incidental?'

'Sorry, sir, I'm not following you,' the Inspector said blankly.

'Look at it like this,' Arbie said helpfully. 'Amy Phelps has been upset by the family "ghost" that she strongly suspects is actually only Murray, paying her back for interfering in his romance with the lovely but beyond-the-pale Doreen. She's even taken a fall down the stairs. She's not happy, to say the least of it. You can bet your last bent farthing that when she turns in at night she's going to lock her door – and maybe her windows too, even though it is summer. You or I would probably do the same thing, in her place, wouldn't we?'

Gorringe nodded impatiently.

Reggie merely swallowed. Hard.

'So Mr Bickersworth needed to find some way to kill her when he himself was locked *out* of the house, and his victim was locked *in* her room. You agree?'

'Yes, yes, but Mr Swift, how did he do it?' Gorringe demanded, reaching the end of his patience at last. 'How did he, or anyone else for that matter, poison Miss Phelps?'

'By poisoning the only thing that she took into that room with her,' Arbie said simply, and spreading his hands in that universal gesture of helplessness. 'It's the only thing he *could* have done, isn't it?'

'But she didn't take anything in with her!' Gorringe exploded in frustration. 'You yourself said that when she went up the stairs that night, she was empty-handed.'

'And so she was,' Arbie said quietly. *'Until she picked up her candle on the upstairs landing table.'*

Gorringe stared at him. Then his eyes began to widen. 'The candle!'

In his chair, Reggie made a slight moan, but when both men looked at him, he was merely sitting stiff-backed and pale, with his lips firmly closed.

'Yes. The candle,' Arbie said sadly, focusing his attention firmly on the Inspector. This accusing-a-chap-of-murder was really the absolute end. It was making him feel quite sick.

'Amy Phelps didn't like gas and preferred to stick to candle-light,' he pressed on, just wanting to get it all over with. 'Reggie knew that – the whole *household* knew that. And he'd seen her retire enough times to know that Mrs Brockhurst left a candle on the landing table so that she could light her way down the unlit corridor to her room. All he had to do was place a candle there that night that was laced with cyanide. And before you ask if that's possible, I asked Uncle if it could be done. And once he'd sobered up after the funeral and set that big brain of his to the problem, he quickly came up with the how and the wherefores and explained it all to me.'

Here Arbie had the grace to grin. 'All of which went right over my head, I'm afraid, as you can imagine. He went on a bit about the melting temperature of wax, and how it would have to be converted to a colourless gas and mentioned various chemical formulas for doing this and that and whatnots. Anyway, I'm sure your own boffins will be able to work it out the same way he did,' he dismissed the technicalities impatiently.

Reggie darted a quick look at the Inspector, and felt sick himself when he saw that the policeman was confidently nodding.

'The upshot is, Mr Bickersworth used his equipment to create a candle with a layer of doctored, poisonous wax just below the top. It would have had to be just below the top, obviously, because of course Amy would have lit the candle immediately in situ at the top of the stairs and the fumes might have started to affect her before she got to her bedroom. If she'd been overcome then, and called out, someone might have seen or heard and come to her aid. And that wouldn't do at all.'

Arbie shook his head miserably. 'No, there *had* to be a short delay before the heat hit the poisoned part. Just enough to allow the lady time to get safely to her room. After that, Miss Phelps would have had to set about getting undressed, maybe have a wash or clean her teeth or what have you, for which she would need to keep the candle burning long enough for it to do its deadly work. And, as a matter of fact, we *do* know that after she got in bed, she kept the candle burning so that she could read.'

Here Arbie reminded him of the evidence of the open book and open pair of glasses on the bedside table. 'Once the burning wick reached the poisoned layer, poisonous gas began to fill the room. We know it was potent, because Miss Phelps died in her bed within seconds. The candle then continued to burn past the deadly layer and back into the normal wax again, and eventually right down to the end, and went out. Leaving the poor lady dead, in bed, in a locked room with no way in or out. It's almost simple, once you think about it.'

The Inspector leaned his head against the back of the chair and thought about it. He noticed that at some point in young Mr

Swift's latest recital, Reggie Bickersworth's shoulders had slumped, and that he looked as if he'd aged about five years.

Carefully, the policeman mulled over Arbie's theory. It certainly had possibilities, but . . . 'Wait a minute!' he yelped. 'If the candle filled the room with poisonous gas, and the windows and doors were all shut, how come you and Miss Coulton-James didn't die the moment you broke in and went inside the murder room?'

Hope flickered briefly across Reggie's face, but quickly died as soon as Arbie responded.

'Yes, that's where I almost got stuck too,' he admitted wearily. 'Until I realised just how clever Mr Bickersworth had been. And the answer, of course, was the skylight.'

'The skylight?' the Inspector said and distinctly heard the older man in the room give another little moan, which was also quickly repressed.

'Yes . . . ' Arbie, whose eyes had flickered briefly to Reggie Bickersworth at this same sound, then quickly away again, fixed his gaze on the Inspector's frowning visage. 'The skylight is too small for anyone to use it as a means of exit or entrance, but its latch is loose, and as a way of airing out the room overnight, it was perfect. All Mr Bickersworth had to do was attach a piece of string to the handle beforehand, making sure that the skylight was close to closed but not latched. And then, once he was sure Miss Phelps was dead, all he had to do was pull on it to lift the skylight open so that the room could begin to air. Then, just before dawn, he reversed the procedure and closed it again. For a lean and still-fit man – and former mountaineer, don't forget – the low undulating roofs of the Old Forge presented no barrier to him. He also told me he was a former Scout Leader, so he knows all about ropes and knots and things. I have no idea what knot would be needed, but I'm sure there's one that allows you to pull on a string in a certain way so that it unravels from the object it's attached to, leaving no evidence it was ever there.'

There was, and the Inspector, as a part-time sailor, could have told him what it was, but he was too distracted by his racing thoughts to bother. Was it possible this youngster had got it right after all?

'Even so, he was taking a risk,' the Inspector said, thoughtfully regarding the now very silent and deflated Reggie. 'What if all the gas hadn't quite evaporated and the person who found her had been taken seriously ill themselves?'

'I know. And as it happens, I don't think all the gas *had* quite gone,' Arbie said, swallowing hard now in remembrance. 'When Val first approached the bed, she went over all queer and nearly fainted. At the time, I put it down to her being light-headed with the shock of it all. But then, well, I have to say, even *I* felt a bit odd when I was standing over the poor woman – because I was nearest to the burnt-out candle! I couldn't quite catch my breath somehow.' He scuffed the ground at his feet, abashed. 'I thought it was because I was in a bit of a funk about things myself, but now I believe we might both have been affected by a little bit of tainted air. Luckily, by then, we'd got the window open behind us, so it wasn't fatal. But when I think back on it . . . ' Arbie shook his head at the narrow escape he and Val had had.

'So, there it is.' He shrugged mightily. 'Miss Phelps is dead, the will has been changed leaving Murray out in the cold, and Mr Bickersworth is sitting pretty and totally unsuspected.'

'But what about Phyllis Thomas's death?' the Inspector asked quietly. 'Did he kill her too?'

At this, the older man winced and shifted on his chair. 'I think this has gone on quite enough. I'll ask you to leave now.'

But neither of his visitors moved, and the Inspector could see that Reggie hadn't really expected them to. There was an unmistakable air of defeat about him that was uncomfortable to dwell on.

269

For a moment Arbie hesitated. 'Well, Inspector, I'm not really sure, to be honest,' he stunned the policeman by saying. 'I think, originally, his plan would have been to wait and see how things stood. And if he found that he could "touch" Phyllis whenever he needed to, and that she was generous and amenable in her new-found wealth . . . well, I'd like to think he would have left it at that.'

In his chair, Reggie swallowed something hard that had risen in his throat.

'On the other hand,' Arbie said unhappily, 'Murray *did* rather play right into his hands by threatening his cousin and making himself look like a "sure thing" if she were to die next. I think we can assume that since Phyllis was willing to tell Val about her cousin's antics, she would have confided in Mr Bickersworth as well. So he *might* have thought that it would be a good idea to strike whilst the iron was hot. He must have been confident that Murray was bound to take the blame for her death. We can only ask him.'

At this, both men looked speculatively at the older man, but Reggie remained mute. In fact, his eyes had got a slightly glazed look now, and the Inspector wasn't totally sure that he'd even heard the young author's latest words. And the policeman could well understand why. Reggie must have thought he'd planned the perfect, clever murder, and the shock of being found out had hit him with all the force of a mortar shell.

'Oh blast it, I just wish Val hadn't advised Phyllis to change her will leaving it all to charity!' Arbie took the Inspector completely by surprise by bursting out so suddenly and vehemently.

'Here, hold hard, sir, don't get so het up. Why on earth should *that* matter anyway?' Gorringe demanded.

'Because, don't you see, everything depends on what charity she left it to, doesn't it?'

'Eh?' the Inspector said, not seeing that at all, and suddenly felt all at sea again. 'As a matter of fact, we're running into some difficulty in finding that out. But surely, the point of Phyllis Thomas's will is that Murray doesn't inherit?'

'Oh no, Inspector, I'm afraid it's just the opposite,' Arbie Swift said. 'It's not who *doesn't* inherit, but who *does*!'

'No, sir, you've lost me again,' the Inspector said, shaking his head.

'You do know that Mr Bickersworth runs an animal charity, don't you?' Arbie said softly. 'One of those outfits dedicated to re-homing orphaned bunnies and various four-footed waifs and strays?'

The Inspector went a trifle pale and turned to stare at the man in question, who had now closed his eyes. As if, by immersing himself in shrouding darkness, he could pretend that none of this was happening.

'And Val *did* say that Phyllis had in mind a charity that her aunt would approve of,' Arbie swept on remorselessly. 'And that Amy Phelps had been in the habit of getting her pets from Mr Bickersworth for years.'

The Inspector groaned. 'Oh, you don't mean to tell me . . . Phyllis might have left the lot to her *godfather*?'

Arbie shrugged unhappily. 'I don't know, Inspector. But I think you'd better find out, don't you? I mean, she might have left it all to the Salvation Army for all we know. And she might have taken an accidental overdose of those sleeping pills . . . ' He trailed off and shrugged helplessly.

'And then again, she might not,' the Inspector finished for him grimly. 'Right, I'm going to light a rocket under my colleagues in Aberdeen,' he said forcefully, startling Arbie considerably, as he had no idea why Aberdeen should poke its nose into all this. 'We need to find that missing solicitor. Then I'm going to ask my boffins to test this poisoned candle theory of yours and to go over this studio and the equipment in here with a fine toothcomb,' he said, looking around at the pleasant room that now didn't seem quite so pleasant at all.

'If Mr Bickersworth *did* make a lethal candle here, he's bound to have left some evidence of it behind, no matter how much he might have thought he'd cleaned up after himself. And now . . .' he said, rising magisterially from his chair, 'I'm going to take Mr Bickersworth to the station and ask him some very hard questions indeed. Come along.'

'Mr Bickersworth, you should have a good solicitor beside you before you make any statement,' Arbie felt compelled to advise him, earning him a rather wrathful glare from the policeman. But Reggie, it seemed, hadn't even heard him. Instead, as the Inspector, one hand firmly on his arm, led him away, he looked too dazed to take much in at all.

CHAPTER TWENTY-ONE

The next morning dawned fine and bright. Uncle was up early and had obviously forgotten that it was his birthday, because the cards and gifts Arbie brought to the breakfast table puzzled him for a few seconds.

He claimed to be only fifty-two. Arbie didn't believe him.

Mrs Privett had cooked him all his favourite dishes and left a wrapped parcel of his favourite tobacco by his plate as her own offering, and Uncle was contentedly smoking his newly filled pipe when they set off from the house a little while later.

'So where's this surprise you've promised me then?' Uncle said, twinkly eyed, as they made their way across the somewhat lacklustre garden towards the green field that sloped down to the river beyond.

'You'll see,' Arbie said, grinning happily, having already spotted in the distance the tell-tale white shape of the small boat tied up by the usually deserted jetty. 'I hope you like it, Uncle. I've had her re-fitted just for you.'

At this, Uncle's eyes slit up speculatively. 'Her, eh? Finally found me that buxom barmaid I've been dreaming . . . er, oh hello, young Val.' He choked off his reprehensible ramblings abruptly, and Arbie spun around to find Val bearing down on him. Even though she wasn't on her bicycle, there was a look in her eyes that again set off 'Ride of the Valkyries' in his mind, and he felt his shoulders go back, ready to take whatever onslaught was coming.

'Ah, Val, lovely to see you.' He presented his most appeasing smile. 'That's a particularly fetching hat you're . . . '

'What's all this about Mr Bickersworth killing himself in his cell last night?' she demanded, barely pausing to nod at his uncle. 'Apparently, Inspector Gorringe arrested him late in the evening and he admitted to killing Amy Phelps and Phyllis, and then hung himself with his shoelaces or something equally awful!'

'Eh?' Arbie squeaked, battered by so much information all at once. 'This is the first I've heard of . . . '

'Oh, don't try and tell me you had nothing to do with it,' she warned him, hands on her hips and her blue eyes flashing. 'I saw Inspector Gorringe this morning when he came to talk to Daddy about something, and he let slip that you and he had had a most enlightening conversation yesterday. Have you been holding back on me, you, you, you *swine*, you?' Val spluttered, all but stamping her foot.

'I think I've just spotted my birthday surprise,' Uncle said hastily, pointing down the field. 'Is that it?' He indicated with his walking stick at the white boat bobbing on the water below, and Arbie nodded mutely. 'In that case, I think I'll check her out. Thanks, m'boy.' He clapped Arbie on the shoulder in a gesture of manly camaraderie. 'I've always liked mucking about on the river. Miss Val.' Uncle tipped his hat to her and then sped off down the field at a good clip, just like the honest-to-goodness yellow lily-livered coward that he was.

Arbie wished bitterly that he was speeding off with him.

'Now look here, Val . . . ' he tried, but she instantly raised a pale, imperious hand, cutting him off.

'No! I don't want to hear any more of your excuses!' Then her shoulders slumped a little. 'Oh, Arbie, I thought we were in this together,' she wailed in a more conciliatory tone. 'If the Inspector was in the mood to finally spill the beans about what's been happening and took you into his confidence that he was about to arrest Mr Bickersworth and how it was all done and so forth, you might at least have come and told me about it afterwards so that I was the first to know.'

Arbie, mortally offended by this slur, opened his mouth to say that the Inspector had done no such jolly thing, and that *he'd* been the one doing all the explaining, but just in time realised the sheer folly of doing so. If Val was this hopping mad already, he was not about to send her boiling over into incandescent rage by telling her just how much he'd kept back from her.

For when he'd finally drummed up the courage to talk to Gorringe about his deliberations it *hadn't* occurred to him that Val ought to be there. He knew that her parents wouldn't thank him for involving her in things any deeper, and there would certainly be talk if her name was linked in any way as being a catalyst to an actual arrest. The newspapers would have a field day as it was! And, damn it, a chap had to a duty to protect the ladies.

Besides, he thought fatalistically, she probably wouldn't have believed he could have worked it all out anyway. Val had always thought him a total dunderhead.

So he hung his head and shuffled his feet. 'I say, Val, I *am* sorry,' he muttered instead. 'I just didn't think of it,' he added feebly.

Val took one look at him, gave a huffy sigh of part exasperation, part despair, tossed her head, snorted a bit and finally stormed off. Arbie watched her go, not sure if he felt glad or sorry that she was apparently finally washing her hands of him once and for all.

He morosely wandered away across the field to join his uncle on the jetty. So, Reggie had decided that he couldn't face a trial, and had done what was euphemistically called 'the decent thing', had he? Arbie didn't blame him. The Inspector must have found the evidence he needed in Reggie's studio and tracked down a copy of Phyllis's will, confirming that she'd left her fortune under his control.

Arbie supposed that justice had been done, but even so, he wished heartily that none of it had ever happened.

He sighed and stepped onto the jetty that his uncle had built, testing the timbers somewhat gingerly, and relieved to find that they seemed solid enough beneath his feet – if not particularly straight. At the sound of his feet, his uncle popped his head out from one of the open boat windows and beamed at him.

'She's a beauty, my boy,' he enthused. 'A bit old-fashioned, but that's no bad thing, and the added daylight you've let into her plus the extra storage spaces for my paints and easels are just right. And the tarpaulin on the floor – perfect. I can paint riverside landscapes "outdoors" but stay nice and dry and warm and out of the wind at the same time! Genuis, my boy, sheer genius! I'll be positively spoilt! Thanks, Arbie m'boy, this is the best birthday present I've ever had!'

His uncle was so over the moon that Arbie's spirits couldn't help but lift a little. The grizzled head retracted momentarily, then almost instantly, popped back out again. 'Oh, and Arbie? The name? Splendid. I nearly choked with laughing. Didn't think you had it in you. You can be a bit of a conservative stick sometimes, you know. But this old girl will get the neighbours' eyes and minds boggling,' he said, affectionately patting the windowsill of the boat. 'She'll soon be notorious on the river for miles around. I dare say all the old biddies and churchmen will try to get me to change her name, but I'll be keel-hauled before I will!'

And with that, his head disappeared again.

Arbie blinked. What on earth was Uncle on about? What was wrong with *The Arty Craft* for a name? He'd thought it rather appropriate himself. It was a craft, and it was going to be piloted by an artist and used to create works of art. What objection could anyone make about that?

Uneasily, he trotted forward to the bow of the boat, where the name would be visible. As he did so, he remembered the deafness of Marcus Finch and that last phone call from him, and he felt his heart plummet.

A deep sense of foreboding and premonition assailed him as he reached the bow and read the resplendent navy-blue italicised writing that proudly declared the vessel's name.

The Crafty Fart.

As the full horror of it hit him, Arbuthnot Swift wondered if he could persuade his publishers that the next volume of *The Gentleman's Guide to Ghost-Hunting* should be set abroad. Far, far abroad. And that he needed to set off on his research trip right away.

THE
GENTLEMAN'S
GUIDE TO
GHOST-HUNTING

BY

MR A.L. SWIFT

Arbie Swift

CHAPTER 4

THE **NETHER BRINTON BANSHEE**

As you will no doubt recall from my previous investigations on the Sussex coast, I had run across the rumour that a particularly rare type of ghostly occurrence was said to be happening a few miles inland in the charming little village of Nether Brinton. And since not all holidays need be taken directly by the sea, I decided to take a small detour to see if the spot might be worth mentioning in this humble guide.

THE LODGINGS

The Farriers' Inn, Nether Brinton - A fine example of a 17th Century inn set amid pleasant scenery, with six rooms available, good feather beds, and plain but decent food.

8/10 on my Swift Scale of Excellence.

THE NETHER BRINTON BANSHEE

THE GHOST IN QUESTION

Banshee - originating from Irish folklore, and also known as 'woman of the fairy mound.' These female spirits are said to herald the death of a family member - usually by wailing, shrieking or keening, but sometimes also by singing an unearthly-sounding song. Legend has it that they can also be heard by anyone unrelated to them, warning them if they are about to undertake something from which they are unlikely to emerge alive. Also known in Scotland, accounts of them are not so common in England.

EQUIPMENT

Throw out all the usual bits and bobs, a good pair of ears - or indeed any ears at all - are all that is required for this peculiar apparition.

AN ACCOUNT OF MY EERIE EAR-SPLITTING ENCOUNTER ADVENTURE

I arrived at this quaint spot on a fresh spring day and instantly made my way to the aforementioned Inn. Not, I assure you, because I was overly anxious to indulge in a touch of liquid refreshment (although I wasn't able to decline an offer of such by the friendly landlord, naturally!) but rather in pursuit of invaluable local knowledge.

As I've already detailed in Chapter 2 - chronicling my efforts to catch sight of the White Lady of Crawley Mansion - by far and away the best source of information about any occurrences in a small village can inevitably be found in the local public house. And in this assertion, I was quickly justified, for I had no more taken a seat under a well-used dartboard, when an old man of some vintage wandered in, and after an introduction by mine host, was only too

THE NETHER BRINTON BANSHEE

willing to oblige me with all the doings of the fearful local legend -
a banshee.

As I'm sure you can well understand, I was most keen, if possible,
to find any evidence of such a rare - if terrifying - being. The old
worthy who told me the tale of this particular Banshee wishes to
remain anonymous, but I can assure you that he was a man who had
lived in the village all his years. And though he was known to have a
vast knowledge of fine spirits of the non-spectral kind, I was assured
that he could weather the effects of fine brandy and malt whisky with
the best of us!

Here, then, is what he told me.

As a lad - like all the children of the village - he had been
told of the Banshee by his parents, who had likewise been told by
their parents, and so on. Thus, the legend probably dates back two
hundred years if not more. And, as children, they were warned that
if they should ever be unlucky enough to hear a lamentable wailing,
they were to stop whatever it was they were doing and hurry home at
once to the safety of their parents and their own hearth.

According to my source, one year, his schoolfriend was actually
saved by the Banshee. She let rip just as he was about to set off
swimming, alone, in the local river. Mindful of the warning, this
lad very sensibly dipped not so much his toe into the water but
rather clambered back into his clothes and headed homeward at a
considerable rate of knots. Later that day, the farmer whose fields
bordered this stretch of the river, was said to be so unnerved by
the incident that he immediately dredged that stretch, and found a
super-abundance of water crowfoot, a particularly dense river weed
common to the area, lurking below the surface. Had the lad become
entangled, it surely would have meant a terrifying end to such a
young and innocent life.

THE NETHER BRINTON BANSHEE

Now, it has become my habit over the course of my investigations to keep an open mind as to the veracity of such accounts, as I'm sure that you, dear reader, being amongst the most discerning and intelligent of individuals, will condone most devoutly! However, it also behoves me, in pursuit of such elusive ghostly prey, to diligently seek out any possible proof that might be unearthed by some diligent and patient experimentations on my part.

That being the case, you can rest assured that after procuring a most delightful and comfortable room at the Inn, and after having partaken of an early supper obligingly arranged for me by the landlord's good lady wife, I resolved to hold a midnight vigil to see what could be made of this 'wailing woman'.

With the exhortations ringing in my ears of several patrons of the Inn, who gave me various snippets of advice on what to do should I encounter their most infamous of denizens (which mostly consisted of running like the Dickens!) I duly made my way out of the village and set off across the fields. I endeavoured to firmly put out of my mind the hair-raising tales they told of some past victims of the wailing woman, which had resulted in one gentleman's hair turning white overnight, whilst another even more unfortunate soul found that he could never eat even the freshest morsel of butter again, since it persisted in turning rancid on his tongue! I had also been advised that the only way to prevent either of these hideous fates befalling me was to wear the helmet from a suit of armour on my head and set forth eating raw onions.

One of my new friends had kindly informed me that a comfortable barn could be found at Hawthorne Dell Farm, and that the farmer of the homestead would have no objection to my presence there, so I set off with a map, my trusty briar thumbstick, and of course, my case of scientific equipment. (Alas, I lamented the fact that I had no method of recording any sounds that I may have heard – but given the fact that a Banshee's hair-raising singing had, on occasion, been said to strike the more faint-hearted dead on the spot, perhaps, dear reader, that is just as well!)

Now, as you may recall from some of my previous exploits, my map-reading skills are not as honed as I would wish, but even a muggins such as myself could hardly fail, over so short a distance, to locate the barn in question, and it was not long before I found myself reposing as comfortably as it is possible to be on a bale of hay.

Picture the scene with me, if you will. The terrain was one of deep, wooded valleys and tightly packed hills, with everywhere lush and green, and the spring barley already giving a good showing. The last skylark had sung his Byronic song, and in the gloaming, I spied a barn owl swooping low over the hedges in search of her prey. Somewhere in the distance, unseen behind a hill, the village church struck nine. The last pink reflections of the now absent sun were fading, and a gibbous moon had taken its place.

THE NETHER BRINTON BANSHEE

All very well and good, I'm sure you're thinking, but where is this all leading? And well may you ask. If you have been industrious in your perusal of my previous chapters, you may by now be aware that for any genuine ghost-hunter, it is a sad but undeniable fact that 99 out of 100 vigils end in abject failure. No ghost ever appears, no poltergeist throws a book or ornament to the floor, no footsteps echo along passages where no human form can be seen. In short, nothing at all happens!

And after all my months of investigations, as you can imagine, I had now become resigned to this sad fate and I was by no means sanguine that this latest endeavour of mine would prove to be any different. So perhaps you can imagine my surprise - and extreme disquiet - when, after barely ten minutes having passed, I heard a sound.

A sound, moreover, that I had certainly never encountered before in my life. On the gentle breeze it came, somewhere to the north-east of my position, very softly at first, so quietly that I had to strain my ears to be sure of it. Indeed, so assiduously did I lean forward in an attempt to hear this phenomenon that I inadvertently pitched off my bale of hay, and only some unintentionally impressive gymnastics on my part, dear reader, prevented me from burrowing my nose into the soil!

I at once abandoned my bale of hay and moved to stand in the immense doorway entrance to the barn, listening intently. And outside, I could hear the sound more clearly.

I now lament my lack of literary talent (which I'm sure you have all been too kind to mention amongst yourselves) and apologise in advance for my poor feeble efforts herewith to explain in mere words something that has to be heard to be properly understood and believed.

But I shall endeavour to do my best. As I stood there in the near-darkness I was aware of the natural soughing of the soft night breeze, and the likewise most natural various rustlings of wildlife in the hedgerow nearby; but above all else, I was very much aware of the utterly unnatural sound of something else. An ululating but in no way strident noise that was almost melodic, but not quite. Throaty, rising and falling in cadence, it continued to wail without ceasing.

Most disconcerting of all, although I could tell, vaguely, the direction from which it seemed to be come, it didn't seem to me that it had any real or substantial point of origin, but seemed rather, to writhe and weave all around me.

I have no shame in admitting that, by this point, my heart had begun to race somewhat, and had I put my hand to the back of my neck, I should have not been at all surprised to find the hairs there were all standing on end!

But was I daunted, dear reader? Well, yes, I was rather! But did I turn tail and run, as all my friends back at the Inn would no doubt have exhorted me so to do? No, I most certainly did not. Instead, I took up my sturdy briar thumbstick and abandoning my equipment, set off in search of the cause of that blood-curdling shrieking. (At this point, I feel obliged to point out to the more cynically minded of you, that I did not leave my equipment in the barn because it was heavy, and that I feared it would slow me down should I decide to change my mind and make a swift, very swift, exit. No, indeed, it was simply because there was nothing in my box of tricks that could have been of any possible use to me. It was too dark to take a photograph, always supposing that the Nether Brinton Banshee would be so obliging as to stop her unholy wailing long enough to strike a pose for me. And as for all the usual tricks of my trade, such as scattering talcum powder underfoot in the hopes of exposing the footsteps of fraudsters or tricksters, that would hardly prove helpful on a breezy night.)

However, even unencumbered, I quickly discovered that finding the fearful lady's exact position was going to be no easy task. The acoustics formed by the hills and valleys bamboozled me, and once or twice I found myself chasing echoes. But one thing was becoming more and more plain – I was definitely getting closer, for the unearthly, mournful wailing, was getting louder and louder.

Now, as I'm sure that it must already have occurred to you, so it occurred to me; that perhaps my friends back at the Inn, either whilst under the influence of too much beer, or merely out of kindness and not wanting me to go home with nothing to show for my time, had arranged this demonstration for my benefit. Well, I can promise you that I kept a wary eye out for any other corporeal beings and an ear out for any muffled laughter or tramping feet but heard no such suspicious activity.

I myself, you may be sure, was careful to keep crouched below the hedge line, and to move very cautiously and quietly!

Finally, I thought I saw, in the distance, a faint, flickering glow, pale orange in colour. It seemed to be coming not far from

a small ramshackle hut, which was itself set underneath a large flowering horse chestnut tree. Not quite sure what to make of this (in none of my research had I come across a 'woman of the fairy mound' who was said to glow) I crept ever closer.

I was, by now, all but crawling along an indent in the ground caused, I suspected, by the farmer's tractor using it as a byway. To one side was a field of barely, and to the other side of this rough track, behind a rough barbed-wire fence, what seemed to me to be open pasture. In this pasture I could make out faint, pale-coloured shapes that I took to be sheep.

At least, I hoped and prayed, dear reader, that that's all they were!

Keeping my eye fixed to the faint glow, I advanced cautiously. Now I have to admit that by this point, my more craven instincts were exhorting me to follow the advice of the locals and make off like a hare (or indeed something even faster) in the opposite direction. But as you, my fellow ghost-hunters are doubtless aware, a faint heart never did bring home the bacon. Or in this case, a first-hand encounter with such a legendary and terrifying entity. So, with this best interest of the humble tome in mind, I crept ever closer.

Then the noise that had kept me such unwanted company,

suddenly stopped. The abrupt cessation of it was almost as shocking as the noise itself. And in the eerie silence – somewhat belatedly – it occurred to me to wonder if the Banshee's warning might have been meant for me, personally. In other words, was my current endeavour one from which I was unlikely to return? This thought, I have to admit, rather made a certain Mr. Arbuthnot Lancelot Swift's good English blood run cold in his veins.

And it was at that precise moment of crisis that I became aware of a presence looming over me, and the sound of harsh, stertorous breathing. You will not be surprised, dear reader, to learn that I leapt to my feet with a blood-curdling yell of my own. You might, however, be as surprised as I was, when I heard a string of curses break over my head that would have made the most coarse of navvies blush. Moreover, being delivered in a most masculine of voices.

'What you 'ere be doing frightening the stuffing out of me, then?' it demanded.

These were the first coherent and curse-free words spoken to me by one Mr Simeon Bartlebass, shepherd of the county, that night we both met, face-to-face, in the fields of Nether Brinton.

Needless to say, after apologising profusely for having given that good man a fright (and forbearing to mention the terrible fright that he'd given me) I gave him an account of myself, and we settled down, companionably at his campfire. And after much hilarity on the part of Mr Bartlebass, he then proceeded to introduce me to the Nether Brinton Banshee – his old family clarinet.

This instrument was an astonishing thing to behold – cracked, misshapen and missing at least two vital components, but it was so obviously the pride and joy of the shepherd that I could do nothing but pretend to admire it and listen (all the time wishing I had copious amounts of cotton wool which I could have stuffed into my suffering ears) as he gave me a proud recital on the wretched thing.

After spending a pleasant hour talking to this most delightful – if unmusical – of men, I bid him goodnight, leaving him to retire to his hut, and spent the rest of the night (totally undisturbed, the more kind-hearted of you will be pleased to learn) – in the barn.

The next morning I returned to the Inn, wherein my landlord listened to my tale of woe with tea, sympathy, and a king amongst smoked kippers that did much to restore my faith in humanity (and my empty stomach).

However, as I was leaving the Inn to set off for the next stop on my itinerary, my landlord had the last word.

'You know, Sir, the most famous account of our Banshee came from the Reverend Wilbercote, nearly ten years ago now. He'd just been in selling raffle tickets here at the bar and was on his way home. He heard her singing loud and clear, and hurried off towards the home of one of his parishioners who was near a hundred years old, and very poorly. And sure 'nuff, the old lady died a'fore morning. And you know what Sir? All that time, Simeon Bartlebass was playing a game of TripleTell in the saloon of my here pub! What's more he won! But then, Simeon always was a man who could handle a billiard cue, right enough. But you see, that meant that it couldn't a'been him and his clarinet that the reverend gentleman heard could it, sir?'

So, dear reader, there you have it, and you must make up your own mind on whether or not my account of the Nether Brinton Banshee intrigues you enough to come down to this part of the world for your next holiday.

Discover more gripping mysteries from Faith Martin with the Ryder and Loveday series.

Coroner Clement Ryder and probationary WPC Trudy Loveday form an unlikely duo when they team up to solve crimes in 1960's Oxford.

DON'T MISS THE LATEST NEWS,
RELEASES AND EXCLUSIVE CONTENT
FROM FAITH MARTIN

SIGN-UP TO HER NEWSLETTER AT
WWW.FAITHMARTIN.CO.UK

Dear Reader,

We hope you enjoyed reading this book. If you did, we'd be so appreciative if you left a review. It really helps us and the author to bring more books like this to you.

Here at HQ Digital we are dedicated to publishing fiction that will keep you turning the pages into the early hours. Don't want to miss a thing? To find out more about our books, promotions, discover exclusive content and enter competitions you can keep in touch in the following ways:

JOIN OUR COMMUNITY:

Sign up to our new email newsletter: http://smarturl.it/SignUpHQ

Read our new blog www.hqstories.co.uk

🐦 https://twitter.com/HQStories

📘 www.facebook.com/HQStories

BUDDING WRITER?

We're also looking for authors to join the HQ Digital family! Find out more here:

https://www.hqstories.co.uk/want-to-write-for-us/

Thanks for reading, from the HQ Digital team